Left Bank

Also by Kate Muir

Suffragette City

Non-fiction
Arms and the Woman
The Insider's Guide to Paris

Left Bank

Kate Muir

headline
review

First published in 2006
by REVIEW

An imprint of Headline Book Publishing

1

Cataloguing in Publication Data is available from the British Library

ISBN 0 7553 2501 X (hardback)
ISBN 0 7553 2696 2 (trade paperback)

Typeset in Sabon by Avon DataSet Ltd,
Bidford-on-Avon, Warwickshire

Printed and bound in Great Britain by
Clays Ltd, St Ives plc

Headline's policy is to use papers that are natural, renewable and
recyclable products and made from wood grown in sustainable
forests. The logging and manufacturing processes are expected to
conform to the environmental regulations of the country of origin.

HEADLINE BOOK PUBLISHING
A division of Hodder Headline
338 Euston Road
London NW1 3BH

www.reviewbooks.co.uk
www.hodderheadline.com

For Barney, Finn and Molly.

PROLOGUE

Madison Malin

Here's the happy family strolling down Main Street, USA, where everything is tiny and in pastel paint, just as Madison remembers it from her childhood. Entranced and revolted, she makes short raids into the barbershop with its candy-striped pole, the Norman Rockwell soda fountain with its counter and stools, and the strident Pepto-Bismol-pink souvenir shops. It's the Malin family's first trip to Play World Paris, the largest theme park in Europe. 'I can't think why we put it off for so long,' says Olivier, darkly. 'It's as shiny and cloying as the cartoon world it's celebrating. It has quite exceeded my expectations.' He points to a cleaner in a furry squirrel costume who is kneeling before them. 'Look – no sooner do you spit out your chewing gum than a cheerful animal character arrives with a spatula and scrapes it off the ground.'

'At PlayWorld, nothing sticks!' says Madison, imitating the voiceover in the theme park's cheerful advertisements, and she grins at the red squirrel. The creature turns his perma-smile mask aggressively towards them, thuds his scraper into a bucket and marches off, his tail bobbing in fury.

The Malins have come here in a spirit of self-conscious irony. How else to bear the day? But Sabine, their seven-year-old daughter, is filled with real awe, and runs joyfully ahead. Behind her, Olivier and Madison laugh together at PlayWorld's vulgarity, its unbridled commercialism, its saccharine endings, its plastic cleanliness, its skyline dominated by a twenty-storey purple inflatable teddy bear in a pose which Olivier notes happily 'comes close to crucifixion.'

The Malins glide to the next PlayZone on a travelator beneath loudspeakers pumping out a medley of 'The Sun Has Got His Hat On' in five European languages. Olivier and Madison give one another sardonic grins, while Sabine swings between her golden-haired mother and her dark, dashing father. The family is a Hollywood-style vision of perfection, and for a moment Madison wishes it reflected the truth. We're getting on unusually well so far today, she thinks. We're relentlessly upbeat, just like PlayWorld. The sun is shining, and there are cries of delight from little children, and cries of disgust from their parents at the prices. 'Welcome to the Fantasy Kingdom,' groans Madison.

'I like it here,' says Olivier. 'The place makes me feel

wonderfully, essentially French.' He turns to his wife, teasing: 'Have you no shame, seeing your sleazy empire of plastic, you purveyors of Anglo-American pulp?' Madison, born in Austin, Texas, affects amused annoyance. She knows Olivier is there both as the father-giving-of-his-precious-time and the philosopher-columnist from the *Nouvel Etat*, looking for something deeper – and printable – from this rare family afternoon out.

'This whole place has been sanitized, completely purged of unhappy endings,' says Madison, shaking hands with a man-sized pink rabbit waving an unfeasibly large carrot. She gives Olivier a curious, melancholy smile, but he fails to notice. He's too busy sifting for ideas for one of his columns or books. 'Yes, yes, it's all about reality being sanitized and sanctified – I could bring that out in an essay about modern childhood's post-religious iconography and semiotics.' He takes out the soft leather notebook he keeps in his pocket, writes, and then snaps back its elastic closure with satisfaction.

Sabine is now circling slowly in a giant pastel teacup, mostly filled with toddlers, while her parents sit on a bench to wait. 'I'm not going on any more baby rides. I want the really fast ones now,' shouts Sabine as her teacup trundles towards them again. Olivier ignores her and reads to Madison from a paperback he has stashed in his jacket. Some American has written a thesis on PlayWorld and Olivier already knows the line he'll be plagiarising from him, a convenient ocean and language away. He reads in heavily accented English:

3

' "PlayWorld is so good at being good that it manifests an evil: so uniformly efficient and courteous, so dependably clean and conscientious, so unfailingly entertaining that it's unreal, and therefore is an agent of pure wickedness." There. That perfectly describes it, doesn't it?'

Madison laughs and nods assurance. She's busy tossing back her long, fairytale hair, and hoping that the resident theme park paparazzo, alerted by the public relations department which has arranged their free passes, will catch the Malin family unawares. A photo of the actress and the philosopher and their pretty daughter on an ordinary day out among the petite bourgeoisie. Madison's working too, just like Olivier, for an actress is never offstage and today her costume is a darted white linen shirt, a metal H for Hermes belt, and perfect Chloé jeans. Sabine is in a dress from Bonpoint of course, while Olivier is wearing his minimalist uniform: an exquisitely tailored black linen Nehru suit and a grey T-shirt. His suits are either linen or fine wool, but always black. He wears one of his twenty grey T-shirts every day, unless he's on television, when he wears white ones, more flattering under the lights.

But today it's Madison who needs lights, action and publicity – *Paris Match* or even *VSD* magazine will do – because forty (actually forty-three) is not an easy age for an actress, and her last film was misunderstood by critics who confused art with pornography. As she watches Sabine go over to a stall to try on an alien mask, Madison wonders at her daughter's boyish tastes, and fondly remembers a simpler time when they did a *Paris*

Match spread with Olivier, five weeks after Sabine was born. They were both tastefully naked in black and white, and Madison's stomach was flat as a crêpe. The cover line was 'Madison and Olivier Malin Present Their Baby Daughter'. Inside there was a large-print quote from Olivier: 'Now I have two loves in my life!' Then he was referring to her; now she's not so sure that those words are true.

A camera whirrs like a mixer in front of them, and a photographer rushes up. Unfortunately, Sabine is caught trying on a poxed green monster head on top of her expensive pink organdie dress, and Madison is laughing at Olivier eating a bucket of frites. This was just not the shot Madison had in mind, but the snapper refuses to return for something more elegant and flattering. 'Shift change,' he says over his shoulder. Madison knows instinctively that the magazines will use the embarrassing picture – this would never happen to Jane Birkin or Charlotte Rampling, she thinks – and snatches the mask from Sabine's head. 'Awww, Anna!' yells Sabine. Madison's eyes widen in irritation, but then she feels a nauseating lurch of guilt.

'I mean Maman,' says Sabine more quietly. 'I need that mask. I love the Alien Brunch Bunch. Pleeeze?'

'No,' says Madison. 'It's expensive rubbish.' She turns it over and sees the price. '*Really* expensive rubbish.'

Olivier raises an eyebrow at her and pulls out some notes to purchase Sabine's temporary happiness. He has never had any qualms about buying love, thinks Madison.

'Do you have to do the opposite of everything I say?' she hisses under her breath at him. 'How's she going to learn the meaning of "no" when you ignore me? You've already bought her that furry bear backpack, the balloon she lost immediately, and an ice cream which turned her tongue blue.'

'What's wrong?' asks Sabine, muffled beneath the mask. 'Are you fighting again?'

Olivier shrugs, in an irritatingly French way. 'Look, Madison, we're at PlayWorld – it's all about the culture of consumption. We must indulge her. We must feed the system.' Madison ignores him, pretending to examine her long blood-red nails. She suddenly notices that they match the talons of the wicked stepmother in a vast Snow White poster above her. She looks from cartoon to reality, and wonders why motherhood seems so ill-fitting, why she always feels as if she's acting a part. She wonders why Anna's name, the nanny's name, comes first to Sabine in moments of need and in anger. Mirror, mirror on the wall, wonders Madison, who does Sabine love most of all?

Of course, the easy solution to children getting their mother's name wrong is staying home, yet Madison cannot face professional and social death. Olivier ground his first wife down to a housewife, whereupon he left her increasingly homely comforts for someone who still had a sense of self: Madison. Olivier is big on equal rights, so long as they cause him no personal inconvenience. He is big on the theory of fatherhood, his pockets are large, but he has never collected Sabine from school.

Left Bank

No one in the little Malin family seems satisfied with the situation. Madison knows that Sabine is smart enough to feel the waves of irritation constantly crackling between her parents. Madison watches as Sabine galumphs inelegantly on a nearby wall, the mysterious opposite of her mother. She sees her daughter's glowing skin, her wild eyes, her legs dotted with boyish bruises from the playground, and feels a rush of love for her.

They have been standing for fifteen minutes in line for the ghost train. It's hot. Late June crowds stinking of fast-food and coconut sun cream surge around them, and Madison, who rarely eats, says she feels faint.

'You should have had some bloody lunch before we left,' snorts Olivier.

'I did,' says Madison.

'Two apples aren't lunch. You're ridiculous.'

Sabine looks from her mother to her father and her forehead wrinkles.

Madison glowers at Olivier. 'You're the one who likes your women thin,' she says. 'But forget it. I'll just get a coffee.'

Sabine starts biting her nails.

Madison picks her way to the coffee stall through the sweaty crowd. These are the wide-bottomed Polyester folks she left Texas twenty years ago to avoid, or at least their European equivalent. She thanks the Lord Almighty for her escape as she watches their fat sons with skinheads, their unsporty daughters in nylon sportswear, their lethargy only broken by consumption.

She sits down under a sun umbrella at the Barista coffee stall, leaving Olivier to ride the ghost train with Sabine. She sips a skim latte slowly, experiencing each calorie.

Soon, over on the ghost train, she can see Olivier and Sabine lurching out of one door of the haunted house, and slamming into another. Olivier looks freaked out, but Sabine is fearless, as usual. He still gets carsick if he's not driving, and the shuddering halts in darkness filled with creepers do not bode well for the bucket of frites. Madison grins. She notes that Olivier's arm is tightly wrapped in terror round Sabine's small, rounded shoulders, which are rippling with delighted shrieks.

'I want a milkshake now,' says Sabine reappearing, towing an ashen Olivier behind her.

'But you just had an ice lolly, honey. Milkshakes are really fattening,' says Madison.

'I want a chocolate milkshake, Maman.'

'If you say please, Sabine,' says Olivier, but his eyes are challenging Madison.

'Pleeeze, Papa,' says Sabine, hugging him, pulling at his hand, and heading for the Barista stall.

'You wanting small, medium, large?' grunts the Eastern-European server.

'Large, please,' says Sabine. Madison looks disapproving and lights a cigarette.

'Pretty girl you daughter, isn't she?' says the Barista greasily to Olivier. 'What age have you got?' he asks, looking down at Sabine.

'Seven and a quarter.'

'Thank you,' says Olivier. 'Now let's go.'

Then it's time for PlayWorld's top attraction, Petit Paris. 'Why go to Paris when you can tour our scale model of the City of Light in half an hour? Climb the Eiffel Tower in seconds! Skip over the Sacré Coeur! Meet the Hunchback in Notre Dame! Stroll the entire Left Bank in a few paces!'

Giggling at the ridiculousness of it all, the Malins mount a fun-sized Petit Paris trolley car, which trundles through model streets a couple of metres wide, past perfect replicas of landmarks at shoulder height. There's the Opéra, dumped bun-like in the centre, while the Sacré Coeur glows icing white on a mini-hill, and the Tour Montparnasse lurks darkly at the bottom. 'But the best thing is, Papa, that you can travel in time,' says Sabine. 'Anna told me so. She's been here twice, you know. Look, look, the guillotine, and Marie Antoinette, and the little doll knitting!'

Petit Paris is peopled by famous Parisians throughout the ages. They peek in at a puppet Proust writing in his corklined room, a mechanised matelot-topped Picasso painting outside the Lapin Agile, and 'Oh Jesus,' says Olivier as they roll down the mini Boulevard Saint Germain. 'Sartre.' And indeed there in the window of the pint-sized Café Flore are Sartre and Simone de Beauvoir dolls, with notebooks, drinking coffee from toy cups, again and again.

Sabine is still disappointed that she couldn't see her own street from the trolley: the Rue du Bac and the Franprix supermarket opposite their apartment. As they draw into the terminus, Madison hops out and purchases a replica bean-baggie Sartre and de Beauvoir couple for Sabine. This is mainly to annoy Olivier, who secretly likes to believe he is the Sartre of the twenty-first century. Madison thinks this is probably true, but not for the same intellectual reasons as Olivier. She likes to tease him with Sartre's words: 'Why did I become a philosopher? Why have I so keenly sought this fame for which I'm still waiting? It's all been to seduce women, basically.' She watches as Olivier turns Sartre over in his hand (usually he turns him over in his head) and removes the doll's pebble glasses and raincoat. With some interest, he discovers de Beauvoir's turban and dress come off, but her body is feature-less rag-doll pink. 'You wouldn't take her to bed,' he says, laughing.

'Don't say that in front of Sabine,' says Madison. Olivier looks hostile, and says nothing for the rest of the ride. Even Sabine is grumpy and bored.

'Can I play with your phone, Papa?'

He hands it over wearily. She presses buttons up and down. 'What's "Junkyard" Papa? Can we go there? I love making things out of junk.'

'Stop it!' snaps Olivier. 'You might dial someone by mistake.'

'Ooh,' says Sabine. 'Can I play Snake II then?'

'Yes, but go and do it over there so we don't hear the infernal beeping.'

Sabine goes off, beeping. Olivier and Madison sit in bleak

silence for a few minutes. Olivier gets out his notebook and scribbles self-importantly.

'This is supposed to be a special day out for Sabine,' says Madison eventually. 'Let's can the fighting, darling.'

They call Sabine over and walk on through PlayWorld's four themed lands 'where you can live out your fantasy adventure without fear of getting hurt.' As a sop to the French nation, there's the Petit Ours flume log ride, but the rest copies the other PlayWorlds in the USA. Sabine spots the Rockin' Rawhide Rollercoaster and runs towards it, whooping cowboy-style. 'I've got to go, Papa, come on!' But Olivier sees the rollercoaster corkscrewing through tunnels in orange fibreglass mountains and throwing itself down ravines. He hears the screams, and his stomach corkscrews in sympathy. He digs his heels in. 'Not a chance,' he says. 'You're not going on there yourself.'

'Papa! You're so mean,' says Sabine. 'It's been rated one of the top five scariest rollercoasters in Europe! Anna told me that. *She* would go with me.' She turns her back on him. 'Maman?' she tries. 'It'll be like that day we rode so fast across the fields at Moulon.'

'No darling, we can't go. Papa's still feeling bad from the ghost train. Besides, it's so windy going through those tunnels that it'll wreck my hair, and I just had it straightened this morning for a Vogue photoshoot tonight.'

Sabine kicks at a litter bin beside the ride and stares at the ground. 'Are you saying no, then?'

'You understand, darling. You don't want me looking a ridiculous mess in the magazine.'

'Oh come on, Madison,' says Olivier. 'You *could* go, whereas I can't possibly. Don't be so selfish.'

'It's not selfish. It's not vanity. It's work, although it's apparently of no importance compared to your own.'

'Well that's just . . .'

Their voices are getting louder. In the meantime, Sabine has headed off with her bear backpack and her PlayWorld pass without a backward glance. She has secured herself a seat, alone, on the Rockin' Rawhide Rollercoaster. It takes a minute for Madison and Oliver to notice, and by the time they reach her, the ride is slowly starting.

'See? I can look after myself,' Sabine shouts down from her seat high on the rails. She has the same defiant look Madison sometimes sees in Olivier. The PlayMate pulls the safety bar down over Sabine's lap.

'You'll see . . .' begins Sabine, but her words are drowned out by the anticipatory squeals of a loud Italian woman and her sons, sitting behind. Olivier shrugs, as usual. Madison is worried. Sabine shoots down the metal rails in a blur, and at that moment, someone recognises Madison and asks for her autograph. Madison smiles. She stands a head higher than most of the women around her: noticeable, Amazonian. A group of French tourists gather, delighted that the Great Mind and the Great Body of the Left Bank have deigned to mix with the commoners. On cue, Olivier puts his arm round his perfect wife, once again confirming his intellectual and sexual prowess, and smiles. The tourists take a photograph of the Malins – Madison's hair is indeed wonderfully shiny today – and wave their thanks beneath the rattling rollercoaster. Olivier and Madison see a pink streak as Sabine whooshes by, shouting 'Yee, hah!'

Madison takes out a long cigarette and lights it elegantly, blowing the smoke out in a sigh. She has calmed down again. 'Darling?' She touches his hand, conciliatory.

'Mmmn?' says Olivier, who has taken out his copy of *Libération* and is studying the book reviews as he waits. Like a small boy, thinks Madison, he always has pocketsful of stuff. But he's trying to avoid talking properly to Madison. He's guilty about something – probably the note to some woman she saw on his email yesterday, the one who is also on his mobile as 'Junkyard' – and he has been oddly shifty recently. He certainly doesn't want to talk about her life. She suspects that even after eight years together, he sometimes prefers her to remain an object rather than a subject. She tries again.

'You know André is considering casting me in the film of Houellebecq's book?'

'Mmmn.'

'But the part is . . . so degrading but so challenging. It's a slapper. It's not pretty.' Her agent was against Madison taking character parts, wanting her to maintain her youthful image for as long as humanly – and cosmetically – possible.

'So what do you think I should do?'

'Ask your publicist or someone. How should I know?' says Olivier, reburying himself in the newspaper.

Madison gives him a death-ray stare which hides her pain. 'Fantastic. Thanks for your help and interest.'

'Oh I didn't mean . . .' Olivier shrugs, putting his arms awkwardly round her in apology.

Their mood plunges down simultaneously with the roller-coaster, and they stand in irritated silence waiting for the ride to stop. One by one the carriages drop their loads back to earth. The Italian family with three sons passes down the ramp, but Sabine is nowhere to be seen. 'Isn't it about time . . .' says Olivier, but the PlayWorld uniformed PlayMates have started slowly loading the rollercoaster for the next ride. 'Hang on,' says Madison to one PlayMate in a cowboy hat, 'my daughter's still on there.'

'No, Madame. It's completely empty now, see. She must have got off,' he says, gesturing below. Madison feels her stomach ice across. 'She'll be in the crowd. Let's look, quick.' They start running in panic among the packed bodies, shouting their daughter's name over and over until Madison's voice cracks, but Sabine is nowhere to be seen. Then Olivier says, 'Come on, Sabine's sensible. Look at the time you lost her in the Bon Marché last winter and she went straight to security. She'll be with the PlayWorld police sooner or later, because she wouldn't go with a stranger. She's too smart. She's a city kid. Anyway, you don't disappear off a moving roller-coaster.'

This thought suddenly makes Madison hysterical, and she screams: 'She's fallen, she's fallen off the rollercoaster.'

Her screams galvanise the staff, who force newcomers to leave their seats on the ride. They put a rope across the rollercoaster entrance, and start muttering on their walkie-talkies. 'Where's your supervisor?' roars Olivier. 'We've got to search that fucking rollercoaster. She could be stuck in a tunnel.' A crowd forms to observe the scene. A few people recognise the Malins, and start taking photographs.

'Fuck off, you fuckers,' says Olivier turning sharply round. 'Leave us alone.' The tourists recoil – Professor Malin is known for his charm, not this.

Suddenly, three security guards in military-style uniforms start ushering the crowd away, and the PlayWorld public relations manager arrives. 'Monsieur Malin, Madame,' he bows his head obsequiously. 'I am so sorry. It appears we have a problem. I am sure your daughter will be found by security in the blink of an eye. Please stay calm and follow me. Now are you quite sure your daughter – what is her name?'

'Sabine.'

'Are you quite sure you didn't just miss Sabine in the crowd? Is there some other attraction she mentioned that she might wander off to?' The PR man fingers his moustache and raises one eyebrow quizzically. His suit is shiny sharkskin.

'She's seven, and she's not stupid,' says Olivier, through gritted teeth. 'She'd wait for us. Always. Now can you search that rollercoaster immediately?'

At last the staff checks every seat in every carriage, every tunnel, every ravine, and under every metre of track. They search the emergency exits inside the fibreglass mountain, and in the engine room. It takes twenty long minutes. They find no trace of Sabine, nothing, except the Sartre and de Beauvoir dolls abandoned under the seat.

Soon the tannoy is blaring: 'Message for Sabine Malin. Please go to a member of the PlayWorld staff, and they will bring you to your Maman and Papa.' This is followed by announcements asking all adults to look out for a little blonde girl in a pink dress. When Madison hears the announcement repeated again and again, she starts to weep. 'She's so little . . .'

Olivier holds her. 'That's not helping, my love,' he says. He reaches into his breast pocket. 'Hey, wait a minute, my phone's gone. Sabine's still got it! Quick, call her on yours.'

Madison's hands are shaking so much she misses Olivier's name on direct dial. Then the phone rings once, twice, and cuts off. They try again. Now there's a message from the mobile phone company saying the number is unavailable.

'Oh shit, shit, what does that mean?' asks Olivier. 'Has someone else got the phone, got her? She would answer it. She loves playing with my phone.'

He looks beseechingly at Madison, as though she might have an answer. 'Let's give the police the number. Maybe they can trace the signal.' Meanwhile, officials and PlayMates mill around the rollercoaster, uselessly engaging in discussion and gesture. Nothing seems to be happening. Madison and Olivier jump each time the phone rings in the public relations man's pocket, but there is no news.

'You stay here,' says Olivier to Madison. 'I'm going to look round myself. I'll be back soon.'

'Please, Monsieur Malin, I think it would be best if you waited here in the office until Sabine is found by our ten-man security team,' says the weasely public relations man.

'Christ. I've got to do something,' says Olivier. 'Why don't you just evacuate the park and we can find her at the gates?'

'I'm afraid that's impossible, Sir. The park will be shutting for the evening in a couple of hours anyway. We don't want people to start panicking. And the financial implications would be serious. I'm sure the call will come soon.'

'Fuck your financial implications. My daughter has disappeared. On one of your rides. Do something!'

By now, Madison is hyperventilating. 'I'm having a panic attack,' she gasps. 'I can't breathe.' A PlayWorld cowgirl offers her a box of tissues and somewhere to sit. This cannot be real. This cannot be real, Madison says to herself, and then aloud, in English. She rocks back and forth on the bench.

Olivier storms out into the crowd. But there are ten, twenty thousand people out there and he looks like he is wading through syrup. Olivier is blocked by endless bloated bodies and inane happy faces eating ice cream. Madison follows him out and keeps seeing flashes of pale pink material in the crowds. Her heart stops, but each time the face is not Sabine's. Madison is horribly, tackily reminded of the glimpses of the red-hooded dwarf in the film '*Don't Look Now*'. She suddenly understands what terror is. It's the worst feeling she's ever had in her life.

An hour later, Olivier and Madison are sitting grey-faced on plastic chairs in the PlayWorld security station. On the table before them lie the Sartre and de Beauvoir dolls. Olivier's head is in his hands. His T-shirt is patched with sweat. Madison stares through her tears into nothing. Her nothing is populated with paedophiles, kidnappers, lunatic murderers. Part of her has been removed, yet she still feels it is there, invisible. She feels a pain which must, she reasons, be that of amputation.

PART I

1

Anna Ayer

In October, just over nine months before Sabine disappeared on the rollercoaster, Anna Ayer arrived at 84 Rue du Bac and rang the 'O. et M. Malin' buzzer outside the double black doors of the carved stone apartment building. She immediately sensed the weight of grandeur therein. A mini door clicked open within the frame of the large double ones, which were only unlocked for oversized items like horses and hearses, and Anna entered the dark arches leading to the sunlit courtyard surrounded by topiary in vast pots.

She was applying for the job as Sabine's nanny – her *British* nanny, which is quite a different thing from those stolid Breton girls the Parisians bring down from the country, or the rollerblading Danish au pairs rented to provide amusement for all generations over the summer. In the seventh arrondissement, a trained British nanny is the equivalent of a mud-spattered Mercedes estate: she adds both reliability and foreign cachet to a Parisian family.

Unfortunately, Anna felt she did not fit the British nanny stereotype. She was an imposter applying for a job which required, surely, a larger, starchier chest, stricter views on discipline and much better grooming. When she saw the grand doors, she worried that she was not sufficiently grand, and she considered turning back, when something scuttled out of the shadows under the arches, flapping. It was a tiny woman with a tweed shawl for wings, steely hair in a tight bun, and thin lips that did not quite meet over her sharp little teeth. She resembled a bat, although, as Anna discovered later, she did not merely have some sort of internal radar that detected all movement in the building, but keen eyesight too.

'A-hah!' said the Bat Lady, pouncing on Anna. '*Bonjour*, Mademoiselle. You'll be here for an interview with Madame Malin for the position of nanny, will you not?'

'Hi. Um, yes. And you are . . .?'

'Madame Canovas.' The Bat Lady seemed put out that someone might be ignorant of her identity.

'Ah,' said Anna, not sure why she should know this. 'I'm Anna Ayer. Pleased to meet you. Are you a friend of the Malins, and where do I . . .'

'No, no, no,' the Bat Lady flapped and coughed. 'Me, I am

Madame Canovas, the *concierge*.' She puffed out her chest with importance, like a small bird. An odd, musty smell emanated from her. 'Go left and take the lift to the sixth floor.'

Anna walked into a marbled hall of mirrors, a compact Versailles, and went over to press the button on the gilded cage of the lift.

'You're five minutes late, you know,' said Madame Canovas, tapping her watch and flapping out into the gloom.

Anna had lived in Paris for four years and already knew of the reputation of Olivier and Madison Malin – they were the unavoidable fodder of late-night cultural television shows (Olivier) and sub-pornographic art house films (Madison). Both were regularly pictured either demonstrating against or dining with government ministers, depending on the Zeitgeist. Their bronzed torsos were generally to be found in Cannes, St Tropez and the celebrity magazines in summer. Olivier's book *Chechnya – Beyond Philosophy* was all over the shops that month. He had recently overtaken Bernard-Henri Lévy as Paris's most popular and telegenic philosopher. Anna kept seeing Olivier's face everywhere: the handsome, heroic philosopher-in-a-flak-jacket. She was not uninterested in checking him out in real life, whether or not she got the job.

As for Madison, her film *Bluetooth* was showing in one tiny cinema on the Left Bank, and was decidedly not Anna's cup of tea. But never mind the celebrity ratings – the practical problem was, that as avowed leftist intellectuals, the Malins were probably too poor to pay a decent whack. Or so she thought until a black-uniformed maid with a frilly white pinny opened the door to a grandiose apartment which covered the entire fifth floor, unlike those below which were more modestly divided in two.

The maid stared at her with narrowed eyes and some distaste, and Anna wondered what on earth she'd done already. 'I suppose you're Mademoiselle Ayer?' snapped the maid, in a foreign accent. 'Come in. You're late, but it is fortunate that Madame Malin is not quite ready. Please take a seat in the salon.'

Before she left, the maid, with habitual movements, unlocked a cabinet and pulled back the doors to display a collection of tiny gold and silver sharp-clawed birds with ruby eyes, plus what looked like a jewel-encrusted Fabergé egg. There was also a miniature gilded piano, with sphinxes for legs; a china toadstool growing from a diamond-studded mound; and other kitsch for the rich. Anna sat gingerly on an overstuffed silk-covered chair (sure to be genuine Louis-something, she thought) and stared at the dozen or so extravagant baubles, wondering what she was supposed to think. Was it to see if she was honest? Would there be a jewel count? And what was a Fabergé egg worth nowadays? Or would there be a memory test, like the ones at parties where the parents cover a tray of objects with a cloth and the kids have to remember them? Or did everyone suffer this display of riches in the great Leftist philosopher's apartment? It was weird.

She pivoted round to see the rest of the vast, curly corniced room. There were thick Persian rugs, and a full-length oil painting of St Sebastian: naked, muscly, and bristling with arrows. Three steps led up to the painting, plus velvet curtains swagged its sides, just in case you missed it. Very posh pornography, Anna thought. There was a breakable Ming-like thing on a pedestal, a Picasso or something Braquish (but you'd definitely say the real McCoy), along with gilded, tasselled couches designed more for endurance than comfort. The room was not short of chandeliers, and also boasted a gilded mirror above a fireplace with big lion paws in swirly red marble.

Anna thought the Malins, as members of the fashionable elite, might have gone for something more minimalist and modern, more Christian Liaigre. But this room smelled of bad feng shui and old, old money, with perhaps a whiff of Dallas gilding thrown in. Even the antique furniture had been restored to perfection. She was sure that sometime after the French Revolution, the Malins had dropped the 'de' or 'comte' from their name, but they'd certainly kept the family silver.

'Here's another one,' shouted a child's voice in French in the corridor. 'Maman, come look!' Sabine ran into the salon and stopped short, for at that time Anna still had three silver hoops in one ear and her bob was still streaked from last night with purple food colouring, always a risk in the rain. At least she'd politely taken the stud out of her tongue for the interview.

'Is that real?' said Sabine, pointing at Anna's hair. 'Are you going to a fancy dress party?' Sabine was probably the most composed six-year-old Anna had seen, the sort of only child that spends most of her time among adults. The little girl was wearing a black turtleneck, jeans and about ten sets of plastic carnival beads. Anna was amused, squatted down to Sabine's level, and replied in French, 'No, I'm here for an interview to be your babysitter. I always look like this. Sometimes much worse.'

Sabine laughed. Madison, who had just entered the room, did not. She was exquisitely polite, but rather formal, with the reserved expression of the recently Botoxed. Although she spoke with a much-dimmed American accent, her intonations and hauteur were exactly that of the *bon-chic-bon-genre* French mothers Anna had previously worked for. Inevitably, Madison was wearing a little Chanel jacket over her Levis. Sabine looked like a miniature version of her mother, except her eyes were brown instead of blue. There was no sign of the father.

There was something in Madison's swift glance up and down that showed she had clearly been hoping for something more Poppins or Norland than Anna, a nanny with a uniform and white cuffs, not dyed hair and blue nail varnish. Anna thought she should probably just leave there and then, but for some reason Madison did not want to entirely rely on appearances, and seemed intent on conducting the interview thoroughly. Anna could tell that her answers were the right ones. After all, she was twenty-two, with four years of experience and some superb references, only two of which she'd written herself.

While Madison asked about her previous jobs and attitudes to discipline, Anna set up her iPod for Sabine to play with. The child put the earphones on and jiggled from side to side on the sofa, humming, and making funny faces at Anna. Madison asked all the usual questions and Anna gave all the usual answers, featuring fresh vegetables, strict homework schedules, and no television before seven o'clock.

'You don't smoke, do you?'

'Not at all,' lied Anna, noting with interest the Marlboros poking out of Madison's Hermès bag. 'I hate the smell, even.' In fact, one of the reasons Anna had moved to Paris was that it was the last civilised place on earth where you could smoke freely.

'Good.'

Anna had not made much effort to dress up for the interview, it being one of five that the agency had sent her on, since it was always as well for employers to see you at your worst, in this case in a faded vintage fifties' dress and cowboy boots. She certainly wasn't a threatening sight for any mother, and especially not one as beautiful as Madison. Madison's mobile phone went. 'Yes, yes, I know I'm late. I'll be there in half an hour or so. No. Yes. Just a facial and a manicure, darling, and make sure you book the Pilates. Bye.' Madison glanced at her watch and now appeared bored with the whole recruiting business. She looked at a paper in front of her where she'd scribbled some notes. Sabine came and sat on Madison's knee, obscuring them.

'And how is your French? You know, for dealing with Sabine's teachers, friends and so on?'

'Just fine,' said Anna in French. 'I was brought up in England, but my father was French, you see?'

'Oh I'm sorry,' said Madison.

'No he's not dead. He just left one day.'

'Oh. Dear me.'

Madison obviously didn't want to pursue an intimate conversation about Anna's relatives, and instead gave an assenting nod. Anna wondered if that meant she'd been offered the job. Madison said: 'If we consider you, Anna – subject to references of course – you have to be available twenty-four hours a day, seven days a week if necessary, because I'm often away for weeks at a time on set, you understand, and Olivier is in the middle of writing a book and does not want to be disturbed with small matters.' They certainly had a strange attitude to childcare. Anna noted that 'small matters' had taken off the iPod and was listening intently. Sabine slipped off her mother's knee and slid behind the sofa. Madison sighed and studied her pale, exquisitely polished nails. Anna studied Madison's nails and wondered what the annual bill for their upkeep was. A thousand Euros? A hundred per nail? She was certainly high maintenance all over. Just looking at her perfection made Anna feel wildly grungy. Madison's voice cut through her thoughts.

'We do insist that you speak only English to Sabine, because Olivier and I want her to remain bilingual, and she's already too dependent on French. Luiza, our housekeeper, has been looking after her until now, and she's from Chechnya, so Sabine's English and French were both suffering.' Anna wondered at this point if Sabine talked to her parents at all, if language was such a problem.

Sabine appeared and handed the iPod back to Anna. 'Thanks, *merci*, *spaciba*,' she said. Madison frowned at her daughter and continued lecturing.

'Luiza will give you a list of preferred foods for Sabine, nothing fatty, because bad habits start young. And you'll also be expected to maintain her wardrobe.'

At this, Anna had a vision of herself with a power drill fixing an armoire, but then realised Madison meant she wanted Sabine's knickers ironed, a strange obsession of many Parisian mothers, she'd noticed. Madison continued: 'Have you any questions?' And before Anna could think of anything, Madison was on her feet: 'Now, your quarters.' Anna flinched at the word quarters – surely somewhere you kept soldiers or slaves – but perhaps Madison had also used English so little lately that she was losing her grip.

She led them to the apartment's kitchen, where the scowling housekeeper Luiza squirted Cif spray aggressively round them, as though Anna might bring some dreadful contamination. Luiza's uniform was crisp and her dark hair pulled back so tightly that her eyes bulged piggily in her steel-rimmed glasses.

'I wouldn't have to wear a uniform, would I?' she said suddenly to Madison.

'No,' said Madison, smiling for the first time. 'That's Luiza's choice. I'm sure, um, what you have on would be appropriate for most occasions, though perhaps not all . . .'

Luiza looked away and opened a cupboard where the cans and bottles were obsessively ranged according to height. Madison brushed by her to a small bolted door in the back wall, which led to the servants' passage.

Anna and Sabine followed Madison's hefty perfume and endless legs up a spiral stone staircase to the *chambres de bonne* in the roof. The corridor smelled of dusty old furniture and, oddly, of apples warming in the sun which slanted through the skylights. 'We own five of the rooms up here, and you may have these two with the interconnecting door. You'll share the bathroom and kitchenette with Luiza.' That'll be fun, thought Anna. Bet she arranges her shampoo with military precision too. 'You can pick out some furniture from the storeroom here. The bed is single.' Madison's streamlined eyebrows rose in silent threat.

Just where has all that down-home Texan hospitality gone, wondered Anna, as Madison continued. 'If you're not required at weekends, you'll use the back stairs, and not enter your room through the kitchen and our apartment.' Sabine was hopping from foot to foot in the corridor, trying to turn the doorhandle, and pulling on Anna's hand. 'Come and look!' Inside, double windows opened out on to a narrow metal fire escape and a view of Paris to die for, over the rooftops to the dome of the Invalides and the Seine, the gold statues of Pont Alexandre III glowing in the late-afternoon sun. Sabine hung right out over the metal rail and pointed out the Eiffel Tower, round the corner almost out of sight. Anna instinctively grabbed a handful of Sabine's jumper and held her steady in case she slipped, while Madison took the other option of screaming: 'Get down, Sabine! Now!'

'Silly Maman. I was really safe. She was holding on to me. You made me jump.'

'Don't you ever do that again,' said Madison, still angry. Sabine ignored her and turned to Anna: 'Anyway, I wish this was my room,' she said, dismissing what Anna later discovered was her white-carpeted princess's chamber four times the size downstairs. Madison's heels tick-tocked across the bare boards and she opened a door which had been knocked through into an identical bedroom. 'Brilliant,' said Anna smiling, 'storage.' Madison looked at her, puzzled. 'For my clothes,' said Anna.

Madison then offered Anna twice her previous salary, and Anna tried to look disappointed but resigned, and asked about holidays. She wondered, though, whether they were offering so much money because of socialist guilt at employing servants, or because the job was going to be gruelling. In previous jobs, Anna had been in the habit of running a profitable vintage clothes stall on Sundays, on the side. And she did not particularly warm to Madison. She struck Anna as the sort of person who had always been so beautiful, she'd never had to be kind, or amusing. But Anna felt confident, given Madison's aura of self-interest and her much-publicised film schedule, that her boss wouldn't be around much. You couldn't stay that perfectly groomed, *and* hang around making mud pies in the park. Chances were that Anna would be able to run her own show,

and she quite liked the kid and she really liked the accommodation, here in the seventh arrondissement. In for a penny, in
for a huge pile of cash, she thought, and agreed to start the job
the next month.

Afterwards, Luiza escorted Anna down the wood-panelled
hallway to the front door, eyeing her suspiciously as though she
might pinch the silver on the way. To her disappointment, Anna
never saw Olivier Malin – clearly childcare was women's
business here – but she heard his rich, ripe-for-radio voice
through the half-open study door. '. . . and tell him if he does
not win the Renaudot prize, I shall be most surprised. I have
spoken to Bourdon only this morning and he agrees about the
need for literature to replace ideologically loaded devices such
as character and plot. Put simply, it is in the bag. . . . No, no,
he will not challenge me, not after what . . . Yes, of course . . .
Now Pauly, to more important matters. I am pondering whether
to have the lemon sole or those juicy little trotters at the Fontaine
de Mars tonight. Which . . .' Anna grinned automatically at
Luiza, acknowledging their below-stairs complicity as eaves-
droppers. Luiza stared back, dead eyed. She opened the front
door and slammed it hard behind Anna, exorcising her.

2

Olivier Malin

Olivier was in Barthélémy's cheese shop on the Rue de Grenelle, his nostrils flaring in delight at the loamy, buttery smell. You could leave the cooking up to the maid, but not the selection of cheeses for a dinner party. Was it not Olivier's favourite foodie, Anthelme Brillat-Savarin, who said back in 1825: 'Dessert without cheese is like a pretty girl with only one eye'? Exactly. Olivier was not merely a popular and unexpectedly handsome philosopher, but what the French call a *gastrophilosophe*: a man who understands that food is for the soul.

In many ways, food is what had started to drive Madison and him apart in their marriage. It was Olivier's fate to have a passion for slim, elegant women, and to fall out of love with them as they either maintained their steely form against his sensual gastronomy or, worse still, ran to fat like his first wife. Olivier believed some women were naturally thin: he preferred not to imagine the maintenance and discipline required. In fact, he dated the decline of his relationship with Madison to the day three years ago when he happened to see her through the window of the Café de la Mairie by St Sulpice having lunch alone – taking alternate bites of a tiny green salad and drags on her cigarette. She'd looked haggard and grey-skinned in the harsh café lights, and had seemed intent on scorching her lustful tastebuds to death.

He shivered at the memory, or perhaps it was the tiled cold of the cheese shop, with its great dark cellar beneath the street cosseting some two hundred cheeses at eight degrees centigrade, with just enough humidity and ventilation to induce ripe perfection in all that unpasturised milk. He thought affectionately of the *affineur* in the cellar, tenderly brushing each soft cheese with wine from its own region, massaging an Epoisses with a little Calvados and crème fraîche. One of the sales ladies bustled up to him in her white coat and matching wellingtons. 'Monsieur Malin, so wonderful to see you. And how is your little girl? We have something that may interest you today, an old Gruyère de Fribourg and have you seen the Mont d'Or? In season now.'

She dug a spoon into the bath of pinkish rind and waved the dripping cheese at Olivier, at such a pitch of ripeness he stepped back, overpowered. The smell brought on a traumatic madeleine moment, and he recalled the day he had taken his fascinatingly working-class girlfriend from the École Normale Supérieure for the weekend to his parents' château in the country. At dinner, when offered the almost-liquid Mont d'Or, she'd stuck a knife in it and sawed messily, instead of using the monogrammed silver spoon provided. She had clearly never progressed beyond cheap brie from Franprix. Olivier's mother had given him – and her – one withering glance, and he'd understood that this was the end of the relationship. He'd been annoyed at the time, but he now realised his mother had been absolutely right.

'Monsieur, the Reblochon is for this evening?' said the saleswoman, pressing possible candidates for softness. Barthélémy prided himself on timing his cheeses to go off, like a gooey bomb, at the exact point of consumption. No wonder he served Matignon and the Elysée Palace too. Olivier tested a chunk of leathery orange Mimoulette, cracked with age, and wavered between two little goats' cheeses, one dry and pungent, the other ripe and swathed in ashes. Sighing, he restricted himself to three cheeses; the palate would be corrupted by more. Indeed, sometimes he served just one cheese if it was particularly delicious in itself. He tasted a few more, for the sake of research, and then everything was tenderly wrapped in waxed paper and placed in the green and white Barthélémy bag. Once outside, Olivier popped his head into the bag for a second and breathed in the great waves of ripe Reblochon, his eyes glazed like a teenage glue-sniffer.

In a sensual trance, Olivier strolled down the Rue de Grenelle. The old walls glowed cream in the autumn sun. People had thrown open their double windows above the curlicued wrought-iron rails, and a dog slurped from the stone dragon waterspouts outside the Musée Maillol. When Olivier passed Dalloyau, he could not ignore the siren call of a tiny leek tart with flaky, butter-ridden pastry. As he pushed the bakery's door to leave, a gamine girl with dark bobbed hair, high heels and a short green belted trenchcoat swept by him, pausing to make curious eye contact for a long moment, in the way men and women do in Paris. Olivier tossed back his locks and gave her his 'Yes, it is I, the famous philosopher' smile. She smiled quickly back, small white teeth in an almond-shaped face, and he watched through the window for a while as she ordered pistachio macaroons. He mused on the possibilities under her tightly belted green coat as he walked home, the tart warm in his jacket pocket.

The sunlight cut suddenly to cool darkness as Olivier stepped over the lintel of the apartment building. He could feel the evil eye of Madame Canovas upon him as he entered the arches, and hear her dry cough. His spine rippled. The concierge had long ago given up twitching her net curtains, and instead had pinned one back with a clothes-peg to create a permanent spyhole. Ever since her husband had left her, without a forwarding address, ten years before, she had been obsessed to near-lunacy with everyone else's business.

Her loyalty to the building's management was unquestioning, and her knowledge of other people's business unsurpassed. Olivier was sure she would have been an informer during the war, given the chance. She got great satisfaction from following orders to the letter.

'Good afternoon,' said Olivier to the gap in the curtains, just to annoy Madame Canovas and indicate his contempt for snooping. This was a mistake, because on cue, she popped out of her dark layer, flapping, holding a bottle of pills and a little black book. Of witchcraft, Olivier presumed. 'Ah, Monsieur Malin, you know I am the soul of discretion, but I just wanted to raise one little matter with you.' She looked round to make sure they were not overheard, and moistened her lipstick-gashed mouth. 'The new nanny. The British girl . . .'

'Yes, what now?' grunted Olivier, putting one foot on the stairs so he wouldn't have to wait for the lift with the old baggage ranting at him. He could feel his leek tart growing cold, and he much preferred it lukewarm.

'Well, not only did this British nanny's delivery truck have to back up right into the courtyard, without previous written permission from the management – I, myself was not even consulted! – but they unloaded – and I am not one to exaggerate, as you know, Monsieur – but they unloaded six clothes rails and *fifty-three* boxes . . .' Here, she consulted her black book. 'Yes, fifty-three. And commandeered the lift for about an hour. For a *chambre de bonne*!'

Olivier tried to interrupt but the concierge rolled on. 'The movers were black, foreign, you know,' confided Madame Canovas, who never let race go unremarked. 'And this new nanny was down there half-naked in a tiny vest, all dusty and sweating – I suppose you know she has a Chinese tattoo on her back, dreadful – helping them lift things. I, personally, would not be so sure that she is the right person for your lovely little Sabine.'

Olivier rolled his eyes, while Madame Canovas rolled on: 'And then there was this chaise longue, covered in cow hide, which got stuck in the lift door. Her taste! God give me strength. There was all this shouting up and down the stairs, too. It disturbed Madame Royan on the third floor who had one of her migraines and she said to me that a mere slip of a girl, a servant, for goodness' sake, should not get above herself like . . .'

'Yes, well, I do apologise if our household has caused you any inconvenience, but I'm sure it wasn't intentional.' Olivier hadn't even set eyes on the girl yet. 'Got. To. Go. Now. Perishables,' said Olivier, gesturing at his bags.

'Ohh. Having a dinner party tonight, are you? For how many? I always think, myself, that Barthélémy's rather expensive, isn't he?' She regarded the bag sourly. 'I prefer the cheese counter at Leclerc myself. Anyway, what time shall I expect . . .'

'Don't worry about it,' said Olivier. 'Goodbye.' He was already running full pelt up the staircase to avoid throttling Madame Canovas.

Olivier was panting by the time he reached the sixth floor. He marched straight down the corridor to the kitchen and dropped the bag with a smile on the counter in front of the maid. 'Hey, Luiza, here's the cheese for tonight, and don't for God's sake put any of it in the fridge this time, OK?' Luiza jumped up, surprised, from the kitchen table. 'Oh, Monsieur Malin, I wasn't expecting you so early.' She started shuffling a couple of recipe books about the table in an agitated way.

'Do you want it all to go on the cheese board, Monsieur?' she asked, carefully placing the bag over something she had been writing.

'Olivier, not Monsieur,' said Olivier in exasperation. He loved service, but he hated dealing with servants in the old-fashioned way. He used the familiar *tu* with Luiza – she was in her mid-twenties, for goodness' sake – but she always used *vous* back. It had been like that for seven years. He had known her brother, her uncle, and her son even, back in Grozny when he was researching his book, but he was still her employer, foremost. Luiza was very traditional that way. So he was always deserving of *vous*. He sighed. It was hard being a socialist with servants.

'Yeah, thanks, put out all the cheeses. And what are you cooking tonight?' Olivier said, sneaking a glance over her shoulder. The papers under the cookery books were entitled: 'Letters from Jenny Marx to Karl, following childbirth', and there was some computer printout on Pliny and health which he couldn't quite make out.

'A ceviche of salmon and lime to start – I've already got that marinading there – and then guinea fowl stuffed with pine nuts, ceps and girolles.' Luiza had picked up French cooking like a native. The variety and luxury of ingredients still thrilled her. She spent half the day down the Rue de Buci with her baskets. 'And I'm not sure about dessert yet – maybe some *pots de crème* with whatever soft fruit is best today at the green market on Boulevard Raspail. Madame loves *pots de crème* . . .'

Luiza trailed off nervously and failed to make eye contact with Olivier, who had moved her shopping bag over and was reading the title of a paper: 'Excavation of the tomb of Tutankhamen's wet-nurse.' Olivier suddenly felt chilled. He looked over at Luiza, who'd started chewing her thumb nail. He thought it best to get back to kitchen matters.

'Sounds great,' said Olivier. 'For eight people – Bourdon and his partner are coming too. Did Madison tell you that? Good.' He wandered off to his study, puzzled. It was fine by him if the staff studied archaeology, Marx and Pliny – Luiza had started some course at night school to make up for the collapse of her education in Chechnya. But Olivier wasn't so keen on the sudden interest in the history of wet-nursing, nor the way she was hiding it like a dirty secret.

Olivier put the staff out of his mind and settled down at his desk to enjoy his leek tart, only wishing he'd bought two. He loved his study, with its soundproofed, lockable green baize door and high steel bookshelves with their attached ladder which glided along on a track. Unlike the rest of the apartment, his room was free of the antiques and hefty gilded paintings which Madison and his mother so favoured. Indeed, grandiose interior decor was about the only matter the two women agreed on. Instead of spindly chairs, he had a wall-length sofa (from the time before he'd fallen out with Starck) and a rectangular slate table which sat eight – or one with lots of papers – which he'd bought down the street in the Conran Shop sale. And, of course, a stainless steel fridge in which he kept film and, at the moment, a case each of chilled Brouilly and Badoit. Oh yes, and some divine little marinaded anchovies he'd got at the Grande Epicerie.

The double windows looked on to the courtyard where wisteria was growing up the lower walls. When Olivier was in the mood, he liked to sit at his table and observe the interior life of 84 Rue du Bac: on the second floor, the wizened Madame Duplessix could be seen watching the racing on television all afternoon, occasionally leaping up and tossing her Zimmer frame aside to phone in a bet. Madame Royan was always trotting out to the pharmacy for expensive panaceas for her various, largely fictional ailments, and indulging in long gossip-sessions with Madame Canovas in the courtyard. Meanwhile, Madame Royan's neighbour, the put-upon Madame Bellan, was regularly in the courtyard by her car unloading dozens of bags from hypermarkets beyond the Périphérique, necessary with five kids and the portly Monsieur Bellan. The most unusual residents were the young couple, the Jeunots on floor five, who appeared from their silhouettes to perform the shower scene from *Psycho* nightly. All this went on under the eternal vigilance of Madame Canovas who, as far as Olivier saw, only left the building for five minutes a day to sneak across the street for her baguette. Right now, she was down in the courtyard having a cigarette and holding someone's mail up to the sunlight in case it held contraband goods.

Kate Muir

Olivier shook his head and swivelled his chair away from the window to face his laptop. He turned off his phones, and bent himself to the burden of the new power elite and life after capitalism, the subject of his latest book. 'The bourgeoisie is still cultivating the notion that democracy is eternal, the only solution, which we see at its extreme in Francis Fukuyama's *The End of History*,' typed Olivier. 'Yet, along with philosophers like Alexander Bard, I have come to believe that representative democracy will be diluted to socio-political icing on a cake which is made up solidly of networks. Bard calls this "the netocracy". Power will come from the control of information, not the politicians of nation states.'

We French, Olivier thought, have been rather slow in coming to terms with the philosophical and political challenges raised by digital media and the Internet, but fortunately the Americans, Swedes and whatnot are well ahead, and conveniently not yet translated here. It meant Olivier had a headstart on a new subject, and frankly, a man can only have so many dealings with the works of Derrida and stay sane. It was time to move on. Besides, the students at his Café Philo sessions in the Café Calvaire at the Opéra were all on to this. It was only a matter of time before it percolated up, and by then he would be master of the new, fashionable technophilosophy.

He pottered happily along in this manner for a few hours. Then he picked up that week's *Nouvel Etat* magazine and turned to his own column, appreciating some of the more toothsome turns of thought again, before returning to his book. He paused only to watch Sabine arriving back from school down below, squirming under a pat from Madame Canovas, and running through the doors to practise skipping with her rope in the courtyard. He was charmed, as though he were a stranger observing his daughter's hair in two sticky-out plaits, her little kilt, and her clean white ankle socks in those round-toed navy strap shoes that respectable Parisian girls have worn for half a century. He felt a wave of love for her, more as a concept than a piece of reality. She could be rather whiny and clingy around him, and he had little time for the horse and fantasy books she wanted him to read to her, preferring something more serious himself. Olivier often announced that he was the sort of man who would make a fantastic father once his daughter was older; he disliked the wet-bottomed tedium of toddlerhood, but once Sabine started grasping concepts, literature and history, he would be there to direct her, to stimulate her growing intelligence.

A figure followed Sabine – the new nanny. It was hard to tell from above, but it seemed to be a small woman in a baseball cap, baggy trousers and trainers. Typical, thought Olivier. Madison's got us a dyke. She had mentioned the purple hair to him after the interview. The thought made him grumpy, the idea that perhaps Madison had selected a nanny on grounds of her unavailability. And as if he would. 'Humph,' he said.

Olivier had just got his concentration back, when the door to his study burst open and Sabine ran in and jumped on him. 'Papa, Papa, look what I made! For you.' She presented him with a tile featuring a ham-fisted painting of a flower. He pulled her on to his lap. 'Oh that's sweet, darling. What kind of flower is it?' Sabine looked at him in exasperation. 'Can't you see it's a lion? Roaring. RAAARRH. Those are his teeth and that's the blood dripping after it's killed a . . .'

'I'm sorry. Have we interrupted you?' said a voice with a slight English accent coming round the door. 'Oh!' she said, recognising him. The nanny looked shocked, and suddenly Olivier realised that she was the gamine girl in the green coat from the bakery, now in working clothes of unpleasant baggy casualness, like some rapper. The brown-eyed stare was the same under the layers, and her bob was stuffed in the baseball cap.

Olivier was puzzled. Why did women do that to themselves, disguise themselves as quite different people? She had been perfectly presentable – indeed rather delectable – a few hours before, and now this?

Then he smiled: 'Olivier Malin. How nice to meet you. Last month when you came for an interview my wife led me to believe you had purple hair. I was expecting someone somewhat different.' He was aware that she knew he'd given her that glance in Dalloyau.

'Sorry. I'm Anna Ayer,' she said, looking down, nervous. 'Sabine's new nanny.'

'Ah,' said Olivier, raising an eyebrow. 'And would that be like the English Jane Eyre?'

'No, I think it's French. But it's spelt Ayer like A.J. No relation.'

He knew Anna meant the philosopher, and stared with new interest at her. She thought he was looking at her hair, and took off her baseball cap.

'It comes, it goes,' said Anna, shrugging. 'The purple, I mean.' She had revealed her small head with its shiny brown bob. 'I'm back to normal now.' She seemed highly embarrassed. Sabine was watching, silent and fascinated. Olivier suddenly wanted them both out of there.

'Could you take Sabine, and in future, eh, Anna, if you could remember I prefer not to be disturbed in my study until after six p.m. . . .' He turned to Sabine, and dangled a little bag of chocolate coins before her as a bribe, which she took. 'Off you go, poppet.'

'And Anna?'

'Yes?'

'Will you have Luiza bring me a pot of coffee?'

Having got the domestic staff in line, Olivier returned to his computer to consider the electronic disenfranchisement of the working classes in the techno age. On a caffeine high, he fell into his stride, pinging out perfectly crafted paragraphs, each cocooning some clever thought. A delicious hour passed unnoticed. Then his bubble burst again as Madison barged in, kicked her heels off, and crashed full length, which was very long in her case, along his sofa.

'I cannot tell you how appalling my day has been!' she began. Olivier tried to finish typing his sentence, a particularly fine sentence, but her voice compelled him to look up. A perfect swathe of bias-cut brown silk covered her body, but her hair had clumped into dirty-blonde rats' tails.

'Oh. What happened? Let me guess. You sacked your hairdresser?' he said, squinting at her, irritated by the interruption.

Madison sounded more Texan, and less French when she was whining: 'Never, just like never am I working with that man again. He's a peasant, with his nasty, big hairy hands and he's an evil dictator behind the camera.' She was referring to one of France's major avant-garde film directors, a man highly respected in critical circles, who just happened to be coming to dinner tonight.

'The pig made me jump into that freezing pond five times. It's September, for God's sake, Olivier. There was mud and weed, and he just stared at my tits through my shirt, fiddling with his zoom, getting a close-up. I said to him, André, I am not some stunt woman. Catherine Deneuve would never do this. Audrey Tautou wouldn't even consider . . .'

'Mmmn.'

Olivier continued typing – he didn't want to lose his deep train of thought – so he hung on while giving Madison an occasional sympathetic nod. She rarely complained about her directors – indeed she loved André – and by the film premiere they were always once again the best of friends. But suddenly his hands were painfully crushed as the screen of his portable computer slammed down, and he looked up to see Madison standing in full avenging blonde Valkyrie mode behind his desk.

'Christ. That fucking hurt. I might lose the chapter,' he said, scrabbling for the save button. 'What was that for?'

'Do you think I'm just wallpaper or something? Is it imposs-ible to engage you in any discussion that does not concern yourself?'

'I was in the middle of a paragraph. I was *writing*. You can't just stop and do another take like a movie. I was inspired – until you tried to break my bloody fingers.' Madison rolled her eyes. Olivier held his head in his hands and said quietly to the desk, 'If only you'd all knock.'

He stood up. 'That's it,' he said huffily. 'I'll have to stop now. I am going to organise dinner.' He walked right past Madison, noting that her flushed cheeks made her look alive and beautiful. At the door he stopped. 'André's a great director, you know, and he does not make mistakes, ever. He storyboards every shot beforehand, so perhaps you should consider suffering just a little for your art, Madison. I know American stars sit being served in their trailers all day, but this is France.' Olivier turned to see Madison's reaction, but she suddenly looked unbelievably tired, too tired to sustain her anger.

'You would think a husband might find it in him to provide some sympathy when his wife is doused five times in icy water, and treated like a whore, never mind the greatness of the director,' she said, her voice catching. 'My head's throbbing. I'm going for a bath.'

But before she could bathe, Sabine thundered along the

parquet corridor. 'Maman! Papa!' Clearly the nanny's shift was over, thought Olivier.

'Don't run like an elephant, darling,' said Madison, by way of greeting.

'Can I come and talk to you in the bath?' said Sabine, jumping around her mother. 'Can you read me *Charlie and the Chocolate Factory*? We won't get it wet this time, I promise.'

'Sabine, I'm so tired . . .' Olivier thought Madison's voice was close to cracking. 'Can't you just give me a minute to myself, darling? I'll read it later. Go help your father. You can arrange the flowers on the table in those two little silver jugs.' Madison then shut the door. Olivier took Sabine's small, warm hand. 'Come on, rabbit.'

Olivier found that Luiza had everything at a peak of efficiency. He let Sabine do the *placement* in different-coloured felt pens in her notebook, and then he wandered into the bedroom to get ready for the evening.

Sabine followed him. She both ran like an elephant, and didn't forget, Olivier noted. Madison appeared, wrapping her wet hair in a towel.

'Maman, will you read me *Charlie and the Chocolate Factory* now? I've been waiting for ages. I want you to read it, in American. Papa's no good at it at all, you know. He sounds really funny.'

'In a minute, darling, I've got to do my make-up. The guests will be here in half an hour.'

Without make-up, Madison's face was still perfect-skinned, a flat classical golden blank which could be redrawn into almost anything, or anyone. Olivier stretched out on the bed in baleful silence, watching Madison create herself. Under stage-style lighting and with professional skill, Olivier's wife made valleys appear under her cheekbones, erased the shadows beneath her eyes, and dosed them with some modern version of belladonna until they sparkled scarily bright. Sabine fiddled with the fascinating tubes and potions on the dressing table, waiting, the book officiously under her arm.

'Stop that,' said Madison sharply. 'You'll break off the end of my lipstick. See, I told you.' Madison snatched the broken brand-new tube from Sabine, who started to cry.

'I'm sorry, Maman.'

'Oh never mind, sweet pea, it doesn't matter,' she said, giving Sabine a hug and a kiss, conveniently before she put her layers of lipstick on. 'Just be more careful. These aren't toys, you know.'

Madison continued her work, sweeping up her newly washed hair into a twist. A high-maintenance appearance is so time-consuming, Olivier thought, delighted to be male.

Madison sealed her lipstick under some kind of plastic coating, so her kisses would leave no print.

'Ooh, what are those? They look weird,' said Sabine. 'Can I try?'

'Eyelash curlers,' said Madison. 'Pass them to me, would you?'

Olivier watched their two blonde heads together as he shaved, with his three-day stubble-maintenance razor, in the bathroom. Eventually Madison was finished, and the results were flawless, perhaps even in her estimation. She looked more thirty than forty-three, Olivier thought.

'Will you read me *Charlie* now? We'd just got to the bit with the Oompah Loompahs . . .'

'Darling, I just have to pick out my shoes. Do you want to help me choose?'

They went to a cupboard in the dressing room with some eighty shoe-cubbies. 'Must be blue,' said Madison, picking out some turquoise snakeskin sandals, 'or silver. Hmmmm.'

She looked paralysed by indecision, as though choosing the right shoes would dictate the course of the whole evening, Olivier thought. Was it because she might just be having dinner that night with both her husband *and* her lover? What better reason did she have to look beautiful? He didn't know whether he was aroused, disgusted or just fascinated by the idea.

'Silver, silver,' said Sabine, trying the red-soled Louboutin sandals on, and clacking around in them. 'Princess shoes!' Madison laid the shoes out, and had just settled down in her bathrobe to read to Sabine, not wanting to crush her dress, when Olivier looked at his watch.

'Sabine, sweetie, will you pop off now and get your pyjamas on?' he said. 'Our friends will be here in a few minutes and you can say hello before you go to bed, as a special treat.'

'But we just started. And I find it so hard to read English on my own . . .'

'Your mother needs to get dressed. Now scoot.' Olivier shooed Sabine gently out.

A heavy silence sagged between Olivier and Madison in the bedroom. Olivier picked up a white shirt from the perfectly laundered pile of six (Luiza was marvellous that way), and pulled it over his head, luxuriating in the silk folds. He tucked it in, undid another button to reveal some chest, and pushed his dark bobbed hair back from his strong cheekbones in the mirror on the armoire. He admired his stubble. There was no doubt in his mind that at forty-four he was as handsome as ever. He felt calm and amenable. He loved hosting parties.

'Can you zip it up for me?' asked Madison in a placating voice. Whatever happened between them privately, they never let it spoil their public persona as a perfect couple. Madison had inserted herself into the shiny pale blue dress with a fishtail hem. With her blonde hair, she looked like something between Brunhilde and a mermaid. Olivier toyed slowly with the zip of her dress, enjoying the heftiness of the lined satin, and the tanned furrow at the bottom of her spine. He had a sudden memory of how much he had once adored Madison. He planted an apologetic kiss on her back and started zipping it in.

Then he saw the label. 'Dior couture?' he said, his voice unable to hide a disapproving tone.

'Sure, honey,' said Madison. 'Who pays the bills?'

Madison's dead daddy paid the bills, which gave Madison a powerful hold on Olivier. The millions were useful, he acknowledged, because philosophy is expensive and unprofitable on the whole, and they would not be living in this style on the money from Olivier's university job at Sciences Po, or his books, or his occasional television appearances. Madison's father, an oily Texas businessman called Vance Rumswagger, had sent his only daughter to finishing school in Switzerland after her mother died. Madison never returned – except for her father's funeral. Vance pined away alone or died of sixty-a-day, depending on whose version you heard. Madison reinvented herself completely, learned grammatically perfect French, dropped her ugly second name altogether, and went from finishing school to sailing school. That mostly involved disporting herself beautifully on yachts and gin palaces in Cannes harbour, where she was inevitably discovered by a Roman Polanski sort who exploited her for his own and the public's pleasure. Olivier fondly remembered many of those early films, particularly *The Turquoise Sea*, and was always slightly surprised that the woman he married had not remained within the confines of those delightful deflowering scripts, but turned out to have a strong will of her own.

The doorbell rang when they were still putting their shoes on – it was Bourdon and his new English lover. 'The English,' snorted Olivier. 'They always come on time, which is far too early.' He stuck his head round the door to check Luiza was attending to them, and went back to splash on some aftershave.

Luiza – who always insisted on wearing traditional uniform, to Olivier's embarrassment and Madison's delight – ushered the guests into the salon, and opened the cabinet filled with the Fabergé collection. The Malins came through the double doors together, a picture of beauty and marital bliss. 'Bourdon, old boy,' said Olivier, hugging his friend.

Bourdon (no one used Ulysse, his first name) kissed Madison on each cheek, and lumbered into the salon. He was at least six feet four, with a huge red beard, and took up a lot of the room.

Luiza silently held out a silver tray with glasses of champagne and whisky to Bourdon and his new boardroom and bedroom find, Horatio Hervey. Hervey had written a graphically sexual, highly intellectual, very fictional romp through Mary Wollestonecraft's revolutionary French years, and Bourdon's company was publishing it in Paris. Olivier noted that Horatio stood at ease in the empty grandeur of the salon – he was clearly used to such rooms at home. He wondered if Horatio had a title of any sort, which he was keeping under wraps. Olivier had a secret fondness for titles, possibly because his family had dropped its own long ago.

'And this must be Horatio,' said Olivier, managing some English and staring at the young man's pout and floppy foppish hair. 'We have heard so much about your new ways with history.'

'He speaks fluent French. Don't you, Horatio?' said Bourdon, clearly proud of his new acquisition, his bulk a strange contrast to the willowy man-boy.

'Delighted to meet you,' said Horatio, bowing his head. His French was perfect, but his accent was appalling. It was clear to

Olivier that Horatio had no intention of giving up his habit of plummy intonation, or indeed his plum-coloured smoking jacket, which he was wearing tonight. Bourdon stroked Horatio's velvet shoulder proprietorially and admired the creamy skin of his unlined neck.

'And what attracted you to Mary Wollestonecraft?' asked Madison, purring in Texan. His wife was always superb at socialising, thought Olivier. She knew just enough about almost everything. 'Was it her writing, or through Shelley, or her daring after the Revolution?' She took the dandyish Horatio into a corner, settled beside him on a tiny Louis XVI sofa, and observed him benignly as he performed his piece.

'Olivier! Darling!' He was smothered in heavy kisses and heady scent. It was Renée Rimbaud, editor of the *Nouvel Etat*. 'Madison! Oh my God, what an exquisite dress. I do not believe it. Where did it come from?'

'Galliano made it for me.'

'At Dior? Oh darling, he just knows you to a T. Was it expensive?'

Madison shrugged. Renée was so vulgar.

'You know,' continued Renée, 'I've been over to see the new Margiela showroom – why, we must, must go together for a bit of girlie shopping, you know.'

'Mmmn,' said Madison flatly. 'I only shop twice a year, once in autumn and once in spring. So – sadly – I'm done.' Olivier watched Renée squirm inwardly in response. She tried to force every woman she met into fake ladies-who-lunch friendship. It was her attempt to conform to how she imagined normal women behaved, but somehow she always struck a wrong note. Olivier knew that Renée was actually a man by instinct, and ran her magazine with ruthless vision. She found it hard to make friends with women, and made desperate attempts to be one of the girls in the most simplistic ways. She was always over-dressed, to compensate for her hard interior, and usually had her small saggy breasts perilously on show. Several paces behind Renée, as usual, stood her tiny husband Paul, a museum curator.

Paul hugged Olivier, his best friend, and then kissed Madison gently on each cheek, mentioning a glowing review – one of the aberrant few – of her latest film. She gave him a kindly smile. Paul left his hand on Madison's shoulder just a little too long, Olivier thought, but then you could never tell what Madison was up to. For instance, André Andrieu had just entered the room, and now she was moving away from Paul and glancing quickly at her reflection in the glass cabinet to check she was indeed beautiful, before floating grandly over to greet the great director, and – as much as possible – to ignore his wife, a grande dame of an actress called Bibi.

'You look incredible,' said André, one of the few men in the room tall enough to look down into Madison's blue eyes, 'I'm sorry you had such a rough time on set today, darling, but I've seen the rushes and I think it was worth every second. It's supposed to be intellectual. We weren't making cheesecake, you know.' Madison blew out a long smoke ring and looked quizzically at André.

'Wait till you see the rushes. They're beautifully lit,' he added, nervously.

Madison suddenly smiled warmly, showing no sign of her earlier wrath about the pond-ducking. She was nothing if not professional, thought Olivier, watching. The portly little Paul had stopped talking to him, and stared distraught at Madison and the film director. André still displayed the strong jaw and body of a leading man, but he had cast all that off for the mental challenge behind the camera. 'Have you had time to think about that book adaptation we discussed last week? It's a dangerous, very uncomfortable narrative, but I think we could crack it together.' He held Madison's gaze, and went on talking. Paul turned his back on them sulkily. Olivier was unsure whether the moment was more embarrassing for him or Paul.

The noise in the room rose, as drink oiled the chattering classes with their clattering glasses. In crisp linen pyjamas, Sabine padded in beneath the crowd, down among endless exquisite shoes and dark male trouser legs. She surfaced beside Olivier, and pulled his D'Artagnan-style sleeve. 'Papa?' she said, but before she could speak, Sabine was crushed in a heavily perfumed hug by Renée. 'Oh, you look just like your mother now! Really growing up, but you've not quite lost that puppy fat yet,' she said, lightly pinching Sabine's cheek. Olivier could see Madison was ready to kill Renée.

'And how's school? Are you performing well?'

'Dunno,' said Sabine. Renée couldn't talk to children either, even though she had two of her own. 'She looks tired, poor thing,' said Renée, turning away, 'I thought she might have played us some piano, but perhaps she's not quite at that standard yet,' she said, gesturing at the *Early Songs* music book on the grand in the corner. Olivier looked round nervously, fearing a possible forced performance, but Sabine had sensibly bailed.

'Night,' said Sabine, grabbing two huge handfuls of cashew nuts from a silver dish as she made for bed, while her mother eyed her worriedly. Olivier knew she was adding up the calories.

They went through the double doors to dine in the neighbouring red-walled room with many silver candelabras and mirrors which shone from Luiza's hard labour. Horatio was talking to Madison about the creative pinnacles of handmade shoe making, gesturing at his own softly shod feet with 'leather like butter'. Olivier could see Madison half listening and watching her own reflection in the mirror, smiling with one movement at both herself and André opposite. Paul Rimbaud looked sick with jealousy. Olivier felt just a touch irritated by all the men paying attention to the glowing Madison – usually it was women flocking to him.

Over the ceviche, there was the usual talk – of the new populist Anglo-American history and whether it was intellectual suicide to be a professor with a television series, of foie gras and early feeding methods of geese, of policy in the Middle East, of Louise Colet's salons, and then, while Luiza-the-immigrant served the guinea fowl in her pinny from the left, they discussed the anguish of asylum seekers in the housing estates beyond the Périphérique, and the racism that pervaded high Paris culture, which was preventing one particular immigrant poet's raw work from being published.

Olivier was engaged in a textbook flirtation with Bibi on his right, partly to annoy Madison, partly because that was what dinner parties were for once you reached a certain age and utter freedom was far too tiring. He loved the elegance of older women, and he still had a pressing need to exercise his charm whenever possible, so he paid careful attention to Bibi's physical and psychological needs. He leaned a little too close, he carefully replaced the fallen napkin on her silky thighs, and he massaged her ego as she moaned about the lack of good parts for strong women. He gestured and touched her hand. Soon the table took on a Rabbelasian tendency. Horatio was feeding Bourdon a particularly choice wild mushroom from his own plate. While bending down for another lost napkin, Olivier had noticed that Madison had momentarily brushed her bare ankle against Paul – her lover? – under the table. Paul looked shocked, then blissfully happy. Madison's skin and breasts became flushed and her eyes sparkled, and she reminded Olivier of the goddess he had married.

Paul was talking intently to Madison about a new biography of Rodin's assistant and lover, the sculptor Camille Claudel, and Madison was spouting what Olivier considered to be a lot of American psycho-drivel. He suddenly felt oddly aggressive towards her. He sometimes preferred it when she remained a statue of serious artistic importance. It was his duty to be the intellectual, and hers, the beauty, and not the other way round.

'Rodin, you know, was erroneously portrayed as a villain in early analysis of Claudel's career, yet there were crushing reproofs and prejudices that came from elsewhere, like . . .'

'Now, Madison, what do you know about that?' interrupted Olivier.

'A great deal,' said Madison, giving him a puzzled stare. 'Particularly the bit when the unfortunate combination of art and repressed womanhood sends her nuts. Now why don't you go check what's going on with the cheese?'

She was right. He would go and remove the top of the Mont d'Or himself, just to check for ripeness and creaminess. When Olivier walked into the kitchen, Sabine was on Luiza's knee in the chair by the big stainless steel stove. Her head was leaning on Luiza's chest as she listened to some complex folk tale, featuring music boxes and strangers in the night. 'Isn't this a bit late, sweetie?' said Olivier gently from the counter, as he cut off the rind. Sabine put her arms round Luiza to hug her goodnight.

Then Madison came in, took one look at the cook and Sabine embracing, and snapped.

'What are you doing up this late? Get straight to bed.' Luiza jumped up as though burned and deposited Sabine on the floor.

'I was frightened, Maman. I had a bad dream about being attacked by lobsters,' said Sabine, her voice wobbling.

Madison relented and took her by the hand. 'You could have come to me,' she said softly.

'I didn't want to want to disturb you. You were so busy this evening.'

'I'll tuck you up quickly, my love,' said Madison, taking Sabine down the corridor. Olivier carried the cheese platter while Luiza followed with the bread. Renée congratulated her on her pintade. 'And what was the extraordinary green, nutty stuffing?'

'Pine nuts, purée of sorrel, and some dandelion leaves.'

'Oh, marvellously nouvelle cuisine.'

'In fact, Madame, it's a seventeenth-century Provençal recipe, and I got it in the library,' said Luiza, without looking back as she disappeared to the kitchen. Reneé looked a little discomfited, but regained her composure once the cheese had gone round.

Meanwhile Paul was in gastrophilosophe heaven. 'Ah, splendid selection of cheeses, and as for the Mont d'Or . . .' he greedily licked some more from his bread, '. . . it is perfection itself. Was it not Antheleme Brillat-Savarin, who said, "Dessert without cheese is like a pretty girl with only one eye"?' Olivier was annoyed. He hated having his pet quotes repeated on him, like half-digested cabbage.

Madison returned to the table and ate three *petits pots de crème* in speedy succession. Paul watched her in awed silence. Suddenly detached from the hubbub of the dinner party, Olivier looked from his best friend to his wife and back again, and wondered how the free pursuit of happiness had brought them here.

3

Madison Malin

Scrunchity, scrunchity, scrunch went Madison's Christian Louboutin heels across the gravel in the Musée Rodin garden on the Rue de Varenne. The great advantage of Louboutin shoes – aside from the fact they give large feet a delicacy previously only achieved by footbinding – is that their soles are always scarlet red, allowing the beholder a sudden flash of the forbidden. In the distance, Paul Rimbaud, director of the Musée Rodin, was hormonally alerted by the signals from her shoes, the modern equivalent of the red A for adulteress. Madison could see Paul marvelling at the tiny cloud of dust raised round each of her perfect ankles. He watched her walk down between the espaliered apple trees until he could clearly no longer bear it. Then he panted up beside her, like a respectful pug.

'From a curatorial standpoint, those red-soled sandals complete you, in the way a red dot or a red handkerchief completes a Corot painting,' he opened, pink with the heat and smiling from ear to ear above his Paisley bow tie, pleased with his theory.

Madison leaned down and tenderly kissed Paul on both cheeks; they were outside after all, and might be seen; why would anyone expect more? Here they were, meeting in a public place, where all who saw would know precisely their intent anyway. But it being Paris, no one would make a fuss about it. Besides, for Madison, there was as much pleasure in the anticipation, the holding back, as there was in the release of the affair, and she had no intention of consummating this one, ever. Lingering was of some importance to a woman whose introduction to love took place rapidly, regularly and roughly beneath the bleachers of a Texas schoolyard with mosquitoes blood-sucking her back.

From behind one of the garden's statues, an overweight American tourist in a polyester tracksuit was videoing Madison with her chignon and cinch-waisted suit as an example of perfect Parisian womanhood. Madison listened to her accent with a shiver of recognition that went back to her childhood, and realised that but a year or so and seventy pounds separated them as fellow Texans, one turned from cheerleader to beauty, the other to blubber. 'Darling, you look just fantastic,' said

Paul, walking across the camera's sights, unaware. 'Are those shoes new?' He looked as though he might bend down to kiss her bare toes.

'Uh huh,' said Madison, all but ignoring his words. She marched briskly on and lit a Marlboro Light. 'Paul, darling, I have been thinking,' she said, blowing the smoke from pouting lips. 'I think I should start a salon in the Rue du Bac – you know, in the old-fashioned sense of Louise Colet, like we were talking about the other night, yet something modern, witty, a little bit dangerous. Halle, that half-Algerian poet, you know, might be a good start, and do you think, perhaps, Benedict Fournier would be an appropriate philosopher? You know, I read his *Ex-Tracts of Modernity* and I thought that his line on Derrida was . . .'

'You would run the most adorable and, of course, intellectually significant salon,' said Paul nodding, his glasses glinting with enthusiasm in the sunlight. 'You, and that wonderful apartment, would be a fantastic draw.' He took advantage of her concentration to slip his arm round her waist. Madison continued, oblivious. Her thin shadow moved along the gravel beside Paul's squat one.

'Early every Wednesday evening, I feel, but not in the summer, obviously. But which architect is making his name now?'

'Jean Nouvel,' said Paul.

'And what about that new curator in the gallery in Ménilmontant? The guy with that installation of plaster casts of erect horse penises? And how did he manage to cast them, do you think?' She grinned. Together, they turned away from the ornamental pool with its stone bodies, and made their way to the gate through the precisely spaced, pollarded trees. Safe from the crowds, Paul squeezed Madison's hand, and sighed wistfully as the sun dappled her hair. 'Paul!' she snapped. 'Concentrate, darling. You must help me, you know all these people.'

'Well, so does Olivier,' said Paul, wiping his hot forehead with a handkerchief that matched his bow tie. Olivier and Paul had been friends for twenty-five years, since university, yet they clearly did not discuss matters of the heart, or of lesser parts. Or perhaps they did, but only in a theoretical manner. Madison presumed that Olivier presumed she was having an affair with Paul, but it was against her husband's code of ethics to mention it to either of them: unlike Sartre, Olivier did not believe in openness and full disclosure. Too well-bred, Madison thought. He's secretly more bourgeois than bohemian. Thus she had engaged in her platonic extra-marital affair two years ago, out of necessity rather than desire: Olivier could not be allowed to sin alone. Oddly the affairs, real for him, fictional for her, had balanced their relationship. The tension kept it half alive – or half dead and malingering, depending on your viewpoint. Madison, with her long history of unquestioning worship from men, and then bitter disappointment with them as partners, thought that was as much as she could hope for. Besides, Paul was respectful, useful, and kind of sweet. He was a friend, perhaps her best friend.

Madison glared at the sculpture of *The Burghers of Calais* before her and continued: 'Olivier doesn't care about any of my projects – except films that feature me naked, which he finds all too amusing. You know, Paul, he'll barely discuss them with me, while I have to listen to his ideas for hours, sometimes in the middle of the night. No, this must be my plan alone. My salon, my life, not his.' Paul nodded understandingly. He was constantly invited places as Renée's husband, rather than in his own right.

Being mistress of a literary and artistic salon, Madison felt, would at last provide escape from being tarred as a 'Texan model-turned-actress' and make her a true Parisian. She worked hard on her own carefully created life story, and had begun this fictional affair with a homely intellectual to improve her image. There was a certain amount of talk about such affairs at the best tables, and there was no question that she was as well-read and smart as most of her *salonistes* would be. It was just that they had the advantage of being ugly. 'Now we shall have lunch and you can write me a list of the artists you think would be most fascinating – and sociable, of course.'

Paul did as he was told. But Madison knew that all he really wanted to do was to take her shoes off in the empty restoration studio behind his office, and worship her on a pedestal along with the other nude sculptures. He had requested that before. But it was not to be. He had just over an hour, and she wanted lunch at the three-star Arnaud. Most of the critics called it the latest cooking, but Paul (and Olivier) considered it a vegetarian nightmare and a rip-off to boot.

Yet as he watched Madison toy with a few matchsticks of truffled celeriac in the expensively beige restaurant, Paul seemed smitten with love. He discussed Fournier with her, but he had only read a magazine article and she an entire book on the subject, so he was slightly out of his depth. Then she wanted to talk about a difficult, much-debated novel which he hadn't even seen, never mind added to the pile of unread works on his bedside table. He discussed his plans to commission a play or monologue on the life of Camille Claudel, to be staged in the Rodin museum among some of the sculptures they created together. 'And I would like the play to continue up until her death.'

'I'm not sure how thrilling thirty years in that lunatic asylum would be on stage, unless you included all that stuff about her only eating raw eggs and unpeeled potatoes for years because she thought someone was going to poison her,' said Madison, giggling.

'You've read everything, Madison,' said Paul. 'How do you manage to read so much?'

'I have to lie around for hours between takes on set. Being all-too-often ornamental in movies, I don't get that many lines,' she said, smiling. 'I hate doing nothing, so I read. Otherwise I might eat, which would be a lot more dangerous.' She extracted some artichoke purée from the lightest of pastry packages, which might possibly contain an unwanted calorie. She could see Paul silently pricing her leftovers.

'Sweetie, I love it here. It's just that I'm squeezing into a particularly narrow set of costumes in my next film. But the food is delicious.'

Madison's mobile started ringing and she scrabbled around her Birkin bag for it. Every time Madison thought about her Birkin, which she did often and with pleasure, she wondered if Hermès would one day name a bag after her. It was a serious ambition.

'Hello? Hello?' It was Olivier, but he must have inadvertently sat on his phone and automatically dialed her.

'I'm very pleased about the German and Dutch rights,' he said, amid much thudding and crackling. 'They're surprisingly big book buyers.' A man's voice rumbled back, talking about lead times and paperbacks. Madison clicked the phone off. 'It's Olivier. He's always doing that. Never remembers to lock it. He keeps it in his back pocket so he sits on it all the time in taxis.'

Paul had his little leather diary out and was concentrating on looking for appropriate characters for her list. He obviously didn't like being interrupted by Olivier, even unintentionally. Madison looked at his suggestions, but she wasn't satisfied. She copied some down, and tapped her Palm Pilot stylus down the length of the list, shaking her head: 'I need it to be less Parisian establishment, and more loose and dangerous. Almost everyone's white and over forty, Paul.'

'Well, so are we,' said Paul.

'Don't say that,' hissed Madison, giggling and looking round. 'I need someone else to help me with this. Someone younger.'

She took out her mobile phone and pressed one of the names on automatic dial. 'Angel' it said.

'Darling, I need your help. Yes. Today, now. Yes, earlier than our appointment. I've had some inspiration. Pick me up at Arnaud in the Seventh in ten minutes ... yeah ... OK ... *Ciao.*'

Paul looked sad. No studio work today, then. 'Is Angel a name, or a description of his role?' he asked, jealous. Madison stood up, laughing, and disappeared into the Ladies just as the enormous bill arrived. Paul hefted his worn credit card on to the plate with a groan. Two lunches at Arnaud in one month were a touch unbelievable. Who had that many A-list vegetarian contacts?

'Oh no, you paid, darling,' said Madison, returning. 'Oh it was my turn, wasn't it? Thank you, anyway,' she said, kissing him. Paul turned his cheek quickly so he could catch the remains of her kiss on his lips, but she drew her head up. 'Sweet man,' she said. 'Perhaps we could see each other after work on Friday? We're not going to the château this weekend, because Olivier's doing a Café Philosophe at Les Phares again. He loves talking to those students.'

Paul nodded: 'Madame Rimbaud had planned to take me to a dull leftist cocktail party at that very hour, but I will have to get unavoidably held up at work ... Will you be wearing more of those exquisite, delicate, red-soled things?'

Madison smiled, and said nothing. A tiny part of her pleasure in this game was that the dreadful Renée might hear rumour of it one day. As they walked outside, two rakish socialist politicians arrived outside the restaurant, and they gave Madison and Paul nods of recognition, watching with increased interest when the quiet of the street was interrupted by the roar of a vast motorbike, the sort with the silencers removed just to annoy. A lean figure upholstered in leather got off, faceless in a black-visored helmet. The biker strode over to Madison, handed her a matching helmet, and thumbed for her to get on the back of the bike. Not a word was spoken. Madison smiled to herself at the little scene. It would do her reputation no harm, she felt.

'Until Friday, darling,' said Madison, blowing Paul a kiss before she closed her visor, hitched up her skirt and hopped on the back of the bike. They left Paul and the politicians standing among the exhaust fumes.

Angélique aimed the bike north to the Seine, and swung so low and fast into the corners that Madison could only see the black tarmac roaring towards her, and feel the wind freezing her bare legs. She wrapped her arms tighter round Angélique's back, and luxuriated in the teenage adrenalin and fear the ride brought, as they roared along the Quai d'Orsay. The engine was so loud that all conversation was impossible. But Madison felt suddenly American on the road, free of stuffy French expectations and *bon-chic-bon-genre* rules. Angélique pulled up near St Sulpice in front of the Decoupage hair salon which she owned, and was helping Madison off the bike, tricky in the four-inch high Louboutins.

'I think they thought you were a man,' giggled Madison. 'It's your big boots. Did you see the faces of those politicians?'

'Ridiculous. Anyway, Maddy, how're you doing?' said Angélique, taking off her helmet, steadying the teetering Madison, and kissing her on both cheeks. 'Who was the little bespectacled fellow that I rescued you from?' It was not the first time Angélique had performed this service.

'Rimbaud, curator at the Rodin.'

'Rimbaud-the-famous-lover? Thought he'd be more glam.'

Madison shrugged and held up her hands in mock despair.

'Sorry. Who am I to talk about appearances?' Angélique slicked a hand through her short hair, pouted her lips and slunk ridiculously as she went through the salon door. 'But I don't know how you can possibly sleep with an ugly man.'

'It's an intellectual relationship,' said Madison.

'Yeah, right,' mocked Angélique. 'What will Madame have today?'

Madison ordered the tiniest of trims, a pedicure and an eyebrow wax, and smiled graciously at the rest of the salon staff. They all smiled back, because Madison was the most regular of customers, and tipped well – fifteen per cent, American style. Angélique had been her hairdresser and friend for ten years now, longer than her marriage, and it was perhaps the more solid relationship of the two. They had risen in parallel stardom, and besides, Angélique had never made a mistake. You might think that long blonde hair is the simplest of styles, requiring no work, but you'd be quite wrong. Madison took out her Palm Pilot again, lay back in the deep leather chair, and told Angélique about her plans for a salon. 'Go on, you move in the finest fashionista circles. And you're not old, yet. You're ten years younger than me, were I to reveal my true age. So who's up and coming? Who's weird, but can still talk properly and won't overdose in my newly recarpeted bathroom?'

'That's a tall order,' said Angélique. 'And are you sure it's still *de rigeur* to carpet bathrooms? Isn't that a bit Dallas?' Madison made a face at her in the mirror. 'Out of the way,' she said to a pretty girl in a white coat who knelt at Madison's feet with a nailfile. 'Can't get it straight if you're right there.' Angélique waved the scissors threateningly at her. The girl moved and squeezed herself under the counter, only her hands popping out from hiding to work reverently on Madison's toes. Above, they continued to talk, oblivious. Angélique provided a list of her too-trendy friends. It helped that Angélique's partner was Henri Mince, an S and M-inclined men's designer at a large couture house, who had made himself famous five years before by staging his own crucifixion with four-inch nails through his hands (but for safety reasons using a more comfortable rope and wooden platform for his feet). Angélique had styled the crown of thorns and filmed the charming scene in front of St Sulpice with a cheap hand-held camera. After about three minutes of crucifixion, her boyfriend had fainted, but no matter. He had the stigmata, and thereafter they both became celebrated throughout Paris.

'How's Henri, anyway?'

'Quite dried out. A new man. Running six sanctimonious miles every morning along the Seine . . .'

'The usual pale polish, Madame?' asked a small voice.

'My, I'd forgotten you were down there. Yes, two coats please. And could you make sure it's properly dry?'

Madison's mobile rang – Olivier had bumped his phone again, so she could overhear everything. 'Madame Paquin!' Olivier was saying. Then there were some mumbles and crunches. She was about to switch it off when she heard a woman's voice say the words, 'Versailles? That'll be eighty Euros.' She turned to Angélique. 'He seems to be buying Versailles for eighty Euros. Is it a model of Versailles? Weird. He should fix the lock on that phone.' She pressed the off button. Angélique was looking at her sadly in the mirror. She said nothing.

'Madison! Darling, I've been meaning to call to thank you for the fabulous dinner last week,' bayed a voice. It was, unfortunately, Renée Rimbaud, snatching a moment between editing and sacking people, her two favourite activities, to have her roots done. She flung herself on Madison (who was in mid eyebrow wax) and kissed the air in the vicinity of her cheeks. Renée was wearing a pencil skirt and a sheer grey blouse through which you could see her bra and her pointy little shoulder blades.

'Renée, how delightful,' lied Madison, resignedly snapping her Palm Pilot shut. She felt oddly guilty seeing Paul's wife so shortly after seeing him. But there was no escape, unless she ran out of the salon with half-painted toes and one bushy eyebrow, and she was starting a new shoot tomorrow. Renée ordered half a head of highlights from Angélique's new stylist Léon.

'I must be finished in an hour and a half, young man. Without fail, I have a meeting,' she announced, and then settled in to prise what information she could out of Madison. First, she tried to soften up her target by providing in exchange all the latest gossip from the Elysée, Matignon, and the mothers outside the best public *lycée* in the sixteenth arrondissement, where Renée kept a *chambre de bonne* for her Filipina maid so as to have an address within the catchment area for her two children. The fact that they really lived in a large *hôtel particulier* in the seventh was everyone's knowledge, but nobody's business. Her left-wing credentials were otherwise impeccable.

'I saw Olivier at Matignon the other day – the magazine was doing a lunch with the prime minister. Is he still going to chair this late-night cultural show with Bourdon? Rumour had it that he was up against Bernard-Henri Lévy for the job ... You know what they're saying – it's all about beauty, not brains, with those philosophers, isn't it?' said Renée, tittering.

Léon stopped his dye brush in mid-air at the mention of Olivier's name and stared in the mirror at Madison, as she spoke sharply: 'You know, Renée, we have separate careers and I don't know everything he's up to, and if something's under negotiation I don't ...'

Angélique leaned over to whisper to Madison: 'Just so you know, Léon, my new stylist, is going out with your little English nanny. Very keen on her.'

'Oh I see,' said Madison, eyeing the stylist, who seemed to be little more than a skinny kid in a tight T-shirt. She decided to be more careful about what she said, just in case.

'Olivier's sure to go down well on screen, with his gorgeous looks,' said Renée, labouring the point as usual. Madison looked at her coldly. She hated her privacy, physical and mental, being invaded at the hairdressers'. She particularly hated talking to Renée. It was the great curse of coupledom – having to socialise with your friends' execrable, inexplicable spouses. There was a silence.

'Shall I do it a touch blonder at the front, to cover that . . .' Léon politely faded out on the word grey.

Renée nodded. Angélique grinned. Madison smiled to herself. She wondered if Renée had any idea how often she saw Paul, but why should she? No crime was being committed. Well, nothing beyond thought-crime, in his case. Renée adjusted her tiny feet in their tiny Ferragamos, and studied Madison's toes undergoing their second coat, her size forty-one sandals on the floor. Madison could tell that Renée, who would rather be talking about the European Union deficit, was about to try some more of what she called 'girly chat'. Her heart sank.

'So flattering, those Louboutins,' said Renée, smiling, and then realising she was being rather rude, she dug herself in deeper. 'Talking of size, do you know that Katrine Duclos has had her breasts enlarged? A wonderful new process, apparently, using injections of foam.'

'Ooh, they say that's marvellous, yes, I've had a couple of

customers with them, obviously I can't say who,' said Angélique. 'But so soft, I hear.' She tipped Madison's chin upwards, trimmed the front of her hair, and winked at her while Renée was rummaging for her trilling phone in the multiple pockets of her Chanel bag.

'No, not now,' said Renée. 'Fix it immediately. Don't waste my time. Use your initiative. I'm in a meeting.' She put down the phone.

'Soft, realistic, and apparently you can still breastfeed through the foam.' Madison looked disturbed. 'Not that you'd want to, of course,' continued Renée. 'I never breastfed – well, I was back at work in ten days in my size eight Chanel, and everyone said it was amazing. But what breastfeeding does to your figure! She looked proudly down at the intact pancakes in her Thierry Mugler blouse. 'You didn't, did you, Madison? No, I remember you were filming three weeks afterwards, and I remember saying to myself how amazingly fast you were back in form.'

'Well, my job didn't exactly allow for it. I did my best,' said Madison. 'But it's a matter of private choice.'

Renée had a strange look on her face. She leant forward and lowered her voice: 'You know the latest thing is to get a wet nurse.'

Léon made a yuk noise. 'No, I assure you, they're making a comeback.' Renée turned. 'Can you make sure you're getting right into the roots with that paintbrush, Léon? Then it lasts longer, since it's so expensive. Anyway, one of the mothers at St Augustine – big career in Paribas – is said to have one. Maternity nurse, night nurse, wet nurse, where do you draw the line, really? And that presenter on Channel 3 news, with the red hair ... definitely. Well, it's very practical. The most interesting thing is that no one is really shocked. Parisian women always used to do it. I'm thinking of commissioning an article, if only I could find someone who would talk.'

'Are you quite finished?' demanded Madison in her deepest, actressy tones. Renée jumped, but Madison was looking down at her feet, apparently addressing the pedicure girl, who scuttled away. Madison quickly put on her sandals and stood up. 'Angélique, darling, I don't have time for a full blow dry. Leave it like that. Goodbye, Renée. Hope to see you soon. Those grey roots are a bore, aren't they? It must take so long. Bye, Angélique, darling. We'll talk on the phone.' She pressed a large note into Angélique's hand and walked out of the door, aware of Renée's stare boring into her back until she was out of sight.

4

Anna Ayer

It was Wednesday afternoon, a half-day for Sabine's school. Anna went out into the crisp autumn for a baguette, stuck it under her arm, and wandered round the corner to St Clothilde school, where she joined the perfectly pressed mothers at the big double doors. The mothers were all suddenly in smart winter coats and high boots, with accessories featuring much purple, whereas two days ago they'd all been in late-summer linen. Anna reckoned there had to be a special *Mères de France* radio announcement they must listen to every morning, in order for such tasteful fashion co-ordination to occur.

The mothers took one look at Anna's short green coat under which she appeared to be wearing nothing but black tights and green shoes, and left an airspace of disapproval around her. Although she'd been in the job for two months, the *Mères de France* remained an unbreachable bastion.

'They're kind of late today, aren't they?' Anna cheerfully asked the blonde highlights in a navy coat with gold buttons beside her.

'Perhaps,' said the mother coldly, immediately turning away.

Anna sighed, and spent some time adjusting the stud in her tongue, just to irritate the *Mères de France*. It wasn't as if there was a problem with her language, which was almost perfect, due to her French dad. It was just that the ladies of the seventh arrondissement thought she was common, and quite probably a dangerous foreign influence on children.

At last Sabine ran out holding hands with her friend Anouk, who was coming home to lunch. Huge backpacks thudded on their narrow shoulders.

'We're late again,' said Sabine.

'The old bag kept us behind for ten minutes to practise our handwriting exercises,' explained Anouk.

'Ooh, that's mean,' agreed Anna, in French.

In unison, the mothers gave her another glacial stare. One should not criticise the French education system, except in private.

The girls skittered around the pavement in huge excitement, although such a playdate was a weekly event. Like tiny sharks, they kept diving at the baguette and tearing off chunks to eat.

'Wait till we get home,' said Anna, holding it high above her head.

'Anna, Anna,' pleaded Sabine, still jumping for the bread. 'Can we go see the wicked witch and her creatures first? Please?'

'Hey, that's not a nice way to talk about Madame Canovas.'

'But Anouk hasn't seen those creepy coal tits she just got. Please, please, Anna?'

'Oh all right, wheedler. Five minutes.'

They knocked on Madame Canovas' door, and not surprisingly, she was peering out from the lace curtain on its glass window, twitching the gold cross round her neck.

'I said to myself, that sounds like my little Sabine coming home from school. My, girls can be noisy on the street nowadays, can't they? It wasn't like that in my day,' she said reprovingly to Anna, while patting Sabine on the head and adding, 'Lovely to see you, young ladies. Come in, come in. Look, we've got a new one called Tito. I went down to the bird market on the Île de la Cité last Saturday – well, I don't like to take too much time off as you know, but I thought the single coal tit needed companionship.' She put her hands round Anouk's and Sabine's shoulders, and they squirmed slightly.

Madame Canovas' two rooms always smelled of gas and overcooked soup, which was not in a cauldron but an orange *le Creuset* pan she'd retrieved burned, and revived, from one of the tenants. Almost no light penetrated the little apartment, such was the thickness of the lace curtains and the forest of knick-knacks and ornaments. Madame Canovas' big black books, in which she recorded spells or perhaps rubbish-collection times, lay on her damask-clothed dining table. Deep in the fug, for the concierge chain-smoked, lurked the bird cages on two stands. One cage contained a black mynah bird, the other three mangy coal tits which looked close to passing out from the cooking fumes. The girls were squealing and poking their fingers through the bars, scared at being in the witch's lair, but thrilled too. The mynah bird seemed to be endlessly repeating the French equivalent of 'damn it', but Anna couldn't be sure and dared not ask.

'Handsome, our little Sabine,' said Madame Canovas creepily stroking the child's hair and talking to Anna in an undertone. She flapped her shawl and stared at the girls. 'As handsome as her father, isn't she? She's got his good bones.' She looked beadily, or perhaps battily, at Anna for any trace of reaction.

'Yeah. Well, I must be getting the girls' lunch. Thanks so much, Madame, for letting us see the birds and stuff,' said Anna, feeling repulsed.

'Not at all, not at all. Don't go yet. Are you sure you girls don't want some blackcurrant pastilles?' She started shuffling through a drawer filled with money-off coupons and ancient sweet tins.

'Lunch,' said Anna, pushing Sabine and Anouk towards the door. 'Sorry.'

'Come again.' Madame Canovas' voice trailed behind them. She fell into a fit of coughing.

In the vestibule, a woman was about to close the lift door, and held it open for them. 'Which floor?' she asked.

'Sixth, please,' said Anna.

'Oh me too. I have an appointment with Monsieur Malin.' For a good seeing to, I expect, thought Anna, because she must have been here before if she knows there's only one apartment on the sixth. The woman had long wavy brown hair, fashionable oblong glasses, crocodile shoes and a flat little briefcase under her arm. Anna would have put her down as a publisher's assistant. Olivier was rumoured to get through a lot of them.

Anna opened the door and pointed down the corridor: 'He's in there, on the left,' said Anna.

'Oh yes, thank you, I wasn't sure,' said the woman, walking confidently to the correct door. Sure you're not sure, thought Anna feeling oddly aggressive, and heading off to the kitchen at the other end of the apartment to prepare lunch.

Luiza had gone to the market at the Rue de Buci, where she could easily spend hours studying the vegetables, but Madison had left careful instructions for the meal, no doubt wanting to impress Anouk's mother, who was married to some executive at Canal +. 'Boiled endive, white fish in milk. Apple purée. Evian. *No biscuits.*'

Madison clearly believed that good – in her case near-anorexic – eating habits began early. Sabine had just a smidgen of normal puppy fat on her, which caused her mother endless angst. 'If she feels that way she should just teach her to smoke nice and early,' laughed Anna to herself as she prepared the official lunch, adding illegal chunks of bread with Nutella at the end.

While the girls munched and chatted, Anna sat dipping torn buttered baguette in her coffee and watching the sun make patterns through the stained-glass window on to the polished parquet in the corridor. She felt time slowing pleasantly, and listened to the creaks and thuds from the *chambres de bonne* above, the sound of a lone piano being expertly practised down on the third floor, and Madame Duplessix on the second squeal through her open window as one of her horses came in at Longchamp. In moments like this, Anna loved the great heaving life of the building itself, and being part of it.

It suddenly reminded her of the noisy four-storey council estate they'd moved to after her father had left them in Manchester when she was nine. He was a long-distance lorry driver, and one morning he'd just driven off in a Tetrapak truck and never returned. All she had left was a black and white photo of him looking rather like a musketeer, and some early holiday snaps, but she suspected he was old now and had a beer belly from the sedentary driving life. She always wondered about him when she saw those 'Les Routiers' signs, or the Tetrapak triangle on juice cartons. After he'd gone Anna, her mother and little sister had to move from a proper house to a concrete building in Chorlton full of life of an admittedly rougher sort than the Rue du Bac. Anna had consoled herself after the loss and the move, by watching everything from her bedroom window with binoculars and writing a diary of the comings and goings of the neighbours like her childhood heroine, *Harriet the Spy*. After a few months observation, she was reassured by the utter lack of other happy families on the estate. Many seemed to be missing fathers, and others had endless dramas featuring changeable male figures. Steady couples just argued all the time. Money made little difference to the unhappy equation – her work as a nanny over the last few years had also confirmed that. Today she gloried in the contrast of her past life with the rich lives being led, the rich polished woods here in Paris, the high ceilings, the elegant double windows with their swirling wrought-iron rails, all reassuring evidence of her escape from the past.

Luiza broke Anna's daydream by storming into the kitchen with half a dozen bags and baskets sprouting fresh herbs and mushrooms.

'Hi Sabine, hi Anouk.' Then Luiza turned to Anna, her face sullen.

'Are you quite finished?' she asked, clearing away Anna's half-full coffee cup. 'I need to unpack.'

'Can we help?' tried Anna.

'No,' said Luiza.

'I give up,' said Anna, to no one in particular.

The girls and Anna left the kitchen and crept past Olivier's oddly silent study on exaggerated tiptoes, and giggled conspiratorially as they slammed the front door and started running down the stairs to go to the Luxembourg Gardens. Anna wondered how much these Parisian kids knew about their parents' double lives, and felt slightly embarrassed.

'The big skipping rope. We've forgotten it. Got to go back,' said Sabine, so they all returned to the apartment to rifle the toy trunk in the hallway. Suddenly, the door of Olivier's study slammed and the brown-haired woman emerged red faced, in tears. She took one furious look at them and shot into the bathroom, slamming the door huffily and giving Anna just enough time to note that the Hermès label of her shirt was now hanging out at the back. Sabine exchanged a knowing glance with Anouk, a look she was far too young to make, even in France, and then they retrieved the skipping rope.

There was much flushing and sniffing from the bathroom. Anna found herself giggling hysterically, along with the little girls. She opened the front door and skipped over the rope a couple of times. Sabine was still standing staring at the bathroom door. 'Let's go, girls,' said Anna skipping again, feeling oddly gleeful. 'Let's take that again from the top – before anything else ridiculous happens.' She suddenly became aware of a movement at the end of the dark corridor behind. It was a wild-haired Olivier, not sure whether to make his eyes wide with surprise, or narrow with loathing, watching her. He marched down the corridor and hissed right in Anna's face, staccato with anger: 'I suggest you take your amusing little display to the children's park where it belongs. Immediately.'

To her disgust, Anna found herself blushing. 'Sure. We'll be right out of your way,' she fumbled and dropped the rope.

'Out. Now. All of you,' said Olivier, slamming the front door behind them, and they were alone outside on the cool marble landing. Anna leaned, a little shaky, against the wall as they waited for the lift. Anouk stood open-mouthed. Sabine was already skipping. 'One-two-three, one-two-three . . . Anna?'

'Yeah? What now?'

'Why do you think Papa wasn't wearing his shirt?'

Later that evening, Anna read some of her old *Harriet the Spy* book to Sabine, and tucked her up in her white linen pyjamas (which had to be ironed every day). The little girl was all warm and sleepy, and her blonde hair smelled of fresh shampoo. Anna hugged her tight, and Sabine kissed her back. When you live mostly alone, far from your family, a little bit of physical affection without complicated emotions is a delightful thing. Anna was beginning to feel genuinely fond of Sabine, and wondered what on earth the child made of the lovers who appeared to parade in and out of her parents' lives. Léon, Anna's boyfriend who worked in Madison's hairdressers', had told her of rumours about Madison too.

She stroked Sabine's hair. 'Goodnight, darling. Sleep tight.' Sabine was clutching her gruesome but much-loved cuddly toy rat.

As Anna turned from the bed, she saw Olivier had slipped in to the room, silent on the thick carpet. He'd been watching them, again, his face dark in the shadows. He had on a fresh white T-shirt for the evening.

'Hello, Anna,' he said, giving her a smile and walking over to his daughter's bed to kiss her goodnight. 'Goodnight, Sabine. Goodnight, Ratty.' Olivier showed no sign of anger or embarrassment about the earlier drama in the hall – indeed, the opposite. A few minutes later, as Anna was gathering Sabine's discarded clothes from the bathroom floor, Oliver appeared and leaned languidly against the doorframe, talking to her as she tidied up. He wanted to know how long she'd been in France, why she spoke the language, what she thought of the novel she had in her bag. Was he buttering her up because he didn't want her to mention this afternoon's drama to Madison, or was he just buttering? But she found him all too easy to talk to, and before long had told him about her father, about the liberating moment when she hitch-hiked into the Porte de Clignancourt, into Paris aged eighteen, and never left.

The front door opened, and Madison's heels came clicking down the parquet. 'Got to go, sadly,' smiled Olivier. He looked at Anna almost tenderly, in what she thought was a fatherly way. Or perhaps that was not his intention.

Anna ran upstairs to her room. Olivier reminded her of her father, but the conversation had also left her pumped up with adrenalin and nerves, which was curious. Her thoughts returned more than she wanted to her employer's earlier shirtlessness, and the fact that, for someone so amazingly ancient, for someone in his forties, it was a tanned and surprisingly muscled chest, tapering to a neat waist. Where did all the food go? Those mini-quiches he always harboured in his pockets seemed to have taken little toll. Perhaps it was because he worked all day and half the night too that he ate all the time, and he drank about ten pots of coffee a day. It was too fascinating, although obviously a sensible person would not want to investigate further. Shedloads of women were already doing that, and look at the terrible ends to which they came . . .

She lay back with a bottle of cold beer on her worn Mies van de Rohe chaise longue, the sole seating in the tiny *chambre de bonne*, apart from at the desk. Anna's theory was that if you couldn't afford much furniture, it should at least be good, and she had trudged the fleamarkets until she found perfection. The room also had a bed that folded into the wall and wooden floorboards that she'd taken the liberty of painting white. It was plain, but pleasing. Her stuff, her vintage clothes, her wild cornucopia of junkmarket finds, was all packed wall-to-wall in the room next door, a sort of props department for the theatre of her life. On the door was a framed poster from a club which said: GOD IS A DJ. YOU ARE THE DANCE FLOOR. LOVE IS THE RHYTHM. Anna sat and stared at the only other decoration on the walls, a black and white poster-sized photograph of herself and Léon, and smiled at him fondly. She'd see him later, but for the moment, something about the day left her feeling out of kilter. Perhaps it was the sight of Olivier so blatantly entertaining a lover in front of his child that disturbed Anna, although Sabine seemed utterly unsurprised. Who knew how much she understood? Perhaps it was useful preparation for French adulthood or adultery. Anna sipped her beer, but she still felt agitated, and couldn't settle down with her book or the television, which was atrocious as usual. She left her door open and wandered down the corridor towards the kitchen she shared with the sulky Luiza.

Luiza's door was open, and Anna couldn't resist going in. She'd only caught glimpses before. Luiza had rather more luxurious premises than her own, with two servants' rooms knocked together and thickly carpeted. Every available surface was covered in tackily framed photos of families and kids, probably Luiza's siblings back home. There was one amateur oil painting of a village among a forest, with garish pink and white houses. The single bed was neatly made, under fake-fur cushions, and the desk was covered in neat piles of paper, Luiza's work from nightschool. There was no clue, however, as to why Luiza seemed to be avoiding, if not openly loathing, Anna, although they had shared this strange little attic together for over two months.

Their kitchen was tiny, and you had to go through it to reach the bathroom. The seeping steam and the stench of rosewater indicated that Luiza was having a bath with the radio on. Anna looked hopefully in the fridge. Luiza had recently labelled her shelf 'Luiza' in what Anna thought was rather a childish way. It wasn't as if Anna was about to nick her tubs of fromage blanc or her cheap vodka anyway. In her own section, Anna found some mangetout, some iffy carrots, a chicken breast and the rice from last night's Chinese takeaway, so she set about making chicken fried rice in a wok, with lots of soy sauce. There was a ton of it, and just as Anna was dishing it out, Luiza emerged glowing, pink as a pig, in fluffy towels from the bathroom.

'Hi, Luiza. I've made loads of this. Would you like some?'

Luiza stared at Anna through her slightly steamed-up glasses as though she were a huge cockroach on the kitchen floor.

'No, thank you very much. I've already eaten. Don't mind me.' Luiza scowled as she took a glass of water, pushed by to her room and slammed the door. The intercom buzzer rang from downstairs. Anna pressed the talk button, hoping it was Léon, but a foreign-sounding voice said 'Luiza? It's Ruslan.'

'It's for you,' shouted Anna. Luiza reappeared and pressed the button to open the door in the street.

Anna sat down to eat at the extended shelf which served as a sort of breakfast bar in the kitchen. A minute later, there was a great thundering of feet on the stairs, and two men burst into the hall, ducking huge bull-like heads under the eaves.

'Hey,' said the first one in heavy accented French. 'Hey, where's Luiza?'

'She's getting dressed,' said Anna, pointing down the corridor and hoping they'd go. Instead they both squeezed into the kitchen. They were so close she could smell their hefty aftershave and the alcohol on their breath, although they weren't drunk.

'Oh. We will wait here then, eh? You are the new nanny? I am Aslan and this is Ruslan.'

Ruslan smiled to reveal a gold tooth, which complemented

his leather jacket and the razor zigzag in his skinhead hair. Anna went back to her stir fry, disquieted by two such large presences in a small room.

Aslan was moving closer to her. 'And your name is?'

'Anna.'

'Oh, I have a sister called Anna. What a strange, um, double coincidence, yes? And are you busy tonight, Anna?'

'What do you think?' said Anna dismissively. Ruslan gave Aslan an exasperated look, and got the vodka out of the fridge. He closed the fridge door and stared for a long time at the list of emergency numbers Madison had stuck to it – her own and Olivier's mobile number, the doctor, Madame Canovas.

Ruslan started work on Anna. 'Do you work for the Malins too? They do well for themselves, don't they? And it is a nice area of the town. You know we work near here at the Barista coffee shop on Grenelle, near . . .'

'You want some?' interrupted Aslan.

'No, she doesn't,' said Luiza, coming in wearing hastily pulled on jeans and a fuzzy jumper with sequin butterflies. She kissed Aslan and Ruslan on both cheeks. While she did this, Aslan continued to stare at Anna with greedy interest, in particular at her extremely short suede skirt.

'I'll just finish this in my room,' said Anna, ducking under Ruslan's meaty arm. She locked her door with care, and ate in front of the television, aware of roars of laughter from the kitchen. She didn't want to be Luiza's best friend, but her level of hostility was weird. Sure, Luiza had been Sabine's nanny for years and maybe missed it, but now she had this fancy title of housekeeper, less work and a double newly carpeted room. And she still saw Sabine. So what was the problem? As Anna puzzled, her mobile phone rang.

'Léon? Where are you?'

'Bath,' he said. 'Stoned,' he continued. 'Long day,' he explained.

'Stay in there. I'll be round in ten minutes.'

Anna ran into her second room to the racks of clothes and hats, threw off her T-shirt and pulled on a swirly seventies' top. She brushed her hair and put on some dark red lipstick. Wrapped up in her coat, she escaped the attic overflowing with vast Chechens, and in five minutes reached the Rue du Pré aux Clercs, half running to beat the cool night air. Léon's apartment was just round the corner from ENA, the École Nationale d' Administration, a breeding ground for the privileged civil servants and politicians he loathed. Léon was not above spitting or dropping lighted cigarette butts from his fifth-floor windows on students he suspected of being Enarques.

Being a hairdresser, Léon felt it necessary to live in the style to which he assumed fashionable French revolutionary hairdressers were accustomed, and had lots of fantastic, minimal pieces of furniture. Indeed they had first met one Sunday morning last year at the Marché Serpette, as they both went to grab the same art deco lamp. Léon shrugged, smiled, and gave way. Anna bought the lamp and they put it by the bedside in Léon's apartment that night. His taste was good, but Anna could never quite get used to his brown leather floor tiles, which necessitated the removal of all footwear at the door. Holding her shoes in one hand, she turned her key. Léon was playing some nasty Bhudda Bar chill-out music at unneighbourly decibels. Anna went into the dark living room and turned down the CD player. 'Hey,' Léon shouted from the bathroom, 'I like it like that. You don't hear the bass otherwise.'

'What about saying, "Hello, darling, had a good day?"' asked Anna.

'Hello, gorgeous,' said Léon, smiling. His pale boyish body lay in the sunken bath. He was elegantly thin, untroubled by muscle except in his arms because he lifted scissors and dryers all day. The bathroom glowed with a dim, blueish light. A joint was burning in the dry soap dish, and Léon was turning the hot tap on with his toes, and peering at the politics pages of *Libération*, which of course prevented him from properly chilling out. It was his usual: 'I mean fuck this fucking prime minister, the smarmy little compromiser, did you see what he said? They are beyond shame and rotten with corruption. The fucking . . .'

'You really need to calm down,' said Anna, removing the newspaper, kissing him, putting the joint to his mouth, and then taking a long drag herself. It was knee-bucklingly strong. You might find hairdressers irritating sometimes, but they had enough exotic customers to source high quality drugs. She took off her clothes, her body ghostly white, and slid in the water at the tap end. Bathwise, it was convenient that Léon was so skinny.

'They're all fucking Enarques, the class that runs this country. Have you seen these percentage figures?' continued Léon, retrieving the paper. Anna began to soap each one of her toes with exaggerated care. Léon always had free samples of the latest expensive soaps and potions, and this was good lavender stuff.

'It could not be more corrupt. Did you hear the prime minister's always had a two-hundred-and-fifty-square-metre "council" apartment in the Rue Jacob? For a thousand Euros a month? It's less than I pay here for seventy-two square metres.'

Léon's rant then petered out. He began bobbing his dark head to the music, and stared vacantly at the blue pencil of light above the mirror. After long abuse, Léon was almost impervious to drugs, but the dope had at last penetrated his central cortex, which left the chances of any sort of physical penetration unlikely, Anna knew from experience. But she still felt slightly aroused, as she had done all afternoon and evening. She began slowly soaping between her legs, while Léon looked on, mildly turned on and mildly amused. Their legs stayed intertwined, brown and white. Anna smiled lazily at him, lay back in the warm water and plunged deep into her own head, following paths into her subconscious. Her eyes closed and her mind opened – inappropriately, incongruously – on a picture of Olivier, quite topless. She lay there with him in the warmth.

Suddenly Léon surfaced like a small, excitable porpoise, and dragged her from the bath into the living room. She felt like she'd been caught in the act, although how could Léon know of thought-crime?

'Oh Léon, I . . .' said Anna, flustered and feeling uncomfortably exposed in the middle of the room.

'C'mon baby. Just lie down,' he said, flicking the bass up on the CD player with his fingertips as he leaned over her, erect, and just a touch menacing. She felt for the first time that there was something oddly repulsive about Léon. Her body had someone else in mind, and he knew it.

'Darling, I don't really feel like it. I'm tired,' said Anna. She felt crap. She took the joint again, resignedly. 'And you've had tons of this and you know how . . .'

'Come on, then, darling,' he continued, paying no attention to her words. He started kissing her, and his tongue tasted like wet tobacco. She turned her head to one side instead and let him kiss her neck and the tattoos on her back while they slid down on to the floor. Léon was rough, squashing Anna uncomfortably under him. She lay passive, like the cold, wet fish she felt herself to be, and waited for time to go by. Léon had shut his eyes, and rocked on in his own world. It was boring, it was uncomfortable, and it was the price she paid for this steady relationship, in a city where she had no one. Anna counted the fourteen recessed spotlights on the ceiling, watched the green lights flicker up and down on the CD player, and sensed the ba-booms of the bass vibrating through the floor and down her spine. Léon grunted and panted, on and on to the steady beat, while Anna lay, detached, self-pitying and angry all at once.

Léon spent his sperm and returned to being his happy hairdresser self. 'I love you. I love you so much,' he said, kissing her on the lips for the first time, and then getting up to pee and roll another joint. 'I'm sorry you didn't come.'

'It's fine.' Lying on the floor, Anna had an out-of-body feeling: she could imagine what she looked like from above, laying there, discarded. She smiled vaguely at Léon, picked herself up slowly and wrapped up in the damp towel he had dropped. She felt her bones had been ground into the floor. On the leather tiles, there was a curious print of her wet body, like the stains left behind on a shroud.

5

Olivier Malin

Olivier was checking the perfection of his nails, because he had a book-signing that evening, when he became increasingly suspicious that someone was watching him. Sabine had sneaked in to his study through the half-open door and for a few minutes had been moving round the floor, sniper style, behind the sofa. Now she was under his desk. 'Ankle biter!' he said. 'There's an ankle biter in the room.'

She wriggled up and sat on his knee, satisfied with her ambush. 'Can I draw with your ink pen, on here? A black knight on a horse? Would you like that?'

'No! Oh my God, not there.' Her pen was poised on the coverleaf of his latest manuscript. 'Here. Here's a new piece of paper.' He let her draw for five minutes, adding a complicated coat of arms and a battleaxe for her, while hugging her on his lap. Normally, Sabine drew zoo animals, but she had some sense that Olivier liked medieval knights, and was trying to please him, engage with him. Or should that be the other way round? Olivier suddenly wondered. But next Sabine wanted to paint their sketch. He suggested she go off and ask Anna.

'Anna's away this evening, and I don't want to paint with Luiza. She's terrible at painting. I want to paint with you.'

'But I've got to go out in fifteen minutes to a book-signing,' said Olivier, distracted, speed dialling for a cab.

'Papa . . .' Sabine looked like she might cry. 'Pleeeze?'

Olivier offered to buy her some real silver paint for her knight next time he was in the art shop on the Rue du Bac, but tonight Sabine was not to be bought off. He gathered his wallet and keys, and reached for his jacket. Sabine was holding it behind her back.

'Painting,' she said, sternly.

'Jacket,' said Olivier, holding his hand out.

'Painting.'

'I can't, darling. Maybe at the weekend. Where's your mother, anyway? Now I need that jacket, it's got my signing pen in it.'

'Take your bloody jacket then,' said Sabine, throwing it down.

'What word did you just use?' shouted Olivier, but Sabine had stormed into her room and slammed the door. He could hear her pushing a chair under the handle, one of her favourite tricks.

'Jesus,' said Olivier. He shouted to Luiza in the laundry room that he was leaving, and slammed the door himself.

Despite pelting January rain, a large queue had formed in the FNAC bookshop in Montparnasse, in anticipation of the arrival of Olivier to sign *Chechnya – Beyond Philosophy*. You might not think such a title would be a crowd-puller, but Olivier had a popular and rather dramatic writing style, plus Bourdon, his publisher, had sensibly suggested the book should include a selection of pictures, many of which showed Olivier looking dashing in a bullet-proof vest against a background of burned-out buildings. For literary types, the crowd seemed exceptionally well turned-out and made-up that evening. The men almost all wore black or wire-rimmed glasses, and the queue also had more than its normal share of young women in long, tight, suede boots. Olivier noted all this with quiet satisfaction as he walked in the side entrance to the signing desk, beside which were teetering piles of his book in hardback. There was a burst of applause. He pushed back his black hair, checked the general crispness of his suit, and forgot about domestic matters.

Waiting at the desk and controlling the crowd was Florence Vallon, the publicity girl from his publishers who had made that unfortunate scene last week in front of Anna and the children. 'I have an announcement,' she said. 'Please could you buy the book first before having it signed? And Professor Malin is so busy that he may not have time to sign copies of his other works. Thank you.' Florence stared strictly through her tortoiseshell glasses at the jockeying crowd with their yellow FNAC bags, and then turned as Olivier arrived. She blushed inadvertently at the sight of him. 'You're late. Again,' she hissed, to cover her embarrassment. Olivier kissed her formally on both cheeks, sat down, and stretched out his long legs under the table. You should never, he mused, become involved with women you work with, for they remain an eternal burden. He smiled sincerely as the fans converged on him. There were more than a hundred people in the line.

'I can't believe I'm meeting you at last!' said a plump, over-nurtured male student with his hair cut in homage to Olivier's. 'I was wondering only last night what you thought about the new network philosophy and here you are to . . .'

'And to whom shall I dedicate it?'

'Eliot, Eliot Nussman, and, oh thank you for all . . .'

'Next!' rapped Florence. Then she looked over at Olivier, her face half hidden by her brown wavy hair, and hissed: 'What do you think you are doing? Since I came round that afternoon, you've turned your phone off, you've ignored all my emails, and it's been a week since . . .'

Olivier remained deaf to Florence and concentrated on the crowd. 'Oh so charming! A paperback of my first book, and well-thumbed too. For an author, that is such a compliment. Thank you. And shall I dedicate it to you? What name shall I . . .?'

A girl melted before him, her long, freshly-shampooed hair sweeping the desk. 'Angelie,' she said weakly. 'I'm Angelie.'

'Angelie.' He rolled the name round his tongue. 'Have I spelled it right? Oh good. Yes, you must come to the Café Philosophe. Yes, you'd be . . .'

The girl nodded, unable to speak, such was her awe.

'Yes, it's every fortnight,' continued Olivier, enjoying himself.

The girl floated away. Olivier's eyes followed her calves and slim ankles.

'How can you treat . . .' growled Florence, all angry, and displaying bony angles in her cashmere jumper.

'Darling, can we talk about it later in the car, because this is not quite the place, is it?' said Olivier, cheerfully signing great loopy O's over and over.

A tall man in a leather jacket with a semi-shaven head reached the front of the queue. He dropped Olivier's book with a thud on the desk, and opened it. He bent over and pushed his face up close to Olivier's. His breath smelled foul.

'See here, here on page 252. Do you see what you say about the Chechen resistance? You make a fucking joke of it, don't you? And here, on page 167 – look what you say.'

'Ah – I'm a philosopher, not a journalist. Those are allegories, you see . . . Yes, well here is not the place for debate, I'm afraid,' said Olivier, gesturing to the lengthening line. 'Would you like me to sign it?'

'I'd like you to burn it,' growled the man. His accent was strange, probably Chechen. Two of the male bookshop staff approached, but the man took one look at them and stormed off out of the door. Olivier was a bit shaken, but Florence looked terrified. 'We have another ten minutes. We can take twenty more only,' she shouted over the hubbub.

'Oh, I can manage a few more than that, my dear. I owe it to them, particularly on a nasty night like this,' said Olivier smiling, pretending to be calm to annoy Florence, and zipping through the volumes before him with his Montblanc. He'd worked on his signature for two years when he was a teen-ager. He still admired its speed and powerful curves. There was almost nothing about Olivier that was not carefully created.

The fans were shoving at the desk, and Florence stepped in front to block them, although she was hopelessly frail for a proper bouncer, and Olivier thought she might faint. She turned to him, scowling. 'We've got to go. You're live at nine o'clock, and the traffic's terrible.' Olivier stood up with finality, and bent his head – a bow to the worshipping crowd.

'Thank you, thank you, my friends. Another time . . .' The fans stood back, suddenly aware of his authority, and Florence and Olivier marched to the door with the bookshop manager fawning in their tailwind. As Olivier left, he had a vague, troubling sense that, out of the corner of his eye, he'd glimpsed the back of Anna's green coat in the fiction section, but when he turned round, no one was there. He thought for just a second about the image she had left in his mind, the first day in Dalloyau, a flash of this other person, gamine and foreign in every way.

*　　*　　*

A limo from Canal Plus television was waiting outside in the darkness, its engine running. They jumped in the back. There was no sign of the unhappy Chechen outside. Florence sat as far from Olivier as possible, on the edge of the leather back seat, squashed against the window.

'Florence?' he asked, while making sure the intercom with the driver was closed off.

'Florence?'

He could see her shoulders shaking. She'd turned her head to look out of the other window into the wet Paris night, the blurred green neon of pharmacy signs, and the washed red of cafés. She was crying silently.

'How could . . . how could you do . . . I . . .'

'Florence, come here.' Olivier tried to grasp her hand, but she pulled it away. The streetlights shimmered by, reflected in the greasy tarmac. The apartments all seemed secretive, shuttered up against the night. He sighed theatrically, stared at nothing in particular, then at his feet, and wondered whether he should have some new shoes made. (He only wore handmade black shoes from Lobb.) Suddenly Florence found her voice, shakily.

'I felt so enriched, so full, I learned so much from you.' She took a great gulping breath. 'And we could have more together and you . . .'

'Darling, it's not like that. You're not being honest with yourself.' He looked across. Florence was paler than usual. Her once-pencil skirt was loose on the hips, and her long crocodile shoes looked truly reptilian on her feet. Her hair seemed to have lost its lustre and her eyes were pink. It is as simple as this, thought Olivier: she has lost her bloom. He took her hand again, and held it in his, stroking it, although he could feel himself taking the steady steps he knew so well, down from attraction to boredom and on to freedom.

'You know I am a married man. I cannot, I just cannot have scenes like that in my home, not in front of my daughter and the staff. I told you never to come there, and what could I do once you were in my office? I have a wife, and I adore you, but there are contingent loves, and permanent loves in my life. I keep these affairs separate, you know that. I told you that a year ago, I told you that from the beginning and I have never lied to you, have I?'

'No. You never lied. To me. You lie to your wife, though.'

'That's not true. We have an arrangement, a mutual arrangement, which suits us, for we want to experience more than one love in life, and you must do that too. For God's sake, you are only twenty-five and you are surrounded by men. You don't need an old man like me.' Olivier smiled.

'I love you,' said Florence, starting to cry again. They waited at the traffic lights while some vast presidential cavalcade went by, a dozen long black cars with flags. They were now very late. 'How can you forget what you said that long afternoon in the autumn, in the Versailles room in the Hôtel Select? You . . .'

What the hell did I say? wondered Olivier, but he interrupted her with: 'Our time together is coming to an end, Florence, and you know that this has run its course. You need to go out in the world, to travel, to leave Paris. You need an adventure, my darling, and you certainly do not need to hang around with an old bore like me,' said Olivier, checking that his nails were clean enough for a television appearance, as they drew up outside the neon-lit entrance of Canal Plus. 'Look, take the studio car on home, for I don't need it and I am meeting Rimbaud later anyway. Go home, Florence, and make a plan to change your life, about which you should call me tomorrow. And if I can help in any way, anywhere . . .' He scrabbled for a hopeful thought to send her off with. He didn't want an unhappy stalker interfering in his life. 'Why not have a big adventure, instead of a small adventure in love? What about the post Laffont have in New York that you told me about? There is nothing to hold you back. I would never hold you back, my darling, everything is before you.' He was met with silence. 'Don't be sad.'

He kissed her on the cheek, already feeling a certain sweet nostalgia for their time together, and slammed the door. Florence's pale face looked unhappily through the window at him, and then the car swept off into the rain and darkness. Olivier walked up the steps into the welcoming light of the television studios, and shook off the weight of Florence with the raindrops that had gathered on the shoulders of his jacket.

He was on the late evening chat show, cheesily entitled *Les Intellos*, with Bourdon, and his rain-ruined hair was going to require some work. He hurried to make-up, where they gave him a quick blow dry. The girl also plucked a few unruly hairs from his eyebrows, and tanned him with a little foundation, which set off his skin nicely against the white T-shirt and dark suit. Olivier understood how women needed to look their best when doing something challenging. He felt exactly the same.

Bourdon was already in the studio. The two of them were there basically to roast a young author from America who had the temerity to write a book entirely made up of sex scenes and call it a work of art. 'It's well known that only the French can do that and get away with it,' noted Olivier, charming the camera. 'There is no profundity here, merely profanity. Where is the intellectual engagement?'

'Uh,' began the author.

'Where is the consciousness, the understanding of the self and of the choices the individual must make?' continued Olivier. 'It's McDo, McSex.'

'Um, that's the point, y'know . . .'

'Banal,' added Bourdon, with crushing finality.

They took about ten minutes to shred the poor stuttering fellow, whose grasp of the subjunctive was hopeless anyway. Then Olivier and Bourdon executed a verbal fencing match on whether the film director Lars von Trier was a fool, a genius, or beyond tedious. Their clashes were a delight to watch, but Olivier felt Bourdon was not on his usual bullying, berating form, so when he had his old friend pinioned with an irrefutable argument, he left him a way out. It was all very gentlemanly, and ended not in tears but cheers from the live studio audience. Olivier glowed after the performance, which once again confirmed his belief that the French intellectual should not be a closeted academic, but someone who publicly engaged with the world, its delights and its problems.

'Are you hungry, old fellow?' said Olivier to Bourdon in the green room afterwards. Bourdon was always hungry. He was a gastrophilosophe of great renown. That was why he was so fat and sleek, like a huge seal. His bulk, his height, his reddish beard, gave him enormous presence. 'Rimbaud and I are meeting at the Fontaine de Mars as usual, and I suspect you may want to join us.'

'No, I fear that I am on a diet,' said Bourdon.

'You are joking, old boy,' said Olivier. 'You have always declared that you would never, ever . . .'

'No,' said Bourdon. 'I have lost ten kilos and I am running on the Champs de Mars with my personal trainer every morning before a very light breakfast of fruit, and Horatio suggested . . .'

'Jesus,' said Olivier. 'You're the last person . . .'

'I'm in love and Horatio has moved in with his wardrobe, which is not insubstantial. And his spaniel Dorothy. And Dorothy's Gucci leather dog basket. What can one do?' sighed Bourdon, raising both hands helplessly in the air, then pulling on his vast cashmere coat. 'He is writing a book on the history of Pierre Frey fabrics in Paris, and as for me, I am in such a febrile state I can barely bring myself to work at all and I may even shave off the beard.'

'Christ.' Bourdon had had many, many lovers in his time, but being wetly in love with an English fop was quite out of order for him, thought Olivier. 'Horatio's almost a teenager. He's from a strange land where they have strange customs, of which we know little, and you presently have him under contract,' said Olivier in a sing-song rant. 'You know better than that, my friend. Don't diet merely for a young man who may well be filling a temporary position. Not eating well means you are cutting off one of your senses. You are blind with love and have lost your sense of taste.' He could not bear to see a mature man suffering from such infantile delusions.

'You're right, but you're wrong as usual, Olivier. I shall not be dissuaded, so I am going home to my céleri remoulade with low-fat dressing,' said Bourdon, picking up his new present – a red briefcase of the softest leather – and stroking it. 'And a bit of the other . . .'

'Slow roast chicken with plump little girolle mushrooms? Seared foie gras?' said Olivier with a last parry, shouting his favourites from the Fontaine de Mars' menu as Bourdon's coat flapped off into a waiting taxi.

Olivier summoned another car and was soon among the darkened grocers and ironmongers of the seventh arrondissement. The Fontaine de Mars appeared, its red-checked half-curtains glowing. Behind another velvet curtain, to keep draughts at bay, were the old wooden tables, the giant cloth napkins, the embrace of the maître d' and the cheerful red face of his best friend Paul Rimbaud with his glass and newspaper.

'There are many things on my mind tonight, old boy, mostly related to the dreadful accident of falling in love,' said Olivier, getting straight to the point. 'Falling in love is cited by many as though they were not to blame themselves, as though fate worked alone.' He told Rimbaud what he considered to be the shameful tale of Bourdon and Horatio. 'Bourdon has gone quite mad, and that little Florence I once mentioned is causing me all kinds of trouble. I am sick of love, its falls, and of people in love, and the over-influence, the over-importance of it all. Why is there this breathless enthusiasm? Why is there this lack of dignity? They should know by now that love is an art, not a bad radio play.'

'Ah,' said Paul. 'You have left another one? There has been a nasty scene and your little intruder in the trio has been expelled again? They always are, aren't they?' Olivier thought Paul sounded just a touch more sharp than sympathetic. Considering that Paul might just possibly be having an affair with Olivier's wife, it was a bit much. But on the other hand, he and Paul went back twenty-five years; he and Madison, eight. Where did loyalty lie?

'Shall we have the seared foie gras?' answered Olivier. 'With baby spinach and caramelised spices? Yes, I'm afraid little Florence became as cloying as a cheap Alsace wine when all the freshness went.'

Paul giggled. 'You should try older women, you know . . .

Let's get the Coteaux du Gennois blanc, talking of wine. And I shall have the foie gras too, followed by Monsieur Duval's own *andouillette* with Chardonnay *jus*.'

'It's true, there comes a time when all this is so exhausting, when the new ceases to amuse. I do not want fidelity, but freedom can be very tiring. I like to be with young people, but it is not as enriching as it once was, you know. Do you know what I mean?'

'Umph, yes,' said Paul, looking rather sweaty in the pinkish light of the restaurant. Olivier stared at him. Usually they discussed world affairs, or Paris literary gossip, but without thinking he had plunged them into a discussion of fidelity and love. Olivier thought better of pursuing the question and continued, his voice slightly tense: 'You see, you have Renée. You are of the same age, the same culture, and you are intellectual partners. I might even call you comrades, with the same intellectual aspirations, but it has not been the same for me . . . and I hesitate to talk of the authentic love of Sartre and de Beauvoir, for I feel the subject has moved from romantic reminiscence to cliché for most observers, but essentially they were partners, working together to fashion a common future, and their love was a product of language – their language, their discussions together. Perhaps having children also precludes that sort of intellectual love in favour of practicality.' He felt a spasm of shame about his treatment of Sabine earlier, and then shook his head and speared a gravy-fattened girolle mushroom. 'Yet, for Madison and I, it is not like that. I fell in love with her for different reasons, I think . . .'

Paul took a great gulp of his wine. 'You mean you do not consider Madison to be your intellectual equal? Yet she's awfully well-read.'

'You think so? I suppose you would know,' said Olivier, regretting immediately that he had almost said the unsayable; that Paul and Madison were involved. 'To me, it seems that the outside of things matter more to her than the inside. She sometimes luxuriates in appearances. She glories in her own and others' beauty, she glories in objects.'

'Not always,' said Paul quietly. 'Besides, in her job so much is about appearance.'

'Yes, but we do not have the relationship I always dreamed of, of a freely chosen partnership of two autonomous beings who hold each other in the highest intellectual esteem. So I am forced to search for the parts that are missing elsewhere.'

'Perhaps your mistake is favouring the younger woman over the older when searching for intellectual esteem?' said Rimbaud, smiling and sawing a stray bristle from his trotter.

'Yes, well, one can't always overcome one's natural instincts to love the young and beautiful, however much one tries.'

'Yes, but you are in the rather wicked habit of eating them up and spitting them out – or so I suspect,' said Paul, his voice teasing. 'You know what Hegel says about those relationships: "each consciousness seeks the death of the other". The effects of love and jealousy are devastating. Now shall we have the *Île flottante* or the *tarte tatin*?'

6

Madison Malin

As they drove up through the avenue of bare laurels, the two-storey windows became yellow rectangles in the night, striped by the black shadows of the ornamental pillars, so from the distance the château looked like a huge jail cell. Olivier skidded the car to a stop on the gravel and jumped out to get their bags. He and Madison hadn't spoken for over an hour, and it was a relief to let the silence out of the car. Sabine was resolutely asleep, already in her pyjamas and bathrobe, and she flopped warm in Madison's arms as she was carried in from the car and up the great double staircase. In the half-light from the fire in the hall and the sconces, Sabine's skin had the same creamy pallor as her ancestors' in the paintings on the walls. Madison breathed in the perfume of strawberry shampoo in her daughter's hair, a smell of her modern childhood which contrasted with the smell of Olivier's home: of woodsmoke, mustiness and damp.

Olivier opened the nursery door for them and quickly disappeared downstairs to pay his respects to his mother, while Madison walked in and laid Sabine on her father's childhood bed, gently peeling off the bathrobe. Sabine growled and disappeared under the quilt and Madison kissed what she could see of her daughter's forehead. In the half-light she could see Olivier's rocking horse, missing its hair tail, and a vast green board with tiny trees and villages where tin Napoleonic soldiers (originally *his* father's) were still lined up for battle. As soon as he became a teenager and a pacifist, Olivier had all but refused to come to the country for holidays. He had stayed holed up in their Paris apartment with his books, and no doubt a girl, if she could be persuaded. So the nursery was preserved in its eternal, stuffy youth.

Madison wandered slowly across to the bathroom, a museum of early plumbing and verdigris from dripping copper pipes, and carefully inspected herself, re-coating her mascara, lipliner and lipstick. In the horrible seventies' fluorescent mirror light, the Malins only concession to modernity, she suddenly saw tiny lines were radiating from her upper lip. They'd have to go straightaway. She would make an appointment with Doctor Giroux on Monday. She lightly sponged on some foundation. Madison always felt it was important to set an example to her mother-in-law with perfect make-up, because Madame Malin favoured blood-red lipstick and death-white powder. Madison put off the inevitable meeting by having a quick cigarette by the bathroom window.

She looked out on the moon illuminating the icy parkland and trees with their trunks caged in iron to stop marauding cattle, and shivered at the prospect of going downstairs. Of all the places in France, this was the one that made her feel most uncomfortable. The oppressive château and its grim inhabitants stretched the new skin Madison had created over twenty years to bursting point. She had painstakingly maintained, polished and educated herself to be a model of Parisian womanhood, but something about the conventionality here made her want to revert to her inner Texan and behave like an extra from *Rawhide*.

'Madison! Why the hell are you taking so long?' Olivier appeared at the door. 'For goodness' sake, my father's waiting in the drawing room for us and you know what he's like, plus the traffic hasn't helped. It's after nine, you know, and he always complains about his stomach if he dines late. Why are we always so fucking late for everything?' Madison smiled to herself, observing Olivier's immediate character change, the stiffening and protective hunching of his shoulders, the increasing formality of his French, as he returned to his old home and habits. But we all remain children in our parents' houses – it's just that Olivier had frozen at a particularly tense and petulant fifteen, which often made Madison want to laugh out loud on their rare visits to the Château de Moulon.

Olivier's mother was calling from downstairs, her voice tight with exasperation. It being a proper family château, the patriarch ruled, was still feared, and must not be kept waiting. Olivier was not the patriarch, and never would be, as the second son. Madison followed Olivier wearily down the staircase. He was texting someone on his mobile as they passed beneath the family crest and motto, now browned to near invisibility, with the arcane words '*Victorioux à touts*' fading away to blood-red dust.

Madame Malin was standing erect and correct beside one of the pillars in the hall, tapping her tiny foot. 'Véronique. How are you?' said Madison, kissing her formally on each cheek. They did not hug. If they had, Madison thought, Madame Malin's thin, brittle bones might crack and she would be left holding a perfectly tailored tweed suit filled with dust. Osteoporosis took terrible revenge on that generation of thin French women who had dined their whole lives on black coffee and cigarettes. Madison's diet was little better, but for a calcium supplement. At least, she thought, I have muscle to hold me up. She had once mistakenly come upon Madame Malin naked in the bathroom, and her body – perfectly trim when clothed – was curtained with empty, unmuscled flesh. She was like some Victorian who could not stand straight without the support of her corsets.

Madison enjoyed these somewhat nasty thoughts – it was how she got through such very long weekends – as her mother-in-law continued to address her with the formal *vous*, unable even after eight years to *tutoyer* the foreigner who had married her son. Still, thought Madison, it may not be a friendly household, but at least it's smoke-friendly. Old Monsieur Malin stunk of cigars, even in the morning. And there he was, Louis, the red-faced toad, standing before the drawing-room fireplace, looking agitated.

'Ah. Ah hah. Whisky, port, eh, or a little Rivesaltes? You are here at last, my dears, and I have no idea why you persist in setting out so late on a Friday night; you see, if you had taken the station road as I advised you, to avoid the . . .'

Madison stopped Monsieur Malin by kissing him, while silently marvelling at his green and yellow checked jacket, of the sort now only worn by French travelling salesmen.

'Madison, well I must say you are looking wonderful, aren't you?' The *tu* lingered too long on his tongue, and the old man's hand lingered too long on her back. Old letch, thought Madison. Then she watched Olivier fawning over his mother. At what point, wondered Madison, do you go from being an agreeable, handsome playboy, to a desirable father, and on to an old eighty-something letch? She turned her attention back to the patriarch, enquiring sweetly about the numbers of (endangered) songbirds he had shot that day on the estate.

'No, no! A deer!' he said, excited. 'A great regal stag, staring at me from the underbrush, in the mist. For a second I hesitated, and then I had him.' He clapped the heels of his hands together sharply, and Madison jumped. 'In fact, m'dear, it's hanging in the game larder, dripping deliciously as we speak and I think we can expect some roasted at tomorrow's lunch, isn't that right, Véronique?'

His wife dutifully assented, and gestured to Madison to sit

down, while continuing to tell Olivier about the shockingly low mores of their nearest neighbours, who lived a good ten miles away. Olivier raised one eyebrow at Madison in ironic but silent protest at the tirade. Madison was not keen to move from the fire and out into the icy steppe of the salon where the painfully upright sofas and chairs lurked in unhappy groupings. Nothing matched, and they really should get it all restored, regilded and re-upholstered, she thought. But there didn't seem to be any money. Just ancestral piles of stuff. Shabby furniture that any self-respecting Texan would toss in a garage sale. She sat down and a responsive cloud of dust rose from the horsehair cushions. She took out a cigarette, and Monsieur Malin was there in a jiffy, ready to light it. He sat down too close to her, exploding more dust. 'My, I do need this drink,' said Madison, smiling her plastic on-camera smile.

While Monsieur Malin warbled on about the creatures he had killed or intended to kill soon, Madison set her face to interested, and thought about the first time she came to the château, nine years ago, to meet the parents. At that time, Olivier was not driving a Mercedes estate with room for a child's bike, but a little black sports car made for two. In this low-slung metal capsule they shot through the dark and the rain; it was thrillingly intimate, like lying speedily in bed together. They were so desperate to make love, they stopped in a lay-by, arriving late and ruffled to the coolest of possible welcomes. Madison immediately got lost coming from her separate bedroom miles from Olivier's, for there were back stairs, front stairs, green baize doors, servants, passages and a tricky business where the second floor became the third when you changed from the main house to the newer wings.

The gong sounded and they went through to dine, just the four of them all lonely at one end of the long polished table. But the grim formality made Madison recall her first time in this room long ago, before she was married. She had changed into a black velvet Cruella-de-Vil dress, which seemed entirely appropriate for the occasion, and Olivier, exquisite in dinner jacket, had taken her arm as they walked down the grand staircase. She remembered being awed and thrilled by the grandeur, the feeling of an ancient ancestral power rooted in this spot for centuries, something that an American, however rich, could never replicate.

Madison had felt both like a princess and a rank impostor. The man she had fallen in love with, the iconoclast, the left-wing intellectual, was also an impostor, for here he was suddenly landed gentry, his title lost in the Revolution, but his sense of entitlement unchanged. They had walked into the dark, candlelit dining room, and as Olivier slammed the door behind them to keep out the Siberian winds of the great hall, large flakes of grey lead paint had floated off the walls, revealing the damp patches of plaster below. The table was set with crusty neighbours and tarnished silver. Olivier had squeezed Madison's hand in sympathy, before he deposited her between his elder brother, Jerome, the treasured son and heir, and a Miss Havisham figure, who had lost her new husband in the war, but kept his vast estate. Jerome, who had Olivier's face stretched into long-jawed horsiness by a fairground funny mirror, had bored her to death with neighing, self-aggrandising tales of his merchant bank in the city. How could two brothers be more unalike?

As rubbery smoked salmon was served with wooden blinis, Miss Havisham had regaled Madison charmingly with tales of her own home. Tales of problems with horse insemination, of wild boars uprooting the celeriac in the walled garden, and of the day Oswald's widow, Diana Mosley, came for luncheon when the cook was off sick, and how Miss Havisham had to prepare some cold chicken and salad, the first time she'd cooked in over five years, but Diana was *so* charming and understanding about it . . .

While Madison was thinking Jesus, fascists, and wondering whether breathing in the lead paint dust would damage her brain, the next course had been served: thick slices of high venison, floating in grease. She had gulped and sawn off a small corner of the meat, catching Olivier's loving and worried eye across the table. Meanwhile, Miss Havisham had rattled on about how she'd been sitting in her private salon one day, and had noticed a strange brown patch appearing on the ceiling. Her housekeeper had told her not to worry about it – the villa was old and damp. But over the days, the brown patch grew and grew, until it appeared to be in the form of the crucified Christ. Miss Havisham thought she was either having a religious vision, or going quite mad, and asked the valet to take a look in the attic upstairs. 'There was a terrible, terrible smell,' Miss

Havisham had said, picking some fennel strands from her snaggly yellow teeth, 'and the door was locked. The valet shouldered it open and there, on the floor, was one of the under-gardeners. He had committed suicide by drinking weed-killer, and the juices from his decomposing body were dripping through the . . .'

At that point, Madison had excused herself from the dining room. She had run down corridors looking for a bathroom, her stomach heaving, and had thrown up the greasy venison and sat tearfully on the cold floor by the bath, listening to the drip of the broken tap. She had wondered why on earth she was there. She'd thought, these are not my people, this is not my world. But it wasn't Olivier's world either, at least only by birthright, and he had rejected much of it. Just not enough. A few minutes later, Olivier had come looking for Madison. He took her in his arms, kissed away her wet tears and said: 'Everything I have become is a reaction to this world, my love. You must always remember that you and I are observers here, not collaborators. But . . . but they are my family: I can't abandon them.' He shrugged and grinned: 'They know not what they do.'

Madison was dragged back to the present by the persistent pawing of her arm by Monsieur Malin, who was talking about some entirely different matter, and vacuuming up a second decanter of red wine. He squeezed her thigh in some excitement and leaned forward to impart what he considered to be thrilling news. 'And for the next course, we have a special treat to celebrate the presence of my beautiful daughter-in-law, and it isn't easy to get them in these times. We have ortolans!'

'Marvellous,' said Olivier. 'I love ortolans. Haven't had them for a couple of years, I think the last time was with Rimbaud at the Académie Française.' Madison felt her stomach clench in anticipation of eating a sparrow – or whatever it was. She could say no, but that would be giving in to Madame Malin, who had no doubt plotted this unpleasant little surprise, knowing Madison's aversion to most flesh. The housekeeper (who was also cook and maid of all work, which explained the dust) served them each with three of the tiny birds, carefully roasted and browned with their little heads on, dull eyes cooked away. Madison had never seen ortolan eaten before, but she realised, as the Malins lifted up their napkins over their faces, that she was going to get away with it.

'Of course one eats them whole,' said Olivier, popping out from behind his napkin, and smiling a mite sadistically at his wife. 'Hence the napkins for politeness.' She could hear the bones crunching in his mouth like cereal under the napkin: 'Mmmn. They taste rather like crispy foie gras.' A look of pleasure welled up in his eyes. 'Mitterrand, rest his soul, chose them for his last meal, with forty oysters. What a wonderful way to go.' Olivier looked expectantly over at Madison, who still hadn't eaten anything. But she was not an actress for nothing, and with a magician's sleight of hand, crushed the little birds one at a time with her fingers, behind her napkin, and emerged chewing nothing. 'Delicious,' she said. 'But I think

Mitterrand's last supper was really creepy. Just typical of him to want to take these tiny lives, to eat live creatures just as his own greedy life was ending. Yuck.'

'I thought you said they were delicious,' said Olivier, now suspicious. Madison smiled and put down her napkin, leaving a small aviary hidden in its folds. The housekeeper found them later and didn't mention them.

'To the contrary, my darling,' said Olivier. 'I think Mitterrand lived a wonderful, full life, loving ideas, loving women, loving books. He is still an inspiration to me. He found meaning in everything, and I know that you only met him once so you wouldn't understand him in the way that I do as a friend.'

'Leftist swine,' said Monsieur Malin helpfully, as he tucked into the cheese.

Olivier ignored him and continued: 'Without Mitterrand's vision on Europe we would . . .'

'Oh come on, Olivier,' interrupted Madison. 'He wasn't exactly a figure of great moral rectitude, was he? Two families simultaneously, and God knows how many other lovers, and he joined the resistance just a little bit too late, didn't he? After getting a medal from the Vichy regime . . .' Monsieur Malin was taken with a coughing fit at the mention of Vichy, while Madame looked darkly at Madison. The in-laws weren't defending Mitterrand, since they were deeply right wing, so what was their problem? Madison stared at Monsieur Malin over the rim of her glass, but he didn't meet her eye. Olivier changed the subject to a discussion of the new Brancusi retrospective in Paris, which he said his parents must come in to see, and Madison forgot the preceding conversation as she was enveloped in a nightmarish vision of the in-laws staying in the apartment, dragging their own brand of frozen, stiff horror into her life.

'Oh no, we never go into Paris in the winter. Too dark and with that terrible traffic, you can never get anywhere on time,' said Madame Malin. And then the conversation jolted duly on, until at last some rancid freezer-tasting lemon sorbet was served, and they all went off to bed reeking of cigar smoke.

Upstairs, Madison and Olivier lay trying to sleep at either edge of the best four-poster guest bed, which had been designed for tiny Europeans, not Amazonian Americans. The sheets were linen, but much mended, with unexpected ridges. The bed also sagged terribly in the middle. You could easily roll down the hill of mattress and find yourself crushed unpleasantly in the valley by your sweaty spouse in the middle of the night. Plus Madison kept sneezing with the dust from the droopy canopy.

'Olivier?' she said after tossing and turning for some time. He grunted.

'What did your father really do in the war? I thought he was in the Resistance? That's what you always said.'

'Vichy,' he said, half asleep. 'And then he joined the Resistance "just a little bit too late" as you would say.' Olivier gave a snort of laughter, which turned almost immediately into a snore. Madison lay frozen by the repulsive news, and by the cold, for Olivier had managed to roll himself in most of the quilt. Why had it taken Olivier eight years to get round to mentioning his father's Vichy career? Was he telling her now because he no longer cared what she thought?

She stared up at the ceiling lit by the remains of the fire in the bedroom grate, depressed, oppressed. An American would just walk out on this rotten family and its foul history, but Europeans seemed to find it impossible to cut and run in the way she had. While Olivier was a pillar of the Left in Paris, a veritable radical whose mobile phone tone was *Bandiera Rossa*, back home he was eternally the second son who wanted approval. Pathetic. Madison wondered why they came here at all, except to let Sabine see her grandparents, and frankly, they weren't up to much in that role either. She fell into a disturbed sleep holed with dreams where Sabine was taken away by menacing tin Napoleonic soldiers, and she was left weeping, watching her daughter disappear into the distance. At her side, Olivier slept like a baby, and snored like a truffling pig.

The next morning was beautiful, partly because of the weather, and partly because Madame Malin had breakfasted in bed, and then spent hours thereafter at her toilette. Then she sat in the library and read the *Figaro*, paying particular attention to the politics – she was clearly the side from which Olivier had inherited his brains. Sabine, Madison and Olivier sat eating breakfast in the tapestried morning room on incongruous white plastic bucket chairs at a matching table from the sixties, all brought here when the Malins felt the pinch and abandoned their apartment on the Île St Louis. Monsieur Malin was there too, but never raised his head from the horse-racing news, for he was capable of little more than grunting in the mornings, given the amount of claret still coursing in his veins.

'I want to go riding on Harmattan. Can I, Maman? I'm tall enough now, aren't I?' said Sabine.

'No, he's sixteen hands, far too big for you. I'll ride him. You stick to the pony.'

'Oh well, if you're going riding, I shall take this opportunity to catch up on a little work this morning,' said Olivier, who was capable of disappearing into the wings of the house for hours, leaving Madison to deal with the in-laws alone. Olivier claimed he was allergic to horses, but no one was quite sure if this was true. There were, Madison had noted, photographs in the family album of him, aged about ten, all gussied up in a little riding coat on a pony.

Monsieur Malin slurped some coffee and suddenly came to life: 'There's a marvellous horse, absolutely marvellous, on great form, he did well in the Arc, you know, running this afternoon in the 3.15 at Longchamps. Will anyone watch it with me?'

'I will, Papi,' said Sabine. 'Can I bet some of my pocket money when you go on the telephone before?'

'Sabine!' said Olivier.

'Well Papi always bets, don't you? What's wrong with that? We made ten Euros on an each-way bet last time.'

'She's a bit young for this,' said Olivier to his father, irritated.

'Ahheerggh,' said Monsieur Malin incomprehensibly as he returned to studying the form.

Olivier's phone beeped vehemently at him from his pocket.

'Infernal things,' said Monsieur Malin, whose home possessed one single large white Bakelite telephone in the study, with the bookmakers' number taped on the wall beside it.

Madison watched smile lines form at the corner of Olivier's mouth as the text message appeared on his screen.

'Who's bothering you at the weekend?' she asked.

'Oh, just a student.' He texted swiftly back, thumbs tapping, grinning, smug.

Yes, it had to be someone young, thought Madison. His older lovers had never texted him. She sighed at the predictability of it all. She cursed her gullibility, her belief that when Olivier had read aloud so charmingly to her in bed from Simone de Beauvoir's *L'Invitée* in this very house nine years ago, for God's sake, the book's premise referred to them. Olivier had considered it very profound as he read: ' "It's impossible to talk about faithfulness and unfaithfulness where we are concerned," said Pierre, drawing Françoise close to him. "You and I are simply one. It's true, you know, neither of us can be explained without the other." '

She crashed down her coffee cup, causing Monsieur Malin to look up startled from the paper, and crumbs to wobble on his moustache. Olivier narrowed his eyes at her, but said nothing. He looked embarrassed and slid his phone into his pocket.

'Let's go, girl,' Madison said to Sabine in cowboy American, intent on excluding Olivier and his father, letches both, she suddenly thought. 'Let's riiide!'

125

*   *   *

Outside, the plain stretched away in a low mist, and white frost draped the box balls on the terrace. The trees were bare before spring, and the ground was crisp. 'Delicious for riding. Come on,' said Madison, and she took Sabine's hand as they walked behind the east wing, past the redbrick walls of the weed-infested potager to the ramshackle stable block, where two rather mature horses and a pony blew white air from their nostrils into the cold. Madison felt comfortable, truly herself, in her riding boots and jeans, with the weight of false relationships of all kinds left behind to fester in the château. She strode into the tack room and grabbed what had once been a fine leather Hermès saddle, now cracked with age, and handed a smaller saddle to Sabine, who staggered brave and uncomplaining under the weight. The horses hadn't been ridden for ages, but Madison had broken quarter-horses antsier than this on their ranch when she was a kid, so she pulled the gelding hard when he reared up and refused the bit. She dragged his head down and stuck her thumb into his mouth until he opened up. He took the bit and was thereafter, like most but not all men, putty in her hands.

'That was cool, Maman,' said Sabine, putting her hat on. She spoke in English, their private language. 'Can you help me up on Pina?'

'No, you're big enough to reach now. I'll hold her and you lift your leg high here into the stirrup and over, yes, well done.'

Sabine looked pleased with her efforts – more than anything, she loved to be independent – and gathered the reins in her little leather gloves. Madison swung herself on to Harmattan, who bucked half-heartedly, and then settled down beneath her. They clopped over the cobblestones in front of the house, and walked out on the lanes through the stubbly fields, past the ponds and into the ancient forest where the kings of France had once hunted deer and wild boar. They walked and trotted for half an hour, hardly talking, until they reached a clearing with a small lake, where there was a little wooden hunting pavilion, in silly sort of Swiss-chalet-style, which must have been built as a rest or picnic stop for noblewomen. They dismounted, and Madison peeked cautiously in through the windows. 'The roof doesn't look very safe. Look at that rotten bit.' But Sabine had already pushed open the door and started poking round the old wood-burning stove. She examined piles of empty beer bottles, and traced graffiti on the wooden table left by children a century ago. Madison followed her, and then they sat comfortably on the bench together, in the play house, watching ducks skid-landing on the lake. Sabine's babysoft cheeks were red from the wind, and her eyes scarily bright.

In the silence, a huge feeling welled up in Madison, the knowledge that whatever happened in her world, however unfaithful Olivier was, she would always have Sabine in all her wonder and complexity, and that her daughter was the most important thing in her life.

'Love you,' said Madison casually, squeezing Sabine's hand. She wasn't particularly good at expressing such emotions.

Sabine hugged her sideways. 'How come, Maman?' she said,

'How come we can't live here all the time? Then we could ride every day and I could have Papa's old room, and I would see you all the time. It's a good idea, isn't it?'

'But darling . . .' began Madison.

'And then you and Papa could be together all the time too, and you wouldn't be so sad, and we could have all this space to play in and this forest and we could build a tree house . . .'

'Sweetie, I've got to work. Papa's got to work. We live in Paris – this isn't our house.'

'Oh fine,' said Sabine huffily. 'Just a stupid idea.' She stomped outside and got on her horse. Madison realised it had been a mistake to teach her to mount by herself when she kicked the pony and rode off, fast.

'Wait. You can't go on your own,' shouted Madison. 'And you're not allowed to gallop. It's too dangerous in these trees.' Sabine just went faster and didn't look back. Madison threw herself up on to Harmattan, and rode swiftly up behind Sabine, whose pony went under the trees rather easily at a canter. Madison and her horse were both bigger specimens, and she had to lie almost flat on his back to avoid the branches poking her eyes out.

'Stop, Sabine!'

'Can't. Won't.'

At last the forest opened up to the pasture nearer the château, and both the horses, stabled for a month, broke into a full gallop. 'Shit,' said Madison, but it was fantastic. The sun had burst low through the mist, and the frost-tipped grass stretched ahead into the distance, as sheep stampeded out of their way.

She caught up with Sabine and rode alongside her, glancing across occasionally at the unadulterated joy on her daughter's face, the excitement which had suddenly enveloped her small life. The horses thundered faster on the hard earth, the blood thundered in Madison's head, and the icy air made her eyes water. She was so happy, so free, so herself; they were mother and daughter in one, combined in a single blur of enormous speed.

In the distance in the garden of the château, a tiny figure was waving both arms at them. Sabine rode one-handed, Western style, and waved back at full gallop. Madison looked at her daughter in astonishment and admiration. As they were about to crash into the walls of the potager, they reigned in their horses together, instinctively, and stopped abruptly, laughing. The figure came running towards them. The horses were lathered with sweat. Sabine leaned down and hugged Pina's neck.

'Well done,' said Madison smiling. 'You don't know you can do that till you've done it. Just don't start by yourself next time.' Sabine beamed back, proud.

Olivier appeared round the wall, red-faced from rage and exertion.

'What the hell do you think you are doing, Madison? I saw you out there. She is six. Six!' he shouted. 'You are irresponsible to the point of insanity. I don't care what you do to yourself, but she's my daughter.'

'Papa!' said Sabine. 'It was the best thing ever.'

7

Anna Ayer

Anna sat on the floor, the wall behind her entirely covered in multi-coloured retro biscuit tins, the words *Petit Écolier* and Lyons competing with brown and gold signage from Fauchon and red canisters from Hédiard. The tins were filled with belts and buttons and scarves, plus other less useful items. Sabine was away at Anouk's house, so in the late afternoon, Anna had settled down in her second *chambre de bonne* to apply triage to her overflowing wardrobe, sorting racks and racks of clothes into three piles: for sale, for wearing and for binning. Although her usual reading was *Vogue* or *Elle*, she had been struggling with Jostein Gaarder's *Sophie's World*, a novel thick with potted philosophy. But she had given up again, this time at the depressing point where Olympe de Gouges was beheaded after the French Revolution for publishing a declaration of the rights of women.

Forget literature – Anna's vast library of vintage dresses and curiosities needed regular maintenance. They were investments as well as vestments, and when fashion moved, she would buy or sell at a friend's stall in the Porte de Vanves every month or so. Generally, she stayed well in profit. But there were many unwearable objects – vast Pucci tops, tiny fifties Dior shoes, and mismatched Chanel buttons – which she could not bear to part with. She picked up a rather garish pink and red fifties dress which had not worked for her – there was far too much bosom to fill.

At that moment, Luiza stomped past Anna's open door, carrying a mug, her face averted. Anna sighed. It was hard enough living alone in Paris without the added delight of a tense and grumpy flatmate, who had to be delicately circumnavigated every day. Even after six months in the Malin household, Anna still had no idea why Luiza was so cold towards her. It had something to do with Sabine and Luiza losing some of her responsibilities, of course it did, but they could not go on like this for ever. Anna suddenly realised the flowery dress in her hands would look perfect on Luiza – she had that fifties curvature, that bosomy shelf, and the red would look good with her dark skin. Anna had a stylist's eye for what suited people, and she could not deny it even this time. To her surprise, she found herself knocking on Luiza's door.

'What is it now? I am on my afternoon off,' grunted Luiza. 'If you're looking for all the messy bottles you left all over the bathroom, they are in your cupboard.' Emboldened by this charm, Anna pushed the door open. Luiza got up from her desk.

'I thought you might suit this,' began Anna, holding out the dress. 'I was going to get rid of it, and then I wondered . . .'

'I don't have any spare money. I send it all to Grozny. I don't waste . . .'

'It's free,' said Anna, exasperated. 'It's a fucking present.' She held the floral dress up against Luiza's dreary nylon uniform. 'Take it. Try it.'

Suddenly Luiza looked almost tearful. Perhaps presents were a rare event in her life. Anna sighed. She left Luiza holding the dress and uttering a grudging thanks.

About ten minutes later, Luiza appeared shyly round the door, wearing the red dress and her furry pink slippers.

'Wow,' said Anna, which covered all possible reactions. 'Here, try these shoes. What size are you?'

Now Luiza looked almost presentable. Her heavy-framed glasses suddenly seemed exactly-right for the fifties.

'Thank you,' she said. 'I'm sorry I . . . It's just that . . .' She looked like she was going to weep again, but then she sniffed, and stood straight in front of Anna's long mirror.

'This was how I used to be,' she said.

'This is how you *are* when you take off that uniform,' said Anna.

Luiza smiled, in a watery way, and sat down on one of Anna's trunks. 'I'm sorry,' she began. 'I haven't been very nice. I was so angry when you came, and I knew it was to teach English to Sabine, I knew in my head that it was fine, but in my heart, I miss her so much. I miss having her sit on my knee, I miss reading to her. I was so bored when I stopped looking after her, until I found other things to take up the time, my college, my recipes . . . And I resent you. No, I resented you, that's the word.'

'But you still see Sabine all the time, and she still . . .'

'Yes, but she was my baby. I look after her from the very first day. And I miss my son, I have a son back home, and it all reminds me . . .'

'Oh shit,' said Anna, as Luiza started sobbing and gulping. Anna put a tentative arm around Luiza's shoulders. 'I didn't know you had a son. Is he the one in the photos in your room? I'm sorry, I thought he was your little brother.'

'No, that's him. Musar. He's nine now.'

'And when you're with Sabine, watching her grow up, thinking of him . . .'

'Yes. It's hard,' said Luiza, clenching her fists and forcing the tears to stop.

'I'd better make some more tea,' said Anna, feeling that the outpouring would be a long one. In her room, Luiza showed Anna endless pictures of Musar in his school uniform, Musar in a yellow football strip. 'He's getting a good education now, and we've got satellite TV,' Luiza said, as though the two goals were parallel. The boy was being raised by his grandmother, while Luiza sent back money to support the extended family.

'We lost our flat in the war, in the shelling, and everything else. My father died, and my brother, so it was left up to me.' Anna noted that there was no mention of Musar's father. She thought it better not to ask.

'How did you come to work here then? Did you know Olivier from Grozny?'

'Yes. He got me a job with the Rimbauds, with Paul and Renée, you know? But it was, oh my God it was so complicated, and she was a total bitch. Came home and sacked me one night, gave me two hours' notice, so I came here and they took me on – I didn't know where else to go. Olivier's a good man, you realise, whatever they say about him.'

'What do they say about him?' asked Anna.

'Oh, you know . . . the usual,' said Luiza, rolling her eyes and offering Anna some slightly stale apple pastries from a tin on the shelf. 'But I owe him a lot – he pays my fare home every year. He likes it when I try out old recipes from the library. He appreciates my cooking.'

'Is that what you're studying at night school? Cooking?' But it turned out that the carefully ordered papers on Luiza's desk were part of her women's history course, an essay on the history of wet-nursing in France.

Now that Luiza had decided to be friendly to Anna, there was no holding her back.

'Anna? I know your French is better than mine. So would

you mind checking it?' Luiza handed her the papers. 'It's very short, only ten pages, and . . .'

'Sure. I'd be delighted. I don't know how much help I'll be, though. You want me to scribble some notes for you? I've got some time before I go out.'

'Thank you, Anna.' Luiza sat proudly in her new red dress, and beamed as Anna went off to read her somewhat muddled prose.

It began: 'It was not until the nineteenth century that wet-nursing became a tendency in all Paris. Labourers, businessmen and artisans send tens of thousands of "Little Parisians" to the countryside to be breastfed. The bourgeoisie did they opposite. They wanted to feed their children at home and imported thousands of peasant breasts from the countryside.'

Well, it would take some sorting, but Anna got the idea. What a weird subject. Maybe it was a Chechen obsession. She read on. Luiza had cited Plato and Jenny Marx on wet-nursing, but the French were the real experts. As usual, Parisians bureaucratised the whole business, with a Bureau for the General Direction of Wet-Nurses, and a penchant for regulations and statistics – eighty thousand babies went to wet-nurses each year in France at the turn of the century. Who knew that it was so common – or so paintable. Luiza had discussed suckling works by Fragonard and Greuze in her paper, and there were photocopies of etchings of an entire lifestyle which died out after World War I and the advent of the bottle. Anna fixed some of the more exotic spelling and grammar, then gave up.

Next, she got down to the serious business of dressing for the evening. She picked out a black vest, pencil-slim trousers, and tied a silk scarf round her waist. It was warming up, even this early in April. She added a vintage jacket and red trainers, and dropped the synopsis back to Luiza's room on the way out. 'I wrote a few notes for you, if that helps. So what got you interested in this?'

Luiza looked down at the papers on her desk and shuffled them. 'Well, uh, it still occasionally happens in Chechnya,' she said, 'particularly when mothers die or get sick, and my own grandmother knew of . . . well, it's a different culture, like France was last century maybe.' Luiza reddened as she spoke, and Anna wondered for a wild second whether Luiza was referring to herself. Had she wet-nursed someone here? Sabine? Would that explain her weird treatment of Anna when she arrived? Or was that too creepy a thought?

All Anna knew was that she wanted to get out of Luiza's pastel low-ceilinged room which smelled of baby powder. She said goodbye, and walked down the stone stairs out into the darkening streets. Ruslan and Aslan, the Barista boys, waved hopefully to her through their steamed-up window on the corner, and she went in to accept their ogling and insinuations in exchange for her usual free latte.

As she left the coffee shop, she saw Madame Canovas bustling towards her on the pavement. The concierge's face was white and sickly looking, and she was wrapped in one of her dark, cabbage-smelling shawls.

'That sort of behaviour is destroying France!' she shrieked, waving her finger at the coffee cup.

'I'm sorry?' said Anna. There was a great deal of flapping, while Madame Canovas lectured her on the 'foreign' Barista chain, which was causing the globalisation of French coffee. It was an evil American invasion of weak, milky, portable fluids, which would put proper French corner cafés out of business.

Anna slurped her drink loudly and waited for the bat lady – who was wearing an extraordinary pink towelling turban – to finish. But she'd only started.

'And where's that little Sabine? I hope someone is picking her up. She's out late, isn't she, for a school night?'

'Yeah, whatever.' Madame Canovas looked sharply at her, not sure if she was being rude. 'I'm off duty now,' explained Anna. 'Someone else is dropping her off.'

'Yes, someone dropped her off the other weekend and there was no one in. She had to wait with me for fifteen minutes.' Madame Canovas actually tut-tutted at this point. 'I was hoping to see her tonight. I have knitted Sabine a lovely navy cardigan – very expensive wool but I got it in a sale – with gold buttons. It's a lot of work, you realise, and I want to try it on her before I finally sew it up.'

'Well, I'm sure you'll spot her coming in. You usually do,' said Anna. 'Must go. Bye.'

God, thought Anna, it's all happening below stairs at 84 Rue du Bac. She was relieved to be out of the grand, oppressive building and the weird intimacies of its relationships. She walked down the Rue de Grenelle, looking up at the first stars struggling to show over the light-polluted city. She passed the pâtisserie, and had an odd, intense flashback to the first moment that she saw Olivier in the doorway; the intensity of his stare. Anna shook her head and passed on, making careful examinations of the windows of Comme des Garçons, Christian Louboutin and Agnès b as she approached the square of St Sulpice where she was meeting Léon after work.

Anna was early, so for a while she watched the ballet of the hairdressing salon through the picture windows: the sweeping and sycophancy of the staff, and the self-interest and preening of the customers. The darkly elegant Angélique, the owner of the salon, had draped herself on the leather sofa by the door and was having some deep conversation on the phone. She didn't seem to work very hard. Léon was still hairdressing, and he hated having his girlfriend around on the premises, but whether this was a territorial thing, or whether he was slightly ashamed of his calling, or ashamed of her, Anna didn't know. So usually they met at the fountain outside, the little one up the hill with stone dragons so worn by the waters they looked like pug dogs. Anna sat hidden in her jacket on the fountain steps, reading *Libé*, and occasionally glancing up into the salon.

Léon was late, because he was ministering to a customer-who-mattered. Anna could tell this, because a whole posse of minions was hovering around the throne, ready to respond to Madame's every need. But clearly someone had brought the wrong brand of mineral water! Madame's face came as close to anger as her thick make-up would allow. No, no, it appeared that Madame liked her Badoit *mixed* with St Yorre, naturally. The coiffing and manicuring continued. But now it appeared that Madame wanted a different colour of nail polish. The hundred or so available were just not good enough, and an assistant was briskly dispatched by Angélique to Chanel down the street. Anna could just imagine Madison causing similar havoc in the salon.

In the meantime, Léon was left alone with his ever-blonde client, who was either twenty or fifty – depending on how close you looked. He ran his fingers and his scissors proprietorially round the nape of her neck, touching and snipping, while keeping eye contact with her in the mirror, and occasionally giving his own buffed arm muscles an admiring glance. Madame appeared to be regaling him with profound details of her life and loves, while Léon nodded understandingly, and tipped her head to one side or the other, according to his whim. Small and trim, in black trousers and a tight pink T-shirt which said 'Simian Society', Léon was often assumed to be gay by his clients. 'I don't deny it. It means they tell me everything, and I mean *everything*,' he'd said smugly to Anna.

The relationship between a Frenchwoman and her hairdresser is one of the most important in life; if the slightest mistake is made, the relationship is guillotined. If, however, the woman and her hairdresser reach that state of silent understanding which results in perfect elegance every time, nothing can tear them apart, Léon had once told Anna. The client will follow her creator faithfully from salon to salon, to the ends of the earth or at least the next arrondissement. This wasn't the case in all countries, Anna thought. For instance, in Chorlton in Manchester where she had grown up, there was only one hairdresser. Indeed, for years, there was only one hairstyle – a feathercut – unless you were over forty, and then you got a perm to go with your bifocals. Anna's French father had such a low opinion of barbers in Manchester that he used to go to London, to the Savoy, to have his hair cut. One day when she was nine, he booked an appointment and never returned, merely phoning in his regrets to his former family. Eventually Anna's mother remarried among her own kind, and got a perm and bifocals.

That would never happen in France, thought Anna, where age is of far less importance than proper maintenance. Look at Léon, enjoying his power over his undeniably beautiful client. Like a classic car, Madame's attraction was preserved by unlimited money and his careful skill. But now he had raised Madame's chair, and had gone round the front, Anna noticed, and was standing beside her legs, his crotch pressed against her thigh as he performed some slow scissor work on her fringe. Then he moved to the other side, and brushed against her again. Madame was looking very relaxed, but Léon gave no indication that he was doing anything out of the ordinary. He stayed pressed there for ages, like a dog in heat clutching at an ankle, Anna thought in disgust.

At that moment, Léon looked over to the window, and Anna ducked deep into her newspaper. Madame checked in the mirror that the back of her head was as perfect as the front, then grandly counted out a pile of Euros as a tip for Léon, smiled, and left. Perhaps Madame liked a little harassment. Perhaps she still thought Léon was gay. Perhaps that was just Paris, thought Anna, where passing glances and touches were free to everyone who wanted with no commitment and even less meaning.

A few minutes later, Léon came out, his leather jacket over his shoulder. 'Darling,' he said, and kissed her lips. He handed her the passenger helmet for his Vespa. 'I've washed my hands, literally, of the rich and spoiled,' he said. 'God, how I hate them. God, how the business needs them.'

'Oh yes, how much you must loathe them,' said Anna, with a hint of sarcasm, and got on the scooter.

Léon looked back at her, slightly disconcerted, and then went on shouting about the film he planned to see, as they puttered through the traffic. Anna wanted to go to one of those English comedies with subtitles and subtleties set in Notting Hill; Léon snorted in horror and said the only possible choice was *Métro-Boulot-Dodo*, a profound, and profoundly depressing critique of the Subway-Slog-Sleep way of life. They argued gently as they chugged on up the Rue de Rennes, packed with honking cars.

'You have no political consciousness, darling, you know,' said Léon, as they stopped at an old café on the Rue Bonaparte. 'But you're delightful. The intellectual debate here just passes you by, doesn't it? It's an English thing.' He tried to kiss her affectionately across the table, but she swatted him away. Since coming to Paris, and particularly since entering employment in such a philosophical household, she had been working on her political consciousness, but she still struggled with the intellectual debate and the jokes in the *Canard Enchaîné*.

She rounded on Léon. He was no more educated than she was, after all. 'Not necessarily. I might just decide not to comment on it. I might just have decided to leave such pretentious matters behind when I moved here. I might just be tired of the arguments.' The waiter appeared. 'But I know that I do want a *bière blanche*.'

Léon ordered the beers and some baguettes and butter, and they dined on these and the free gherkins and peanuts on the table. The café was quiet; too grotty for the tourist beat, but pleasing with its funny old oil paintings, all badly executed, its brown panelled walls, and its grumpy staff. It was the sort of place where one felt a traitor for not smoking, so Anna shared Léon's roll-up.

'How is it going, up there in the servants' quarters?' asked Léon, gesturing in the direction of the Rue du Bac. He seemed to think Anna's service job was menial, whereas his was art. 'Does Little Miss Malin require her knickers ironed, and her homework done by you in best copperplate?'

'No. Her mother likes that sort of thing – well, you've seen what she's like in the salon – but Sabine's fine. I like her. I've looked after a lot worse. She's nice to hang out with – we go places, funny little museums, the Jardin d'Acclimatation, places that I'd never go near in my regular life, and she questions everything, and everyone. She's a total tomboy, and almost normal, given the inadequacies of her parents.'

'Which particular inadequacies?' asked Léon, loudly crunching on his gherkin. 'I could name some myself as a member of the public.' He sprayed out bits of gherkin as he spoke. 'Shall I start with the actress or the philosopher?'

'No, don't bother,' said Anna, faintly disgusted. 'You've told me before. But the problem for Sabine is that her parents are just never there. And when they are, they're, like, so self-absorbed. I suppose they think of her more as a pet, something to pat. It's as though some selfish couple – like Simone de Beauvoir and Jean Paul Sartre – were landed with a child. The Malins are so self-obsessed, so interested in their own careers and brains, yeah, that the idea of disturbing themselves to do some fingerpainting with her is an inconceivable thought. In fact, I often wonder if they even intended to conceive her . . . I don't know. The Dad is typical of most rich Parisian fathers I see round here, sort of distant but nice when it comes down to it, and of course, engaged in a load of dangerous liaisons. The mother seems obsessed with appearances of all sorts. More French than the French, if you know what I mean?'

'Nice body, though.'

'That's very politically correct of you to say so. You know Madison maintains that by consuming nothing but Marlboros and dessert.'

'Bit like my diet,' said Léon, paying the waiter from his fat wodge of tips. Anna was pleased Madame from the hairdressers had inadvertently bought her dinner. 'Shall we go?' he said. 'The programme begins in fifteen minutes. There's a controversial ten-minute short on Iraq beforehand that I don't want to miss.'

'Yeah, right,' groaned Anna in English. Hanging out with so-called intellectuals in Paris was hard going. She got as slowly as possible on to the back of the bike in the dark streets, while Léon revved impatiently.

The cinema was small, arty and damp. In the queue, Léon was delighted to find two of his fellow revolutionaries, Philippe and Mattias, and arranged to go drinking with them afterwards. They were students at Sciences Po, and considered themselves rather radical for befriending a hairdresser and a nanny. They were both twenty-one, almost interchangeable in their wire-rimmed glasses and T-shirts with things like 'Faust' written across them. They did not wash sufficiently, and their love affairs were invariably disastrous, or non-starters. They looked to the more experienced Léon for advice on these matters.

Léon took Anna's hand, possessively. He was always very amorous in dark theatres, whatever the film, however ghastly or political. And certainly during the Iraqi short, and the excruciating tedium of *Métro-Boulot-Dodo*, Anna could only welcome the distraction of his attentions. She liked kissing in the dark – it reminded her of the pleasures of being fourteen again. Besides, the one time she happened to look up, she saw a rat walk across the floor two rows ahead in the half-empty auditorium.

Métro-Boulot-Dodo was entirely filmed on one day in the Gare St Lazare in black and white, with the disaffected, dulled commuter as star turn. For at least ten minutes, or perhaps hours, the film showed endless sad and harried faces going through the platform turnstiles: ger-klunk, ger-klunk. Then the cameraman followed a briefcase at low level, in real time, as it bought a ticket, a croissant, went to the gents, peed for thirty-five seconds, and didn't wash its hands. And so on, and on.

'Jesus. Well that's ninety minutes of my life I'm not going to regain,' said Anna, as they sat afterwards drinking steadily round a table in the all-night Café Marron on St Germain. Mattias gave Léon a knowing glance and said kindly, patron-isingly: 'Let me explain, Anna.'

Mattias talked for some time about commuter-computers, anomie, Weber and the atomisation of society, pausing now and then to ask whether she understood. Anna drained her beer and dragged her fingers across the pile of her purple velour seat. 'Of course she understands what you're saying,' said Léon, as though Anna wasn't there. 'Her dad's French. Whether she understands the concepts, well that's a different matter.'

'I'm going for a pee, boys,' said Anna, exasperated. 'Just keep talking as you were. You probably won't notice I've gone. I'm just a girl.' The men gave one another significant glances, and continued their conversation, while she marched off downstairs, to what she knew were some of the grubbiest, most consistently flooded toilets around. She vowed to stay there in the stench for five minutes until she felt less angry. She looked in the mirror hoping, as usual, to see Audrey Hepburn, but instead she saw a bright-eyed, feverish-looking person. And Hepburn never wore trainers. Anna sighed and brushed her dark brown hair forward to cover her red cheeks, but her bob wasn't quite long enough.

She took her lipstick and mascara from her pocket and re-made up her face, wondering whether Léon and his friends were ridiculous, or whether she was just a bit drunk and ignorant. She had a feeling that if she'd ever been to university, she could confidently dismiss them as pretentious gits, but with her limited knowledge in the particular areas of French film and French men, she just wasn't sure. And she loved Léon, or she thought she did. She just preferred him when he didn't have friends to show off to, and concentrated his attentions, mostly lewd, on her.

She shut the bathroom door and walked unwillingly upstairs into the orange lights, the thumping music, the screaming, the shouting, the fug of smoke. The café was packed, it being Friday night, and she squeezed and pushed her way back to their table, where she discovered she'd lost her stool. Her white bike helmet sat alone on the floor.

'What did you do with my chair, guys?'

'Oh shit, someone's taken it. We didn't notice,' said Léon.

'Come and sit on the banquette between me and Mattias. There's room if we squeeze.'

The boys had more drinks and were *still* talking about the film. The conversation turned to commuter carriages, being shut up in them morning and night, and thence to parallels of cattle trucks and the Holocaust. 'Oh for God's sake,' roared Anna, suddenly enraged. 'Why don't you just fucking grow up. It was a bad film about a boring train station. It had no deep parallels, and you're just using it as a subject to intellectually wank around.'

'Ooh la la,' said Philippe, in a voice hefty with irony. 'Mary Poppins is annoyed. Better get her a drink.' He started singing: 'A spoonful of sugar makes the medicine go down', in bad English.

Léon scowled Philippe into silence, and took a gentler, but more irritating, line himself as Philippe got up to fetch her another beer. 'Darling, you're a bit overwrought.' He stroked her hair. 'You're so beautiful.' Which was Parisian code, Anna thought, for 'you're so thick'. 'I love you, you know,' he continued.

Meanwhile Mattias put his arm around her shoulder from the other side of the squashed banquette, and she felt his thigh press against hers: 'Hey, let's be friends again. We'll talk about something else.' Mattias smelled of sweat and damp anorak. He had a red boil on his neck. He frowned, searching for a helpful thought. 'You know, Léon is always saying how fantastic you are at . . .' and then he stopped, moved his arm lower down her back, and nudged Léon. 'Have you ever been in a three-some?'

'Oh for fuck's sake,' said Anna, turning on Léon, who had been watching Mattias's movements with amused interest. Could there be a more clichéd bunch of Frenchmen? She looked livid. 'Do you regale your little student friends with every detail of our lives? Do you tell them about all your conquests?' Then suddenly her anger reached a higher pitch. 'Do you tell them how you rub like a dog against the grande madames of the seventh when you cut their hair? Do you . . .'

But she stopped, because Léon, socialist, egalitarian, revolutionary and now mortally embarrassed person, had slapped her hard across the face. Philippe spilled the beer he was carrying, Mattias gaped, and then they both looked rather excited. Anna picked up her jacket and stumbled over the crash helmet as she tried to escape the three predatory faces staring at up her. She picked up the helmet. It felt heavy in her hand and suddenly she turned and lobbed it hard into Léon's lap. When she looked back through the café window from outside, he was still doubled up in pain.

Anna started running, fast, anywhere, up from the Boulevard St Germain towards the river because here people, staring people, kept getting in her way, bumping her. She was crying, but she barely needed to breathe, such was the adrenalin racing in her, and within a few minutes she was stopped by the cold stone balustrade of the Seine. She stopped crying and leaned over it, calming herself as she watched the wobbling reflections of buildings in the thick brown water.

'Fucking sex-saturated city,' she said aloud, but no one heard. There was something almost gruelling about being a woman in your twenties in Paris; you were propositioned all the time, by the Barista boys, the men in the street, your boyfriend, your boyfriend's friends . . . She groaned, and tried to remember why on earth she had come here. She stood still, staring at the Seine. Upriver was Nôtre Dame all floodlit and fancy, demanding attention. Glowing tourist boats idled by, their multilingual commentary booming stupidly in the clear air, the sound of chatter and clinking glasses drifting across the water. Down the river Anna saw endless bridges, and the lights swooping on the quays, the trees punctuating the stone walls. At that moment, she loved the city a great deal more than its inhabitants.

'Fuck him,' she thought. 'Fuck him and his adolescent friends when I have all this.' She tied her jacket round her waist and loped off, following the riverbank. At first she just heard the thunder of blood in her ears and saw the passing lines of the paving stones beneath her as she ran faster and faster. She often ran round the Luxembourg Gardens, so she eventually found a comfortable, steady pace. Tourists turned and stared at the madwoman running among them at night. Then Anna began to look up as she ran by the river. On the other side, the great Samaritaine department store hove into view, like a lightship. She ran along the Quai Voltaire, and opposite, the Louvre went on, and on, wing after golden stone wing.

Before the Quai d'Orsay, she turned down towards the boulevard, past Gaya Rive Gauche, where Olivier was regularly to be found eating oysters, past the taxidermist Deyrolle where a stuffed camel looked sadly out at her, and the coils of a white rattlesnake seemed fluorescent in the darkness. Her legs began to hurt and her body needed oxygen.

As Anna crossed over the Boulevard St Germain again, two miles from where she had started, she was struck by the silence of the Rue du Bac in its *bon-chic-bon-genre* dullness. No late-night whooping. No late-night walking, even. It was as though a neutron bomb of respectability had cleared the streets. On the empty stage set, the only sound was of her gasping breath. Anna slowed to a walk, and felt that her anger and agitation were exhausted too.

It was about one in the morning when Anna tapped in the code and clicked open the front door of the great dark building, her home. The lights were all off at the front, replaced by the blind eyes of shutters behind wrought-iron balconies. She crept past the Madame Canovas' window, where a night light still shone, ever-vigilant. As Anna passed the crack in the net curtains, she saw the concierge scribbling something in a book. Beyond, in the marble hallway, Anna slowly regained her breath. She was too shattered to climb six flights up the back stairs, and opted to risk Madison's wrath by taking the lift and creeping through the sleeping house to the door which led up to her attic room. She was still warm, even stripped down to her vest. She pushed the lift button, wiped her face on her jacket and pressed her cheek against the cool marble while she waited.

The birdcage lift creaked and wheezed, but the apartment was silent, the gold mouldings and architraves shining eerily in the moonlight coming through the stained-glass windows in the hallway. Because Anna was still drunk on running and beer, she had the feeling she had entered a church, and froze for a moment in the pools of red and green reflected light on the floor, waiting for a revelation. She shook herself back into reality, took off her shoes and carried them down the corridor, creeping past the bedrooms and Olivier's study to the kitchen.

Just as she opened the back stair door, a deep voice said: 'Ah hah, you might prove useful here.' Anna jumped. Olivier was standing in the hallway watching her, his black shadow silhouetted in the light coming from the study behind him.

Anna thought he was angry about her being in the apartment so late. She sensed trouble. It was always a nightmare eventually, living under someone else's roof. 'Oh, sorry, didn't mean to disturb you so late. Couldn't face the six flights of stairs and . . .' Then she realised Olivier had not been sleeping and still had on his grey T-shirt and trousers. He was pulling one of his all-nighters at his desk.

Indeed, Olivier looked positively delighted to see her: 'You didn't disturb me at all. I'm still working, and Madison's on location. Would you mind coming into the study for a second? There's something you might be able to translate for me. I've been struggling with it for hours. Very much in the vernacular.

Do you have a moment?' Olivier gave an ironic smile which indicated that he knew his employee had nothing better to do in the middle of the night. Some hanks of dark hair hung over his face, and he pushed them away. He looked exhausted, but his eyes were bright with obsession and some caffeine or amphetamine to get him through the night – he swore in interviews that chemistry and literature went together and always had.

Anna followed him into the dim study. Her reading and writing skills seemed to be popular today, but she felt pleased that Olivier valued her thoughts – more than her bloody boyfriend did. Olivier pushed a magazine across to her into the pool of light on the desk. 'That whole page. The piece is in English, but I can't make sense of it at all. Can you?' It was someone's thesis, about hackers, networks and 'technofuturism' but it seemed to be mostly written in American ghetto-fabulous slang. Anna stared at it for a while and got the sense. She was still a bit breathless. 'This basically says that hacker culture will always remain anti-establishment; that its language and the new netspeak will exclude the old. It's sort of a new English-ghetto-Esperanto, it's the language of the clubs, of black music – does that make sense? – and he's using it to show . . .' A tiny bead of sweat dripped from Anna's forehead and plopped on the page. 'Sorry. I've been running.' She continued the translation '. . . to show the possible exclusiveness of such a language . . .'

'Don't worry. Take your time. Running where?'

'Running away,' said Anna.

'Ah,' said Olivier encouragingly, and downed his pen, waiting with what appeared to be great interest for more revelation. 'Who or what were you running away from?' His voice suddenly became concerned. 'Did someone try to attack you, Anna?'

'No, no, I just ran to get it out of my head. Now let me get back to this and I'll finish it for you.' Anna went on for some minutes with her translation, bent over in the pool of light. Inside she was wondering: what the hell am I doing here at one in the morning alone with this man?

'What's "it" if you don't mind me asking?' said Olivier, unexpectedly interrupting her from the sofa by the desk, his face in shadow so she could not see if he was watching her. Anna pulled up the thin strap of her vest which had fallen down. She felt sure she could feel Olivier staring at the little Japanese symbols tattooed between her shoulder blades.

'It was some guy, never mind,' said Anna. She suddenly felt upset again. This really wasn't any of his business. 'Do you see this here? This bit contradicts itself, unless I'm understanding it wrongly.' Olivier stood up and leant over behind her to look at the text. She felt her back tense up. She turned round, aware of how close he was. Olivier was staring at her as though he had stopped hearing the meaning of the words and was thinking of something else entirely. His finger suddenly outlined the tattoo on her back. Anna flinched, scalded, and turned to confront him. There seemed to be men everywhere this evening, touching.

'What do . . .'

'What does that sign mean?' said Olivier, amused and nonchalant, taking his hands back, putting them schoolboyishly in his pockets, and moving away until he was in front of her across the desk.

Anna looked at him severely. 'These tattoos are Japanese symbols for peace and balance, and . . . well they're not working.' Olivier gave her a sympathetic smile, and then looked down with some interest at the tiny bumps of her nipples now rising through the vest. She was in too much of a muddle to know why anything was happening. Then he noticed the red mark on her cheek, and asked softly: 'Anna? What's that? Who did this?' He was beside her again.

Olivier's concern made her throat contract in a prelude to crying. He sounded so adult and fatherly, while being quite the opposite, she reminded herself. 'Can I help you with this tomorrow? I have not had a good night,' she said, standing up shakily and holding the corner of the desk.

'Are you tired?' asked Olivier. Anna noticed he was addressing her suddenly with *tu*, instead of *vous*.

She shook her head. 'No. I'm too disturbed to sleep.'

Olivier turned and surveyed her, dark eyed, in a questioning silence. 'You want to talk about it? To a foreigner, a stranger? An impartial stranger?' He smiled, more kind than predatory now. 'Sit down,' he said, and Anna found that she had.

She felt uncomfortable that the employer-employee relationship had suddenly turned into something different, and she was not sure precisely what, although it was both liberating and tempting. Olivier seemed aware of her unease. 'I'll get us some water. You're still rather hot. And perhaps some wine,' he said, studying the condition of both Anna and the nicely chilled Brouilly in his office fridge.

Olivier opened the bottle of wine, poured two glasses, and filled two more with water, then came and sank deep into the sofa beside her.

'Talk to me,' he said. 'Talk to me, Anna. I'm a trained philosopher, you know, years of experience. I can analyse any moral dilemma and provide a solution in moments.' He gave her an ironic smile. 'Drink this, and this, that's my prescription so far.' Anna drank the water, and then took the wine. She glanced quickly at his half-illuminated profile beside her: his strong nose, like some Roman emperor, and the deep sockets from which his eyes watched everything.

'Now . . .' said Olivier.

'I've a question,' interrupted Anna. 'Have you seen *Métro-Boulot-Dodo*?'

'Uh huh,' said Olivier, slightly puzzled.

'And what did you think of it?'

'Well, it's a load of pretentious trash and I walked out after fifteen minutes. Why?'

Anna smiled at him for the first time that night. 'That's what I wanted to hear.'

8

Olivier Malin

By eight o'clock at the Café Calvaire nobody could get through the doors, so thick was the Friday-night crowd. Bodies blacked out the windows which normally overlooked the polluted crossroads of the Opéra. Immobilised customers, smoking with the ferocity of youth, passed notes above each other's heads to order double espressos and beers. The volume of talk rose in anticipation. Then the Messiah appeared in his crisp white T-shirt and perfectly tailored black suit. And lo, the crowd parted before him and his escort, a waiter wearing a T-shirt with the words: 'A Café for Socrates'.

Olivier acknowledged the applause with a brisk nod that bordered on a bow, flicked back his hair, and perched on a bar stool above his acolytes. There were fifteen or so different 'Café Philo' nights around Paris now, but Olivier's had been the first, and was still the most popular. Combining the skills of a game-show host and an intellectual, he rounded up subjects for the evening's impromptu philosophical debate. 'Utopia: What's the Point?' suggested one woman. 'Should You Spit in the Soup?' shouted another. 'Chechnya: Beyond Philosophy,' suggested a thuggish-looking skinhead in a Nike football jacket at the bar.

'I think I've written enough on that, as many of you will know,' said Olivier, smirking at those who nodded in the front row. 'We're looking for a more universal topic here.'

'What's not universal about the oppression and corruption of a great people? What about this human propensity for fucking up, for self-abuse, as a nation?' growled the skinhead's ursine mate slightly inarticulately from beneath an LA Lakers baseball cap. He sounded Chechen himself, Olivier thought. Or something. You never knew. But one thing is certain: you can always spot a recent immigrant by the quantity of designer sports labels he wears. 'True,' said Olivier smoothly, 'but we might get bogged down in detail on Chechnya. I'm not sure that everyone here is expert enough on the subject.' He smiled patronisingly and waved his hand for the next offering.

'The Immorality of Fidelity,' offered a man in black leather, grabbing the microphone. Olivier perked up a little at that one, and wrote it on his list, but then his attention was drawn to something more fascinating in the front row. 'Professor Malin?' called a languid classical beauty, who was there most Fridays,

'What about: Only the Unique is Other?' Olivier turned his gaze full beam upon the beauty, and acceded to her request.

Then they were off. Olivier clarified and moderated, as spotty, raw boy-students at the front jostled for the microphone, while the middle-aged further back took notes and plotted clever one-liners. The crowd picked at the meanings of 'unique' and 'Other' as though they were scabs. A drunk at the back shouted at Olivier: 'It doesn't make any sense, this. You're talking bollocks.'

'Precisely,' said Olivier. He liked it when the discussion got a bit rough. 'That's the whole point. "Only the unique is Other" is a phrase from the philosopher Levinas, and if a great philosopher can produce something so unclear, then that should make us all think about glib statements. Next?'

'There's a whole baggage of sexism here, which you're letting him off with,' said a girl with what Olivier presumed was lesbotically short hair. 'He characterised the feminine in terms of alterity, thereby assuming the male perspective all the time.'

'Good point. Do you think he was an existentialist, given this sort of statement?'

'No, Levinas was never an existentialist, but there's a lot of existentialism in his writings, such as that little nausea essay, whatsitcalled?'

'*Evasion*,' said Olivier.

'Right,' said the girl. The boys at the front clearly felt they were being excluded, and waded in again. The overheated debate continued for about forty minutes, until the languid beauty got up and moaned that the discussion was being corrupted 'by ignoramuses who don't even know enough Hegel or Kant to pass the philosophy section of the Bac.' Olivier forgot his earlier crush on her, in order to crush her.

'Philosophy's for ordinary people, not just academics. That's why we're here, talking.' He looked up, modestly, sincerely, forgetting there were no cameras to appreciate this. A statement was about to be made. 'Philosophy's got a role to play in the divide between rich and poor, the growth of technology and the threatening of democracy. Philosophy gives reason a chance. It's a chance to stay on the riverbank and not be swept away by the river of superstition which leads to hate, passivity and exclusion.'

At the word exclusion, the beauty turned pale, and there was a burst of applause. Olivier flicked his hair and scanned the crowd as he waited for the noise to die down. At the back of the café, Olivier saw a delicate face he recognised slightly, and he grinned automatically across the room. Unsmiling, the dark-haired girl lifted a hand and an eyebrow to acknowledge him, and he realised it was Anna. He had hardly seen her around the house for the last month or so, not since they had talked into the night. She had been avoiding his gaze at home, but tonight she had obviously been watching for some time, for two espresso cups and an ashtray sat before her. He felt a rush of desire for her. But Anna's eyes left his, and she drew on her cigarette and slowly blew smoke up towards the ornate, yellowing, pressed-tin ceiling of the café. Olivier took the next topic, on morality and power. 'I'll throw that one open to the floor,' he said, pointing at a glinty-spectacled, pushy student from one of his classes at Sciences Po. He was bound to pontificate for some time. Olivier took a moment to think.

Why is she here? he wondered. He was both complimented by Anna's presence – she wouldn't be his first philosophical groupie – and a little perturbed. He didn't like the way she looked so calculatingly at him. In potential liaisons, Olivier liked to make the running, to be in control, and he thought he had been the other night when they had talked in his study. But now he felt like he was under the 'nannycam', so to speak. Anna's attention was directed at the student speaking, while her fingernails drummed on the table.

The bespectacled student was deep in the argument about Christianity and sexuality: 'Sexuality – for which we can often read sin – is confessed, encoded and turned into discourse, controlled by the power of the Church.'

A foreign accent came from the back: 'But wasn't it Foucault who suggested somewhere that prohibition and censorship are not the most important forms of power, but in fact a sign of its limits?' It was Anna's voice. Most unlikely. Olivier stared. It was a fair point, but what was she doing? Applying for a post as teacher's pet? He had never considered her stupid, perhaps because he'd never considered her mind without paying rather more attention to her body. With some interest, he watched her delicate-boned face redden with embarrassment.

The student fought back, but Anna bravely tried again. Her voice trembled a little as she said: 'You're assuming that power works from the top down, but sometimes, it's from the centre to the outside. It's not so simple, or so . . . so patriarchal as you portray it.' The student, now very irritated, sat down. Then he got up again and started babbling.

'Thank you. That's enough,' said Olivier, with a slightly incredulous tone in his voice, looking over at Anna with his eyebrows raised in amusement. 'That's all we have time for tonight – in fact we've overrun. Next week, we'll take a new topic, so be ready with suggestions. And if you need an argument before then, you can also attend the midweek Café Philo with Professor Jaures at Le Robinet in the fifteenth.' Olivier sat down to boisterous applause. Fans of both sexes formed a posse around him as he started to walk between the tables. Each wanted a sliver of his attention, to be part of his intellectual and physical glow of confidence, and each tried to get a word in. Olivier gagged slightly on the hefty perfume half the women seemed to be wearing, and autographed a few of his books, brought dog-eared by dogged fans.

He looked round confidently for Anna among his entourage, but she did not appear. Her table was empty, a small tip lying on the bill, and in the ashtray, two cigarette stubs, stained with dark lipstick. To his surprise, Olivier felt an unpleasant, almost teenage pang of disappointment in his stomach. The café was suddenly stifling him. He brushed off the students who were crawling over him brandishing theories, and pulled on his black jacket. He decided to clear his mind by walking home alone across the bridge to the Left Bank in the warm May night.

He crossed the Avenue de l'Opéra briskly and headed directly down the Rue St Roch which led to the Tuileries and the Seine. Usually Olivier felt uplifted by the students' adulation and the adrenalin rush of thinking on his feet – sometimes, the crowd could be disturbingly combative – but tonight, striding past the rickety old buildings and printers, he felt an underlying irritation, which he put down to Anna's unexpected presence. It was bad enough to be spied on by the domestic staff, but it would appear they'd all been reading philosophy, twentieth-century works in the nanny's case, and Plato and Marx in the maid's case last year. Was it catching or something? And what was a nanny doing being a nanny when she knew a very obscure line from Foucault? She had talked Foucault, and disappeared. She had spurned him, he thought. So irritating.

There was nothing Olivier enjoyed more – other than a perfect meal – than the pursuit of love; extra-marital love, nowadays. He adored the initial meeting, the obsession, the seduction, the discovery of a new body and a new mind, and he was always fascinated by the part of himself, the new Frenchman, that emerged from each fresh conquest. He liked the chance to reinvent himself, to be a slightly different character in each short-running drama. (Long-running dramas were generally bothersome, and interfered with his comfortable home life, which he had no intention of jeopardising.)

His pleasant thoughts were interrupted by a commotion behind him. Under a street light further up the Rue St Roch, two bulky men stood, arguing and shouting aggressively in a foreign language. Olivier recognised them as the Chechens from the Café Calvaire. He quickened his pace, but soon they drew up close behind him. Suddenly the yelling stopped.

'Ooh, it's the great philosopher,' said one, brushing roughly by Olivier on the pavement just as a car came by and prevented him stepping on to the safety of the road. They walked so close he could hear the nylon rustle of their sports trousers. The men laughed and walked on, arguing again. Olivier preferred to pull his punches in debates than elsewhere, so he slowed his pace and watched them until they safely turned the corner on to the Rue de Rivoli and disappeared. He felt slightly shaky. He suddenly remembered he hadn't eaten that evening, and put the uneasy feeling down to that.

Was there not a little bar here with barrels outside, just up a side street off the main road, that did a delicious plate of mixed charcuterie? He peered into the darkness ahead, looking for the lights of the bar, and carefully checking for the aggressive men. Instead he saw a female figure in a short trenchcoat walking quickly along the crossing of the Rue de Rivoli, a block ahead. He knew from the proportions of the waist, the length of the legs and the way she moved that it was Anna. Olivier ran up behind her. She started and turned at the sound of his feet.

'Ah Anna! There you are in your famous green coat. I remember it from the day I first saw you,' said Olivier, skidding to a halt beside her. 'Now what do you mean by coming to watch me? I wasn't aware that you had any interest in philosophy.' Just as he said that, Olivier had a sudden memory of Anna's fluent translation of the English philosophy paper the other night. Maybe she did have some kind of grasp of the subject. Anna was smiling, coolly observing his flustered appearance. 'Hello, Professor Malin,' she said, laughing at him. He looked irritated. 'Olivier?' she said, more kindly. 'I just wanted to see what you got up to by night. There was nothing on television . . . French television! Dreadful.'

They fell into step, and Olivier asked about Foucault (of whom he was very fond). Anna explained that she'd picked up Olivier's *Magazine Littéraire* in the kitchen, and taken it to the launderette with her, where she was forced to read it for two hours. And she'd struggled with this article on Foucault and power. 'I'd quite forgotten it all until that sanctimonious little git annoyed me, and the arguments came flooding back. In fact I didn't understand half of them, any of them, really. But Frenchmen! Dreadful. He was all puffed up with importance. Was what I said wrong? I was just guessing.'

'What you said made perfect sense.' Olivier thought it rather sweet that Anna had tried to read up on his subject. In fact, it was very promising in all sorts of ways.

'Hey, did you see the Chechen guys from the Barista Bar in our street turned up at the Café Philo? They are so weird,' said Anna. 'They're called – let me get this right – Ruslan and Aslan. They're funny.'

Olivier repressed a shudder. 'Oh, perhaps, yes,' he said. They walked on down the Rue St Roch in a slightly uneasy silence, then turned up a side street. Their shoulders jostled on the narrow pavement before a lighted doorway. 'Now, my dear, I

am quite starving. I'm just going in here for a beer to recover –
and a plate of their very good charcuterie. Perhaps you might
join me?' said Olivier.

'Sure,' said Anna. The confidence with which she answered
signalled to Olivier that there had been some profound change
in their relationship, incubated, perhaps, during the long, late
night in his study.

The little *gargotte*, a neighbourhood restaurant with gingham
curtains at the windows, was filled with portly men knocking
back beer. By the door, two old ladies in spectacles and pearls
sat with kirs and walking sticks primly before them. Olivier
headed for a red vinyl banquette in a corner of the dim, ochre-
smoked backroom, and the waiter set out knives and forks on
the paper tablecloth. Just one other couple were eating in the
alcove beside them.

'I am so mega-starving,' said Anna, flinging off her coat and
turning hungrily, loudly to their waiter. 'What I need, desperately, is a *bière blanche* and some of that *jambon de Bayonne*
you've got hanging over there, and garlic *saucisson*, and some
little gherkins. And lots of bread please.' Olivier was silenced,
since she had spoken of all his unspoken desires. 'Me too,' he
said, almost weakly, 'but just a regular beer.'

Olivier sat down. 'Anna? You are a gastronomic goddess.'
Anna looked at him boldly, smiling. 'Madison's mostly vegetarian, isn't she?'

My God, so that was where they were already, thought Olivier.

The subtle, gentle beginnings of their friendship in the household were suddenly laid bare, out in the open world. There was about to be some direct competition. But they were very different, these women in his life. Perhaps they tasted different too, a gastronomic ocean apart. For instance, he would characterise Madison as long and lemony, rather sharp. Whereas Anna was small, dark, and probably deliciously chocolatey. He suspected he would know the truth of that all too soon, and he smiled.

He studied the girl across the table. Anna wore a dark top and a tiny brown and orange suede patchwork skirt, and her bob swung back and forth as she talked. To Olivier she looked foreign, un-French: the skirt was shiny with age, secondhand from the sixties. There was both a delicacy and a raw otherness about her that Olivier needed to explore, only the unique is Other being the theme of the evening so far. Anna was still rabbiting away, oblivious. 'The vegetarian thing must be hard for you, sometimes. I've always liked that medieval idea that there are certain temperaments connected to different foods . . .'

Olivier supplied the rest of the theory and plunged deep into gastrophilosophy until their order arrived and they both fell upon the red meat. They were feverish. Anna tore off lengths of the dried ham, with its still-bloody smell, and held the strips high above her lips before reeling them in. She was disgustingly, thrillingly free of the manners of a Frenchwoman. Olivier watched her small tongue with its strange silver stud appear and disappear, while he carefully rolled each of his salami slices into a cylinder, and let the raw taste permeate him in small bites. He felt the stirrings of a bizarre variety of desires that he couldn't quite describe.

Anna reached for the baguette at the same time as Olivier and their fingers touched. A force field formed over the table, where every gesture took on a secondary meaning only they could feel. Olivier tore off two equal chunks of bread, and passed her one. The waiter brought fresh unsalted butter in a little dish, and being British, Anna slathered it all on her bread. Olivier continued to pile the charcuterie on dry bread. Then Anna held her butter-loaded baguette to his mouth and said: 'Eat. Your nation isn't always correct on these culinary matters.' Olivier did as he was told, and it seemed at that moment that this mix of food and life could not be more simple or perfect.

Anna watched him, a smile of sheer pleasure on her face, and bit a little gherkin murderously in half and crunched its remains. 'I like it here,' she said, surveying the restaurant, then surveying Olivier as though he were a particularly fine cut of meat. Olivier felt excitement, and just a sliver of uneasy fear. Then Anna took his hand in hers, and brought it to her mouth, and slowly sucked on his meat-salty fingers, her eyes steadfastly, amusedly on his, almost challenging him.

Olivier closed his own eyes for a second, wanting to reject the foreign mix of romance and Tom Jones comedy for something more serious, and above all to gain control of the situation. He much preferred to seduce, rather than be seduced so obviously. He took his fingers away, cupped her small chin in his hand and held her like that as he kissed her across the table for so long that the ladies with the kirs and walking sticks looked as if they might cheer the small soap opera which had unexpectedly blossomed that night in the café.

She bit down on his tongue, in the midst of their kisses. Olivier was taken aback by her roughness. 'What are you . . .' he began, stopping for a moment to catch his breath. While his mind was attempting to raise itself above the thrilling vulgarity of it all, his body was fully engaged. He was aware of a fierceness there, definitely more carnivorous than vegetarian. He stared at Anna. Her dark eyes were shining, and her cheeks were flushed. Her teeth looked strangely sharp. He pulled away. He had some enquiries to make. He drank some beer, slowly, in silence. She waited.

'First you spy on me, then you spurn me, and now you snack on me? You owe me an explanation.'

'I was hungry,' said Anna. 'Also, I like charcuterie a great deal, particularly a well-cured *jambon de Bayonne*. In my room, I sometimes keep a whole Napoli salami and just slice . . .' Olivier imagined her all alone in her room, kissed her again, and fed her the last few slivers of salami with his fingertips. He kept eating the *jambon de Bayonne*, even though he was sated, because he was suffering a worse hunger.

It was after eleven, and the café was emptying. Looking rather regretful at leaving the scene of the drama, the two old ladies picked up their sticks and walked into the night, hats carefully secured. Now there was just a rowdy crowd of men round the bar, and not a woman in sight. The waiter brought more beers and then joined the crowd drinking and talking, leaving Olivier and Anna alone in the background. Olivier slid round and joined Anna on her side of the banquette, putting his arms around her. She was small, firm, and eminently possessable.

'I'm not sure if that's proper,' she said, pulling his arm lower. 'The customers might complain if they saw.' She took his hand, and slid it down to touch her legs beneath the tablecloth and beneath her skirt. They stayed drinking, talking, touching, combustible in the smoky backroom, until midnight came, when the proprietor started stacking chairs pointedly on tables and sweeping around their feet. Olivier called for the bill and whispered: 'I want to be true to myself, true to you. I have to make love to you. It's knowledge we must both have. Otherwise we will face an inner disharmony which will . . .'

'Yeah, I know,' said Anna, cutting in, confidently. 'You've wanted to for ages. But I have to go home, and you can't come there. Luiza's next door.'

'I would take you to a hotel, my darling, but there's nothing round here, and Madison was expecting me two hours ago. Perhaps we . . .'

'That's life,' said Anna, shrugging. The cooling night air conspired to return them to reality as they left the café.

'My darling,' said Olivier, temporarily solving both problems by pulling Anna into a shop doorway, enveloping her in a warm hug, and kissing her beneath a huge sign which read: 'We print announcements for births, weddings, and deaths. Serving all your needs in this life and the next!'

'My needs,' he said pointing at the sign, smiling. 'My needs are unmet. I need you now.' His fingers found her nipples, stiff, through her shirt. They stood kissing for some time, the strange metal shape of her tongue-stud surprising him, and he pressed himself against Anna, into the warm V-shape of her legs.

'What you need is a brisk walk in the fresh air,' said Anna, abruptly setting off across the avenue towards the Tuileries and the bridge. Olivier caught up with her, uncomfortable, discomfited. He was not best pleased with the way Anna was being so direct, brusque and horribly attractive to him. It was very British. And it really wasn't the weather quite yet for outdoor seduction, although Olivier did have fond memories of certain spots in the arches down by the Seine. The gravel was silver in the moonlight, and huge, sculpted heads and horsemen looked down upon them. A policeman gave them the kindly nod that policemen give to lovers late at night, and hand in hand they crossed the river over to the Quai d'Orsay and the top of the empty Rue du Bac.

Normally, despite being six feet tall, Olivier walked shoulder-to-shoulder with Madison in her heels, and he suddenly felt a strange tenderness looking down upon Anna's shining hair as they walked. Again he pulled Anna towards him, in the long windowed entrance to the taxidermists', Deyrolle, and they kissed under the glassy eyes of the camel and the white rattlesnake which had seen Anna run by in a flurry of anger only a few weeks before. While they went into the doorway as lovers, a few moments later they emerged separately as strangers, seeing the shadow of 84 Rue du Bac looming ahead.

'The all-knowing Madame Canovas has infra-red sight, I have reason to believe, from previous encounters,' said Olivier. 'We must be careful.' They tapped in the code and crept into the ornate vestibule by the lift and the stairs. Olivier opened the lift door. 'Come on,' he whispered.

'No. I've got to go up the stairs. Staff entrance, you know. Upstairs, downstairs, as we say in England.' Anna smiled and curled her lip almost imperceptibly. 'Goodnight, Olivier,' she said. He watched Anna go, followed by her doubles, the endless reflections in the hall mirrors of girls in green coats, all intent on leaving him unsatisfied.

'I'll phone you on your mobile.' Olivier paused, and grinned. 'We must talk.'

The night light suddenly snapped off in Madame Canovas' apartment across the courtyard. Olivier raised his eyebrows in resignation, and watched as the last flap of Anna's coat disappeared up the servants' staircase.

Olivier felt a gaping painful hole at his side where Anna had been. Usually his reactions to the ups and downs of seduction were much more intellectual. But like a doctor observing new symptoms in a patient, Olivier laid out his needy, heady feelings one by one, and his diagnosis was worrying. He felt ambiguous about Anna's curious tendency to take the initiative. He remembered once, during his eight-year marriage with Madison, when he conceived a passion for one of Paris's older, but incredibly elegant and witty hostesses. He had haunted her salon, and made endless exquisite and subtle approaches to her over lunch privately, and publicly too, over dinner when her husband was but a few seats away. He had been happy then, just walking behind her, savouring the airstream of her scent. Then one day, he had arrived early, alone at the salon, and she'd kissed him hello on the mouth with her dry red lipstick and then started opening the buttons of her silk shirt. And suddenly, now that he'd stopped running to her, now that she'd turned round and approached him, he was repulsed. The obsession had withered that very second.

And here was a new situation. Not repulsive, but certainly disturbing, for Frenchwomen instinctively know how to handle these things, the dance back and forth, the glances, the delicate wordings. Olivier was less sure about handling something foreign, meatier, more pungent. And so local. Of course, Olivier had never believed that fidelity had anything whatsoever to do with love, and he knew he had a duty to explore whatever passion led him to, while remaining within the social confines of his relationship with Madison. Sex alone was not enough for him, for he thought the best thing about falling in love was the falling in love itself – now who said that, he wondered, as he slipped quietly into the dimly lit bedroom.

In the crack of yellow light from the hall, he could see that Madison was asleep, gloriously Ophelia-like, floating in the ripples of the white sheets, her golden hair around her, breathing gently. Olivier took all his clothes off and stood there with his desire for another still showing reproachfully, grumpily. He pulled the sheet down just a little and looked at Madison's breasts, strangely white, waxy and saucer-like in the near-dark. She suddenly seemed to be a giantess. Sighing, but desperate to escape his bodily demands, he started kissing Madison method-ically, gently. She groaned, pushed him away, and rolled over, displaying the pearl-like path of her long spine. Olivier, unabashed, kissed each vertebrae down and down until he found himself by a backward path between her legs and underneath the sheets. He went on kissing. He closed his eyes and imagined himself elsewhere, under a second-hand suede miniskirt in an alleyway. Or something tawdry and wonderful like that.

He worked hard, efficiently, for he had known the specific mechanics of Madison's body for a long time. More encouraging noises came from above, as her body moved in rhythm with his. Then they were joined, and he was making love to Anna, quickly, roughly and darkly, with Madison falling away from him into the void, her part in the act quite forgotten.

'Oh my darling, I'm sorry, I just went too . . .'

'Don't worry, honey. There'll always be another time . . .' said Madison. 'Now, if you don't mind, I'll just go back to what I was doing before you came in.'

She rolled over, shut her eyes, and that appeared to be that.

Olivier walked slowly into the adjoining bathroom, the tiles cold on his feet now the heating was off. He didn't switch on the light. As he was peeing, he looked through the window, up and across to the mansard roof, three windows along from the left, the room where Anna lived. Her light was still on. A shadow passed the blind, then nothing. He stood there for five minutes watching, wanting, before creeping back into the bedroom. Madison was asleep again. He could tell by her soft breathing. He lay his head on the pillow, looked across at her, saw her damp eyelashes and dark sockets, and wondered for a moment if she'd been crying. Then he, too, rolled over and forgot.

9

Madison Malin

Madison rose in the dark at six, and immediately Olivier spreadeagled himself in a reflexive, sleeping movement across the whole bed. She saw his strong face in profile in the light from the bathroom, his skin brown even in winter, his expression contented, and she thought: why does he sleep so peacefully? She knew that last night he had taken something from her, but she was not sure what. She felt degraded and melancholy without being able to put her finger on the problem. While she was bathing – for freshness is everything on a filmset, especially at an age when the cracks begin to show – Sabine appeared in a Batman costume.

'Maman!'

'Ssh, don't shout. Your father's still asleep next door. What are you doing up at this time, and why are you wearing that thing?'

'Fancy dress day at school, for Mother Teresa's charity. I've been ready since five, playing on the computer. All the other girls are going as Sleeping Beauty, Rapunzel or Barbie, but Guillaume and I are both superheroes with secret powers. I'm going to wear my black riding boots and this mask. Do you want to come to the parade after school? All the mums are coming and . . .'

'I'm on set until five, darling, in some godforsaken field way up near Amiens.'

'Oh, yeah, right.' Sabine was pulling on her dusty riding boots. 'Well, Anna will come. She bought me this costume in Monoprix with her own money. Is it true that you pay her lots of money every week to look after me? Anouk said that. Anyway, Anna said I didn't have to be a princess if I didn't want to be and that there were far too many princesses around in silly pink dresses for her liking.'

'I don't need to know what Anna's liking is. The costume looks highly flammable, however, so be careful.' Madison was finding the emotional subtext of the conversation too disturbing at this time in the morning, especially before coffee. 'Will you pass me that lavender conditioner over there?'

Madison looked down in the bath at her smooth body, a tribute to the Rue du Bac's finest skin spa and her Pilates teacher. It was good enough for a nude scene today, especially with careful lighting, and anyway, André preferred suggestion to full-frontal vulgarity. She got out and massaged herself all over with body lotion.

'Can I have some?' said Sabine. Madison gave her a tiny, expensive dollop, and Sabine rubbed the cream on her riding boots until they were shiny. 'Nah, nah, nah, nah Bat-man!' she sang, pleased.

'You're funny,' said Madison, laughing and getting dressed.

She stood in the kitchen, a vision of perfection, and waited until seven when Anna staggered down the stairs from her *chambre de bonne*, dark-eyed with exhaustion, in her tracksuit. That girl should really sort herself out, thought Madison, and then she might be quite attractive. Anna and Sabine – wearing her Batman eye mask with some difficulty as she ate – immediately got into some complicated conversation about the best cereal in terms of numbers of plastic freebies in the box, with Anna arguing strongly for Weetos, and Sabine for Shreddies. Madison said goodbye. Sometimes, she thought, it was better to have a young nanny to do some things, because frankly her own interest in superheroes and Weetos was limited.

Sabine's tastes were always unpredictable. Last week she had taken her as a special treat to a fashion show, in the Cirque d'Hiver, with fabulous wild birds and models. Madison had thought Sabine would have been a charming companion and accessory. Instead she had wriggled and was utterly bored and grumpy. They had argued, and Sabine had stormed into her room when they got home, kicked the door shut, and jammed the handle.

Madison sighed and walked to the corner. She was early for the car that was taking her to the filmset, and so went into the Barista takeaway coffee shop. 'Madame,' said the steroid-muscled guy behind the counter. 'What a pleasure it is to see you.' He looked her up and down. 'What would you like today?'

'A small skinny soy latte,' said Madison, once again pleased that American coffee habits had taken France by stealth.

'Aslan? Skinny soy for the lovely lady.'

Madison leaned on the zinc counter while the milk frothed. 'Pardon me, but where is the name Aslan from? Is it from the Narnia books?'

'Nah, no books in it. I'm Aslan and he's Ruslan. Our mother liked the way it rhymed. We're from Chechnya – well, your husband knows all about Chechnya, doesn't he? Seen him on the TV.' He grinned at her, showing a solid gold front tooth. Madison was a little disconcerted that he knew exactly who she was. 'Chechens run all the Baristas round Paris now – they call us the latte mafia.' Madison smiled. There was something amusing and rather exciting about the pair of them, with their pumped-up weightlifter's bodies, razored haircuts, and the way they moved lightly in neat leather trainers. The car hooted outside. She proffered a note. 'Come again soon, lady,' said Aslan, winking at her.

The drive through Paris and into Picardie was interminably boring, past the high rises of the Périphérique and through undistinguished flatlands punctuated by crumbling concreted churches, all built to the same pattern in the 1920s after everything was razed in World War I. Madison did not look out the window, but sipped her breakfast, the latte, and made final plans for her first salon, plans Olivier knew nothing of. Then she read a few pages of a biography of Beckett, her on-set beach reading, until they passed a sign which said: 'Military Base. Authorised Personnel Only. Danger of Explosions.'

'Hey, Maddy,' said some assistant rigger, as she got out of the car. 'Generators have gone down, the big lights on the crane have fused, and it's a fucking nightmare.'

'So nothing out of the ordinary, then. Good to see you,' said Madison, happily. Somehow, once she was at work, even the rough was generally smooth – well, apart from the time André made her plunge five times in the frozen duckpond. But she loved the isolation of each filmset, the months of camaraderie, the fact there was nowhere else to go, and that most of the time you couldn't even be called on your mobile phone. Heaven. Work was the one place where she could really be herself and have time to think.

The filming of *Soldier, Soldier* was taking place on a disused army base, where the crew had redug the First World War trenches with some accuracy. In fact, Madison suspected some of the boots, shrapnel and twisted wire on the raw earth were from long ago, and not props at all. Apparently they had found an unexploded bomb when they brought in the mechanical diggers. The mud was genuine, which is why everyone on the crew wore Aigle wellingtons, including Madison. She splashed through the car park towards a camouflaged metal arc, a disused bomb shelter which was make-up and costumes. This was a low-budget film, without Hollywood trailers and pretensions. Three old school buses propped up on bricks served as dressing rooms, one of which had two armchairs rescued from skips. Madison liked it that way. She had been in only one gross-budget American thriller – in which, inevitably, she was carefully coiffed, then raped and murdered. She'd hated every moment of it, all that business of sulking in one's trailer with plastic containers of organic wild-rice salad, being a starlet. The French were much more egalitarian about it all.

There were dozens of extras in grey-blue mud-spattered uniforms, standing and having their make-up done at speed, but for the so-called stars there were plastic chairs in front of trestle tables with lit-up mirrors, and even Pampers babywipes for make-up removal. Sellotaped to the long walls of the shelter were photocopies of war photographs, the soldiers displaying a vast array of handlebar and other interesting moustaches. A medical booklet from 1914 showed diagrams of the correct way to bandage a head and an eye – André Andrieu, the director, liked total accuracy where possible. Madison sat down in front of the mirror, and while she waited for the next make-up girl to be free, she tried on a variety of moustaches from a dusty crate beside her. She was a natural mimic. 'Something more ginger for me, do you think?' she said to the soldier-boy next to her, who was giggling through the fake blood caking his face.

'Stay still!' said the make-up girl, but Madison had an exceptional talent, largely unnoticed, for comedy, and continued her Germanic moustache routine until all the soldiers and crew were hysterical. Then in the mirror she saw André standing in the doorway, watching her with interest. He turned and disappeared.

Madison got some coffee from an urn which boiled its sticky brown gloop all day long, sat down to take her turn, and marvelled once again at how long it took to do the 'no make-up' look. Then she squished herself into a corset, lace-up boots and a nurse's uniform with a stupid white hat. Her scene that morning was in an unheated tent, supposedly behind the lines, where she had to lie very tenderly, in a sort of motherly way, alongside a shell-shocked nineteen-year-old who had lost his leg below the knee and was dying. It was supposed to be night, lit by oil lamps, and she was personally not convinced that any germ-alert nurse would sensibly share a bed with someone bearing a gangrenous, smelly stump.

When she arrived, the soldier-boy was already in bed under the sheets, and they were testing the lamplight with Polaroids. 'That's all we can do until the generators come on. Should be about five minutes,' the assistant rigger told her.

'It's fucking freezing in here this morning. It doesn't feel at all like May,' said Madison.

'Uh huh,' said André, snuggling deeper into his huge blackdown jacket. 'You'll have an authentic reason to get in bed with him.' The generators cranked back on, followed by the lights and the cameras. No heating, though. Madison was still icy in her thin cotton uniform. She tried to look cheerful and briskly nurse-like.

'Whaddya reckon he smells like? Just for veracity, you know?' said Madison. The soldier, an extra she'd never seen before, giggled.

'Terrible,' said André. 'So do your stiff upper lip thing while being tender at the same time. Get in. And again!'

She got in beside the soldier once, twice, then seven times. The make-up girl, in a huge, jealous-making woolly jumper, kept daubing Madison's nose with powder. André was pacing round the bed: 'No, closer. You need to be closer so I have your faces together in line on the pillow,' said André. 'Again.' He spent about ten minutes between each shot adjusting the light and the angle. Then they tried again.

This time she squeezed right into the young man on the narrow hospital cot, and then jumped up.

'Oh my God, it's real!'

'What? Fuck. You just spoiled a great shot. I had the shadows just right on your faces,' growled André.

'His stump. It's a stump!' Then Madison remembered her Southern manners and said: 'I am so sorry, honey. It's just it was rather a surprise suddenly feeling where your leg stopped. I mean that it really stopped.'

'Oh, it doesn't matter at all,' said the soldier-extra. 'This is how I make my living – they get real veracity in the shots with me. Anyway, it's wonderful working with you – I remember seeing you when I was little in *The Turquoise Sea*.'

Madison got back into the bed and turned her face towards the soldier's on the pillow, and slowly smiled.

'That's it, cut,' said André, happy at last. 'Lunch.'

They all put on their wellingtons and trudged through the mud and light sleet towards a white tent in the distance. Inside, there were long tables decked with enough food for a wedding – the French film unions expected no less, Madison sniffed – but then she loaded up her plate with five different kinds of crudités, a little smoked salmon, and some olives. She sat at one of the paper-covered tables with André, the stumpy soldier, a lighting technician, and a Ministry of Defence historian who had turned up to give advice on the authenticity of the set. Madison liked the way you never knew who you were going to end up talking to at lunch, and that there was no divide between stars and the crew. The Ministry of Defence man looked rather excited to see her, though. He was eating skate in black butter with capers, while André was walloping into a huge plate of veal stew with fennel.

'This chef is known to be one of the finest in the film business,' said André, drinking some of the Gamay that was left on every table. 'I'll work on any budget, so long as it includes his cooking.'

The Ministry of Defence man made a truffling noise. Madison looked over and said: 'Have you spotted any serious historical mistakes, then?'

'Ah,' he said. 'There is the question of tidiness in the trenches. The German and French trenches look the same here, but in reality, the Germans maintained their ladders better, and kept everything neatly. Whereas the French put up silly signs, jokes, photographs, and even set little shrines into the mud walls.'

'I could have guessed that,' said Madison grinning, going up for a dark chocolate mousse.

By the end of the afternoon, Madison was grey-blue with cold, almost matching the soldiers' uniforms. André's perfectionism took no account whatsoever of human suffering. But she knew the scene had worked when she saw the rushes. Shattered, she lurched over to one of the school buses that served as a trailer and curled up in the brown nylon armchair, drinking Diet Coke and reading the Beckett biography. She felt unaccountably happy. And it was nearly time to knock off for the day.

André came in, moaning. 'I'm exhausted. My eyes have gone all watery looking at that screen. I can't tell what's good and what's bad any more. But I do know you were fantastic, and very resilient, given all that mud and shit.' He kissed the top of her head as she sat. 'You want a beer?' He took two from the little fridge in the corner and plonked one on the table in front of her.

'What're you going to do when we've finished, Madison? What's coming up?'

'Another Ferrone film.' Madison shrugged, resigned.

André looked closely down at her. 'Let me guess. You're playing the mistress? Of a corrupt politician? There's a lot of very expensive black underwear?'

'You got it. Except the male politician wears the black lace underwear and dies on the job.' Madison took another sip of her beer. 'But it's good money.'

'You don't really need to do things for money. And then?'

'And then I don't know.'

'I could use you . . .'

'You already do. You abuse me all day.' Madison smiled.

'I'm doing a Beckett, *Happy Days*, next year in Paris. I haven't done theatre for ten years, and I, well, I'm just thinking about it, would feel less alone if it were you I was directing. I know how you work, and when I saw you mucking around with those moustaches in the make-up trailer, I realised how funny you might be if . . .'

'You want me to play a mad wrinkly pensioner covered in muck up to my neck?'

'Yes. It just came to me. I hadn't thought about you at all before for the part.'

'Christ,' said Madison, insulted and complimented at once.

'You'd need some hefty make-up . . .'

'I'd be out of a job afterwards. You play ingenues, mistresses, then mothers, and then it's only a short step to grandmothers and unemployment.'

'Or an alternative route.'

Madison shrugged.

'Well, think about it, Madison. You *are* reading his biography, I notice. *Ciao.*'

Madison thought about it all the way back in the car to Paris, and although she was rather tickled by the idea of sustaining two hours alone on stage in a pile of sand, she knew it would be the end of her film career. Except as a character actor, which was an equally unpleasant thought.

She switched on her mobile phone. '17 missed calls,' it flashed. 'Press for options.' She knew her options would be feeling guilty or harassed, but these were not available on the phone. Instead she played them all back: Luiza with a plumbing problem; Anna with two potential playdates for Sabine; Anna again with a leak in a ceiling somewhere; Darphin Spa ringing to say she'd missed her facial; three hang-ups from Paul Rimbaud; her personal trainer re-scheduling a missed Pilates session; Sabine wanting help with volcanoes for science; a call from her hairdresser Angélique; another from Renée, asking her to lunch – and with Renée, lunch was never free – it was torture; Luiza again; Olivier complaining that Anna and Luiza kept ringing to complain to him; her agent, twice; a dire mother from Sabine's school; Olivier asking where on earth she bloody well was.

Madison shut her eyes and tried not to exist for five minutes until they drew up outside the apartment building. She tapped in the security code, but before she was through the door, Madame Canovas was upon her in a flurry of shawls, lamentations and halitosis.

'A most terrible thing has happened! It is an absolute emergency, imperative that something is done immediately.' Madame Canovas fell into a burst of dramatic coughing, and then wheezed on: 'The Robichons on floor five have been informed but they are not home yet, so I took the liberty of letting myself in to their apartment once we realised it was coming through to the fourth floor, and a sight more appalling I have never . . .'

'Stop!' said Madison. 'What is actually the problem, Madame?'

'You cannot mean that you have not been informed! But surely Luiza or Anna told you: the bath, your bath, has been leaking, not through one floor, but two, and had I not been vigilant, we would all have been flooded until . . .'

'Did anyone call a plumber?'

'Ah, that I don't know, Madame Malin, but in my opinion . . .'

'I'll go straight in and find out. Thank you, Madame Canovas, and I'm sorry to have caused you any trouble.' Madison knew from experience that if Madame Canovas was left unappreciated or unplacated, there was hell to pay. Your mail could easily get lost for weeks, for instance. Madison dived in the lift and Luiza met her at the door and explained about the burst pipe under the bath and how they'd turned off the water, but the plumber hadn't yet turned up. Olivier was lecturing today at Sciences Po, so he was no help. Domestic matters were generally beneath him.

'Fine,' said Madison. 'Now the water's off we don't need to panic. Call the plumber again to see where he is, Luiza. And where's Anna?'

Luiza gestured towards Sabine's bedroom and peered hopefully at Madison though her cooking-spattered glasses. 'And, um, I have an evening class in half an hour so if you wouldn't mind?'

Madison's phone went again. It was a mother from Sabine's school. She signaled yes to Luiza, wondering what on earth the maid was studying. Meanwhile a text came in from Olivier asking her to bring his bow tie to the premiere they were to attend at nine o'clock that night. Madison rang him back to ask where the tie was. She could hear a loud bar or café in the background.

'Thought you had lectures this evening?'

'Oh, um, yes, I'll be back in class again in an hour. I'm just waiting for a colleague. See you later.'

Who was he with now? wondered Madison. There was something in his guilty voice that made her feel upset and uneasy. There were still seams of her original passion for Olivier hidden deep inside her, and sometimes one touched the surface, painfully.

Feeling grimly burdened by life, Madison marched along the corridor to Sabine's room. She could hear giggles. 'And I've packed this African tablecloth with the giraffes on it, for making a tent or picnics or wearing as a cloak. It's a *multi-purpose* tablecloth, you see. I have this bag ready at all times, just in case. See, this is my special equipment – a torch and this screwdriver which came in a cracker, and my supplies: these chocolate coins that Papa gave me, I've saved them for emergencies, and my army water bottle. And Ratty.'

Madison stopped behind the open door and listened.

'You're well equipped, then,' said Anna, her voice close to laughter. 'Where are you going?'

'New York, of course.'

'Of course,' said Anna. 'Where else?'

Madison walked in. There was a sudden shuffling as Sabine shoved her red backpack under the bed and then stood up, trying to look innocent.

'Hi, Maman.'

Madison gave Anna a knowing look, but she thought it best to let Sabine keep her secret.

'Do you mind if I have an hour's break before babysitting tonight? I've just got to quickly meet someone down the road,' said Anna.

Madison agreed, and took Sabine off to tackle her project on volcanoes. Anna had obviously begun the work with Sabine, because the kitchen table was covered with spilled paint and cardboard. 'Got to finish it for tomorrow. Look!' Sabine was pulling on Madison's jacket, which she had not yet taken off. Sabine was waving a brush dripping orange paint.

'Watch my coat! It's Armani!' shouted Madison.

'Ooh,' said Sabine, 'sorry. Now I've done the earth green and brown, sort of swirly orange for the fiery lava, but what colour would the smoke in the crater be? Pink? And then I need to label all the parts.'

'Maybe the smoke's grey. Didn't they tell you? Wait. I don't know anything about volcanoes, and we don't have a book, do we?' asked Madison. 'Why don't you look it up on Papa's computer while I see to the leak?'

Madison was setting Sabine up at the computer – only to find that her daughter was much more technically competent than she was – when she noticed piles of scrunched-up hand-written letters in Olivier's bin. She was not a prying person, but there was something about the numbers of letters and the vicious way they had been crushed that drew her. She unfolded one, and saw that it was filled with lots of angry ravings from someone called Florence. This Florence seemed particularly prolific, but then Olivier got a lot of crazy mail. She threw the letter away, and her phone rang again. It was Paul. 'Darling Madison,' he said by way of greeting. 'Could we meet at the . . .'

'Not unless you can weld pipes, honey,' growled Madison. 'I'll call you later. The doorbell's going.'

Madame Canovas arrived with the plumber, just as Sabine reappeared with her hands painted yellow up to the wrists.

'Hand stars! Everywhere!' she said.

'I said to myself that I had better inspect with my own eyes, for this is a matter for the whole building,' said Madame Canovas, marching briskly towards the bathroom. The plumber followed, lugubrious. 'I'm on double time after six,' he said helpfully.

'Ceiling downstairs will have to be replastered, I'm sure,' said Madame Canovas. Sabine had left huge yellow handprints on the kitchen door handle, the study door, and no doubt on Olivier's computer.

Madison turned on her. 'Stop making this mess immediately! Go and wash your hands. This isn't how you go about a school project.'

Sabine looked at her with a challenging grin. 'No water. The water's off.'

Madison saw a bottle of Badoit sparkling water on the kitchen shelf, and started dousing Sabine's hands and wiping them with a dish towel. The paint was tough to remove, she was rough, and Sabine began crying.

'Maman, Madame Duclos said we have to finish the volcano and label it for tomorrow. Oww, that's sore where you're rubbing.'

'Well, we'll finish it later, or tomorrow morning. I don't have time now. Get into your pyjamas.'

'But you leave at seven in the mornings.'

'Your father will just have to help for once, then.'

A PR person rang to ask Madison to be in a charity fundraiser on television.

'Your joint's gone. I'll have to weld it,' said the plumber.

'I've trouble with my joints,' said Madison to the PR person on the phone. 'Call me tomorrow.'

Madame Canovas was about to launch into another performance, so Madison literally – but politely – pushed her out of the door, and she flapped off down the stairs in a tremendous huff.

'Maman?'

'Yes?'

'I've got my pyjamas on. Will you read me *Charlie and the Chocolate Factory*?'

'Darling, I've got ten minutes to get ready and I've got to call a taxi to take me to the première.'

Madison sat on the trunk in the hall and put her head in her hands.

'Poor Maman,' said Sabine, patting her. 'I'll help. I'll call the taxi for you.' She took Madison's phone. 'Papa showed me how to do it – you just scroll down to "taxi" and press the green button, and tell them when and they automatically know where to come.'

'Automatically,' said Madison, smiling at her seven-year-old competence. 'In ten minutes, thank you, Monsieur,' said Sabine into the phone.

Next, there was a call waiting. It was Madison's agent, fixing up an interview with *Vogue*. 'And wear something fantastic tonight. There are ten camera crews coming.'

Anna burst through the door, late, her eyes bright, her breath smelling of beer and mints. She took over Sabine and the plumber, while Madison went to her wardrobe. Her dress was missing. Her Valentino. She searched under all her coats and ripped open the plastic on everything from the dry cleaners. Then she remembered that Luiza, being super-competent, had taken three of her evening dresses to the dry cleaners last week. Madison sat on the bed and took ten deep breaths. Somehow the Valentino was the only right dress for tonight. She pressed the mute button on her phone. She regrouped, found Olivier's bow tie, and put on her faithful blue satin fishtail Galliano. She brushed her hair and hairsprayed it while hanging her head upside down for a minute, resulting in instant bounce. She'd do her make-up in the car.

The car drew up a few minutes later outside the university buildings of Sciences Po, and Olivier hopped in, looking fresh and handsome in his dinner jacket.

'Darling,' he said, kissing her, his breath smelling of beer and mints. 'Did you bring my tie? You look at bit hot and bothered.'

'That is a fair assessment. I'll tell you later exactly what happened while you were *lecturing*, but I've warpaint to put on.' Madison could feel she was on the edge of breaking down and screaming. After all that had happened this evening, all the irritation and hassle, Olivier was sitting there all cool and calm, smelling of beer and mints. Just like Anna had been. They couldn't possibly . . . no one would be that deceitful, surely?

'Madison?' Oliver was watching her expression. 'What's wrong?'

'Suffice it to say that I am neither a good mother, nor a good plumber. I feel like I'm schizophrenic – I love my work, but the minute I get home, everything falls apart and I turn into a psychopath.'

'Darling!' said Olivier. 'Don't be silly. What can I do to help?'

'It's a bit late now, but you should learn to do some home repairs with your soft philosopher's hands and be able to label all the parts of an active volcano by seven a.m. tomorrow.'

'What?' said Olivier, puzzled.

Madison gave him a dark look and then performed a small, steady-handed miracle as the chauffeur raced round corners and across the Seine to the Palais de Chaillot, where Madison's first Ferrone film was premiering.

She fixed her lip gloss just as the car drew to a sleek halt at the red carpet outside the floodlit Palais. Madison and Olivier got out, paused to beam for the cameras, and then walked slowly hand in hand down the line of paparazzi, lingering to make witty remarks and sign autographs. The train of Madison's turquoise dress contrasted most photogenically with the red carpet. The cameras caught the Malins as they gave one another a loving look before turning to go inside. 'Paris's Perfect Couple,' said the headline in *VSD* magazine.

10

Anna Ayer

However great his fervour, Olivier was not the sort of man who could make love on an empty stomach or a mere sandwich. He also, Anna suspected, liked a preamble. Just as his philosophical arguments meandered winsomely before coming in for the critical kill, so he enjoyed a circuitous route to seduction. He wrote the script beforehand in his head, for in his middle-aged way, he needed to control the situation. Yet these thoughts did not stop Anna agreeing on the phone to meet Olivier and play the part for the first time in Labrousse, a little steak restaurant in the dirty, perspiring streets behind the Gare St Lazare. Few people went to Labrousse intentionally: it merely captured those waiting for trains with time to pass, and a few regular shopkeepers at lunchtime. It looked dull enough from the outside to have featured in that seminal film *Métro-Boulot-Dodo*.

Olivier was sitting in a smoke-fugged corner of the restaurant, under an ugly carved mahogany mirror. He was engrossed in *Le Monde*, with a half-empty glass of red wine suspended in his long fingers. The story which had caught his attention and stopped his drinking hand mid-air was also making his eyebrows rise and fall. As she watched, Anna was pleased that the world still mattered so immediately to him; that his compulsions extended beyond the physical. His jaw jutted in anger at the newspaper, and then softened to a smile as Anna appeared before him, dressed all in black. He looked her up and down, amused. 'For a funeral or just a *petit mort*?' he asked softly as he stood up to kiss her.

Anna laughed, yet in contrast to their last meal, she found herself nervous, experiencing the same anticipatory breathlessness she'd once felt during a panic attack on a plane landing with a faulty engine in a storm. Naturally, she gave no sign of this being the case. What threw her was the unnatural aspect of this assignation – that it was devoid of mystery, except in the style of its execution. The name of the little hotel where the act would take place, for instance, still remained unknown to her, but the length of their small drama was decided: it must finish by half past three in time for her to pick up Sabine from school – after coming, after Anna's pre-ordained *petit mort*, about which he was inordinately confident. All their time together was snatched: a drink for an hour before his première and her babysitting; a moment in the Jardin du Luxembourg after work. Clearly, the upper middle-class French were used to timetabling their passion and pocketing it as neatly and traditionally as they dressed.

'Is absolutely everyone you know having an affair of some sort?'

'Not constantly,' mused Olivier, taking the question very seriously. 'But there is no one who has not had their little adventure, as we say here. Or so I suspect. I suspect it even of my wife, but it is a husband's duty to suspect his wife and do nothing about it, isn't it? Anything else would be uncivilised.'

'I've got no idea. Who writes these rules?'

'Nothing is ever written down. It's all in the imagination, you see.'

Olivier kissed her across the table to emphasise his point.

Anna already felt that slight out-of-body experience, as though her feelings – which were in interesting turmoil – were being relayed to her second-hand. The waiter arrived bearing his huge moustache and their plates. Olivier managed to speak and eat with equal gusto, sometimes both at the same time. Anna only half listened, instead observing his hands talking, his features moving as though in a silent film. Although she saw him almost every day, while working she did not risk observing him closely like this.

They had ordered rare steaks. Anna drank some wine. Olivier took her hand as though reading the palm and stroked the pulse point at her wrist, tracing the blue lines of the veins. She could see Olivier watching her fast breathing in what she now felt was a too-tight jacket, which fastened high up the neck with tiny flat pearl buttons.

'Where did you buy that? It's old, isn't it?' said Olivier, touching the slightly shiny gaberdine of the cuff.

'The second-hand market at Porte de Vanves. I think it's theatrical, principal boy, you know.'

She drank some more and felt a calm beginning to flood through her. Olivier ate some steak and watched the red juice pool from the cut on his plate. He touched her bobbed hair. 'All in all, you look like a young priest.'

How could words be so disturbing? But they were, perversely. Under the table, her leg pressed lightly against Olivier's, connecting them. Paris cafés were designed with tiny tables and chairs, perhaps for this very purpose. Close up, she could see the crows' feet round his eyes, the wrinkles on his forehead, and the darkness in his eyes.

'So where might we be going a little later?'

'The Hôtel Select, which is not particularly grand but is rather famous in its own way. Perhaps you have read Busson's *Lost Station*? There's a scene in it set there when the heroine . . .'

'Nope.'

'Well, the Hôtel Select will be fascinating for you, then, for it is the best of its kind and there aren't many left like it. No, I hear it is all vulgar Americanised Ibis and Holiday Inns now – unless you have a little apartment stashed away somewhere – and as with all chains, there is no sense of occasion.'

While Anna felt the shadow of sin, of what-she-was-about-to-receive hanging over her, Olivier seemed to have confronted the forbidden before. While she wondered what fresh heaven or hell the curiously named Hôtel Select would bring, he rattled on, outlining his theory of life after top-down capitalism, and how the netocracy would consume democracy. She could make little sense of his arguments, but she felt pleased that he expected her to grasp them, somehow. He was old, older, but not patronising, not like Léon had been. He had no need to patronise, nothing to prove. He looked very satisfied, his mind filled with ideas, his stomach filled with flesh and blood, with more to come. Olivier gestured over to the waiter, wiped his mouth with a napkin and intertwined his legs with hers under the table. 'A steak with a pat of thyme butter, a pichet of house red, a double espresso and a square of dark chocolate,' he said, before ordering coffee. 'What more could a man want?'

'Dessert,' said Anna dryly, in some way hoping she could derail the timetable for love just a little. Olivier looked surprised, but not annoyed, as she ordered a crème brulée. '*Bonne continuation*,' said the waiter as he served her. Olivier refused to share the crème brulée with her, and instead watched with anthropological interest her technique for cracking the crisp burnt-sugar top and burrowing beneath in the cream. She ate slowly, at first out of desire to slow proceedings, and then out of desire, because it was too good to rush.

'The true test of a restaurant is its crème brulée,' observed Olivier grandly, watching Anna lick her spoon, providing a sighting of her tongue stud. 'Although this is an unprepossessing place, the food is what my friend Claude Lebey – you know that food critic? – would call "correct". Do you see the sign on the wall over there?'

Anna looked across. There was a large oval sticker with the words 'Member of the Society for the Protection of Eggs Mayonnaise'. She snorted, and then immediately wondered if a Frenchwoman would snort during such an assignation. Olivier was laughing. 'You see, here is an ordinary restaurant, a bistro of no importance, yet it is preserving traditional foods, as they should be, unadulterated by all this "fusion food", these foreign influences. Here, the patron still respects the *terroir*, the roots of food in France.'

Anna was only surprised that he didn't say '*la belle France*', so patriotic did he sound. 'Yeah, but eggs mayonnaise? All cold and white with slimy Hellmann's?'

'No, no, no. You have clearly had a bad experience which has scarred you.' He leaned forward, as though imparting a state secret. 'Let me explain. The lettuce leaves should be whole, alluring, providing a crunchy background, and the eggs should be boiled for ten minutes – but no longer. Three halves look most pleasing on the plate. The mayonnaise should be fresh and eggy, with the right consistency: it should cover, yet not be too liquid, rather like a tablecloth draping the eggs. It is far from simple. Yet egg mayonnaise is dying out, just like pig's trotters, a good onion soup, blood sausages . . .' He looked genuinely mournful, and very appealing. 'So hard to get them now. By defending eggs mayonnaise, this emblem of bistro cooking, we defend the bistro. The threat, as Monsieur Lebey says, is not really to *cuisine de terroir*, native cooking, but to *cuisine de trottoir*, pavement cooking.'

Anna sat mesmerised by this poem to gastronomy. In her experience, food lovers were good lovers. Olivier's voice rumbled low and soothing, the sort one might use for calming wild animals, or talking a prisoner down off a jail roof. Anna felt trancey, as though she were on ecstasy. She lit a cigarette, blew the smoke out slowly, and waited for the world to steady.

Olivier paid, the waiter held out his jacket, and they left the soupy fug of the restaurant for the summer breeze outside. '*Bonne continuation*,' murmured Olivier in Anna's ear as they turned the corner and walked hand in hand up the hill to the hotel. Anna felt a cold spasm of fear run from her head down to the end of her spine, where it met a contradictory warm tide rising. She stopped and kissed him, and they stood still, embracing, for a long time, as passing Parisians looked upon them with approval.

'Let's move, before we become a Carrier Bresson photograph,' said Olivier, and Anna giggled. They turned into a steep street of ripped flyposters on boarded-up shops, and open shops where everything was on sale, the bargain of a lifetime, for one day only, today. They looked out of place among the cheerful coloured bustle: Anna was goth-pale, while Olivier was wearing sunglasses, which made him all the more noticeable as a celebrity intellectual. Perhaps this was intentional, since Olivier was only exercising his divine right as a Frenchman to the *cinq à sept*, or in this case, the twelve-thirty to three-thirty slot. (Anna had read that heavy traffic had put the end to the *cinq à sept* at those precise hours.)

And now Anna was suddenly part of the Parisian world of sex, lies and subterfuge. She had never slept with a married man before, never wanted to. But now, she did, with a visceral need. Every so often nagging guilt about Madison and Sabine, particularly Sabine, would surface, and have to be subdued, subsumed beneath her obsession with Olivier. To be honest, Anna didn't care that much about Madison – she didn't like her high-handed iciness, but she liked Sabine. Unfortunately, she liked Olivier a great deal more.

Clearly Olivier had no such compunctions. As if anyone would have minded his little liaison! As if anyone would not respect him for honouring passion over the dull quotidian! Besides, those who live the high life of the mind must also know the low life of the body. Or so Anna imagined that Olivier assured himself on such occasions. But she was suffering from a gnawing desire for him, which had been quietly eating away at her for months and needed to be assuaged with reality, not dreams. There was no choice. Afterwards, she would decide whether good or harm would come from it.

* * *

The Hôtel Select overlooked the rail tracks fanning out from the station, and the warm air was filled with diesel fumes and the clank and thunder of metal below. The hotel was an inauspicious skinny building with knobbly green glass in its old double doors and a sign so miniature no tourist would find it. Which was the point. 'I can't believe places like this still exist,' said Anna. 'You're so retro.'

'I'm not retro, my darling. I'm genuinely old fashioned. This is a quality establishment. You'll see.'

Anna approached the door cautiously, with the same awe and trepidation she used to have when entering dark, incensed churches as a child. Olivier approached the door cheerfully, and she wondered if he was thinking of other piquant afternoons spent there. Then he spotted that the *boulangerie* next door was open. 'We must, we absolutely must have one of those,' he said, disappearing suddenly from Anna's side into the shop, where they did a particularly delicious loaf – indeed the window display boasted a gold medal from the Distinguished Order of Master Bakers – in a circular plaited shape. Olivier tossed the ring of bread on his arm, took off his dark glasses, and bounced up the steps of the Hôtel Select. Anna wondered if there would be a game of sexual deck quoits featuring the loaf, but suppressed her laughter. She felt that a Frenchwoman would not make a joke at this point.

Inside the little hotel was dimly, grimly lit like any other, with flowered wallpaper and a rackety, caged lift. The foyer reeked of pine air freshener and *Joy de Patou*. Inside what appeared to be a ticket office, a bespectacled, respectable woman looked up from her desk. Her grey face burst into life when she saw Olivier. '*Ah, bonjour Monsieur!* How fortunate we are to have you!'

'Madame Paquin! So delightful to see you after so long.' Anna wondered precisely how long ago and how often Olivier had frequented Madame Paquin's establishment.

'And which room would you and the young lady prefer today? Number five is sadly already taken, although if you'd rung . . .' She shook her head in sorrow and folded some intricate tapestry cushion she was sewing to one side.

'A little chinoiserie will be just fine, Madame,' said Olivier.

'Ah. Number three . . .' She took the key from one of ten hooks behind her, and pushed it through the grille to Olivier. In return, he laid four twenty Euro notes flat on the counter and smoothed them with his hand. 'Until later,' he said, 'and perhaps a bottle of red?' He added another note. Madame Paquin swiftly gathered up the money, nodded, and folded her arms, observing Anna's appearance with some disapprobation.

Olivier concertinaed the metal diamonds of the lift door and ushered Anna into the tiny space, with barely room for one. She immediately felt caged and breathless. She wanted to run out. Olivier must have seen the thought flit across her eyes, because he took her hand again and said: 'It's fine. Don't worry. It's fine. It'll be most amusing for you.' He started kissing her as the lift rose four floors through the darkness, carrying the smell of warm bread with it. 'What I love about you is you are completely authentic,' said Olivier, kissing her up against the flock wallpaper of the upstairs corridor. 'Remember what Sartre said, that to act in bad faith is to turn away from the authentic choosing of oneself and act in conformity with a stereotype, but you are always you, coming from some essential centre.'

'I think that's more Northern grit than authenticity, but I'll take your word for it.'

Anna could think of plenty of stereotypes for herself, slut and adventuress being two, but either way she was impelled to go ahead, because it was there, because it was possible, because it was Parisian. She had worries, of course. Would the sheets be clean, and what on earth was behind door number three? Olivier unlocked it and flung open the door with a flourish. There were black-lacquered walls lit by red lanterns, the dim light from which perhaps disguised the worn furniture. In the sliver of sun that came in below the pulled blind, Anna could see that the room was bizarrely glamorous: Chinese silks on the bed, kimonos on the walls, a beautifully upholstered chaise longue, and huge willow-pattern vases which looked like they came from the discount store Tati rather than the Far East. The effect was dramatic.

'Madame Paquin prides herself on her upholstery and the individuality of her decoration – and her pristine sheets. She used to work in the theatre, and all the directors and intellectuals come here, perhaps because it's so traditional, a perfect stage set for little adventures,' said Olivier, holding her in his arms. 'Each room is different.' He tipped her chin up so she looked him in the eye, whereupon she couldn't breathe any more. She thought she might sway like some corseted Victorian about to faint, until Olivier began the laborious process of undoing the twenty-one buttons on her jacket. 'There are certain disadvantages to these vintage garments you persist in wearing,' he said kissing each sliver of flesh as it was revealed. His hands were long, with hairy knuckles. He slid down to unzip her long boots and trousers, with the meticulous attention of a valet. She hadn't worn socks. Socks are not sexy. 'Unfortunately we missed room number five, "Versailles",' sighed Olivier.

And then he stopped talking, and knelt stroking the iridescent white of the insides of her thighs. She looked down upon his dark head and felt lengths of hair brushing her skin. In the distance, the traffic roared and tiny trains made metallic thunks of coupling in the goods yard. He smelled of cinnamon and loamy earth. 'What's "Versailles" like?' whispered Anna, sliding Olivier's T-shirt over his head, and studying his chest, fingering a few grey hairs among the black. Her bra fell in a curl on the floor. ' "Versailles"', said Olivier, 'is the hall of mirrors – on the walls, on the door, everywhere, and there's a disconcertingly large one on the ceiling with a very ornate gilt frame which looks like it might plunge on to the bed at any moment, crushing those . . .' But she interrupted him, slipping a small pale pink nipple into his mouth, then arching slowly backwards in his arms on to the sheets.

She closed her eyes and seas of warm red and orange swept by. Outside, his fingerprints left a Braille trail up and down her body, and made a meticulous, stroking examination of the tattoo on her back. Some of his fingertips had little roughnesses on the skin, and she could identify each one in different places, carefully mapping the first expedition, feeling deeper. And then, with an almost unbearable lightness of touch, he seemed to be causing her to levitate from the bed, which was not true, but in some way the planes of horizontal and vertical were shifting in the room, red silks looming and swooshing, and time flatlining. She felt a warm electricity of pins and needles in her toes, which travelled up and up into her head, pulsating, until there was a thunder of blood and waves broke in the orange-red and swept down. Only after that did she touch him.

She became a bend of white over Olivier's straight brown frame. His skin seemed to be stretched over stone, hers over wire. He was heavy with strength and reality; she was insubstantial. He tasted salty, and she began a languid conversation with her mouth, suggesting, then abandoning. She floated over him, coming and going, listening to his breathing, his half-words, his unspoken clues, and instinctively following them. But hands came and held her face and brought it up opposite his, and she looked into his eyes in silence until the colours, rising again inside her head, made her close them. Now his hands were on her waist, lifting her upon him, and she felt the astonishing relief of the emptiness, in her head, in her body, being filled. Then they became a complicated puzzle of movement out of which suddenly emerged a beatific calm. As the blood stopped thumping in Anna's head, she again heard the faraway trains whistling, the tannoy announcements in the distance, and the sound of Olivier's breath in her ear as she lay on his shoulder. Anna kept her eyes tightly shut, suddenly realising that there were unshed tears in them. She felt his fingers brushing across her damp lashes. 'My love,' he said. 'My love.'

They lay staring silently in the way that lovers do. Anna noticed tiny wrinkles on the brown skin in front of his ears, and felt saddened by the distance between their ages and lives. On the other hand, in bed they interlocked, and the divide could be crossed by flesh into perfection, and that should never be dismissed or forgotten. She had not known anything as clear as this before.

There was a discreet tap at the door. Anna jumped, feeling invaded, but Olivier wrapped a towel around his waist and retrieved a bottle of cheap red wine and two tumblers from an invisible Madame Paquin. 'How did she know when to . . .'

'She always knows. Years of experience.' They sat up against the pillows with their tumblers. 'You have made me alive again, my love. You have brought me into the here and now. We are at the centre of the richness, fullness and ambiguity of human existence,' said Olivier, for whom a simple phrase like 'I love you' would never be complicated enough. Anna suddenly wondered if he was thinking in his ambiguity of Madison, but she suspected no thoughts of his wife crossed his mind, for he was living a separate moment in time, in his here and now, for which he would not feel guilty later.

But there was little time to pause for thought, so Anna and

Olivier broke the bread, and drank the wine from each other's mouths until they needed to make love again, differently, because this was no longer the first time and they were armed with knowledge.

They took a taxi back to the Left Bank together. The long avenues of the city appeared to be celebrating them, decked out early for Bastille Day, with a series of tricolour flags and banners. Anna wanted the afternoon to repeat forever in a loop, but suddenly they stopped in a quiet street off the Boulevard St Germain, a discreet few blocks from Sabine's school. Anna began to open the car door, but Olivier pulled her back for one more moment. 'I can't bear to let you go. Anyway, you're ten minutes early for Sabine.' He held her face in his hands, and kissed her one more time. 'Until next week, my love?' He smiled as the door began to close.

'Until next week,' she whispered, wondering if her legs would hold her up. She felt as if she was giving off a strange glow of happiness, which even strangers might see.

'Anna! It's me! Oh, it's Papa!' Sabine was rushing towards the taxi. 'Hi. You're early. We were at the park.' She was followed along the pavement by a crocodile of schoolchildren accompanied by two nuns in black habits holding footballs.

'Get back into line, Sabine!' shouted one of the nuns, and nodded severely into the taxi at Olivier. He looked nervously around, then got out. To rush off would have been even more embarrassing.

'Thank you, Sister,' said Olivier, squaring up to the nun. 'We'll just take her home from here.' They walked with Sabine between them, holding both their hands. Of course, there is nothing illegal about being in a taxi with your employer – why, he could just have been giving Anna a lift. Unless Sabine saw . . .

'Why were you holding Anna's head in the taxi when I came along?'

Olivier's face darkened. He gave Anna a swift glance above Sabine. Anna started gabbling the first thing that came into her head.

'Ah, that's because I've got to go to the dentist. He was looking at my sore tooth.'

'Oh,' said Sabine, looking sideways at Anna, with her father's knowing eyes. 'Yes, I hate going to the dentist . . .' Olivier interrupted her: 'Now, because you've been particularly good at school this term, there's going to be a special treat at the start of the holidays,' said Olivier quickly, stopping her train of thought. 'Guess what it is?'

'We're going to get a puppy?' squealed Sabine.

Olivier looked over at Anna, exasperated.

'No, guess again, my little rabbit.' Sabine tried a variety of tacks, quite forgetting the earlier scene in the taxi, until Olivier revealed that he was going to take her and Madison to PlayWorld Paris next weekend. Sabine started jumping up and down in delight – she had fought a long campaign for this, Anna knew, against Olivier's icy contempt for PlayWorld's vulgarity and Americana.

'Next weekend, really?' said Sabine, scarcely able to believe her luck.

'The Rockin' Rawhide rollercoaster is one of the top five scariest ones in Europe – I've been on it,' said Anna, knowing Sabine's taste for danger.

'Are you going to come with us?' asked Sabine, excited.

'No, just your maman and papa,' said Anna, catching Olivier's eye. 'I'm going on the train to Amsterdam next weekend – they have the best clubs.' Olivier, to her delight, looked just a touch disconcerted.

They were almost back at the Rue du Bac. Anna thought it was best that they were not seen together any more, and made an excuse that she was going back to the school to fetch Sabine's music bag. Olivier gave her an anguished glance, and Anna walked off. What had they done? Had they been caught – or not? And besides, did anyone care in this family, in this city?

A nun stood at the school door as Anna came out from the cloakroom with Sabine's music bag. The nun smelled stale, of the musty wood of churches. 'Thank you, Sister,' said Anna, and turned her eyes away, knowing that the nun had watched her with Olivier in the taxi, worried that she might somehow discover her to be see-through, that her wickedness was visible to all. She walked away, stunned by the cliché of it, the sheer *Belle de Jour*-ness of the experience; the older man, the love hotel, the prying eyes of the nuns. Father I have sinned, thought Anna. Father I have sinned with the father. And then she shrugged, the way a Frenchwoman might.

PART II

11

Madison Malin

'We do suggest you wait in a complimentary luxury suite in our Pink Princess Hotel until your daughter is found. Best to stay nearby, eh?' smiles the unctuous PlayWorld PR man. 'I can personally assure you, Monsieur and Madame Malin, that we have teams of the best-trained security guards searching throughout the theme park, and it is only a matter of time before they succeed, I am absolutely sure.'

'Oh wait a minute,' says Olivier, his eyes narrowing in anger. 'You mean the police haven't got here yet? When the hell did you call them? You mean for nearly two hours your so-called beefcake security men, your "PlayMates", have been running around like headless chickens while anything could be happening to my daughter?'

He lunges across the security office at the PR man and grabs both his shoulders. 'What the fuck do you think you're doing here, you sycophantic little creep? It's not PlayWorld, you know. It's real. They need to put up roadblocks. They need to . . .'

'Olivier, don't make it worse,' says Madison, looking nauseous. Olivier shakes the little man until his moustache twitches and his piggy eyes bulge with fear. Suddenly Olivier drops him and lets him speak, in a nervous squeak.

'We filed a report with the police over an hour ago, Monsieur Malin, after we searched the rollercoaster and found nothing. It's just that the Marne-le-Vallée police tend to let us deal with these problems ourselves, with our excellent record of past successes. I must assure you the PlayMate security men are fully competent.'

'Shut up,' says Olivier, ice in his voice. He speaks slowly and dangerously. 'Just get us out of here.' He starts punching numbers on Madison's mobile.

'Oh dear, oh dear, please don't ring the newspapers yet,' whimpers the PR man. 'These matters are very sensitive, and require careful consideration. Besides, there's the question of media harassment for a couple of your status.' Beads of sweat pop out on his greasy forehead.

'Like I said,' shouts Olivier. 'Shut. The. Fuck. Up.' He holds the phone to his ear. 'Newsdesk, please. I want to talk to Thibault.'

Madison lays a warning hand on Olivier's shoulder. 'Are you sure you want to do that now? They might find her soon.'

'Let me handle this. The more people that are looking for her the better,' says Olivier. The PR man shakes and nervously brushes his moustache. He makes one more attempt, directing his words to Madison, hoping she will be more amenable: 'What if, say, there were kidnappers about to call who did not want publicity and put certain conditions on . . .?'

Madison's skin goes from grey to green at the mention of kidnapping. In her head she revisits old newspaper pictures of the dark hole under a floor with one soiled mattress where some paedophile kidnapped girls and kept them for . . . but she stops the thought. It's not going to help now. Instead, she ignores the PR slimeball and retrieves her mobile from Olivier, who has finished his call. Perhaps some miracle will occur, and Sabine will turn up on the doorstep at Rue du Bac. She can't understand why she didn't think of this before – after all, there was all that silly business of Sabine showing Anna her little backpack for running off to America. She calls Luiza, who throws down the phone in her room, and runs down to look in the apartment. Two minutes later, Luiza calls back, hysterical.

'Aieee! My baby, she's not here. There's nothing, no one, no messages on the answermachine. There's no one here. Where is she?' Great sobs come down the phone.

'Oh my baby.' Madison can no longer make out what Luiza is saying, or what language she is speaking. This is not helping. 'Call me if you hear anything,' Madison says, and cuts her off.

She tries Madame Canovas, but it is Sunday, and she always allows herself a rare desertion of her post for evening mass. Madison calls Anna, who is clearly in a bar somewhere, given the electronic dance music and roaring in the background.

'Anna. This is important. Go outside where you can hear me. I want you to go home, right now.'

'Hey, what's the big problem? It's the weekend. I haven't . . . you don't think we . . .' Anna sounds oddly guilty. 'Hang on, I'm going outside. Signal's crap in here.'

Olivier is sitting with his head in his hands. He looks up sharply at the mention of Anna. Suddenly the line becomes clear. 'Listen, Anna,' says Madison, 'Sabine's disappeared. She was on the rollercoaster one moment and gone the next. She may have been kidnapped. She may be . . .' and here, Madison takes a desperate gulp of air.

'Oh my God,' says Anna. 'Oh my God.'

'She may just be lost and come home herself somehow. Or maybe the Paris police will bring her home.'

Madison can't speak any more, because a lump has sealed her throat.

Anna's voice suddenly sounds tiny. 'This is terrible. I'm leaving now, Madison, but I'm in Amsterdam right now. For the weekend, clubbing. I'll call Luiza. I'll try to get the night bus, or the first one tomorrow. Shit. What can I do? Is there anything I can do?'

'In Amsterdam? Forget it. Nothing. Bye.' Madison rings off. 'Call waiting!' says her phone. It's her agent, Jean-Claude. He is not best pleased.

'Where the hell are you? I stick my neck out with *Vogue* to get you this photoshoot when they wanted Audrey Tautou instead, and you're a bloody hour late. Your dresses are all here, but are you too grand to be on time or what? The photographer is livid. He says you're not so famous that you can . . .'

'Jean-Claude, that's enough. My daughter's disappeared in PlayWorld Paris. It's an emergency. Cancel everything.' She presses the end call button.

She stares at the bleak white walls and fluorescent lights of the office. She shuts her eyes. The word 'if' forms again and again, huge in Madison's head. If only she had gone with Sabine on the rollercoaster. If only she had not cared about keeping her hair smooth and perfect for a fucking photoshoot. If only Olivier didn't get motion sickness. If only one of them had put Sabine first.

Olivier turns menacingly again towards the PR man, who makes sure he stays out of reach, slithering behind a burly PlayMate bouncer. Olivier strides to the door, and Madison follows, screaming inside with frustration, unsure whether Olivier's anger and urgency is getting them anywhere. What is the logical thing to do now? What ought to happen now? she wonders. Her watch says two hours have passed. What can happen to a child in two hours?

A little crowd of well-wishers, or perhaps voyeurs, has formed outside the PlayWorld security station by the time Madison and

Olivier emerge into the open air. The news has obviously gone round the theme park that their daughter has disappeared from the Rockin' Rawhide rollercoaster. No one asks for autographs, and a strange hush comes over the staring crowd as the Malins climb into the security minibus. Olivier holds Madison's hand painfully tight as they drive along. Soon she pulls her hand away and sees the red marks of his nails in her palm. She stares out of the window as the garish neon signs of the theme park start to come on, throbbing pink and green like something out of a horror or porn movie: 'The Hottest Rides In Town!', 'Kingsize Kebabs', 'Experience the Thrill of the Wall of Death!'

The Pink Princess Hotel looms above the rest of the theme park. The five floodlit salmon-coloured towers with silver roofs and Rapunzel-style shutters camouflage what is essentially an ugly breeze-block motel. The PR and security men leave them for a moment 'to freshen up' in their five-star suite, which has 'The Rose of Romance – Honeymoon Palace' instead of a number on the pink door. The room stinks of cigarettes and peach air freshener. Madison promptly throws up in the bathroom and rests her head against the cool tiles of the wall.

When she comes out a few minutes later, the taste of ashes still in her mouth, the suite's living room is swarming with detectives in smartly cut suits: the Marne-le-Vallée police, the Paris police, all yammering at once. Suddenly the situation is of the utmost importance. Two celebrities are involved. Everyone wants a piece of the crime.

'Madame Malin!' says a policeman as sleek and blubbery as

a seal. 'So sad to meet you under such distressing conditions. I have always admired your performance in *The Turquoise* . . .'

'Yesss?' hisses Madison through gritted teeth. The policeman shrivels slightly.

'Ah. Would you like to sit down, Madame? Could you possibly tell us the colours and labels of your daughter's clothes? Monsieur Malin was rather vague.'

'I'll stand, thank you,' says Madison. 'Pink Bonpoint dress, aged six to eight, this summer's collection. White sandals.'

'Underwear?' asks the policeman cautiously.

Madison looks nauseous again. 'White.'

An Inspector Teze from Paris emerges from the crowd and introduces himself. He's older, and so is his crumpled suit. Madison immediately feels confidence in him. The inspector dismisses the rest of the police pack downstairs. He asks the Malins for a photograph of Sabine to circulate to all police stations and airports. Madison pulls last year's school photograph from her purse. Sabine has yellow plaits sticking out, with an uneven, spiky fringe she chopped herself. Until that moment, Madison had thought the photograph was scruffy, but adorable. Now it's beautiful beyond belief. 'She's only six in the picture and her hair isn't usually . . .' Madison chokes up again.

'Never mind, it's a start,' says the inspector, snapping the photo with his phone and messaging someone to disseminate the image everywhere. He sits down on the sofa, which is shaped like a pair of red lips, and says: 'Now tell me everything that happened; everything and everyone you saw, from the beginning.'

American-style club sandwiches are delivered by room service, and they slowly begin to curl as the Malins tell the story. There's really nothing to say: no suspicious strangers, no curious incidents, no one following them. Just a normal family day out. Inspector Teze looks long and hard through his black-framed glasses at Olivier and Madison and is silent for a while.

'I'd prefer not to ask this, but is there anyone in Paris – think about your neighbours, acquaintances, your associates at work – is there anyone who has shown an unhealthy interest in Sabine? Is there anyone who holds something against you, someone who is disgruntled, who might have cause to . . .'

'Inspector, this is an isolated incident at a theme park, for God's sake. I'm a philosopher, not a billionaire. It's got nothing to do with our life in Paris,' says Olivier. Then he becomes less confident. 'Has it?' he asks Madison. She shrugs.

'Olivier has his enemies,' she says, slowly blowing out smoke from her cigarette.

'What precisely do you mean?' says Olivier sharply.

'Come on! Look at what they say about you in print. Can you imagine what they think in private?'

Olivier stares bitterly at her. His T-shirt looks grimy and wrinkled, and so does his skin. Madison tries to assuage his irritation: 'Well, perhaps it could be us both. People see our life together, our public profile. Maybe they're envious. Maybe they think we're rich and they can gain something . . .'

'Oh don't be asinine,' growls Olivier.

'We mustn't discount any possibility, however unlikely,

Monsieur Malin,' says the inspector, severely. 'She wouldn't have run away for any reason, would she?'

'From PlayWorld, when she's been campaigning to get here for months?' said Olivier, his voice full of sarcasm. 'It was a big treat. And she disappeared off a *moving rollercoaster*, Inspector.'

There's a knock at the door of the Rose of Romance suite.

'Monsieur, we found this. Was it what you were looking for?'

A policewoman holds out a transparent bag containing a green monster mask.

'Oh Jesus,' says Madison. 'It's her Alien Brunch Bunch mask.' She reaches out to grab it, as though touching the ugly rubber will bring her closer to Sabine.

'No! There may be fingerprints,' says Inspector Teze, pulling the bag away.

'Where exactly did you find it?' asks Olivier.

'Main Street USA, near the exit to the south car park,' says the policewoman. 'We're doing a full search, and we've shut the theme park.'

'The mask: it means she got off the rollercoaster with someone, doesn't it? She must have walked with a stranger, but why did no one see?' asks Madison.

'We're not coming to any conclusions yet, Madame. The investigation has just begun,' says Inspector Teze.

'Well, you'd better get on with it, then,' snaps Madison, and walks into the bedroom and slams the door. She can hear Olivier saying in a low voice that his wife is under a great deal of pressure. He asks where they should proceed next. Inspector Teze says he needs Olivier to look through a crucial hour of video footage, shot by the PlayWorld security cameras.

Olivier pokes his head round the bedroom door: 'Madison? I'm going to see this video replay, in case I can recognise her. Call me if anything happens.'

Madison is sitting on the bed staring into space and holding a bottle of water. 'I . . .' she begins. 'Why? Why, Olivier? How can this have happened to us?'

'I don't know, darling. I don't know. Be brave. Be sensible.'

Madison takes her shoes off, throws the red lacy heart cushions on to the floor, and falls on the shiny purple quilt, her head pounding, waiting into the evening for the phone to ring. For the first time in over twenty years she wants to call for her own mother, her long-dead mother. She wants someone else, a proper adult, to be responsible for this, to deal with it somehow. She curls up, in real agony, praying that Sabine is not in pain, or horribly frightened. Madison thinks about fate, chance and punishment, and wonders what kind of mother she is – or was. She knew that none of this would have happened – whatever horror this is – if she or Olivier had been closer to Sabine, both physically and mentally. Did Madison understand what mattered most and least to Sabine? She suddenly thought back to herself at seven, and remembered just how much she quietly saw and understood of the adult world. In some way, Sabine's parents had failed her, abandoned her in their distraction, their obsession with their own problems. They had left space for someone else to intervene. Madison presses hard on her temples in an attempt to contain the pain.

The empty theme park's lights reflect through the open curtains on to the ceiling of the room: pink, green, orange, red, pink, an endless sickening sequence. From deep in the hotel comes the pounding music from tourists doing the Chicken Dance. Who on earth would come for their honeymoon here, a honeymoon in hell?

And there's another story . . . the one Madison's trying not to think about for even a second, the story told to her by Renée – who else? – who said she heard it from a PR man who had left PlayWorld six months ago. 'It's one of those urban myths, of course,' Renée had said, 'but it went like this: there's a little boy who disappears in the crowds at PlayWorld, and no one can find him. His parents think he's dead or abducted. Then a week later, he fetches up at a police station in the bad part of Ménilmontant, and he seems dazed but fine – except there's a long scar on his back. Someone has removed one of his kidneys. PlayWorld hushed it all up, of course. Paid the family a lot of money not to talk to the newspapers. But we journalists, we hear everything.' The thought forces Madison into a foetal position on the bed. She can't bear to be alive while Sabine may be suffering.

Olivier returns, red-eyed, freaked with frustration, and says he's not sure – maybe he did glimpse Sabine's pink dress in the crowd near the south gate, and maybe he didn't. 'I realised that she's so small, adults would completely block her out in a video.'

'She's so small, yes,' says Madison, biting her lip to stop

herself crying. 'She's too small for this to happen to her.' She calls Luiza again; but nothing has changed, except the level of Luiza's hysteria. Olivier is silent, staring at his hands, his energy and hope draining away. Madison passes Olivier a bottle of water from the minibar and stares at him as he sits in the changing coloured light on the bed, radiating darkness. She wishes she had never met him. But all she says is: 'I need another cigarette.'

Madison thinks about the selfishness, the disregard for others, that comes with Olivier's ridiculous existentialist justifications of his behaviour. She wonders about his soft moral core and worries that lesser evils attract larger ones. Perhaps there's some twisted ex-lover out there who has taken Sabine. She fears that they are cursed, that somehow they deserve this, that there is a dark pall over the Rue du Bac. But Sabine doesn't deserve this, whatever it is. She has done no wrong. Madison keeps seeing Sabine in her mind's eye riding wildly across the countryside at her grandparents' house, her blonde hair flying, and the look of joy on her face. Then she remembers all the times she failed to read to Sabine, talk to Sabine, play with Sabine. The last trip she made alone with her daughter was that godforsaken fashion show, and they had fought afterwards.

The phone rings, and they both jump, but it's just the police, with little to say. There are various adult fingerprints on Sabine's alien mask – probably the stallholder's – but none match those on the police database. Madison puts down the phone and relays the detail to Olivier who is now pacing up and down the room. He takes eight steps across, and eight back, eight across, eight back. Eventually, Madison locks herself in the hotel bathroom to get away from his brooding presence. She sees herself in the fluorescent light of the bathroom mirror, and it is not a pretty sight, internally or externally. For the first time she spots a vein in the middle of her forehead, throbbing with stress, and the lines like plaster cracks around her eyes where her foundation has run and merged with her mascara. She washes it all off and goes out, red-eyed, bare-skinned, raw inside. In the meantime, Olivier has taken four miniature vodkas and gins from the minibar and poured them into a tumbler with some tonic.

'You hate gin,' says Madison.

'Sometimes I like it. You don't know everything about me, you know. Want some?' says Olivier, tossing it back. 'Anyway, why aren't they calling? Where's that Teze guy?'

Madison shrugs, and stands, her hands hanging limply.

'Come here,' he says, from the bed. Madison lies down beside Olivier, and he takes her hand. 'It will be all right, darling. It must be,' he says, but his voice catches. They lie on their backs for some of the night, dozing for no more than a few minutes, and Madison thinks that their frozen, clothed bodies on the bed must, from above, look like a dead king and queen on a medieval tombstone. Every so often they are brought to life by the telephone, and then left in purgatory again.

Eventually the neon is replaced by dawn, and the Pink Princess reception gives them an unnecessary 6 a.m. wake-up call. They order coffee from room service. Minutes later, there are the sounds outside of 'The Sun Has Got His Hat On', followed by a voice shouting 'Wakey, wakey! Your Rise and Shine breakfast! Room service!' They answer the door and a man in a purple bunny costume says: 'As the occupants of one of our premier suites in the Pink Princess's Hotel, your alarm call comes in the form of a PlayWorld character! Top of the morning to you. Top of the morning to you-hoo!'

Madison quickly takes the coffee tray.

'Fuck off,' says Olivier to the purple bunny. 'Just fuck the hell off.' And he slams the door.

A few minutes later, there's a knock. The bunny is back.

'Sorry, Monsieur, I've just started my shift. I didn't know about . . . but I am supposed to give you the newspapers. Part of the five-star service.'

The bunny nervously hands Olivier the bundle. On top of the pile is *Le Figaro*, and inside, on page five, is a short story with the headline: 'Philosopher's Daughter Disappears', followed by the line: 'Police refuse to rule out kidnapping at PlayWorld Paris.'

There's a small picture, too, the latest one taken by the park paparazzi, of Sabine holding the monster mask, Olivier eating frites from a bag, and Madison looking frosty. The happy family is walking down Main Street, USA.

12

Olivier Malin

The Rue du Bac is slick and metallic with rain as Olivier and Madison arrive just before seven in the morning. The sixth floor of their apartment building has a wide-eyed, startled air, its shutters left open, while those below are still closed. The place seems achingly empty to Olivier. A deathly cold crawls up his spine, and he shuts his eyes, thinking of his only child, where she might be, what she might be suffering. Madison is in her own world of agony and seems to be literally wringing her hands red on her lap. The Malins are silent as they leave their car in the garage. They stare pale and hollow-eyed at one another across the bare landscape of their collapsed relationship and suddenly childless family. What is there left to say?

Throughout the journey Olivier has been repeating rhythmically in his head: 'Sa-bine, Sa-bine, Sa-bine.' There are a thousand things he has failed to tell her, to teach her. He can't remember when he last talked to her properly. Not in the car to PlayWorld, when he played the child-friendly New World Symphony to hide the tension between himself and Madison. He last touched Sabine when he had his arm around her tense, excited shoulders, during the ride on the ghost train. It hurts just remembering her physical presence, her warm pyjamas and sleep-mussed hair when she climbs into bed with them on a rare weekend morning when they are not up early. Olivier knows he had the choice to engage with Sabine, and he did not. If he believed in God he would ask now for a second chance, but he believes only in his own rationality, which is disintegrating. He constantly shakes his head, trying to dispel the throbbing.

And why did they go to PlayWorld at all? Because he was desperately trying to distract Sabine, hoping she would forget about seeing him in the taxi with Anna. It is his fault. A red wall of shame swims before Olivier's eyes. Through it he notices a lone photographer, dozing on a collapsible stool next to their front door. The man snaps to attention and starts taking pictures as they arrive, his flash illuminating the dull morning. He asks if there's any news. Olivier ducks away and stamps in the door code. Suddenly they're in the silence of the hallway, the traffic noise banished. There's just their breathing and the melancholy sound of rain dripping from the plants on to the cobbles of the courtyard.

The quiet is shattered by a great jangling of keys, a sliding of bolts, and Madame Canovas catapults from her lair amid shawls and remonstrations.

'And about time too. I was shocked, shocked. It was just fortunate that I was vigilant. To think that you would have left your daughter like this, without having the sense, the decency to call and check there was someone here? I myself was astounded, and I said to Madame Royan: "What sort of people are these to send her home by herself with no one . . ."'

'She's here? Madison, she's here!' shouts Olivier, and runs into the concierge's apartment.

'Mind you, it's not the first time this has happened. Oh no,' continues Madame Canovas, coughing and wheezing as Madison pushes past her too. 'That other night I had to look after Sabine for an hour when her friend dropped her back. And what sort of nanny is *that woman*? I will tell you, she's not a nanny, she's a whore . . .' Here she peters out, because her audience has disappeared and there are screams and tears coming from her front room.

Olivier is holding Sabine in his arms, and crying with relief. Madison is wrapped round them both, her face buried in her daughter's hair. The three become one.

'Sabine, Sabine,' says Madison, and holds the child's face in her hands, feeling the softness of her baby skin. Olivier smells the underlying smell Sabine's had since birth of freshly baked bread. It's the best feeling in the world: she's all there, she's alive, and Olivier feels a huge physical surge of joy and relief rising through him. He turns and holds Madison tight too, for a long time. Her eyes are shut and tears are pouring out from under their lids.

Sabine begins to cry too now, but she looks slightly surprised, as though she can't understand quite what all the fuss is about. Indeed, when Olivier entered the room, his daughter was perfectly composed, sitting at Madame Canovas' polished table, sipping a bowl of hot chocolate and eating bread from a basket lined with paper doilies.

Sabine looks like a creature from another time, in a pink-sprigged cotton nightgown which is far too long for her and faintly redolent of mothballs. Her face is twisted with fear. 'I'm sorry, Maman, Papa, I'm so sorry. I didn't know you'd be so worried. I thought you'd come home but you didn't come and . . .' Her voice is lost in the sound of crying now. Madison kneels down face to face with Sabine and holds her.

'It doesn't matter, my darling. We're not angry. We're just so happy you're here. We thought you were . . .' She gives a long, ragged sigh. 'But how did you get here? What happened?'

Madame Canovas stands listening behind them, wearing a strange pink towelling turban, her arms folded over her striped apron, clacking her rosary beads censoriously. Sabine explains that she simply got off the rollercoaster, called a taxi to PlayWorld on Olivier's mobile account, and went home. 'It was on the list in his phone, see, just like the time I called a taxi for Maman. And I was so angry, and you were arguing again and again and it went black inside my head. I don't really know why I was so angry, but I wanted to come home and be with Anna – and then she wasn't there and I was so frightened.' Sabine starts wailing, and then bites on her knuckles to stop. 'The taxi man was very nice and he left me with Madame Canovas.'

'Well, obviously my suspicions were aroused,' says Madame Canovas, getting ready for some high-operatic action. 'I said to myself, what sort of people are these who can throw their child, alone, into a taxi – the driver was black, for goodness' sake – and send her home to an empty house? It is fortunate that I did not call the police and report this incident of neglect. I, myself . . .'

'She ran away! Don't you *understand*, Madame? We didn't know where she was – all night. It's in the papers, the police are involved,' shouts Olivier. 'We had the night from hell at PlayWorld. Why didn't you think to call us, you stupid . . .'

'I don't know who you think you are calling stupid in these circumstances, Monsieur Malin,' interrupts Madame Canovas, drawing herself up to her full four feet eleven inches, her head pecking towards him like a bantam, bathing him in her halitotic breath. 'It would appear to me that it is you and Madame who have behaved stupidly, while I have been a good Samaritan, taking in this child from the street in her hour of need.'

Olivier is rolling his eyes. Madison frowns at him. The concierge continues. 'I did call – your apartment and your mobile, which was switched off. I went upstairs, but the apartment was empty. And your maid was out when Sabine arrived – and then she came back late with one of those appalling men from the Barista Bar – those *chambres de bonne* are full of sluts, mark my words – so I did not think that was an appropriate place for an innocent child to be. And', Madame Canovas added, glowering at Madison, '*she* would never give me her mobile number. Also, if you remember, Monsieur, *she* refused to leave me your keys after *she* accused me of snooping when . . .'

Madison looks ethereal with exhaustion. 'Let's just call the police and our friends to say Sabine's safe and then get upstairs. Thank you very much for looking after her, Madame. I'm just sorry such an event had to occur.' She pulls her phone out and starts punching the numbers.

'Sabine is not a child of Mary, you know. She is a child of Paris and that is much more dangerous,' says Madame Canovas, cryptically.

Olivier takes Sabine's hand. 'Come on, rabbit, let's go.' They put on Sabine's dress which has been ironed and folded, and her bear backpack from which Olivier retrieves his phone. 'Papa? I lost my Alien Brunch Bunch mask.'

'I know. The police know. Half of Paris knows.' Olivier suddenly thinks what a fool he was to tell the newspapers so precipitately of Sabine's disappearance. 'You'll get it back.'

In the lift up, Sabine starts jabbering about her night with Madame Canovas: the strange smells of her cooking; the squawking of her birds; the stale liqueur chocolates from last Christmas that she offered as a treat. In the middle of the night,

Sabine awoke to find Madame Canovas dressed all in white, standing by the camp bed, stroking her hair and holding her hand. 'I pretended to be asleep, Papa. She's Madame Creepy, you know, that's what Anouk says. And Madame Canovas said lots of weird stuff to me about God. And she's going bald, eeeuch. I saw her without that towel on.'

As he unlocks the apartment, Olivier feels sickened. He finds everything about Madame Canovas cloying and repulsive and he has a feeling she did not make the greatest effort to contact them or Luiza because she wanted to have Sabine to herself for the night to fill her empty, narrow life. And just at that moment, a tear-stained, ruffled Luiza comes galloping down the service stairs and sweeps Sabine up in her arms in the hall. 'My silly baby. Your maman told me you ran away. I was so worried. Shall I make you some muffins, little one? With chocolate chips?'

'That'll solve it,' groans Olivier, and sits down at the kitchen table with his thumping head in his hands while Luiza and Sabine muck around. But Sabine occasionally glances nervously at him out of the corner of her eye – she knows their conversation is not finished. Olivier feels so relieved, but at the same time freakishly disturbed. For a long night he had thought there was something horribly wrong with the outside world – but now he realises there is something horribly wrong with his own family.

Perhaps he is to blame. Children don't run away without a reason; certainly not a child as smart and sensitive as Sabine.

Luiza puts a coffee in front of him and reads his thoughts: 'Don't you worry, Monsieur Malin – it's not the first time a child has run away – they don't really understand what they're doing. She does not know how much she has, my baby.' Olivier nods in agreement. He is so at a loss he will take advice from anyone, even the maid. Then his world lurches again as Anna appears in the kitchen with Madison. Anna's eyes are huge, black-bagged with lack of sleep, and she's carrying a little rucksack. Sabine runs to her nanny and holds her in a sort of rugby-tackle hug round the legs. They stay like that for a long time, and Anna's tears fall on her hair. Olivier can't bear it. He watches, his eyes watering.

'I worried about you all night on the bus. All night,' says Anna quietly.

'I missed you,' says Sabine. 'I came to find you and you weren't here. I didn't think you would let me down too.'

Olivier feels a schizophrenic ripping of any emotional balance that remained in his head: what have I done, as a father, as a lover? Exactly how have I let Sabine down? Does she know about us, about Anna and I? But why would she have run away to Anna, then? Madison has hardly entered his calculations, but with a swift glance up he sees the scene through her eyes, the psychological pain of being branded with the words 'Inadequate Mother'. What is it in her face? Jealousy? Fear? She must see a twentysomething, flighty girl who has been paid to look after Sabine for less than a year, yet has made an enormous emotional bond with her. And her father, if only

Madison knew. How flawed, how desperate were they as a family that a stranger could have such power?

Madison takes Sabine on her knee and hugs her tight.

'I love you,' says Madison, tucking Sabine's hair behind her ears so she can see the face she nearly lost. 'Nothing scary like this is ever going to happen again. I'm going to keep you safe.'

'Maman,' says Sabine, and buries her head in Madison's neck.

Luiza pours coffee for them all. Anna's hands shake as she holds the cup. Olivier catches Anna's gaze just once, and his eyes burn with suffering. Lines hatch on his forehead.

'Oh Jesus,' says Anna, and then looks at Sabine. 'Excuse me.' She lets out a long breath which she must have been holding for hours. Madison takes a packet of chocolate-topped Petit Ecolier biscuits from the cupboard, and starts sharing them with Sabine. Olivier hasn't seen his wife eat biscuits for years.

But it's clear that Madison wants what Olivier is dreading: to be alone with her daughter. His wife puts on her warmest smile: 'Anna, Luiza, thank you so much for everything you've done, for your support. Now we are just going to go off and have some time together, as a family.' Anna looks quizzically at her, kisses Sabine, and walks out of the door, very slowly. Madison looks after her, bitterly.

Now they are in Sabine's bedroom, the unhappy family of three. Olivier doesn't know what to say. Silently, Madison pulls a little red backpack from under the bed and shows Olivier the somewhat inadequate contents of her daughter's running away kit: the tablecloth, the water bottle, the chocolate coins, a map of Paris, the cuddly rat. She stands tall like a judge over Sabine, who is sitting tearfully on the bed, in the dock, clutching her knees to her chest in self protection. She grabs the furry rat and hugs it close.

'I thought it was just a game, your backpack, but it was real,' says Madison. Then she sits down next to Sabine, sighs, and puts a hand on her shoulder. 'You have to tell us everything, my darling. You have to tell us so we can fix whatever is wrong and this will never happen again.'

'Why did you do it, baby?' asks Olivier, crouching in front of her. 'What did you think would happen?'

But what has happened is, on the whole, unspoken and inexplicable. Sabine herself cannot enumerate why, Olivier guesses. She just knows there is something rotten in the state of the Rue du Bac, something that weighs upon her and disconcerts her. The undercurrents, the adult games, are beyond her understanding, but the fact that she wants more of her parents, more of their time, is clear. She looks at them, pink-eyed, pleading silently.

'Anna . . .' says Sabine, and Olivier feels his blood stop pumping with the fear that she will reveal his affair. 'Anna's always there. I thought she would be there but she wasn't.'

'But sweetie, why did you leave us like that? We were at PlayWorld, for goodness' sake. Anything could have . . .' begins Madison.

'You were fighting. And anyway, you're always leaving me in

the middle of things and going off, so it was my turn to leave you and go off. So there!' shouts Sabine, and runs off into her bathroom, slamming the door and locking it.

'Shit,' says Olivier quietly.

Madison goes to the bathroom door and in a tremulous voice, tries to calm Sabine. A few minutes later there's the sound of the bolt being unlocked, and now Sabine and Madison are holding each other, Madison kneeling on the floor.

Olivier looks down at the sobbing, howling pair and realises that the only way out of this madness must be his parting from Anna, despite the most promising of beginnings. The household and the family cannot function under such a strain. But his relationship with Madison requires major surgery. His frustration with the situation suddenly turns to anger with Sabine: 'You stupid little idiot. You could have been killed, kidnapped. What did you think we would think? You're so selfish, you only thought of yourself.' He sees Madison's warning glare.

Sabine is getting increasingly hysterical: 'I . . . I just wanted to go away. I thought it was going to be the best day of my life and it was so horrible, you were so mean to Maman, you were both so grumpy. I'm sorry.' Her voice goes into a scream: 'I'm sorry!' and she buries her head in the bed.

'We're sorry too,' says Madison, holding her. Olivier feels he's carrying so much guilt he can't hold anything else. Madison's piety is making him livid too.

'Look, we're not going to sort this out in half an hour. Indeed, it may take a lifetime,' snaps Olivier at his wife. 'So I think we should be as normal as possible. Why doesn't Sabine get back to school – she'll only be an hour late – and you go and do your postponed photo shoot, I'll get back to work – I must make the finishing touches to the last chapter on technocracy – and we'll see Sabine at four o'clock. OK?'

Madison looks at him as though he were the antichrist. 'Can't. You. See?' she enunciates. 'Can't you see that everything has changed? That everything will have to change? I'm not going anywhere this morning. Sabine's not going anywhere. Maybe later.'

'Fine,' says Olivier. 'Whatever.' He kisses and hugs Sabine. 'You be good, you hear me, and I'll see you this afternoon.'

Sealed in his study, Olivier tries to write, but he keeps staring out into the damp, dripping summer day. Madame Canovas is in the courtyard – wearing a rainmate and a see-through plastic poncho with the word 'Lourdes' on the back – carefully trimming the box balls with her nail-scissors. The irritating sight of the concierge reminds Olivier of the sheer foolishness of his situation. He feels ashamed. For someone who is usually so good at reading women's moods, he is puzzled that he failed when it came to the simple case of his daughter. Was it because he didn't notice her enough? Or was Madison at fault? Doesn't a child need its mother most?

Olivier sighs and wearily works his phone, leaving messages with friends about Sabine's reappearance. He tells Paul Rimbaud how he feels pathetic: pathetic for making such a fuss, and pathetic for being such an insensitive father. Paul cheers him up with tales of Renée's hands-off parenting: last week he discovered his wife didn't even know the name of the children's doctor, or of any of their little friends. 'We've got a weekday nanny and a weekend nanny, and *you're* worried?'

'The nanny's not the problem. Well, she *is* the problem. But mostly I'm the problem . . .'

'Articulate words from one of our great modern philosophers,' snorts Paul. 'Are you, um . . .'

'Yes. I am. We are.'

'Oh dear,' says Paul. His voice has gone from amused to horribly cold. 'Under the same roof is a little . . .'

'I know, I know, Paul. I cannot stop myself – I am a man possessed. You see, she is the woman in my head, constantly in my consciousness . . .'

'Olivier? I don't want to know any more. It's not my business. You may be assured of my discretion, however. I'm just glad Sabine is back.' He rings off.

Anna is becoming a problem for Olivier, he knows it. Even before Sabine ran away, he felt tension had increased in the apartment. Olivier supposes that he smells differently and smiles differently when he is in love, and Madison senses this all too well after eight years. Even his fellow *gastrophilosophes*, like Bourdon, have been wondering if he had become a hermit, and Olivier is losing weight, favouring passion over food. He is in the grip of terrible jealousy for once; the casual affair is one thing, but the household affair is a deeper, darker matter. He instinctively knows when Anna is somewhere else in the building, her lovely flesh inaccessible to him. His longings are tested all day, and then in the evening, Anna is often hard to pin down, her phone off, and Olivier suspects she might still be seeing that dreadful hairdresser.

Olivier wearily climbs the ladder to his bookshelves and takes down a huge pile of reference books and philosophy texts. It will be impossible to write well today, this distracted, so he will organise all his notes. At lunchtime, he hears Madison and Sabine preparing to leave for school, and he slips out to kiss his daughter again, to confirm her reality.

The afternoon drags on, through hundreds of dire footnotes and an unbearable headache. Olivier dozes off for a moment at his desk, and wakes two hours later. He shakes his muddled head like a dog coming out of water, goes to the window, throws it open and gulps in the air. He stares blankly out at the cobbles steaming in the sun and the clipped topiary. Suddenly Anna appears from the back stairs, pale and worried-looking, hauling a huge carpet bag and a heavy leather trunk on wheels. Olivier stares, horrified, as she crosses the courtyard. She's leaving. She's walking out on him.

Olivier runs for the door. Madison is standing in the hall.

'Where are you . . .' begins Madison.

'I've got to, um, go down to the university and get a reference book there.' He takes his laminated library card from his pocket and waves it.

'I think we need to talk, Olivier. We need to spend some time asking ourselves some questions before we speak to Sabine again, properly.'

'Yes, absolutely. Later. This is essential work. I'll be back in an hour.'

Madison shrugs and looks at him with contempt. Olivier doesn't have time to care. Outside, the lift is agonisingly slow in coming, so he runs down the stairs, barging past Madame Canovas coming in with her baguette at the front door.

'Monsieur,' she begins. 'I have been worrying all morning. I would like to apologise if . . .'

'Christ,' says Olivier, exasperated beyond reason. 'Not now.'

Now the concierge looks like she's going to cry and leans out of the door to watch him run frantically down the street. Olivier doesn't worry about who sees him because he fears the worst, losing Anna. He didn't know that he cared so much, so viscerally, until she walked out. He feels the freefalling emptiness of abandonment for the second time in twenty-four hours. He looks all around, panicking in case Anna has disappeared in a taxi, but then he sees her – a tiny figure in a flowered summer dress struggling with her huge trunk in the far distance near the Métro. Olivier heads up the Rue du Bac, but first Madame Bellan gets in his way with her Sunday ready-roast chicken from the butchers' and starts asking about Sabine, and then two mothers with toddlers in prams double-park across the pavement.

'Get out of the way,' Olivier growls, his eyes and hair wild, and one of the toddlers starts crying. But Anna is being sucked into the maw of the underground and he might never see her again . . .

'Anna! Anna!' he shouts, his voice breaking.

She turns round, stops, and calmly waits until he arrives at her side, panting.

'Olivier?'

'Where on earth are you going? You can't leave. You can't leave me. Why haven't you told me about this?'

'Told you about what?' says Anna, puzzled.

Olivier finds himself wrapping his arms around her, her head against his chest, his lips on the softness of the nape of her neck. He closes his eyes.

'Don't leave, Anna. I love you.' There, he's said it. He didn't know he was going to say it. He hardly knows her. 'I love you,' he repeats, confirming it. 'You are the woman in my life.'

Anna looks stunned. 'Oh my God,' she says slowly. He notices that she does not say that she loves him, not yet. She smiles, embarrassed. 'Olivier, my darling, I wasn't leaving. I wasn't leaving you. I'm taking all this down to the little antique shop by Porte de Vanves. You get a lot for an old Vuitton leather trunk like this.'

Olivier starts to laugh. Soon they can't stop laughing. He kisses Anna again and again beneath the curlicued art nouveau sign outside the station. For the second time, he has escaped the horror of losing someone he loves. Perhaps the disappearance of Sabine has made his emotions all too clear: everything is suddenly in focus. Together, Olivier and Anna make a beautiful Paris postcard, the lovers entwined on the Métro steps under sun-dappled trees. The only hitch is that Madame Canovas is peering beadily at them through the green railings.

'You dropped this, Monsieur,' she says, convulsed by coughs. 'While you were running.'

Madame Canovas holds out Olivier's library card as though it were contaminated with anthrax. She smiles at them both, a death's-head smile, and walks weakly off.

For the rest of the day, Olivier feels queasy with the fear of Madame Canovas, sitting like a resentful bomb under the building, coughing and ticking. Anna has escaped to her junk shop, while he is left to face the dissonant music. Still, Sabine is back from school, and Olivier feels a rush of joy and relief as he reads to her before bedtime.

'Hey, rabbit,' he says, tucking her in. Sabine gives a little shudder, as though the residue of a day of crying is still escaping from her body. Olivier hugs her tighter. 'Hey, calm down. You're fine, you're back with us. It's OK. Nothing bad's going to happen again.' Sabine quietens.

'Do you think I'm bad?'

'No. It was all a big mistake, a small problem with unexpected exponential growth.'

Sabine looks puzzled. Madison comes in to say goodnight.

'I'm glad I'm back in my own house with Rat and Owly and Anna and Luiza!' says Sabine, suddenly cheerful.

'With everyone,' nods Madison, and Olivier sees that she is painfully noting this list of Sabine's objects of affection.

Later, Sabine sleeps, pale but peaceful in the arms of her toy rat, while Madison sneaks in to check on her constantly, the way she did when her daughter was newly born. Normally, thinks Olivier, Madison has a cigarette as soon as Sabine goes to bed, but tonight she doesn't seem to want one. Like some priest in his black suit, Olivier stands in the dim light at the bottom of Sabine's princess bed and whispers to Madison. 'It's a resurrection, as though she's returned from the dead.' He falls silent and sits down on the end of the bed. He looks terrible, sleep-deprived and dried out into wrinkles. 'Oh Madison. What did we do to deserve this?' He looks from Sabine to Madison, and back again. His long fingers violently rub at his temples and forehead, as though to erase everything in his head. 'How long have I been writing about angst, about this sense of dread, about despair, boredom, nausea and absurdity? I've written whole books on it, but only now do I come to understand even something of the meaning of those words.'

'Olivier?' says Madison. 'Get a life.'

He's insulted, but then she takes his hand. 'She's home, and it's going to be all right, isn't it? We're going to be all right.' Olivier nods, and smiles strangely, the corners of his mouth turning down rather than up.

When all seems calm, Olivier declares war on his hunger and rushes off to the Bon Marché Grande Épicerie before it closes.

He returns with essential supplies: purple oil-soaked olives, raw beef carpaccio, some Ossau Iraty cheese, *Pain Poilâne* and a tedious vegetable tart for Madison. He forgets to buy milk, but he does remember a box of eight macaroons in Sabine's favourite flavours: pale green pistachio, coffee, chocolate, and pink strawberry, all tied with ribbon. He leaves the offering beside her bed for her to find in the morning.

'Breakfast,' he says happily. 'And we won't even ask her to brush her teeth.' Madison smiles at him, her eyes full of life again. They open a bottle of Olivier's best Pouilly Fumée from his wine cellar downstairs, and sit opposite each other in the rarely used salon. The doors of the red-lacquered Chinese cabinet stand wide open, and the jewelled ornaments shine in the spotlights. Madison takes a huge gulp of wine. She curls up with her bare feet tucked under her on the stiff-backed velvet sofa. 'This is so uncomfortable. We should chuck it.' Olivier stares at her.

'Really? Muugh?' says Olivier, whose mouth is now full of newly sliced charcuterie from the paper bags gracing the little gilt coffee table. Madison's phone keeps beeping – messages she has failed to pick up all day from Paul Rimbaud, and other friends. She plays them back. One is from the spa in the Rue du Bac where she has her monthly facial and a Botox injection scheduled for the next day. She texts: 'Sorry, too busy. Cancel all appointments.' Olivier reads over her shoulder and stands tearing off huge chunks of bread and leaving crumbs all over the Aubusson rug. Normally this would irritate Madison, he knows, but instead she shrugs, leans over to the coffee table, grabs some bread, pulls up a slice of beef carpaccio, and nibbles it.

'Huh?' says Olivier, his eyebrows disappearing. 'Do you know what you're eating? It's meat. *Dead meat.* One of God's former creatures.'

'Yes,' says Madison. 'It's surprisingly good. I've never had it before. I don't think carpaccio was around much before I gave up the ways of the flesh.'

'Weird,' says Olivier, shaking his head. 'This has all had a most peculiar effect on you.' Madison is humming 'I can see clearly now the rain has gone', under her breath and munching away. Olivier, from the depths of his dark French soul, can't believe she thinks so simplistically, so obviously.

'Do you think Sabine needs some kind of therapy? Should we all go to see someone?' he ventures.

Madison snorts. 'I don't think we need therapists to tell us to behave like a normal family. Look, honey, I just care that Sabine has been returned to me, like a gift, and I won't waste this second chance to be with her, and be her mother: daily, ordinarily.'

'Oh, for God's sake,' snaps Olivier. 'It's not as if we were cruel to her.'

'There's a kind of quiet cruelty . . .'

'Oh poor little rich girl syndrome? Don't be so fucking obvious.'

'Well, is there something else? Something I don't know about?' asks Madison, deflated, lost.

Olivier shakes his head. He daren't speak. There's too much swimming around in his head. Anyway, Madison is talking, on and on, about how she sees it all laid out in black and white – perhaps more a dull grey – that she has not been there enough, that during the months when she went off filming abroad, that during the evenings when she was out late, Sabine, out of necessity, formed other ties, almost as strong as those with her parents.

'And maybe what they say is true about not breastfeeding enough . . . oh, but let's not go there,' says Madison. 'We can't all be perfect. Yet it's as simple as this: quantity time, not low-quality time with a harassed mother, is what you register when you are seven. You appreciate the people who play Dinosaur Monopoly with you for two hours, especially if you don't know your cheerful companions are paid for the pleasure.' They sit in silence, guilty words falling to the floor around them.

'I'm so tired,' says Madison. Olivier comes to sit by her on the sofa, in some sort of solidarity.

'Shall we get some sleep?' asks Olivier.

Madison's eyes are watering again. She pushes Olivier's hair away from his face and kisses him, gently, sadly, repeatedly. Olivier feels unexpectedly uncomfortable. Her touch is some-how repulsive. For Madison, their physical togetherness is a release, but for him it seems to be a return to marital captivity. Or perhaps he is just exhausted beyond understanding. He pulls away from her breast, her embrace.

'No, I just can't, my love. I'm so sorry, not tonight. I have to be alone for a moment – I have to analyse this. Plus we're both exhausted.'

He can hardly bear the damaged look in Madison's eyes, or her cheerfully courageous voice: 'That's OK, darling. I was thinking, anyway, of going to sleep in Sabine's room, on the pull-out bed. I don't want her to wake up alone.'

Olivier's veins are still running with adrenalin and espresso, so he sits in his study under the green-shaded brass light on his desk, and tries to figure a way through the rickety maze of his life. High across the courtyard, the light goes on in Anna's room, and Olivier sees her silhouette walk to the window and look down. He stands by the curtain, unseen and filled with longing, knowing a meeting would be inappropriate and plain stupid.

Then a great anger wells up in him, followed by waves of frustration, and he starts kicking the bookcases and filing cabinets on the wall, until the metal dents. Madison rushes in, bleary eyed. 'What's wrong?'

'What do you fucking think's wrong?' snaps Olivier, rubbing an injured toe.

13

Anna Ayer

Madame Canovas stalks Anna's dreams: a sinister, laughing dwarf lurking in bat-infested corners all over Paris. Indeed, when Anna wakes in a pool of sweat at three in the morning, alone in her room, she feels that her sleeping subconscious has exaggerated very little: the concierge is her personal nightmare. Madame Canovas' knowledge of her affair with the master of the house will soon percolate upstairs via coffee with Madame Bellan and Madame Royan, until it reaches the top floor.

The alarm clock jerks Anna from a belated heavy sleep at seven-thirty. She scrabbles into yesterday's wrinkled dress, cleans her teeth and runs downstairs. Madison is in the kitchen with Luiza, and there's a smell of freshly baked brioche and coffee.

Madison looks wonderfully well-slept, soft and beautiful in the morning light. She's just wearing jeans and one of Olivier's grey T-shirts, but the sight of his shirt on her makes Anna's stomach churn with resentment.

Madison is smiling at her, all friendly: 'Oh Anna! I'm sorry you had to get up so early. I forgot to say I'm taking Sabine to school this morning. Can you still pick her up, though, this afternoon, when I'm at work? I'm just going in to have a word with her teacher. Still, since you're here you must have some of this fantastic brioche.' Anna feels a second stab of jealousy – now she feels that the child is going to be taken away from her too. Her strong attachment to Sabine – unlike any of the children in her previous jobs – became all too clear to her during that long, grim night on the rattling bus from Amsterdam. Or perhaps she sees Sabine in Olivier, and Olivier in Sabine.

'You look tired,' interrupts Madison. 'It's been hard for us all.' The worst thing about Madison's sympathy is that Anna knows it is genuine. It's just that yesterday everything shifted; that her relationship with Olivier, which Anna had tried to compartmentalise as a game, an adventure, has suddenly become all too real. Just because of a few words.

Sabine bounds in, comically bent beneath her *cartable*, her vast French schoolbag. She waves cheerfully to Anna because she is stuffing her mouth full of buttery brioche.

'That's the third one,' says Madison, and then she shrugs and laughs. 'Come on, honey. We've got a lot to do. Let's get to school.'

Left Bank

When they have gone, Luiza and Anna clear up the kitchen and then sit, drinking coffee, both feeling stupidly redundant. Olivier walks in, nods perfunctorily at them both, and grabs a double espresso which he drinks in one gulp. He scribbles a note on the kitchen pad, folds it, and hands it to Anna. 'Some stationery that Sabine needs for school. Can you get it this morning? I'd get it myself but I'm off to lecture at Sciences Po. Thanks.' He walks out and they hear the front door slam. Anna feels her eyes watering. What's wrong, though? Why should he acknowledge her in front of Luiza? But it's still hopeless – they have been caught by Madame Canovas, and everything must come to an end. The rich, juicy complexities of her life are now flattened into a dull plain that stretches on for ever. She thinks about her duplicitous relationship with Sabine, and with Olivier, and hates herself and the deception she has perpetuated. Why did she come here? Why did she ever get involved with this disturbed family, this man, this child? Anna's stomach knots.

She slouches slowly downstairs to go to the Bon Marché for the stationery. In the vestibule, on cue, is Madame Canovas, fit to burst with the knowledge of Olivier and Anna's affair. The concierge is agitated, but also so exhausted that her eyes seem huge black holes. She has her rosary – the one blessed by the Pope – in one hand, and wears a new green turban.

Madame Canovas' smug delight in the whole disaster depresses Anna even more. 'How we suffer! How we all suffer! Oh dear, oh dear. Oh poor Monsieur and Madame. Have you seen the papers?' Her eyebrows disappear up into the turban and she actually tuts. She is almost hysterical. 'The public humiliation for the family! It makes everyone look quite ridiculous. Everyone. You know, I have always had reservations about a young girl being brought up like that, and now look what happens! Oh dear, you must be so distressed yourself. Or worried about your position, perhaps? Have you thought about going to confession at the chapel down the street?' Here, Madame Canovas allows herself a knowing smile, before returning to her lament. 'Oh that poor, poor little girl. Oh Mother of God, what will we all do?'

Anna thinks silence is the best policy, as she restrains the urge to deck the repulsive Madame Canovas. The concierge coughs constantly as she drags her big shopping basket to the door, repeating her 'Pray for us. Poor, poor little girl' mantra, and adding, puzzlingly, 'And of course there is all the cleaning to do, very, very important, so I am going to Franprix for Cif, bleach, pine polish, and what else was there? And I have a half-price coupon for the Cif. I must get everything spick and span, you see. I must make everything shine. All must be in order.'

She disappears across the street, shaking her head, talking to her rosary, her shawl flapping in the wind. Anna is annoyed, and suddenly wonders if her latest sins have been written up in the black books. She tries Madame Canovas' door, which is locked, of course, and then peers through the pinned-back net curtain. The notebooks are in a neat pile and everything seems normal in the dim front parlour – except it is unbelievably tidy and clean. The jugs on the dresser are obsessively lined up in order of size, the ornaments are gleaming, the garish Virgin Mary mini-shrine is lit, the dark floor is shiny with wax polish you can smell even outside, and the silver candlesticks have been rubbed so that they glow beneath black, funereal candles.

Anna sighs and slams the front door behind her. In the street she grumpily checks the shopping list. No mention of stationery, but Olivier would like her to meet him in the Musée Maillol in the Rue de Grenelle at eleven. She feels an immense surge of joy. Despite the fact that Olivier's already seen her looking raddled this morning, she runs back upstairs to change and do her make-up. There's not much time.

The Musée Maillol is opposite their local bakery, but Anna has never ventured beyond the stone dragon fountains outside. It is cool and calm in the museum. She pays and stands in a carefully selected green sixties' dress under the words '*Fondation Dina Vierny*', desultorily reading a leaflet about Vierny, Maillol's lover and an art dealer who preserved his legacy. In paintings, Vierny looks so young, full-lipped and gorgeous, while Maillol's photograph shows an old prune in a beret and beard.

'My love.' It is Olivier, bright-eyed, excited. He kisses her on both cheeks with exaggerated formality. Anna feels dizzy, unreal, and somehow embarrassed about being with Olivier like this, so near to the house. What should she say? They start walking though the galleries, past the breasty bronzes produced by Maillol, past pretty little things by Bonnard, Gauguin and Matisse.

'Are you mad?' whispers Anna. 'Anyone could see us here.' But Olivier smiles and says that the place is full of foreign tourists on a weekday. Anna is worried about Madame Canovas, but Olivier just shrugs. Parisians don't tell, he says. Affairs merit an *omertà*-style silence. 'Maybe you *want* to get caught,' says Anna, looking sideways at Olivier who is eyeing a primitivist painting of a fat farmer's wife on a ladder. 'We've been seen twice, so how could it be worse?'

He turns to stare at her. 'Perhaps you're right. Who knows what the subconscious – or indeed the conscious mind – is doing here, when we take these risks. As Sartre said, "Desire does not come to consciousness as heat comes to the piece of iron which I hold near the flame. Consciousness chooses itself as desire."'

'And you have chosen me?'

'Yes.'

'I love you, Olivier. What are we going to do?'

He kisses her, full of boyish happiness. There's no one to see, not enough guards for the warren of little deserted galleries.

'We are going to do exactly what we've been doing, of course,' he says.

'But Olivier, your daughter ran away two days ago. Doesn't that change everything? What if . . . I mean, don't you and Madison have to stay together for her? Is it right to be doing this? Should I go and work somewhere else?'

'She ran away to find you, remember. You of all people can't walk out on her. She needs you.' Olivier's voice sounds tight. 'I need you.'

Anna looks at him in silence. A dark, pained shadow passes over his face.

'And I can't leave Madison. Not right now, not after this.'

They talk about Sabine, the reasons why she may have run off. They don't entirely blame themselves – Madison's shadow floats over the whole conversation. Olivier seems upset, but then suddenly perks up, and gives Anna a lecture on the rules of the great French affair. He cites the fine example of former President Mitterrand who had affairs all over the Left Bank. 'Look around you in the seventh, and there's the Rue Frederic le Play apartment where Mitterrand's mistress Anne Pingeot – lovely woman – and Mazarine, their daughter, were guarded by the state, paid for by the state. They named Mazarine after the street where they began their affair. And then there was that Swedish journalist Mitterrand supposedly had a son with, who lived on the Île St Louis – near my parents' old apartment – and the police would block off the entire street while he was visiting. Such a bother – but no one said anything, least of all his wife. It's not the done thing.'

Anna suddenly wonders if Olivier is investing so much in their affair because the rest of his life is a mess. He is clinging to the one thing that works, that gives him simple happiness, but at what cost? And who will pay?

Olivier is standing in front of a beautiful portrait of Vierny, painted by Maillol. She wears a red dress on a green background, and her dark hair is wrapped round her head in a plait. 'Dina Vierny was just fifteen when she met Maillol,' he announces. 'She was his model, then his muse and lover. She stayed with him until he was old, until he died in a car accident. Did their ages matter?'

'Does forty-five and twenty-three matter, you mean?' asks Anna, laughing.

'All I'm saying is that a serious relationship is not impossible, despite a wide difference in age. Indeed it can be all the richer for it. Maillol was perhaps not a genius, but he was a good artist with a great woman behind him. Without her, his legacy would have disappeared.'

Anna, as she was supposed to, immediately saw herself as Olivier's muse. Perhaps he would eventually leave Madison. And what of the blonde ice maiden, anyway? Did she deserve him? What sort of mother was she? Anna had no real idea, since she tended to hand over Sabine and disappear. But the relationship between mother and daughter was certainly complicated, prone to tantrums on both sides. Léon had once told Anna about a strange conversation Madison and Renée had had in the hairdressers about breastfeeding. It made Anna speculate scarily about Madison, and Luiza, with her son left in Grozny and her recent essay on wet-nursing. Such a strange subject to choose.

'The green in this painting, and her dark hair, reminds me of you, of the day I first saw you on this very street in your little green coat,' says Olivier. He takes her hand. 'All this has made me realise we must live for now, and not in a limbo of waiting. We owe it to ourselves to experiment before it is too late. We must accept the truth, and not deny it.' They find themselves alone in the basement, beneath Ilya Kabakov's Soviet installation, *The Communal Kitchen*. Battered pots, sieves and spoons sway on strings above their heads, all lit by weak bare bulbs. Each family has a labelled cupboard to prevent pilfering. The conversation and sour arguments of the invisible inhabitants of the building play endlessly. It reminds Anna of the Rue du Bac at its most oppressive; the watchfulness of Madame Canovas, the nosy neighbours, the inescapable communal family life.

'It says it's the domestic gulag,' says Olivier, grinning. He pulls Anna into a corner and kisses her to the point of delirium. She sways in his arms, floating back under the pressure of his mouth.

'We can't do this here,' she says, forcing herself to pull away.

'I know we can't. I have a lecture in fifteen minutes.'

Anna feels shaky, disappointed, unbalanced by desire. She wants to be with him now.

'I love you, you know,' says Olivier. 'Meet me at the Hôtel Select on Friday, at noon.' And with that, he disappears through the doors into the Rue de Grenelle. Anna watches his dark figure for a moment through the glass, as he heads into Dalloyau for some delicious little pastry. Whatever the circumstances, Olivier's appetites go unchanged. Anna buys the green and red postcard of Dina Vierny, and walks back to the apartment. She is filled with a desperate need to sleep.

As she opens the outside door, a large black bird with an orange beak dive-bombs her and then swoops off. Anna screams. The bird flies up to a ledge in the courtyard and taunts her, saying: 'Dammit. Dammit' in French. Then she realises it isn't a scene from the domestic gulag. It's Madame Canovas' mynah bird on the loose.

Anna nearly slips running through the vestibule, its tiles still wet with lemon-fresh bleach. Anna knocks on the concierge's door. This is usually unnecessary, given Madame Canovas' radar, but she appears to be deep in her own world, cutting a story from the newspaper and pasting it in one of her black books. Beside her is a pile of neatly stamped and addressed envelopes. She keeps murmuring, 'Oh Mary, conceived without sin, pray for us who have recourse to thee . . .' and other religious incantations over and over. Anna tells her the bird has escaped.

'No, no, he has not escaped. Nino is free at last!' says Madame Canovas, her eyes bright and feverish. She is taking off her apron and hanging it up. She leans, exhausted against the door for a moment.

'Won't he die in the wild? Be set upon by Paris pigeons?'

'No, St Catherine loved pigeons,' says Madame Canovas, inexplicably. 'This is the best way. I have no one to take him, you see. And Milo and Tito have flown away too! They were so happy, fluttering into the blue sky above.' Anna assumes she means the weird coal tits. 'Sabine loved my birds,' adds Madame Canovas, wistfully. She's talking about Sabine in the past tense, thinks Anna, feeling a shiver in the back of her neck.

'But Sabine's fine. She's back at school today,' says Anna.

'Yes, yes, I know, of course I know. But anything could

happen.' And with that, Madame Canovas gathers her letters and bustles out of the door past Anna to the street.

'I am off, you see, to light a candle at the Chapel of the Miraculous Medal down the road, and to write a petition to St Catherine,' says Madame Canovas. She's twitching a small gold medal on a chain round her neck, thousands of which Anna knew were sold to tourists each year at the shrine to St Catherine Labouré on the Rue du Bac. Anna's been in there, down the passage to the dark, gloomy chapel, filled with pilgrims off tour buses. They want to see where St Catherine, then a novice nun, had a vision of the Virgin, and a late-night chat with her. The Virgin asked her to have the medal made, and its copies have sold and sold.

'Poor, poor girl. I blame myself for the night of suffering for her parents,' continues Madame Canovas. 'So much to do, so much to do . . .' she mutters, going out into the street and turning right towards the chapel and shrine beside the Bon Marché. St Catherine is buried under the altar of the chapel, beneath a whopping statue of the Virgin. The nuns sell postcards of engravings of the apparitions depicted with puffs of smoke and halos, plus St Catherine herself in black robes and a giant white kite-like headdress. Still, Anna is not unfond of St Catherine. She often takes Sabine to play at the sandpit and slides among the espaliered fruit trees of the nuns' old walled vegetable garden, now named for the saint. But clearly St Catherine's importance to the increasingly fanatical concierge is of quite a different order. Has the stolen night with Sabine or the knowledge of Anna's affair with Olivier totally unhinged Madame Canovas? Anna can't remember her ever making so little sense.

Upstairs in her room, Anna's heart is beating too fast. It is lunchtime, but she is too edgy to eat. She lies on her bed and tries to sleep, but the emptiness is oppressive: she needs to be with someone. She knocks on Luiza's door. Luiza is sitting on the bed, holding two framed photographs, one of Sabine, and the other of her son Musar in his school uniform. The boy is terribly handsome, skinny, and not at all like Luiza. Anna also looks at the picture of Sabine – she's got Madison's hair almost like a wig over Olivier's eyes and strong-boned face. Anna plonks herself in Luiza's armchair, with its cheap, shiny cushions, and explains about Madame Canovas. 'She's behaving really weirdly; I mean weirder than her normal weird. She's polished her entire apartment, released those disgusting birds to die in the wild, and now she's run off to worship at the shrine of St Catherine. Do you think they've sacked her at last?'

'You know, Madame Canovas saw me come in the night Sabine was lost, and didn't even tell me she was there with her,' says Luiza.

'Oh my God, how creepy is that?'

But then Luiza explains she was with Aslan. 'He stayed the night, when I didn't want to be alone.'

Anna gives a knowing smile. It is about time Luiza enjoyed

herself. She wonders which Barista brother it is – the big one or the small one – they blur in her head.

'And afterwards, after he'd gone, I felt, I don't know, bad, wrong. I felt guilty about Musar.'

She puts her son's photo down, and bites her lip.

'But is his father . . .' ventures Anna.

'His father's dead, for all I know, for all I care,' snaps Luiza. 'His father was a Russian soldier, and he disappeared that night, for ever. Some people in Grozny had a problem with that, with me. And money, there is always the question of money, so it was better for me to be here out of the way, earning. And Musar goes to a good school, he is well-provided for, he's a good reader, very clever at maths.' Her voice cracks a little, but she seems intent on continuing. Anna goes to sit beside Luiza on the bed, puts an arm around her. She wonders if Luiza was raped by the soldier.

'And so when Sabine was lost the other night I understood that when I touch her, when I am with her, I am with Musar too. It is more complicated than you can imagine.' She rubs a long-healed burn on her bare arm, which Anna had always thought must have happened when Luiza was cooking. Now she is not so sure.

Anna picks up the child's photo. 'He's very handsome. What age was he when you came to Paris?'

'Eleven months. I was still breastfeeding him.' Luiza is in floods of tears now. 'I still had . . .'

'And is that why . . . did you . . . did you feed Sabine?' Anna regrets the words as soon as she utters them.

Luiza is jolted out of crying. 'What made you think that? Oh my God, no, not her! No, Madison was obsessive about it – she sent her breast milk by FedEx from the film set, frozen for bottles. I just did all the getting up at night. No.' Then she looks up warily at Anna. 'But you're right. I did breastfeed Renée Rimbaud's son Guillaume – you've seen him, he's a big boy now. Renée went back to work at the magazine after two weeks and formula made him ill, so we came to what she called "an arrangement". A well-paid arrangement. Do you think that's terrible?'

Anna is too shocked to say anything, particularly something sensible. Her first thoughts are for Luiza, how fucked up and crap her life must be, to want, to need to do that. 'No, um. I've heard of other working mothers doing it in Paris. Just never met someone who actually was the . . .' Anna can't actually say the word wet-nurse. It sounds far too old fashioned and weird. She is secretly rather repulsed by the idea, and somehow ashamed that she had imagined Madison was the sort of mother who would hire a wet-nurse. It does not surprise her about Renée, from what she's seen of the woman's cack-handed childcare on visits to the apartment. In fact she once overheard Olivier joking with Madison that Renée was really a man – with ovaries.

'How I wish I'd never done it,' continues Luiza. 'Guillaume was a lovely baby, but Renée was madly jealous and madly demanding. She's a crazy woman. We had a terrible fight when she wanted to let him cry one night, to train him. And that's when she sacked me, and I had nowhere to go, no work permit. Paul called Olivier behind Renée's back, and they took me on as the cleaner, just before Sabine was born.'

'It's not been easy for you, has it?' says Anna, giving her a hug. Luiza becomes tearful again. She seems terribly flustered about Aslan's overnight visit, or perhaps ashamed, yet it seems that Aslan is the first person she has slept with in years.

'But it was so nice to talk in my own language. I got a bit drunk – I'm not very good with vodka. He's coming again tonight and I'm worried.'

She explains to Anna that Aslan himself is not the problem – he is, apparently, 'a fine, muscled man'. The problem is his visceral loathing for Olivier and the Malin family, because of Olivier's book on Chechnya. According to Aslan, *Chechnya – Beyond Philosophy* is too flippant, and displays a widespread ignorance of the full suffering of the Chechen people.

'He hates Olivier's book, hates him, hates the idea that I work for him. He has his reasons – Aslan found his other brother dead in a pit during the war and . . .' Luiza suddenly looks worried. 'You must never tell him what I told you about the Russian soldier.'

'I won't. Can't you just tell him that you're doing a job, and he's doing a job selling coffee, and that the rest doesn't matter if you get on together?'

'You don't know what it's like to have a complicated past. You just think history's something you learn in school.'

Anna looks insulted and gets up. Luiza grabs her hand. 'I'm

sorry. I didn't mean that. Thank you for talking to me. I needed to talk so much.'

Anna is still burdened by her own secrets, but now she's carrying Luiza's too. She sighs. 'I've got to go now to pick Sabine up from school.' Anna looks out of the window. It's oppressively hot, and the sky has gone yellow-grey, the sign of a summer storm. She stares unseeing into the middle distance. She hears a bird squawking harshly above, the distant sound of Madame Canovas mumbling and praying to herself, and then there's silence. Suddenly a huge black shape flapping cloth flies past Luiza's open window and lands with a heavy thud below. Anna screams and they both hang out to look down into the courtyard. There's a pile of black clothing on the ground. Pale legs splay out from beneath it. A wet, dark stain is spreading from the green turban across the cobblestones.

14

Madison Malin

Yellow fluorescent police tape squares off the stained spot where Madame Canovas fell to her death yesterday. From the window Madison can see white chalk marks outlining an angel on the cobbles, where the body once lay: Madame Canovas' shawl gave her the wings in death that she needed in life. The black mynah bird is still cawing from one of the stone window ledges above – a gothic detail which Madame Canovas quite possibly intended. It is as though the concierge is still watching every movement in the Rue du Bac through her witch's familiar. Madison shivers with an overdose of caffeine and trepidation. Madison was never fond of the concierge – indeed the opposite – but her death confirms the terrifying feeling that nothing is logical or explicable any more. There is no sequence of events, no cause and effect, just chaos falling from the sky.

Madame Duplessix, Madame Bellan and Madame Royan and their shopping bags have formed a circle downstairs. The neighbours' faces are severe, then expressive, as they engage in a marathon gossip. The words 'suicide', 'in all my born days', 'priest', and 'a truly religious woman' float up to Madison through the open window. But the neighbours are certainly not consumed by grief. Indeed, the only person who really wept for Madame Canovas' was Sabine. Her parents could not keep the manner of the death from her, because by the time she came home from school yesterday, the building was heaving with policemen. But children are strangely resilient, thinks Madison. Sabine wailed in agony for an hour, an inconsolable sadness that consumed her so much she lay face down on the floor. Then she rose, ate a huge dinner and watched *The Simpsons* as though nothing whatsoever had happened. By bedtime she was cheerful again, wearing her pyjama bottoms on her head like a turban and charming imaginary snakes, in the form of dirty socks, out of the laundry basket. Madison found herself giggling hysterically with her daughter in relief. Sabine made no further mention of Madame Canovas, merely giving the courtyard a nervous backward glance as she went to school this morning.

Madison shuts her eyes, because an uncomfortable thought is pressing upon her: was Madame Canovas' suicide – and it must be suicide – encouraged in some way by her guilt about harbouring Sabine for the night while her parents thought she had been abducted? But that was no crime, so why did she go for this final walk on the roof? Was she depressed? She was certainly deranged, that much Madison can vouch for.

The phone goes again, and Madison ignores it because she knows it is her agent, apoplectic because she is refusing to go to Romania – the new no-frills Hollywood – for four weeks' filming. She can't bear to leave Sabine for that long again, not until their family life steadies somehow, until children stay safe at home and concierges stop falling from the sky. Besides, she was to have played a thirty-year-old, which was stretching it a bit. A text comes up on her phone. Her agent knows she is there. 'They'll sue you to hell for breach of contract . . . You are crazy.'

Madison smiles. Quite soon her agent will be suing her too, for breach of contract, because they are about to part ways. The days, Madison has decided, of playing blonde mistresses in ridiculous underwear are over. Her last few nights have been mostly sleepless, but they have given her time to look at her life, and the lives of those around her. When you face disappearance and death head on, vanity falls right off the radar. Fear illuminates what matters, and leaves the rest in shadow, perhaps forever. Besides, yesterday she saw in the *Figaro* that an actress in a long-running play at the Bastille had taken a heroin overdose and gone into rehab. Madison suddenly felt that fate was on her side. She rang the play's director, an old acquaintance, and asked him if he needed a new fiftysomething sexually repressed headmistress to replace her. The director was stunned.

'You? You play an old trout in tweed like . . . well, whatever takes your fancy. Come and read with everyone else tomorrow. You never know.'

Still, before she leaves for the audition, Madison stands before the mirror, slightly at a loss. The hand holding her blusher brush falters, and she wonders what on earth to do with her make-up and her hair: she hasn't played an unglamorous part in twenty years. But she wants this role. It's weighty, and the theatrical hours will suit – she can be in Paris, see as much as possible of Sabine during the day, and as little as possible of Olivier in the evening. Sad, but perfect. She has detected something different in Olivier recently, not just because of the crisis with Sabine. He has never rejected her before like this, or seemed so distant. Maybe it will pass, but she is not going to sit around waiting for him. She's not going to pretend she has a lover any more. It's a question of dignity.

In the courtyard, Madame Bellan and Madame Royan nod approvingly at Madison's black suit and severe bun – they think she is showing respect for Madame Canovas, and do not realise she is dressed down for the audition. A raddled-looking detective in a shabby suit pops his head out of the concierge's apartment as Madison's high heels click by. He beckons her inside.

'Ah, you would be Madame Malin, am I right in assuming?' Madison nods. 'So delighted to meet you,' continues the detective, pumping her hand for just a little too long, 'but in such sorry circumstances.' He has a worn, intelligent face. He introduces himself as Inspector Biran, in charge of the

270

investigation into Madame Canovas' death for the coroner's office. 'I so admired you in *The Turquoise Sea*. I never thought I would . . .' He shakes his head, as though to ward off some impending madness. 'But to the point. Could you possibly come by to talk to me later? I am interviewing all the neighbours. Has to be done for the records.'

Madison nods her assent, and asks the inspector what he thinks has happened. 'Well, it's not written in stone yet, but between you and me, Madame, it's obviously suicide. Of course we'll need to wait until there's an autopsy and official report, but you knew she had terminal cancer, didn't you? Lungs. All those menthol cigarettes. All those drugs.' He gestures behind him to a shelf where a dozen white vials of pills are carefully lined up in order of height.

'My God. Lung cancer? No, not at all. Although that would explain . . .'

'She didn't tell anyone in the building she was ill?'

'Well, perhaps her friends, but not us.'

'I'm having trouble finding her friends, to be honest with you, Madame Malin. Or her relations. The suicide note is addressed: "To whom it may concern", which is unusual.'

'Oh goodness,' says Madison, simultaneously horrified and intrigued. 'Oh, we'll have to talk later, Inspector. My car is waiting outside.'

Inspector Biran sits back down at the table in Madame Canovas' front parlour. He frowns and continues sticking yellow Post-It notes into significant pages in the concierge's black books.

* * *

At the audition, Madison has one of those glorious moments where she knows, just knows that she will win the part. The second she sees three pages of the script, a voice comes into her head and a vision of Olivier's brittle, haughty mother coupled with the thrillingly hidden sexual mores of Miss Jean Brodie. She hears the director and producer shuffling in the darkness of the empty auditorium, talking desultorily. They have not exactly been filled with enthusiasm for her audition so far. But the theatre smells reassuringly of old popcorn and a damp fustiness – Madison hasn't done theatre for years, and she is seized with sudden nerves. Her adrenalin starts pumping; the script is shaking in her hands. Then she walks out into the spotlight, inhabits the headmistress, and everything flows. Madison realises that there are all these other people inside her, desperate for air. She is full of voices. This is the first of many.

When she finishes, there is an awed silence. The director, who is not one to mince his words, says: 'Well fuck me, Madison. I had no idea you could do that.'

'Thank you. I had no idea either.'

'But it looked as though you'd been playing the part for weeks.'

'Have you ever seen *The Prime of Miss Jean Brodie*? It's not exactly popular in France. But if you had, you'd know that in this part, I am in my prime.' She laughs. The director comes on stage, and kisses her, with new enthusiasm, on both cheeks.

'How soon can you start? I'll can the understudy. How soon can you learn the part? It's long.'

'I can rehearse with the cast this week and start on Monday,' says Madison.

'Sold. I'm printing the playbills now,' says the director. 'Madison? You are a goddess. I thought the play was about to go under.'

She walks out into the dancing sunlight and traffic circling the Bastille, and finds herself in the Café des Phares. Madison starts studying the script, and orders a sandwich and large *kir vin blanc*. She never drinks at lunchtime.

She gets back in time to pick Sabine up from school, leaving Anna underemployed, sulky and bored at home, sorting Sabine's laundry and sewing nametapes on her shirts.

Sabine is naturally suspicious of her mother's unexpected reappearance in her life.

'Where's Anna? Are you going to come every day? Anna usually buys a baguette on the way home from school, you see, and sometimes we . . .'

'Are you hungry?'

'Totally desperate.'

'Baguette it is, then. But not every day.'

Madison starts talking to Sabine about Madame Canovas. Fortunately, Sabine, due to her Catholic schooling, is, for the moment, a firm believer in heaven, and convinced the concierge has gone there. Madison privately thinks purgatory might be more appropriate, so Madame Canovas could watch people going up and down all day and take censorious notes. Poor old busybody – maybe her illness turned her sour. But Sabine appears sanguine about the whole situation – she's just worried about the fate of Madame Canovas' birds.

Madison takes Sabine back home and is about to leave her in the kitchen with Anna and Luiza, who has made a huge, delicious-smelling stew, afloat with mystery items. Sitting on the kitchen window ledge is Madame Canovas' mynah bird, looking rather bedraggled. 'Dammit,' it says weakly. 'Dammit.'

Luiza gives Sabine some bread and sunflower seeds to put out on the ledge, and the bird flies off, frightened, and then returns and gobbles the lot.

'I want him to live with us,' says Sabine. She has always wanted a pet, usually a puppy, but she has also campaigned for a python from time to time.

'Well, he's not going far in the wild, is he?' says Madison. 'Not with that vocabulary. But I suspect he – or is it she? – smells when caged.'

'I'll clean him out,' offers Luiza. 'I like birds.'

'That detective downstairs,' begins Anna. 'He's been up asking us lots of weird questions about Madame Canovas, about what I saw. He's quite rude.'

'Oh, do you think so?' says Madison.

'Please, pleeeze can we keep him, Maman?' interrupts Sabine. Madison shrugs her assent – she doesn't want the bird to go the way of its owner. Sabine is delighted – the only problem is capturing her pet. It turns out that this is simply done. Madison goes down to the concierge's apartment to get the bird's cage. Inspector Biran looks up, glassy eyed from his reading of Madame Canovas' black books, and snaps to attention. He fishes the ornate cage out of the gloomy backroom and hands it to Madison, looking adoringly at her.

'Madame? Could you possibly pop down for a word later? And Monsieur Malin?'

'Olivier's showing no sign of appearing today. He always goes to his office at Sciences Po when domestic life looks too tricky . . .' Madison stops speaking – that's not the sort of thing she normally says to strangers, but she supposes there is something compellingly confessional about a policeman.

'I see,' says Inspector Biran with some interest. 'Well, whenever *you* have a moment, Madame.'

Upstairs, Madison places the cage by the kitchen window, fills up the water and feeding trays, and in a few seconds, the stupid bird moves in, swearing quietly to itself.

'Does anyone know what he's called?'

'I think he's called Nino,' says Anna.

'Well, I'm going to call him Rover and teach him to say woof,' says Sabine, very seriously.

'You're weird,' says Madison, and is seized with laughter. She stops when she sees Anna staring at her. Madison cannot quite gauge what the look means.

*   *   *

Inspector Biran pulls out a chair for Madison in the concierge's apartment. His rumpled jacket hangs over the other chair. He has set up office on the parlour table, which shines like a mirror and reeks of pine polish. Madame Canovas' spells and potions are being examined: the fat black books and phials of pills. The inspector asks Madison a variety of questions about the concierge's recent behaviour, and whether anyone else has been seen in the building. Madison has little to tell him. What she wants to know is whether Sabine's disappearance affected Madame Canovas. She asks him if there's anything in the suicide note about her neighbours.

'Oh, just take a look and see what you make of it.' He hands her the note, in fine copperplate on peach stationery with little forget-me-nots at the top. 'I shouldn't really be showing you this, but she doesn't appear to have any living relatives as far as I can see, so what the hell.' The inspector sits back, and with a wry glance at the wide selection of lung-cancer pills, lights a Gitanes. He offers another to Madison, who hesitates, then refuses, sighing.

The inspector gives her a sympathetic look. 'You've had quite a time of it, haven't you, with your daughter running off too? And I hear she spent the night with Madame Canovas, which is rather curious.'

'Yes. Who knows . . .'

Madison busies herself with the three-page note. It begins: 'To Whom It May Concern: I am dying of a terrible disease, a burden laid upon me by God for reasons only He knows, but reasons I humbly accept as His servant. I have tried to work for the forces of righteousness here in this position which I have held for thirty-one years, yet my purpose has not always been fully understood.'

The inspector looks over her shoulder, rolls his eyes and says that as far as he can see, it is all the fevered witterings of a dying woman. Maybe the cancer had got to her brain – or perhaps her strange night with Sabine just pushed her right over the top. Literally. Madison grimaces. There's little else of note, except the funeral arrangements and that Madame Canovas announces she is leaving all her worldly goods to the Fontainbleau bird sanctuary. She adds that she hopes the management will consider that she has left her apartment 'scrupulously clean and in very good order.'

'Skip to the end,' says the inspector. 'There's something about her leaving a gold medal for your daughter. It's here in an envelope too. It's fake gold, by the way.' Madison reads on: 'I now leave this Miraculous Medal which I have had myself for the last thirty-years, to an innocent child, Sabine Malin, daughter of Monsieur and Madame Malin of Floor 5, 84 Rue du Bac, so that she may wear it to safeguard her against accidents. As the Holy Mother said: "Graces will abound for those who wear this medal with confidence."'

'Madame Canovas should have worn it more often herself, then,' says Inspector Biran. Madison raises an eyebrow at him. 'You appear to have formed an instant opinion of the dead.'

'I feel I know her already through these diaries,' says the

inspector, smiling. 'Well, they're not so much diaries as logs of all human life in the building: who came, who went, who argued, and above all why. Almost Proustian in their detail.' He reads her a random entry: ' "28 October. Two foreign men, skinhead hair, one quite dark, visit seventh floor 19.14 hours. Leave noisily – perhaps drunk? – 21.30 hours." Racist, wasn't she? Anyone who is an "immigrant" or "dark" gets logged.'

The inspector drums his nails on the table. 'I hardly need to investigate further, but it has all been most compelling. Here.' He pushes Madame Canovas' tawdry metal medal across the table to Madison. There's an M on the back, presumably for Mary, and two religious hearts, one encircled with thorns, one pierced with a dagger. On the medal's front is the Virgin and the words "Oh Mary conceived without sin, pray for us who have recourse to thee!"'

'Why couldn't she just pray more, instead of jumping off the roof?' asks Madison. She fingers the medal and then slips it into her jacket pocket.

As Madison stands up to leave, the inspector says, 'Can I ask you a favour, Madame Malin? Would you mind signing this for me?' He goes to fetch his battered brown briefcase and pulls out an old, carefully folded poster from *The Turquoise Sea*. A twenty-year-old Madison languishes sulkily on a beach in a short red gingham dress. 'I stole home at lunchtime to get it. I hope you don't mind . . .'

Madison laughs and signs. 'Of course I don't. I just find that photo frighteningly, disturbingly young. It can't be me.'

'Oh but it is you, I see it in all your expressions.' The inspector clears his throat. 'Excuse me.' He folds the poster, as though it were some religious relic. While he goes to put it in his bag in the back, Madison's eye catches another entry in the diary, open on the table: 'Friday 29 April. 00.45 hours M. Malin returns late, closely followed by Mlle. Ayer...' Madison jerks back in her seat when Inspector Biran reappears. He looks from Madison to the diary entry in silence, as though computing something. The clock on the mantelpiece clunks.

'You know, Madame Malin, I deeply respect you, not just for your films. I can tell you're an honest person, while those surrounding you perhaps are not as full of integrity. Now, I just must go to the café to fetch another coffee, because I have more work to do here. I will be back in five minutes. Would you mind waiting, and you can just sign a short statement when I return?'

The inspector gives her an agonised look, smiles kindly, and walks out. The front door clicks behind him. Madison watches her hand with its pale pink nails stretch out towards the diary. Her heart is thumping horribly. She knows that she will regret what she is about to do.

Soon after the entry when Olivier and Anna arrive home late at a curiously similar time, there are others: '7 May, 14.30 hours. M. Malin visits the *chambres de bonne* again. Returns 15.30 hours. Complains of plumbing problem.' The coincidences build up, or so it seems to Madison.

The stiff, schoolmarmish handwriting continues. One entry

details the day the building's manager had come to inspect some old, leaking radiators in the Malins' apartment. There was a woman's voice and laughter coming from M. Malin's locked study, but no one opened the door when Madame Canovas knocked. 'Study radiator still in need of inspection,' noted the diary.

Madison shrugs. What does it all prove? Nothing, really, or so she hopes. But other odd incidents and glances between Olivier and Anna are starting to make sense. She dismisses the thought and flicks to the end of the unfinished diary, morbidly curious to read Madame Canovas' final entry. But there's just a list of various cleaning materials she requires, and a cutting from the newspaper about Sabine's disappearance. The day before, however, the page is entirely filled and marked with a Post-It. The breathless conclusion sees M. Malin and Mlle Ayer in each other's arms on the steps of the Métro.

Madison throws the book at the wall, smashing one of Madame Canovas' best china jugs. She sits with her head in her hands, filling up with blinding, red-hot anger. She feels nauseated too, revolted by the idea that this sleaze has been going on around her daughter, in her house. In her bed? Or perhaps Sabine knew. Perhaps that was why she ran off. Madison wants to kill Olivier. She wants to wring Anna's duplicitous little neck. She's ready to . . .

'Hello. I'm, um, back.' Inspector Biran takes one glance at Madison, who is deathly white, with two feverish red spots on her cheeks, and knows what she has done, and what he has done.

'I'm sorry,' he says, looking almost tearful himself. 'So sorry. I didn't know what was the right thing to do. You should forget that . . .'

'Forget? I shall not be forgetting anything.' Madison rises up, taller than the inspector, an avenging Amazon. 'Thank you, Inspector. You did the right thing. Can we finish our business in the morning?'

'Of course, Madame Malin,' says the inspector. 'Of course.' He watches in horror as Madison runs up the stairs, her metal heels clattering like knives on the marble.

Madison stops at the apartment door, grasping desperately for some calm. She had always known that Olivier was not entirely faithful, but this time he has turned the knife in a wound in the very centre of their life and their home. She is shaking with shock and anger, but she cannot let Sabine hear what she is going to say. She lets herself into the apartment, listening. Everything suddenly seems to be in slow motion. She hears the dishes clinking as Luiza cleans up in the kitchen, and Anna and Sabine singing 'What shall we do with the drunken sailor?' in the bathroom, amid splashes. She walks steadily and deliberately into the kitchen and asks Luiza to take over bathtime and to ask Anna to come into the salon. Luiza takes one nervous look at her and scuttles away.

Madison sits opposite the painting of St Sebastian and for once in her life, really feels his pain. Anna walks in, relaxed. 'Hi. What did they say about Madame Canovas?' Then she sees Madison's livid white skin. 'What's wrong? Are you all right?'

'How *could* you?' shouts Madison, her face now a few inches from Anna's. 'How could you abuse my trust? Violate my home, my husband, my child? No wonder Sabine ran away. You have poisoned our lives, our family. You sleazy little whore.'

Madison's hands are clenched, white-knuckled by her sides. She has never wanted to hit someone so much. Anna looks absolutely terrified. She doesn't even try to deny it.

'Oh my God, I'm so sorry. Oh my God.' She descends into tears on a chair. Madison grabs her wrist and pulls her up, face to face.

'How long has this been going on? Does Sabine know?'

Anna shakes her head and bites her lip.

Madison looks at her in contempt. 'Of course, who the hell doesn't know? Even Madame Canovas bloody well knew.'

Anna says nothing and looks at her feet. 'Answer me,' says Madison. 'How long has this been going on?'

'A few months. Sabine doesn't . . . It was just . . .'

'It was just what? A game? Did you think only of yourself? You are unbelievably selfish.' Madison looks over at Anna's shocked expression. 'And stupid.'

'But Olivier . . .'

At the mention of Olivier's name, Madison suddenly wants to bawl like a baby. She feels she could have handled him having some distant affair, away from home, as he no doubt has had, but *this*? On her own doorstep, in her face. She will not let Anna see her tears, though. Madison holds her head up high and looks down at Anna. She takes a deep breath and enunciates each icy word. 'I have nothing else to say. You pack tonight, you leave tomorrow. I do not want you anywhere near my daughter or this apartment again, ever. Do I make myself clear?'

Madison opens the door to the attic stairs, and waits for her to step out.

'I'm sor . . .' begins Anna. 'Can I just say goodbye to Sabine, I . . .'

She just doesn't get it, thinks Madison.

'Get. Out. Of. My. House. Now,' says Madison, through gritted teeth. She opens the back door, and slams it behind Anna.

Luiza edges out of the bathroom and looks in anguish at Madison.

'Oh don't tell me you knew too?' says Madison, exasperated. 'I can see it in your face. Just get Sabine into bed and put on a story CD for her. I'll be in later to say goodnight.' Madison goes into Olivier's study, and raids his fridge, which always contains fine wine. She opens what looks like the most expensive bottle, and pours herself a glass. Then she puts her head down on his desk and cries for a long time. She feels utterly humiliated.

When the front door clicks open an hour later, Madison can tell that Olivier has already been alerted by telephone about the discovery of his crime, because he creeps gingerly into the apartment, as though trying not to disturb its equilibrium. Madison looks out of the study door. Olivier is silhouetted in black against the twilight, hesitating. She strides down the long hall towards him. His face registers a series of emotions, which stop suddenly on fear.

'I'm not going to ask you anything,' Madison begins. 'It is beneath my dignity to do that.'

'But there's nothing . . .'

'Anna is leaving in the morning and she will not see Sabine again. The rest is your problem.' Madison looks disdainfully at him. 'All you need to know is that my trust has been utterly violated, and so has that of my daughter. Your daughter.' She turns away in disgust.

'Madison?' says Olivier, putting a hand on her shoulder.

'Don't touch me!'

'Madison . . . it was just a mistake, a silly dalliance that got out of hand. It's of no significance. I didn't mean to hurt you, or Sabine. You know what it is like for me. I must experiment, I must find my limits . . . Oh God, I'm sorry. I didn't know what I was doing.'

'Of course you fucking knew what you were doing. You have no moral centre, no core, and you justify it with all that philosophical crap. You write and talk about ethics and principles in the world, but at home, you have none. None whatsoever.'

'I resent that . . .' begins Olivier, but Madison interrupts.

'You can resent all you want, but I'm not discussing this any more tonight. I shall be sleeping on the spare bed in Sabine's room, and you can sleep where and with whom you like.'

'Oh Jesus,' says Olivier. He leans shakily against the hall wall. Madison shuts the door of Sabine's room, excluding him.

She slumps into Sabine's armchair, her legs like jelly, and cries a little bit more, until there is nothing left, until she is calm and empty. Half an hour later, Madison gets up, washes her face in the adjoining bathroom, and walks over to Sabine. Her daughter is deliciously abandoned in sleep, with her arms thrown wide on the pillow, her skin soft and rosy. Madison kisses her gently, half a dozen times, being careful not to wake her.

The evening is humid, so Madison reopens the door to the hall for some air, and watches as the stained glass of the windows pattern the floor in the moonlight. The jewel-coloured reflections disappear and reappear as clouds pass over, tracking time. Soon Madison is lying in white sheets on a single mattress across from Sabine, watching her body gently rise and fall under the covers, and luxuriating in her closeness, her safety. Madison's love for Sabine burns as though it were sunlight focused through a magnifying glass.

15

Olivier Malin

Meanwhile back at the château, Olivier is hunkering down, hoping to ride out the Texas tornado which lurks inside Madison. They decided that getting away from Paris for the weekend might help Sabine, given the apartment's unfortunate associations, and the lingering shadow of Madame Canovas. For Olivier, it is also a chance to escape the domestic gulag. He knows from past arguments that Madison is less likely to stick a fork in his face or break his little finger in the refined atmosphere of his parent's home. There is nothing crosser than a Southern belle when crossed: those beautiful manners are quite left behind. At least, thinks Olivier, Madison will have to behave well in public. At least there is the comfort of keeping up appearances for his parents as well as for Sabine. Besides, this is the last time they can come down together for the weekend as a family, since Madison has acquired some dreadful job in the theatre which involves working every night except Sundays. Was that prescient, or well-organised? Did she take the job before she found out about Anna? The thought makes Olivier queasy again. His stomach has not been right for days, a sign of very serious emotional disturbance.

He tries to distract himself with the newspaper, but even in the bright morning room of the Château de Moulon, there is no escape: Olivier's mother takes all the celebrity magazines, mostly in order to moan about the demise of the upper classes and proper etiquette. She has left *Paris Match* magazine prominently open on the white plastic table with the newspapers. There is a double-page spread which starts with that charming black and white photo of the Malins naked together after Sabine's birth; then the PlayWorld shot with Sabine in the alien mask and a paragraph about her temporary disappearance – 'a domestic mix-up' – and ending with a snatched picture of their three backs running from the apartment into the car last week with the headline: 'The Malin Family Together Again!'

Olivier thinks that at present his family will win the Tolstoy prize for most varied and complicated unhappiness. Although he has vowed that he will never see Anna again, and scourged himself profusely before Madison, the Malins can barely speak to each other, while desperately trying to be as normal and loving as possible to their daughter. Last night Sabine came into their bedroom twice, weeping and calling for them, but at the same time, asleep. She talked deliriously of a huge black bird, sweeping down and sticking its sharp claws into her arm. The night before, she wet her bed for the first time in years, and cried out for Anna. Olivier put her back to bed, changed the sheets, calmed her, and lay back down, sleepless with his burden of guilt.

He felt wretched, lying there beside Madison as she slept serenely. Being in bed together will not cure what lies between them, and Olivier fears that one day soon he will have to prove his verbal commitment to Madison, to no one but Madison, with a physical performance. At the moment, he can't bear the idea. They lie together in this lie for reasons of propriety, but there is an electric fence running down the middle of the bed, which only they can see.

The dead weight of Anna is crushing them: the infernal, internal affair. And it is not just Anna – it is years of other affairs and misunderstandings, layers of rotten flesh that need to be cut away to return to the bones of their relationship. Olivier's not sure he has the strength to do it, although every time he sees Sabine, or hears her voice, he is deeply ashamed.

He leans back in the white plastic bucket seat at the breakfast table and stares at the faded medieval tapestry which covers the entire wall behind. In a field of dark flowers there is an army returning from war. At the front is a victorious knight, bloodsodden and exhausted, looking up at his distant damsel who is now more décolletée than in distress. And why on earth is the damsel holding up a large goose – or is it a fat white baby? But the simplistic tapestry conspires, like everything else, to remind him of the inadequacy of his own relationship. He and Madison have survived this horrible lost-and-found time together. To any normal couple, what they have been through recently might eventually bring strength and reaffirmation. Instead, Olivier feels a grey weariness, and a sense of aching, physical deprivation. Although he has declared to Madison that his affair is over for ever, Olivier is still in mourning for Anna, but his grief must remain private. Worse still, Madison is coldly resigned. 'All that matters now is Sabine,' she says. This makes Olivier a great deal more nervous than if they'd had a screaming row, as they always did in the past. Madison's an unexploded, buried mine, and he's dancing carefully around her. It's a nightmare. The château is full of nightmares.

Across from him, Madison looks composed and beautiful, her skin shining, bare of make-up. She's drinking her coffee, luxuriating in the sight of the sunlight dappling the back of Sabine's head as she sits crosslegged on the floor. Olivier tightens his jaw and drops the offending *Paris Match* in the wastebasket. He doesn't even want to share the air with Madison, because it is so full of unexpressed hurt and tension. 'Come on, rabbit,' he says to Sabine. 'Let's go for a walk and feed the ducks with these. We'll see if they sink.' He picks up some rock-hard croissants from the basket – yesterday's, which his mother always has the maid re-heat for economy. He gives one of the croissants a tap on the table to prove their solidity to Sabine. It used to be one of their jokes.

'Oh Papa, no, not yet. I've got to finish this droid battle first. I'm at level three!'

Sabine's head goes back down to her Gameboy. Olivier sighs and looks over for support at Madison, who remains ostentatiously glued to the script of her new play. Because, for the moment, Olivier cannot say no to Sabine, he agreed on Friday to her long-held demand – always previously refused – for a Gameboy. Naturally, she is playing with it non-stop. Her parents have to drag her away to enforce quality time upon her. When Madison tried to read her the previously much-requested *Charlie and the Chocolate Factory* last night, Sabine just said 'No thanks, that's baby stuff.' The situation is now so bad that she will only leave the Gameboy to bet on the horses with her grandfather. Perhaps Sabine's also sick of intense adult company, when previously there was very little. Perhaps it's her reaction, her withdrawal into a safe, busy, virtual world. The Gameboy and the visit to her grandparents are an attempt to return to normality, but for her parents, it is a return to hell.

Olivier's mother Véronique arrives, heralded by a noxious cloud of perfume, and pancaked white with powder after the morning application. She hands Olivier his mobile, which she's nosily answered. 'It's that inspector, darling.' Madame Malin sits next to Madison and pours some almost-cold coffee – she would never consider wasting it by ordering a new pot.

'How are you, Véronique? You don't usually come down to

breakfast,' says Madison, too chummily, using the intimate *tu*, which Madame Malin prefers to reserve for blood relatives. Olivier watches Madame Malin suppress a frown, but Madison keeps at it: 'Stick to the baguette, Véronique, that's my tip. The croissants are puzzlingly hard. I think your maid must've got them mixed up with yesterday's.' Madison smiles sweetly and returns to her paper. Madame Malin suffers a horrible coughing fit.

Then the matriarch recovers and attacks, 'Does the child have to wear that thing to breakfast?'

Sabine looks up for a second and grins. She is wearing the Bart Simpson T-shirt which Anouk gave her two days ago.

'Yes, I'm afraid *the child* has to wear *that thing*,' says Madison, wryly. 'It's a gift from a friend. And Sabine prefers it to Bonpoint.' She pauses. 'Do you watch *The Simpsons* much out here, Véronique? It's a fantastic insight into the American mind.'

Madame Malin shakes her head, disgusted, and pours herself more cold coffee.

Olivier is still talking on the phone to Inspector Biran, who is not entirely popular with him, following what he suspects is the mass dissemination of Madame Canovas' diaries in the name of justice. 'No funeral for a couple of weeks until the investigation's closed, but he says it's just paperwork now,' Olivier announces to everyone. His mother has taken a particularly ghoulish interest in Madame Canovas' death, but he wishes she would shut up in front of Sabine.

*   *   *

Olivier leaves his women battling silently – Sabine with her droids, and his mother and Madison with each other – and goes outside on to the cobblestones in front of the château. He breathes in the hot, dusty air and its stench of mown grass, and walks for a long time without noticing where he is going. There is a creeping weight on his shoulders. Guilt is the opposite of freedom, and if there is one thing Olivier hates, it is not being free, intellectually or emotionally. Emotionally, he is trapped right now, unable to breathe, so he needs his intellectual freedom all the more. He wants to hide and write his troubles away, but he knows he has to stand around playing this ham role in his self-created family drama. At least for the weekend. He kicks the stones at the edge of a stubbly wheatfield which stretches boringly away.

There is a sudden clatter of hooves on the cobblestones behind the château, and Madison and Sabine emerge on two horses. In the distance he sees their long limbs and the blonde hair coming out underneath their velvet hats. They ride swiftly off into the woods, liberated, together. Olivier feels unexpectedly envious of them. He stands by the side of the millpond and throws stones hard into the water like a small, sulking boy. There is nowhere to direct his anger and frustration. He hates himself, and he hates Madison. He doesn't want to live in this eternal, uncomfortable compromise which is bad for him and probably worse for Madison, if only she would admit it. Yet he is holding back: he cannot bear to hurt Sabine. Not now.

Left Bank

As Olivier stares at the green duckweed oppressively covering the pond, and the fast-closing air holes made by his stones, a deep melancholy descends on him. He feels that the only way to lift the suffocating gloom is by talking to Anna, just to hear for a moment tiny traces of her Mancunian accent underneath the French, to enter the simplicity and directness of her world. He can't just switch off his obsession at will. His phone itches in his pocket. He has promised Madison he will not call Anna, but he has told Anna a slightly different story – that they must have a cooling-off period, time to think.

Olivier scrolls through to his code word for Anna, Junkyard, and nearly presses the call button. He knows Anna is staying with friends somewhere in Paris; he worries that she is alone and upset – or worse still, in some nightclub. He can't stop thinking tenderly about her, but instead he controls himself and calls Paul Rimbaud. Olivier starts talking about adultery while he continues stoning the pond in punishment.

In the elaborate language Olivier prefers, Paul advises that it is not Anna that Olivier loves, but the aesthetic idea of love. Anna is anyone. She doesn't matter. 'We all love the idea of being in love. Remember that moment in Kierkegaard's *Repetition*, when the young man can't sustain his eroto-aesthetic love for a girl due to his sense of higher calling, a calling to poetry. The girl isn't a reality for him, but just the occasion for awakening his poetic impulse. Your problem is that you have a lot of those impulses. About one a year for a new woman, a new aesthetic impulse, if I'm right.'

Olivier clears his throat, and then says nothing. Paul continues: 'You're moved by the imaginative idea of love, to which love in a concrete sense is sacrificed. Unless this one's different . . .'

'Yes, I think that may well be the problem.'

'Look at me,' says Paul. 'I have always played with the idea of a woman, never the reality, but in a way the imagination is more satisfying. I've been utterly faithful to Renée throughout our marriage. I've never had an affair, except in my head.' Olivier is shocked, because this alters the whole imagined balance of his relationship with Madison.

'You've never . . . honestly?'

'Honestly,' says Paul.

'I thought in our circle we all . . .' begins Olivier.

'But it's not for want of trying,' adds Paul and he laughs, sadly.

Olivier is puzzled. He had always thought, in his heart of hearts, that Madison had been having an affair with Rimbaud; a long affair. Somehow he didn't mind that, the idea that they both had contingent loves, that it was all fair among friends. He had thought that such possibilities lay unspoken alongside their relationship – well, they had with his first wife. Indeed, Olivier had hoped that Paul might make some kind of confession, give an indication of something going on. But now there's this great moral imbalance, now Madison is utterly in the right, and Olivier is in the wrong. He rings off, his uneasiness heightened, but then he concludes, comfortably to himself, that Madison probably had an affair with someone else entirely.

Left Bank

*　*　*

When Olivier returns to the house much later, Sabine is in the kitchen making pastry with Eugenie the maid. Neither wants his help. He goes upstairs and hears Madison laughing on the phone to someone. 'Yes, of course, darling,' she's saying. 'I'll do it. I'll do anything for you, you know that.'

He walks in the bedroom door, and she hurriedly says goodbye to the person. Olivier suddenly feels jealous. 'Who was that?'

'Oh, just a work thing,' she says, and changes into her oldest jeans for Sunday lunch, just to annoy Madame Malin, who always puts on a proper dress, and insists that Monsieur Malin wears a tie, even if just the two of them are dining alone.

'Madison?' says Olivier.

'Uh huh?' she says as she pulls a T-shirt over her head.

'I know what we said about Anna, and that's behind us now, but do you remember long ago when we first met how we talked about having contingent loves, and one central relationship which would stand the test of time?'

'Oh here we go.'

Olivier frowns at her. 'Well, I thought we had in some way, like so many others around us in Paris, come to an unsaid arrangement, which if it works makes a marriage more profound, more durable.'

'You said "unsaid".'

'Oh come on, Madison, you're an adult. You're not blind. You understood.'

'Early on, perhaps, but I would just like to point out that your Sartres and De Beauvoirs did not have children.'

'They didn't want to.'

'Do you know how many abortions she had to have to keep him?'

'That's beside the point.'

'I think at times she might have been angrier than you'll ever know. Their perfection is in your imagination; I'm sure it's the same with all those relationships. I read all their biographies and her novels when I was a teenager in Texas, and believed in them, but now I'm older, now that I have a child, they seem so flawed. Except the bit when she says "The most mediocre of males feels himself a demigod as compared with women."'

Olivier holds his throbbing head and groans. 'That's another punch below the solar plexus. What more can I say? I'm sorry, I'm trying to make it better, but I can only do that with your help. Before . . . before what happened with Anna,' he mumbles the last few words. 'I mean before that, were you happy, or were you just . . .'

'I don't know. I will try, but what I feel now is frozen. All my emotional reserves are used up. I feel our relationship is in suspension until someone melts. And it may not be me.' She looks sadly at him. 'I still feel betrayed and humiliated. And I don't know whether time will heal.'

'Or reveal,' says Olivier.

'I have nothing to reveal to you, Olivier. Unfortunately. And I have some vacuuming to do.'

Olivier is exhausted by their conversation, and mystified. He has never seen Madison and a vacuum cleaner in the same room, let alone working together. He follows her, pulling on his jacket for lunch, down to the drawing room, where his father Louis is having a pre-prandial cigar.

'Urh hurlh!' grunts Monsieur Malin, by way of greeting. 'My dears! A little sherry perhaps?'

Madison shakes her head, tosses the sofa cushions on to the floor, and lifts an antediluvian Hoover with a ballooning grey bag on to the stiff sofa. 'Dust mites,' she shouts over the racket. 'Years, no, centuries of dead skin. Dead aristocratic skin. Going to give them all a good clean. Been dying to do this for ages.' She bangs Monsieur Malin's armchair with her hand for effect, and a grey cloud rises.

Monsieur Malin jumps up in horror, as though the dust has passed unnoticed for the last seventy years, and enthusiastically joins Madison by throwing more cushions down. 'Must tell Véronique to speak to that maid! Such slapdash work.'

'Why don't *you* speak to the maid, Louis?' smiles Madison. 'Her name is Eugenie, isn't it?' Monsieur Malin is not sure whether or not he is being ticked off.

Madame Malin arrives at the peak of the chaos. Olivier is standing at the window, ignoring it all, knocking back a second stiff sherry. Monsieur Malin is vigorously battering cushions with the poker from the fire. Sabine has made a vast den in the upholstery, so she can play her Gameboy undisturbed.

'What on earth?' Madame Malin coughs in the fug of cigar smoke and dust.

'Appalling dust mites. Got to be careful. Allergies, you know,' says Madison, smiling. 'We'll be done in five minutes. It might be worth getting some of this reupholstered, you know.'

Madame Malin unplugs the Hoover, which gives a strangled wheeze. 'Luncheon is served,' she says, in a sub-zero voice. She ushers them into the dining room. 'It's pheasant. Well-hung, just as Louis likes it.' Olivier looks over at Madison with some sympathy and shrugs. He wandered by the old tiled game larder early this morning, and saw the pheasants hanging up, one somewhat maggoty, all pungent.

'Back in a moment,' says Madison. 'Just start without me.' She returns almost immediately, and when the starter is over, everyone else is served with unpleasant pheasant in a greasy sauce by Eugenie, while two plates of fluffy, steaming scrambled eggs are suddenly provided for Sabine and Madison.

'Nothing like fresh farm eggs, is there?' says Madison. 'I hope you don't mind, Véronique, but, well, I just hate pheasant. In fact I hate all game. It's only taken me eight years to tell you this, but now seems to be the right moment.'

Sabine snorts into her napkin. Madame Malin looks livid – and lost. 'I . . . we . . .'

'You do what you like, m'dear. We're very old fashioned here,' says Monsieur Malin patting her hand. 'I think we'll need another carafe of wine.' Olivier sighs and refills his glass for the third time.

Madison starts talking about the re-mastered version of *Le Chagrin et La Pitié*, the documentary on France's collaborationist tendencies during World War II, now out on DVD. Olivier gets terribly interested in the subject, until Sabine asks: 'What does collaboration mean?' and Monsieur Malin goes even redder than he usually does when he's got two carafes of wine inside him.

They take coffee in the drawing room in an uneasy silence, interrupted only by the gloomy tick of the vast gilded clock on the mantelpiece. Shafts of sun come in the window, illuminating the millions of newly risen dust motes. Madame Malin is reading the *Figaro* women's food page. Olivier looks over her shoulder at the extraordinary headlines: 'The Leek: A Green Goddess' and 'The Crayfish: How it Runs, How it Runs!' His mother is glued, not surprisingly, to an article about the 'aristocratic' Noirmoutier potato. 'The expensive Noirmoutier is to the potato family what Château Lafite is to Bordeaux: the very best. If he'd tasted it, Baudelaire wouldn't have succumbed to opium and Verlaine would have given up absinthe.' Olivier is impressed. He makes a mental note of the potato's name.

Meanwhile, Madison is reading what Olivier knows to be an absolutely disgusting, semi-pornographic book by Houellebecq. At least his mother has no idea of this. Sabine is on the Gameboy, of course, and Monsieur Malin is snoring, his chins vibrating into his cravat. Olivier picks the least painful remaining armchair and idly picks up *Libération* at the page where Madison left it. It's a long article by a distinguished member of the *Académie Française* about the merits of the philosopher's cafés in Paris, and how they are spreading round the world. Olivier feels, as a leader in the Café Philo revolution, that he has done much to democratise intellectual debate. He smiles to himself and scans quickly down for his name. He finds it in the fourth paragraph:

The Café Philo movement, which has been so lauded by non-academics, has in fact resulted in a deterioration of the level of debate. The tendency is to the lowest common denominator, and the café discussions are used to express degraded rivalries, conflicts and power plays. Particularly ludicrous is the cult of the compère/professor – the worst example being the media-hungry Olivier Malin, the colossus who bestrides the Café Calvaire, where rational thought is sloppily allowed to give way to emotion. The core of philosophy has been evacuated, dispensing with all intellectual hard work, and leaving vague discourses against unemployment, unfairness, and exclusion, in an atmosphere of superficiality and self-aggrandisement.

'Bastard,' says Oliver.
'Pardon?' says Madame Malin.
'Madison, did you see this ridiculous piece about me and the philosophy cafés?'
'Oh, I missed that. No, I was actually looking at that little review of the film, you know, *Soldier, Soldier*, on the back.

André's delighted. I just talked to him.'

Olivier turns over the arts section and finds the review of André Andrieu's World War I movie. It's described as 'powerful and challenging'. Of particular interest is the 'smouldering, ambiguous, sophisticated' performance of his wife.

'That's marvellous,' says Olivier. 'I'm so pleased for you. That sort of critical praise has been a long time in coming.' He means what he says, but he's also swallowing the bile that comes with jealousy, something he's never experienced in reference to Madison's work before. The room suddenly seems hot and oppressive. He looks at his mother and father and thinks they would look good stuck permanently in their armchairs in the window of the taxidermist Deyrolle in the Rue du Bac.

'I've got some work to do. I'll be in the study.'

In his father's study, Olivier shuts the door, and crumples into a chair among the manly smells of leather and cigar smoke. His fingers caress the spines of the beautifully bound books which he has read most of, and Monsieur Malin, almost none. Indeed, Olivier wholly credits his father for his desire to lead a life of the mind; opposites react. The big white phone sits like a skull on the desk, and Olivier watches as his fingers abandon the books of their own accord and start tracing Anna's number on the old circular dial.

When he gets through and hears her lovely, lonely voice, he suddenly does not know what to say. But his subconscious has been busy these last few days, and somehow the resurrection of his daughter has brought clarity to his life. Also Madison is no longer the woman he married; she is someone quite different. He no longer wants to float on, wasting time.

'Christ,' says Anna. 'What do you mean by that? Isn't it a bit early to . . .'

'My darling, I know now that by adopting a form of love where I make no commitments, there is no true resolution or unification of the self. I want to end all this duplicity. I want us to have authenticity together. Listen, Anna, I want to make a commitment to you. It's that simple. Then no one needs to live with the pain and deceit of compromise.'

'Are you saying that you're going to leave Madison? And what about Sabine?'

'Being honest with her is better in the long run. But it can't happen immediately. We will have to go on secretly like this for a while. But at least we are no longer in the same building. We can be together when you find an apartment.'

There is silence at the other end of the phone. Anna starts crying. 'It's awful. I love you and I don't know what to do. I'm not exactly apartment hunting. I'm sleeping on Aslan and Ruslan's sofabed now and I don't have anywhere to go, or a job. I don't even have a reference.'

Olivier says he will write her a wonderful one, and give her money until she finds a job.

'I don't want your money. I don't want to be paid for. I'm all over the place. I don't know what I'm doing. I have to think for a while, Olivier. I'm frightened.'

'My darling, don't be frightened. Trust me, it'll be fine. I'll call you tomorrow, and I'll be with you in Paris the day after.'

He can hear her sobbing.

'It'll be all right, Anna, my love. It'll be wonderful.'

Olivier puts down the phone and stares at a photo of his father and mother from the late 1970s, all buttoned up and conspicuously in hate with each other. He cannot live that life. He must do the opposite. He cannot settle down comfortably and live with his mistakes.

Olivier is left undisturbed and escapes into the glorious freedom of his head for hours, writing an impassioned defence of the Café Philo movement, which he emails from his mobile and computer to the opinion section of *Libération*. At seven o'clock he rises from the desk, and goes to find Sabine. He follows the electronic beeps and dings down the upstairs corridor, until he finds her sitting on the floor of his childhood bedroom, loading another programme into her godforsaken Gameboy.

'Halt! Go no further! Desist!'

'Hi, Papa. What are you talking about?'

'Stop loading more crapulous programmes into that Gameboy. It will eat your mind. It is mechanical claptrap. I can't believe I ever agreed to you having one.'

Sabine looks near to tears.

'It's brilliant, Papa. Don't say that.'

Olivier relents and kisses the back of her neck as she bends over the console, her thumbs a blur as she flicks the buttons.

'It's your bathtime, rabbit. Just put it down for a moment. You can't do it all the time.'

Sabine looks hard at Olivier as she takes off her T-shirt and he runs the bath in the room off the old nursery. 'If you were little you'd want a Gameboy. Anouk has one and so does her brother and . . .'

'Just because everyone has something doesn't mean it's good.'

Sabine picks up a handful of the tin soldiers scattered across the green-painted board, with its papier mâché mountains carefully built up by Olivier long ago. 'It's like what you did with those toy armies, in the olden days before they had electricity. It's about battles and weapons and . . .

'. . . strategy,' finishes Olivier. 'You're right. And we did have electricity. I'm not that ancient.'

'What's strategy, Papa?'

'I'll teach you chess and then you'll understand.' He smiles at her and lifts her over the high side of the old roll-top bath. Sabine splashes around and rubs the green marks where the brass taps have dripped for years.

'Why did Madame Canovas die, Papa?'

Olivier feels a nervous twitch going across the back of his neck. 'Because she was sick, rabbit. She had a disease that wasn't getting any better. I just wish she'd told us.' Sabine looks as though she might cry.

'Did Anna leave because I ran away? Was she angry with me?'

'No, darling, no, of course not. She just had to take another job. Nannies don't stay for ever.'

'Luiza has.'

'That's true. Well, I'm sure you'll see Anna again, or she'll write you a postcard.'

'Maman said she was never coming back. Does Anna hate me? Did I do something bad?'

Olivier hugs her tight for a long time and reassures her that everyone loves her very much, particularly him, and that she has nothing to do with the recent troubles.

'Are you sure? I'm not sure. I don't understand,' says Sabine, frowning, but then she ends the conversation by starting to blow bubbles underwater. He watches as Sabine's hair floats out in beautiful waves. 'I love you,' he says. Sabine smiles. Olivier collapses exhausted on the bathroom stool, beneath the peeling Paisley wallpaper, and starts to bite his nails.

16

Anna Ayer

Anna peers groggily out from beneath the duvet. Somehow, the backs of her eyes hurt, and her tongue tastes of ashtray. Ruslan is heading towards the kitchenette in his greying boxer shorts. He is muscled and werewolf-hairy, even on his back. In contrast, his head is mostly shaven, leaving two dark zigzags at the side. The fearsome sight makes Anna duck quickly back beneath the covers of the sofabed. The living room stinks of cigarettes, spilled beer and fetid male pheromones. Anna does not intend to rely on Aslan and Ruslan's kind hospitality for long.

Ruslan is now holding a cup of instant coffee worryingly close to Anna's head. She sits painfully up. 'Aww. I feel like my skull has been trepanned. I never usually drink vodka.' She takes the cup. 'Thank you.'

'What is this "trepanned"?'

'It's when people use a dentist's drill to make a hole in their skull to let in more oxygen. They say trepanning makes your brain work better – or it kills you.'

'Interesting,' says Ruslan, very seriously.

The coffee is disgusting. How can they work in an espresso bar and serve stuff like this at home? And what a home – the sixth floor of a concrete-box apartment building with a broken lift by Montparnasse station. The crockery in the cupboard vibrates when the trains go by. The floral wallpaper fights with a huge Free Chechnya poster. Still, what else can she do? When your accommodation goes with your job and your belongings are in storage in a warehouse on the Périphérique, life can feel very precarious. Anna's not sure that Olivier understands how serious all this is for her, as he weekends in his fancy château.

Aslan appears, yawning, in his nylon tracksuit. It's past eleven in the morning.

'Hi. Where's Luiza?' asks Anna.

'She's in bed watching those videos I got sent from Grozny. It is some soap opera she has been missing for years. She'll probably be at it all day,' says Aslan.

'She didn't drink as much as you did last night,' says Ruslan, grinning. 'You were very, um, impressive.'

Anna groans.

Ruslan sits on the arm of the sofabed and pats her shoulder.

We obviously became good mates last night, thinks Anna, shared lots of stories. But which stories?

'Those bastards have given you a bad time. You know, Anna, if you have trouble with Monsieur Malin, we're always here to help, aren't we, Aslan?' He winks at his brother.

Across the room Aslan is lying on his back on the brown carpet, lifting some unbelievably heavy weights on a bar, and grunting like an ox.

'Gruuugh. That man has pissed you around. And he writes a lot of fucking crap,' observes Aslan, stopping his repetitions to point at Olivier's *Chechnya – Beyond Philosophy*, which sits with a pile of SAS-style thrillers in French and English. 'You should give him the dump, you know. Gruuugh.'

'I think he's the one who's dumped me. Or perhaps he didn't.' Anna shrugs. 'He keeps changing his mind. And I certainly don't know what I'm doing. I just need a job and I need a place for all my stuff.'

At last Ruslan has thought to cover his hairy pelt with jeans and a T-shirt, which makes Anna more comfortable. He speaks rapidly to Aslan in a language Anna doesn't understand.

'We're going to be very busy today,' he says to her, grinning.

'I thought the coffee bar was shut on Sundays?'

'Oh, we're, uh, working at another branch. See you later.'

The Barista boys leave, looking rather silly in matching wraparound sunglasses. Anna lurches in her vest and pants into the kitchen, and flagellates herself by washing a week's worth of dishes, and cleaning up the furry blue-green mould in the sink.

She takes a shower, finds some clean clothes in her rucksack, and feels only marginally better. Luiza is still slobbing in Aslan's bed watching the television. She must be very keen on him to sleep in those grubby purple sheets, Anna thinks, but she is pleased that Luiza has at last found a boyfriend of sorts. It's just his grotty surroundings that are the problem. Anna can't bear being in the stifling flat for a second longer. 'I'm going for some shopping. See you later.'

Anna walks out of the building's back entrance into the high-noon light of the barren cement plaza above Montparnasse station. She leans against a graffiti-splattered wall, and watches her hands shaking as she tries to light a cigarette. The hangover perfectly fits her mood.

'Shit,' she says. 'Shit, shit, shit.'

Surrounded by bleak concrete, she feels profoundly alone. Of course Anna has friends in Paris – from the stall, from nightclubs, some other nannies – but there's not one really sensible, honest adult she can talk to. There's no safe place to hide for a few days and be fed, cosseted, and told not to worry. She's certainly not going back to Manchester to the beige bifocal world of her mother and stepfather, and her boring sister Julie – that's a special outpost of hell she only checks into once a year for Christmas Day. Anna wants sympathy without judgement, but who do you tell when you have so many secrets? What would her father say, wherever he is? He's a Frenchman after all, with a knowledge of this world and its workings. Anna wonders about him more and more. Maybe he's dead. But maybe he's different from the rest of her grim family. Maybe he would understand.

Bizarrely, she hears the thunks and plocks of tennis being played. She wanders towards the noise, and behind some green screens, she sees a set of all-weather courts stuck incongruously above the railtracks heading west. The players sweat in the canyon of offices and flats, sucking in pollution, worried that if they hit a ball too hard, it will end up on a train roof somewhere in Brittany. Anna flops on a bench in the sun and listens to the steady rhythms of play. Her thoughts go madly back and forth along with the balls.

'This is the final call for the *TGV Atlantique* on Platform Five,' says the station loudspeaker system below the tennis courts, and Anna wonders for a long minute whether it might be best just to get on that train south and start a new life. Maybe her father lives at the end of one of these train lines. Or here in Paris, even. She could find him, if he is alive. There can't be that many Ayers in France. But he might not want to see her. After all, he was the one who left without a forwarding address.

She wanders desultorily out into Montparnasse, through the late afternoon traffic, until she is irresistibly drawn to the pink and blue portals of Tati: half department store, half drug, with its glorious, tacky bargains. She shops as therapy, tempted to fill ten of those heavenly pink-checked plastic bags with silk wedding dresses for next to nothing, and custard-coloured stilettos. The prices are silly. She purchases tons of stuff she doesn't need or have room for as a homeless person: orange fishnet tights at one Euro; the stilettos; a lime-green vest for two Euros; a set of nesting woks for Ruslan and Aslan; and a nodding battery-operated dalmatian for Luiza to give secretly to Sabine for her as a goodbye present. Emboldened, she marches into the Fnac bookshop and buys two self-help manuals, including *Love is a Drug – How to Detox* and a book on *Tracing Your Family Tree*. Thus laden, she sights the red and gold awning of La Coupole, the famous old café which has conveniently placed itself in her path. She does not want to go back to the grim flat. 'Hair of the dog,' says Anna to herself and staggers in under her bags. She finds herself ordering a Dubonnet and ice at the counter. She has never been in the Coupole before. Nor has she tasted Dubonnet, but somehow it seems to be the moment for both.

Anna sits up at the bar smoking beside a few men who are reading newspapers, and opens the family tree book. The brasserie is stuffier and more impersonal than she imagined it; not at all degenerate in the hands of its new owners, the Flo restaurant chain. But the mosaic floor with its art deco brown triangles and black semicircles is still there. The room stretches into infinity, its mirrors, glowing lights and brass punctuated by naïve paintings on greenish pillars. Anna likes the way older couples sit together on the banquette at one side of the white-clothed tables, preferring observation to conversation. Waiters sweep by holding precarious silver platters of oysters on crushed ice high above their heads.

After a second Dubonnet, she finds herself texting Olivier, who is probably driving back from the château. 'In Coupole. All alone. Wish you were here. Wish everything was simpler. Your Anna.' There is no reply. Five minutes later, she calls Luiza. There's no point in sitting moping alone when you can have company.

'I can't come now,' says Luiza. 'I'm cooking a bouillabaisse for the boys. Aslan said he'd bring some extra special bottles of wine to go with it.' But Anna dreads to think of breathing fish fumes all night from the sofabed.

'Stuff that. We'll finish it later. Come down to the Coupole for a drink.'

Luiza has never heard of the Coupole. 'You know, it's the big café on Boulevard de Montparnasse, touristy, famous?'

Luiza still seems puzzled. 'It's round the corner from Tati,' says Anna.

'Oh right, near Tati, of course I know it,' says Luiza, immediately understanding. 'I'll be there in ten minutes.' It does not surprise Anna at all that Luiza shops regularly at Tati. Where else could she possibly come by all those fluffy, sequinned, pastel jumpers or that tan handbag with the pink rhinestone studs? And then Anna rebukes herself, suddenly realising that Luiza shops economically because she sends most of her money home for her son.

When Luiza arrives, Anna orders her a vodka Martini. Luiza takes it suspiciously, and sits nervously up on the bar stool, as

312

though she's never negotiated one before. They discuss Madame Canovas, Olivier and Sabine. Luiza is going to look after Sabine again, when Madison's not there, and Anna somehow does not mind that so much as being replaced by a stranger.

'Do you think Madison will stick out being supermum for long, or do you reckon she'll disappear again on some film?' asks Anna, hoping Luiza will badmouth Madison.

'No. I think she means it. She's got some new job in Paris.'

But Anna knows Luiza will be glad to have Sabine back; she remembers her initial jealousy. The Martini starts working, and Luiza begins talking, as usual, about her son.

'If I get married one day,' she says, 'maybe I be able to bring Musar to Paris to live – and go to a good Lycée.'

'Are you in love with Aslan, then?' asks Anna, getting straight to the point.

'Don't be funny – I have only been with him a week. That is not love.'

Anna orders more drinks. 'So you got together the night Sabine disappeared?'

Luiza nods. 'I was crying so much, and he took me home, and helped me check to see if she was in the apartment, and then we talked, and . . .' She smiles. 'Who knows what will happen. They've lived crazy, sad lives, Ruslan and Aslan. They're older than you'd think. They're in their thirties, they've seen a lot of killing, a lot of violence. Aslan's fought hard for everything, here and there.' They fall silent. Five women in bright skirts rush by them, heading downstairs to the basement dance hall.

'But what about you? What about you and Olivier? Will you go on like this, in secret?' Anna shrugs. Luiza ploughs on. 'I've watched you look at each other. And he used to stand often in the evenings in his study staring up at the *chambres de bonne* for a long, long time. I didn't think he was looking at my window.' Luiza grins.

'Christ,' says Anna. 'Were we that obvious?'

'There's always been someone. They don't love each other, Monsieur and Madame. I'm not sure that they ever have.'

Anna feels a burst of optimism, and then shakes herself, trying to lift some of the tension in her shoulders. Luiza has the mesmerised look of someone who is not used to alcohol. Tango music vibrates up from the tea dance below. More curiously dressed men and women go into the basement.

'Come on,' says Anna. 'We're going dancing. Downstairs.'

'But I can't dance,' says Luiza. 'And I'm wearing trainers and they're all in fancy dresses.'

'Tati will provide,' says Anna, dragging her into the Ladies. A few moments later they emerge, Luiza in the yellow stiletto sandals, half a size too big, and Anna in the lime-green vest. In the basement, night has already fallen, and the old dance floor is lit by red and green lights. Sixtysomething couples, immaculately dressed, are doing the full *Come-Dancing* Paso Doble, while twenty-year-olds are mucking around, joyously messing up the steps. Everyone is extremely hot. Anna pulls Luiza – red-faced with embarrassment – on to the dance floor. They whirl and birl, all energy, no technique, and soon they're having a fantastic time. Young men grab them by the waist and spin them, and so long as one person knows the steps, it seems to work. There's a South American band, which describes itself as an orchestra – accordions, double bass, violin, piano, brass – making wild, live music. There aren't enough male partners, so Luiza and Anna end up dancing together, exhibiting their glorious incompetence and joy to all. At last, it's seven o'clock, and the tea dance ends. They walk back in the warm summer evening down Boulevard de Montparnasse, each filled with strange hope.

Anna's phone goes. It's Olivier. He's hysterical. The apartment has been burgled while they were away for the weekend at the château. There is no sign of a forced entry, but Olivier's oldest and most expensive wines – his best Margaux, his Château Smith-Haut-Lafite, his Château Yquem and his particularly fine 1995 Le Pin – are gone for ever. Plus Madison's jewellery and the Fabergé ornaments. But Olivier seems most upset that his study has been trashed – there are papers everywhere, files mashed into the ground, and coffee poured into his computer. It is something more vindictive than an ordinary burglary, and it was all easily done when there was no concierge to watch.

'Oh my darling, I'm so sorry,' says Anna. 'What can I do?'

'I just wanted you to know, because the police will be checking anyone who has keys, anyone who might have had a grievance.'

'You can't possibly think . . .' begins Anna, outraged. 'I posted my keys in the letterbox the day I left.'

'I know. Of course I don't think that. I love you. But I want you to be safe from all this. I want you to know what to say when the police come round.'

'I'm not sure I have anywhere for them to come round to,' says Anna, her voice catching.

'Oh my darling. Look, I'll ring tomorrow. I've got to go. Madison's coming.'

Anna explains the situation to Luiza. 'Poor Olivier. It's not just that they've taken expensive stuff, but they've trashed his study, and ruined his computer. What burglar would do that?'

Then Anna thinks of Ruslan and Aslan. A picture comes into her head of the evening months ago when she went to the Café Philo and saw the Barista boys across the crowd, barracking Olivier about Chechnya. Then afterwards they jostled him in the street. But why would anyone get that angry about a mere book, for goodness' sake? Still . . .

'Luiza? Where are your house keys?'

Luiza suddenly goes white. She starts searching wildly through her rhinestone-studded handbag. Her keys – all the keys to her *chambre de bonne*, to the front, apartment and cellar doors of 84 Rue du Bac – are gone.

'Shit,' says Anna.

'The bastards,' says Luiza.

17

Madison Malin

'This is not merely a burglary – it is an attack on my freedom of speech. If a philosopher cannot honestly express his views, that is an atrocious indictment of society.' Olivier is pacing dramatically up and down his study, his hair flying. 'But yet I feel this appalling guilt: that you and Sabine have both suffered this intrusion because of me, because of my writings.'

'It's a burglary, Olivier, not a fatwa,' says Madison, exasperated by his histrionics. 'If it was a fatwa, they wouldn't have taken all my jewellery.'

Olivier presses his hands to his throbbing temples. 'But the attack on my work, my computer . . .'

'Maybe they just knocked over a cup of coffee. Anyway, I've

317

just rung a techie to come round and dry out your hard disk and try it in another machine. You mean to say you didn't make a copy as you went along?' Olivier squirms a little. 'Well, of course, I have most of my work backed up . . . but it is the principle of the thing.'

Now that they have changed the locks, Madison finds herself less freaked out by the burglary than she expected. She discovers that she just does not care that much about losing her jewellery or all those Fabergé ornaments, carefully collected over a dozen years. What she does find frightening is the idea that Anna might have copied her keys and given them to someone in revenge. Is it not all too coincidental: who else would have known that they were away for the weekend and that there was no concierge? But when she suggests this to Olivier, he goes ballistic with indignation, and slams his study door.

'I'll leave it to the police, then,' says Madison through the door.

In the hall, she can still hear Olivier shouting down the phone to his editor, Renée Rimbaud, that she must run an article by him on 'Thoughtcrime and Punishment'.

'There is this human propensity for cruelty, Renée, which progressive thinkers like myself are loath to acknowledge, especially when it comes in their own door. Was there something, one phrase, one assumption that was wrong, that drew them to visit their horrors on his house?'

Madison groans, wanders off to the salon, and stares inside the empty lacquered cabinet where her collection of ornaments used to be. Whatever happens, she thinks, Olivier likes to make himself the centre of the drama. Yet he is still behaving like a child, taking no real responsibility for his actions as a writer – or as a father. They say people remain childlike until they have children, but Olivier does not seem to have made that emotional leap yet. That is partly what makes him so attractive: his passions, his impulsiveness, his amusing needs. But there comes a time when the wind of tolerance changes and blows against you in all sorts of ways, and this is Olivier's time, thinks Madison. She strokes the empty cabinet's painted top – if she rips out the shelves it will make a fine place to hide the television.

Madison looks at her watch. It is nearly lunchtime, and *Le Monde* will be out by now with the first review of her as the lead as the headmistress in the play at the Bastille. She decides she will go downstairs to the café on the corner, and if the paper happens to be there on the zinc, she may quickly glance at it. Her stomach churns all the way down in the lift, but she need not have worried. The café owner is behind the counter, and starts making her an espresso on sight. 'A splendid write-up, Madame Malin, if I may be so bold.' Madison smiles from ear to ear. The café owner finds himself blushing, for no good reason. Madison finishes the coffee, and then casually flicks through the arts pages. A warm weight of confidence settles upon her.

She suddenly wants to share the review with Olivier. She runs upstairs, but there is no one in the study. On Olivier's desk there are sheets of paper, covered in doodles and reams of infatuation. On the top is a final, much-worked, philosophic love poem to someone. Madison knows instantly that it is not for her. The small breasts being eulogised just don't meet her description.

She bumps into Olivier in the hall. 'Just went to the kitchen to find some *Pain Poilâne* and that particularly nice little garlic sausage from the greenmarket, plus a few olives marinated in lemon oil. You want some?' He waves a bulging sandwich at her.

Madison shakes her head, unable to speak. She is pale, despite her make-up. She is holding Oliver's best Montblanc pen, uncapped, like a dagger. Olivier looks at her nervously, suddenly worried that she might stab him with it. She clears her throat: 'I just needed a fountain pen for Sabine to practise her writing.' Her voice is flat, holding back anger. She walks away with exaggerated calm. Olivier might, just for once, do the decent thing and hide the trail of his duplicity.

Downstairs in the courtyard, there is a great grinding and creaking as the huge double doors open to allow in a removal truck. The Jeunots on floor four have clearly had enough of the building's new tendency to disappearances, death and desecration. Madame Canovas has still not been laid to rest, metaphorically or physically.

The concierge's funeral takes place two weeks later, after much bureaucracy and investigation. Everyone is relieved that

Madame Canovas' death was declared 'accidental', despite her well-organised departure. It's better that way, for the church.

Madison and Olivier arrive together at the cemetery at Montparnasse, which is gorgeous in the dappled light beneath huge silver-barked trees. Over the stone tombs and sun-warmed sculpture, the Lego-like Montparnasse Tower rises incongruously. The summer air is heavy with the scent of flowers and pollution. Madison also detects the smell of mothballs from rarely aired funeral garments. There are, in total, eight mourners for Madame Canovas – two conscripted nuns from the convent on the Rue du Bac, a strange young man in a suit, and a few dutiful neighbours: the Malins, Monsieur Bellan, Madame Royan and Madame Duplessix, beetling gaily about on her Zimmer. Olivier always looks as if he is going to a funeral, in his uniform of black and white, so Madison narrows the terrible mothball stench down to Madame Royan who is wearing a dark, bag-like dress with a fur collar, and is weeping copiously, possibly about something entirely divorced from the passing of the concierge.

Madison herself isn't grieving – she just feels slightly numb behind the veil of her black straw hat. She realises that now no one will ever know whether poor, old, mad, mean-spirited Madame Canovas had any hidden attractions, but it would certainly appear that she did not have many friends. Everyone else by the grave – an expensive central plot presciently booked by the concierge twenty years ago – seems very composed, except when the porcine priest describes Madame Canovas as 'the life and soul of the building' and Olivier snorts. Still, Madison is glad Sabine is at school and not here.

On their way out, the Malins walk past the unknown sharp-suited mourner, and give him a friendly nod. 'Gérard Solange. Just paying my respects. I didn't know Madame Canovas well,' he says. Madison smiles. Olivier curls his lip in disgust and strides past the man.

'What's your problem?' asks Madison when they are out of hearing.

'Didn't you notice his *Front National* tiepin? Repulsive little Lepeniste,' snarls Olivier.

'That does not surprise me one bit,' says Madison. 'Do you think she was a party member?'

Olivier nods.

Now they are beside the shared grave of de Beauvoir and Sartre by the far wall. Olivier, though not a religious man, does like to worship his god whenever possible, and stands by Sartre's tombstone in wordless communication. De Beauvoir's fans are by far the most enthusiastic, Madison notices as she takes off her hat. They have left flowers, notes, and more mysteriously, old *Métro* tickets and single rolled cigarettes: essentials in the afterlife. She feels a sudden desire to pick one up and sit on Simone's grave to smoke it, but she hasn't touched a cigarette since Sabine returned. To keep her mind off the craving, she teases Olivier.

'Perhaps, after twenty years, you should think about dropping the black-suit, white-shirt thing except for funerals. What about some autumnal tones? They would suit your complexion.' She points to a postcard propped up on Sartre's grave. 'Even *he* wore dirty-old-man raincoats, and at the height of fashion, those dreadful mock-suede car coats with fur collars.'

'You know that my exterior is of no importance to me,' says Olivier grandly, who recently threw a hissy fit when Luiza slightly singed the collar of his designer white silk shirt while ironing. 'I only require simplicity, like a monk.'

'Yeah, right,' says Madison, laughing. But she is also looking at the two names together for ever on the simple headstone – Sartre above, de Beauvoir below some years later – and wondering if she would want to share a public eternity with Olivier. She knows all too well that Sartre and de Beauvoir had their contingent loves, but they were soulmates. She can't say that about Olivier. Not any more. Nor does she want contingent loves for herself. No Paul Rimbauds, no desire to be anyone's mistress. No desire for deception.

Olivier scowls out the window as they ride in a taxi to the Rue du Bac in uncomfortable silence. Madison leaves Olivier and walks round to the Rue de Grenelle to pick up Sabine from school. Among the *bon-chic-bon-genre* mothers, she stands out, tall and magnificent in her tightly belted black suit. A ripple of respect goes through the crowd – Parisians know serious tailoring when they see it – and various mothers come up to chat to Madison, in a way they never did when Anna was at the school doors. Behind, Madison can hear the gossips talking:

'*She*'s less thin than she was,' says one. 'Yes, but she looks good on it. A little flesh is better, especially when one is *a certain age*,' says another. Madison smiles benignly at everyone, and arranges to take five small girls to the cinema on Wednesday, the next half-day. Then she and Sabine walk slowly down the Rue de Grenelle, examining brass ships' telescopes in the antique shop windows, saying little, holding hands.

'We *have* to go to the Rodin garden today, Maman,' orders Sabine. Then she lowers her voice to a whisper. Madison has to bend down to hear. 'You can see my map of the dens there if you want, but it's secret. Only Anouk and I know, so you mustn't let on to the other mothers where we are hiding.' Sabine gives her a significant look. Madison nods, as seriously as possible. As a *Mère de France* – someone who has patriotically increased the population – Madison gets free entry to the Rodin Museum and its grounds. Of particular interest to Sabine are the two vast sandpits for children at the end of the gardens, behind the ornamental pool, where everyone meets. The place is also perilously close to the offices of Paul Rimbaud, but Madison hopes to slip by unnoticed. She's more interested in Sabine's carefully folded mystery map, each area of bushes labelled with a girl's name in shiny gel pen, plus sites of buried treasure. Madison suddenly feels cheerfully tearful about being let in on the secret, the breakthrough, she supposes, after three weeks of near-silent, slightly embarrassed walks with Sabine to various parks.

Madison likes this life, with its new, slower rhythms. She

finds it very hard, however, to get up in the morning, because when her play finishes at eleven, she is on an adrenaline high and has to unwind after midnight in various little restaurants around the Bastille with the rest of the cast. Otherwise, she comes home wired, wanting something – sex, maybe, but not with Olivier.

But this downshifting from films to an obscure play has not harmed her career. To the contrary: her part in André Andrieu's film *Soldier, Soldier* is still being critically acclaimed, and now she's suddenly had the courage to accept three roles that her agent thought were 'very bad news indeed' before she sacked him. The more unavailable she is, the more the calls start coming in. In the autumn she will play an increasingly loony, aging Camille Claudel in a film about the sculptress and Rodin; appear as an old slapper in a TV dramatisation of Houellebecq's book; and next year there will be Beckett's *Happy Days*, directed by Andrieu on the Paris stage. Plus there is the relief of playing the weird or ugly on stage, playing older women, who require little beauty maintenance. When the Botox in Madison's forehead runs out, she doesn't replace it. Expression takes over from repression. It feels most peculiar, as though she is melting.

Madison wriggles her newly liberated forehead up and down as she watches Sabine play hide-and-seek in the bushes with her friends. Each time Sabine disappears, Madison's heart stops for a millisecond, but then she is gradually realising that they cannot live with eternal vigilance, and hides her fear.

She's taken her high-heeled shoes off, and is walking barefoot in the sand, talking to one of the other mothers, when a small man appears between the espaliered beech hedges, panting. There are sweat patches under the arms of his linen suit. It's Paul Rimbaud. Madison hasn't seen him alone for months, although he came to Sunday lunch last week, when Renée gave her a lecture on good parenting, and Madison kept a straight face – just. Paul waves to Sabine, and kisses Madison with some enthusiasm. The other *Mères de France* stare. Madison is pleased to see Paul's friendly face, but finds his intimacy cloying.

'Darling, I saw you in the distance from my office window. I thought, "I recognise that elegant walk." And I was right. But why are you all in black? It's too beautiful a day.' He sits on the bench, picks up her shoes from the ground, and caresses them, peering at the label, the red interiors and soles. Madison gives him an exasperated look and explains about Madame Canovas' funeral. Paul reluctantly puts down the shoes, and pats her shoulder.

'I hope for your sake that that's the end of all this craziness – Sabine, Madame Canovas, the burglary . . .'

'And the small problem with Anna,' adds Madison.

'I find it hard when you both confide in me,' says Paul, grimacing nervously. 'But Olivier did mention a little . . .'

'I think it was a lot, but never mind.'

At this point. Paul makes a last, desperate play for Madison. Should she not have an affair too? And would he not be the ideal candidate? He declares his total adoration, his worship, his willingness to . . .

'Do you want an ice cream, Sabine?' interrupts Madison, as her daughter walks over. She gives Sabine money to run to the café, and then turns to Paul.

'I'm not going to be false any more. I'm going to be honest. And that means I'm never going to fall in love with you, or sleep with you just for the sake of some supposed parity with Olivier, if it can be called that. I don't believe in that kind of marriage; I've tried to, as you know, but it doesn't work for me. Maybe I'm an old-fashioned born-again Texan under all this.'

Paul mops his forehead sadly with his spotted handkerchief as she continues. 'I feel I led you to believe that I was keener than I am; that there might be something, and I'm sorry. I'm sorry for being so artificial. But I love being with you, talking to you, and I'd like to stay your friend if it's not too painful.'

'Thanks,' says Paul. 'Thank. You. Very. Much. You know for years I've . . .'

'I bought a Zoom Rocket and Anouk has a Monster Slurpee,' says a purple-lipped Sabine, arriving back with a dripping lolly. 'Do you want to taste it?' Madison advises the girls to eat in their den, and they go off again.

'I'm sorry,' she says to Paul. 'But that's how it is . . .'

He is silent for a while, and his glasses require a meticulous polishing. 'As a friend, which I now am, apparently,' he says, 'as a friend, I think you should leave Olivier. Now.'

'But we're just trying . . .' Madison hesitates. 'And I must think of Sabine. Besides, he says – not that I entirely believe him – that it's over with Anna, that we should begin again.'

'And again. And again,' says Paul. He looks hard at her. 'Can't you see what he is? Can't you see that he will never change, that something in him never fully developed? Olivier is rational when it comes to writing, to intellectual matters, but sexually his superego never took over. Maybe his *maman* didn't love him enough, whatever . . .'

'Yeah, anyone would guess that, but what do you mean by all this Freudian stuff?' asks Madison.

'When it comes to love, to sex – and they are usually one for him – he knows no judgements of value. Olivier seeks satisfaction without regard for the circumstances of reality. He seeks novelty, he seeks pleasure. He always will. He always has.'

Madison groans. 'I knew that, really. I just wish you hadn't voiced it.'

Paul shrugs. 'As a *friend* it is my duty to be honest.'

'Beast,' says Madison, laughing, and kissing him goodbye.

They return home, and Madison struggles over Sabine's maths homework until dinnertime. Madison is naturally bad at maths, but her head is swirling with so many thoughts she cannot concentrate. So once Sabine is off eating with Luiza, Madison does what any woman would in this situation: she confides in her hairdresser. The confidence is so sensitive, however, it must take place in Madison's apartment. She calls Angélique to meet her there before she goes over to the theatre. It would not do to have the whole salon listening in. A quarter of an hour later, the two of them are sitting over a glass of wine in the Malins' apartment. The two women talk about everything – Sabine, Olivier's affair with Anna, and the other affairs which were rumoured or dreamed of.

'I didn't like to say, Maddy,' says Angélique, her brush hovering. 'I know we have an unwritten code of honour among Parisians about affairs, but when you told me one day that Olivier – remember when you overheard him by mistake on the phone – was trying to buy Versailles for eighty Euros, I was afraid to tell you that Versailles was a room in the Hôtel Select, this famously kitschy love hotel which I myself have frequented in the past. But now it doesn't matter.'

'I'm not so sure,' says Madison.

'I thought you were making one last bid for monogamy – or at least friendship. For yourselves, for Sabine?'

Madison's words catch in her throat. She feels as though she might cry, quite possibly hysterically. 'I don't think living in this unhappy atmosphere is good for Sabine. I think that's partly why she ran away.'

Angélique nods and gets out her scissors. She's trained at handling these situations. 'The usual, Madame?' she says, after knocking back some more wine.

'Yes,' says Madison. 'No, no, no, in fact. No. Chop it off.' Thus Madison, liberating herself from her hair like a 1920s flapper, gets a grown-up bob.

'And do you want me to dye this tiny white streak coming through here, Maddy?'

'Leave it. Well, leave it for now. We'll attack it if I lose courage.'

'Ooh, very Susan Sontag. Very intellectual,' says Angélique, smiling. 'You *are* going to leave him, aren't you?'

'How do you know? *I* don't even know what I'm doing.'

'When a woman gets as radical a haircut as this, it is always a *sign*,' says Angélique 'Congratulations. He is a fool.'

Madison looks at Angélique with narrowed eyes.

'OK, OK. He's a fool, but he has good hair.'

Madison is laughing, melting again with relief.

'You should keep the apartment, but get rid of Olivier's grim ancestral furniture. He can move into that rental on the floor below or somewhere, where those people moved out,' says Angélique, all practicality. Madison had been quietly thinking this too, but was afraid to discuss it. Angélique advises her to get shot of the Louis XVI chairs, the gilded picture frames, the Persian rugs. Minimalism is the thing, and one needs space for a salon to breathe. 'It's old-fashioned and stifling. It makes me think of carpet slippers and fat pug dogs. It's not you. Never was. Declutter – get rid of your husband, and all this stuff.'

Her world and coiffure turned upside down, Madison gets in the taxi to the theatre, barely recognising her new reflection in the windows, puzzling over the person she has suddenly become. But this person has been lurking beneath Madison's skin, quietly waiting to come out for some time. Madison has always felt until now that she was somehow acting her life, trying to escape her dusty Texan roots by becoming a perfect French beauty; marrying a celebrated Paris intellectual; performing as part of a public couple; ensuring her daughter was *bien élevée* – well brought up. And in the end, it all stank of superficiality.

How she will explain all this to Olivier, she does not know. The right words refuse to form in her mind. Rather sweetly, Olivier is coming to see her in the show tonight – clearly the reviews over the last two weeks were good enough to merit this rare act of loyalty.

When Madison appears wigless at the stage door, surrounded by autograph seekers, he's somewhat surprised.

'What the . . .?' says Olivier, when he sees her long hair has disappeared.

'New regime,' says Madison.

'Well, it suits you, but I wish you'd asked me first.'

'Why?' says Madison. Olivier shrugs.

'I've lived with those long, golden tresses for eight years. I'd become attached to them.'

'Not that attached,' she says, severely. Olivier gives her a pleading-but-charming look, like a chastised puppy. Madison rolls her eyes.

They take a taxi to St Germain and walk down the boulevard in the cooling night air, past endless tourist couples in the Flore and the Lipp who all look sickeningly on the point of proposing to each other, because they think that is what Paris is for. It all serves to emphasise for Madison the emptiness that lies between her and Olivier. Outside Gaya Rive Gauche, there's a man in blue overalls shucking oysters. 'I'm starving,' says Madison. 'Let's go in.'

Olivier follows her into the quiet little expensive restaurant. The owl-spectacled Maître d' hovers happily at their side, for Olivier is a famously good customer. The Maître d' reveals that he has an exquisite sole that should be served with nothing but a touch of lemon butter, yet can hardly be compared with the glories of the tuna and wild salmon tartare with fresh herbs, and did he mention the scallop ceviche?

Olivier, who has been tense as a stalking cat, suddenly looks like his old self, and enquires after the precise contents of the seafood risotto. Madison sits in benign silence – she usually has the salad and the crème brulée here – and then suddenly orders them a dozen *Fines de Claires* oysters.

'But I can't manage that many,' warns Olivier.

'They're not for you.'

'But you don't eat oysters.'

'I did once. I do now.'

Olivier looks on, terrified and fascinated, as Madison eats a dozen live oysters and the juice drips down her chin. 'Ever since I stopped smoking, the world has become a gastronomic paradise,' she says, grinning. There's much provocative slurping, and at one point she shuts her eyes to experience the full Atlantic taste.

'Where the hell did you come from?' asks Olivier, because it is clearly someone else's soul in a body that looks like Madison's, only increasingly curvier. He leans forward, interested in the unexpected display of hunger and sensuality. He seems fascinated by her in a way he hasn't been for a long time.

'It's like this,' says Madison, wiping her lips, putting down her napkin with some finality. 'And let me put it in your terms. Let me put it in the words of the woman I have failed to be for you. Do you remember when Simone de Beauvoir talked about how much she hated the life of the bourgeoisie? Something like: "We hated Sunday crowds, proper ladies and gentlemen, the provinces, family life, children, and all varieties of humanism." Now I know you love your child, you love Sabine, but as for the rest, it's true, isn't it? You hate daily, dull life. You can't live with it without subverting it somehow.'

'Well, I must dispute your thesis that . . .' begins Olivier. But Madison has been writing this speech, she realises, for years.

'I am, at base, a Texan. I am provincial, and proud of it. And I was never going to be the de Beauvoir to your Sartre, if that was what you wanted. I have been your lover as fully as anyone could be, and for a number of years, but I will never be your soulmate, the one that holds you steady as contingent relationships come and go. And you are not my soulmate. There isn't enough there between us, and it's not just language and culture: it's in the essence of us both. We could be lovers, but we could never be best friends. We are intelligent in different ways, but we are not intellectual equals. I love you for what there was, and as Sabine's father, but I can't stay with you in emptiness together, even for her sake. I just think it would be better for her if we were separate, and not living in an unhappy compromise.'

Madison stops, takes a deep breath, and realises her hands are shaking. She looks across and sees an extraordinary thing happen: Olivier's eyes are filling with tears. She's only seen him cry once before, the night Sabine disappeared. He looks grave, and pained.

'I don't want to hurt Sabine,' he says, his voice catching. 'She's had enough to go through.'

'We've already hurt her enough. Do you think she's blind and deaf, that she doesn't sense the disharmony between us? A child's image of herself mirrors that of her family, and we're not an image to be proud of at the moment. She lives with anxiety, inconsistency, when we could offer her honesty: two homes, two parents who love her.' Madison feels she is about to cry too. 'You know it's the truth,' she adds. Her pulse is racing, and she is light-headed. But she also feels this great wave of clarity and strength. It's decided. Olivier takes a huge gulp of his wine, and moves some crumbs around the tablecloth. He says nothing. Madison feels she has to fill the space. 'I'm sorry if I've been cold, or controlling, or just plain dull, but it's become clear to me in the last few weeks that I have been trying to fit into a skin I imagined for myself years ago, and I am not that person. And you colluded in the building of that person, and in order to leave her behind, I must leave you too.'

Olivier laughs nervously: 'You sound like you've been

possessed by the Devil.' He takes her hand across the table and smiles tentatively. 'You've very wise, Madison. And you're probably right. If I may put it once again in terms I understand, Sartre says love is the desire to capture the other's freedom, to enchant and ensnare the other's subjectivity. Love is an unrealisable ideal, doomed to failure . . .'

'Unless the lovers are equally free,' interrupts Madison. 'Unfortunately we couldn't love the way we wanted to, because we had separate ideas of what a relationship should be. And still do.'

'Let's go home, Madison,' says Olivier, sighing.

It's past midnight by the time they reach the double doors of 84 Rue du Bac. The lights are all off, for the new Brazilian concierge – who is inevitably called Carmen – does not believe in constant vigilance. The window that Madame Canovas used to spy from is now filled with a bouquet of pink and yellow plastic flowers. Olivier and Madison walk upstairs into the apartment, and as they enter, Luiza pops her head wearily out of the kitchen, nods, and disappears upstairs to her room.

Then the air is heavy and silent between Olivier and Madison, and the high-ceilinged rooms are filled with the shadows of their past. Tonight, they will sleep together for the last time. In unspoken agreement, they walk down the corridor to Sabine's room, and stand together by her bed. Her calm and beautiful face is just visible in the street light coming through the shutters. Olivier reaches out to stroke Sabine's hair, and she stirs a little. Madison is crying without making a sound.

18

Anna Ayer

In the Luxembourg Gardens the gravel shines garish white in the midday sun as Anna frogmarches herself down the long path. The trees alongside her are all pollarded, hugging their shade meanly to their trunks. She feels a weariness in her step, an unwillingness to take this road to a final meeting with Olivier. She lights a cigarette, examines her melancholic symptoms – unexplained crying, loss of concentration, lack of purpose – and concludes that her season of seduction is well and truly over.

As she passes the ornamental pond in front of the Luxembourg Palace, she mourns not only her time with Olivier, but also with Sabine. The sight of overdressed rich kids poking toy sailboats with sticks, a nostalgia-postcard of how childhood should be, reminds her of the moment when she and Sabine rolled up their trousers, dived in to rescue their boat, and were evicted by the park guards. Then there are the asthmatic ponies for hire between the dusty trees, and the carousel where Sabine would compete with her friends to catch the hoops on a rod as the painted horses whirled round and round. Anna sighs, and tries to refill her lungs with the hot air, but nothing lifts the weight pressing down on her.

Olivier is at a café table outside by the puppet theatre, staring unseeing into the middle distance. There are shadows under his eyes and his cheekbones are more pronounced – and handsome. Anna has not seen him for over a fortnight: they have only spoken quickly on the phone. She stops behind a tree to smooth down her fifties' flowered dress and gorges herself secretly on the sight of Olivier, letting all her weaknesses flood out before she has to go forward and be strong. But there is already a lump in her throat. It's the worst possible way to begin this conversation.

'Anna,' he calls, 'Anna', rolling the word pleasurably round his tongue. 'Anna, come here', and he smiles and kisses her softly and pulls a metal park chair out opposite him. 'My love,' he says, and leans forward, intense. She sees the muscles of his arms grow taut in his grey T-shirt. 'How are you? I'm so sorry everything has had to be so complicated. I am sorry you had to be the one who suffered.'

'I'm fine,' lies Anna. 'I've been missing you. It's odd not seeing you, not catching even a glimpse of you every day.'

He takes both her hands across the table and holds her gaze. It's devastating, like a schoolyard no-blinking competition, and penetrating in every way. Anna feels a fierce physical craving for him, but she also knows what he is going to say, one of two things, and they are both equally awful: that they should end the relationship for good, or that they should continue in secret.

'I can't live like this,' she says, pre-empting him. 'I can't live a half-life in your shadow, waiting. You know?'

'I know.' He smiles. 'I know, my darling', and he kisses her again. Anna suddenly feels he is relishing this too much. Is she being toyed with? Is he enjoying the little drama?

'Let's get this over with, then,' she says, pulling away. A waiter hovers by them, unnoticed, takes stock, and sensibly disappears.

'There's nothing to get over,' says Olivier with a huge grin. 'I'm free. I've moved out. Madison and I are separating. I can be with you all the time. Day and night and night and day, and even in bed for long, late afternoons if you're not too busy . . .'

Anna cannot at first believe that he is serious. After all, she knows that there have been half a dozen affairs, and Olivier has stayed put in his marriage each time. She makes this point, as delicately as possible.

'But you are different, Anna. What we have is different – this is not a passing liaison – it is a meeting of two minds across cultures, across ages . . .'

'And two bodies,' says Anna sharply. Suddenly, it is clear: 'Did she throw you out, then?'

Olivier jerks back as though she has punched him. 'Don't be ridiculous. This is my decision, and it's the right one. I cannot live with compromise or deceit any more. Too much of my life has been wasted with that. And I can be more honest with Sabine.'

'Sabine,' says Anna shaking her head. 'Oh God, poor Sabine.'

'Well, you don't have to come and be her wicked stepmother. But Sabine is your friend, and she trusts and respects you. I mean, of all the people ... you couldn't be better for her.' Olivier seems delighted with the convenience of it all, and explains that he has moved into the apartment below his own, the one on the fourth floor recently vacated by the Jeunots who left in horror at the neighbours, despite their own predilection for strange shower scenes by the window.

'I moved in two days ago, but it seemed so empty without you. And it is clear to me that I cannot be without you ever, for you have awakened impulses in me that I thought were lost and dried up. Together we will find truth and self-realisation. You are the woman in my life. There is no other.'

He wraps his arms around Anna, and pulls her close. The waiter arrives, clears his throat loudly, and then shrugs and walks off again. 'I love you. I love you, Anna,' says Olivier, and for a moment Anna feels the weight of worry and insecurity slide off her. She feels as if she has come home, that Olivier will look after her. But something rankles, something feels wrong. She pulls away from the suffocating wrapping of his arms. There's nothing worse than getting exactly what you want, what you've dreamed of. Also, at twenty-three, does she want to be a stepmother, a homey, wifelike creature? 'Olivier, I'm just at a loss here. I don't know what to do,' she says. 'It's a big decision.' Olivier looks hurt and slightly amazed. 'I don't mean that in a bad way, it's just it's too much. I was expecting the worst. I wasn't expecting this, you . . . I can't hold it all in my head.'

'Take your time,' says Olivier, smiling benignly. He obviously considers her doubts to be a mere hiccup. 'Our bed isn't being delivered until next week. You can come slowly. Indeed, I will make it my business to have you come, slowly.'

Anna feels exasperated. Innuendo is not what she wants right now. So she tells Olivier a story, a short story of the man in her life, of the day that her father rang them at home in Manchester to say he wasn't coming home and drove off into the far distance in his lorry. Now, she says, she needs to find the ending to that story. Sabine's disappearance made Anna think all the more about her father who disappeared. Plus, being tossed out into the street with her suitcases made Anna realise that she wanted to find her roots, wherever they were. A permanent man in her life. And thanks to the glorious pedantry and accuracy of French bureaucracy, it has taken her less than a week to relocate her father, a Monsieur Pierre Ayer, in Le Havre.

'Good Lord,' says Oliver. 'Have you called him?'

'Yes. He was shocked, and then very sweet, a bit embarrassed, you know? And he has a new wife and two children there.'

'Hmmn,' says Olivier, indicating that he knows the evil ways of men. 'So he never contacted you at all?'

'My mother was very angry and stuff. She completely erased him from our lives and never spoke about him. I don't know whether there was any mail. There're only a few photos left.'

'And what does he do in Le Havre, this Monsieur Ayer?'

'He's a senior manager at the Tetrapak carton depot.'

Olivier shrugs, and raises an eyebrow.

This irritates Anna. 'Whoever and whatever he is, I need to know what happened to this man, my father. I need to know where I came from, what I am. I need to know all this before I make any other decisions.' She wishes Olivier would give her some encouragement. But he is silent. 'So I'm taking the two o'clock train from St Lazare this afternoon.' She looks at her watch. 'And I've got to go.' She stands up with her hands at her sides, unsure.

Olivier kisses her again. 'I'm glad you're going. You need to go – and to come back. Back to me.'

'I don't know, Olivier. I just don't know what I'm doing.' Anna walks off, so he can't see she is crying. Behind her, she can still hear his deep voice, calling the waiter over, and sadly ordering the eggs mayonnaise.

The train to Le Havre is an old one, with curious panelled compartments and disturbing wheezes and clanks. As they pull out of the Gare St Lazare, Anna suddenly sees the rackety building of the Hôtel Select high above the tracks, home to

Versailles, and to those passionate afternoons with Olivier. Would it be the same living together, day to day, steeped in the ordinariness of each other's lives? But then, reasons Anna, Oliver is not ordinary. He is not a domesticated male. He is by no means safe.

But she also feels that she is being sucked back into a difficult, uncomfortable place. In the last three weeks away from the Rue du Bac, she has felt relieved that all the lying and subterfuge is over. She does not want to be part of the darkness that seems to surround the Malin family, the constant chain of disasters. And she certainly does not want to take out the rubbish from Olivier's new apartment and meet an icy Madison on the stairs. Olivier's plans are all too creepily convenient and intimate. On the other hand, chances like this, chances to love, are rare.

Funnily enough, that's what Luiza just said to her yesterday. 'I have to take my chance with him.' She was talking about Aslan, Aslan-the-burglar, but Luiza didn't believe that. Her keys were lying on the chest of drawers in the boys' apartment when they returned that day, and although Aslan and Ruslan were far too cheerful, they revealed nothing.

When Luiza tackled Aslan directly, as they lay in bed that night, he said how insulted and horrified he was that Luiza could possibly think such a thing of a man of integrity, of principle, of a man who had fought for his country. Luiza let it pass. 'I love him. I'm lonely,' she said, her face strained.

Anna finds Luiza's behaviour annoying, but is she any better? She loves Olivier. She is lonely, homeless and rootless, her clothes in storage, sleeping in a grubby *chambre de bonne* by Nôtre Dame, taking casual babysitting jobs. To go against the soothing flow, to not move in with Olivier, would be the hardest decision.

Perhaps the day will give her new perspective. Anna takes out a photograph, taken fifteen years ago, of herself and her father in bathing suits on Blackpool beach. Pierre Ayer is dark, devilishly handsome, and ox-like from lifting heavy loads and steering that vast wheel up in the cab with its sleeping platform in the roof. Anna has a sudden flashback of sitting on her father's knee in the truck, pretending to drive it, unable to turn the wheel at all. She has few other memories – he wasn't home very often; always on the road. He was a distant, glamorous, foreign figure who brought her back costumed dolls, stiff, ugly things with felt shoes and lace collars from the different European countries he visited. Where did the dolls go? Did her mother throw them all away? Anna decides against calling Manchester to find out, or indeed mentioning any of this to her mother, who is settled into dull grey coupledom with Anna's kind but tedious stepfather. She puts the photograph back in her notebook, beside the green and red postcard of the Dina Vierny, Maillol's muse. She is not sure which of these images represents her now.

Outside, the landscape is becoming more flat and estuarine. The grasses are parched yellow and the sky is greying. In the distance Anna sees a bridge arching over what must be the Seine as it enters the sea. She is nervous now, yet her father – Papa? Pierre? They sound equally wrong – seemed so welcoming on the phone. He even asked her to come to spend the entire weekend with his family, his other family, her half-sister and brother. She said just dinner would be fine.

How do you dress as a dutiful daughter to a less-than-devoted father? Anna looks down at her vintage ensemble, which seems fine. Her tattoos are decently covered. On second thoughts, she takes her tongue stud out and puts it in her purse. No need to scare them first time round. Utilitarian concrete buildings fill the view – Le Havre, she knows, was levelled in the war, and looks like it was replaced with breeze blocks in about five minutes. The train stops, and the whistles and bustle of the station begin. Anna sits still in the carriage, wondering for a moment if she should just turn around and take the next train home.

Outside Le Havre station, Anna is disoriented. She asks for directions to Tetrapak, and a man points down to the docks, half a kilometre away. Eventually she arrives in the cacophony of the shipping terminal, the air filled with salt breezes and spilled diesel. Through criss-crossing forklift trucks and huge orange metal sea containers, she is directed to a Portakabin. Obviously the job of senior manager at Tetrapak cartons is not as grand as it sounded on the phone. She knocks on the door and a tarty-looking secretary ushers her in. He's there, her father, behind a wooden desk covered with messy papers, a half-eaten ham baguette, and an empty beer bottle. Anna knows it is him, because she recognises the features and hair from her photograph, but the body has been pneumatically inflated, a bloated version of his youth.

'Anna?' He rises with some difficulty from his chair, and squeezes her in a huge embrace which smells of old sweat and new salami.

'Let me look at you! My daughter! My, how you've changed, I can't believe it's you! And your sister Julie? How is she?'

Anna is staring at him, unable to speak. He suddenly goes silent, his bonhomie deflating. 'I'm sorry I never . . .' He wipes his forehead with his sleeve. His hair has gone grey at the temples, but it is still beautifully cut, though not, Anna suspects, by the barber at the Savoy, her father's last known appearance in England.

Then Anna unfreezes, and remembers her manners, for in these times of sheer wrongness and agony, manners are very useful. She asks after his family, his children, his job, as though he were a complete stranger. Then she finds herself sliding the Blackpool beach photograph across the desk towards him.

'Oh my! I remember that. I've put on a bit of weight since then, haven't I? But you look marvellous. Fit and healthy.'

Anna says nothing. Her brain feels thick with some sort of glue. Her voice isn't working.

'Coffee? Tea? Or perhaps you drink Coke? And I usually have a cake at this time of day.' The secretary brings in some dry, unappetising pastries, which Anna ignores. They talk of practical sensible matters: Pierre's new house and patio (she can't bring herself to use the word father), Anna's various jobs as a nanny in Paris, her sister's taxi business in Manchester. Pierre's shirt buttons are straining to hold in his girth, and Anna finds her eyes drawn to the yellowish patches under his arms. She feels queasy, disappointed, and looks desperately away, ashamed that appearance is of such importance to her. Underneath, he may be wonderful, she encourages herself. On the shelf, there's a photograph of a podgy teenage boy and a half-naked girl wearing lots of make-up and jewellery.

Anna picks it up. 'Is this . . .'

'Yes, that's your brother and sister, Sylvie and Philippe! Sylvie's what, eighteen now, and Philippe's thirteen.'

Anna does some swift calculations. 'So you . . . my God, you had another family at the same time as us.'

'Well, not exactly a family, but Marceline and I did have "a little accident", shall we say.' He gives Anna a sickly sweet smile. 'And then we had Philippe when we got married, after your mother and I broke up.'

'You didn't "break up". You disappeared,' says Anna, bitterly.

Pierre laughs and shakes his head. 'Is that what your mother told you? Oh dear. Oh dear. Well, I'm glad you're here to hear my side of the story.'

'Why did you leave her, then?'

'I was unhappy. We were wrong for each other, your mother and I. How can you get to know someone when you just see them on weekends? And then I met Marceline here in Le Harve, on a trip.' He proudly shows Anna a photograph of an orange-tanned blonde with vast teeth. Marceline's cleavage bursts forth from her too-tight silver top. 'And I passed through every week, and soon . . . well, I felt more at home with her, here. I never fitted in in Manchester. I didn't like that street we lived in at all, all those Blacks and Pakis. And as for the food? Fish and chips? I had to choose, and I chose Marceline and *la belle France*, but I was too ashamed to tell you. Perhaps you understand. Indeed, the very fact that you have moved here makes me think we are very similar.'

They're now heading home for dinner in Pierre's battered Renault. As the traffic goes into gridlock just outside the docks, Anna suddenly has a burst of clarity and thinks: I'm stuck in a car that stinks of cigarettes and wet dog, with a racist bigamist who is my father! She smiles politely at Pierre, and then coughs.

'I hope you don't mind the dog hair, dear,' he says. 'I breed Alsatians in my spare time. There's a lucrative market here for guard dogs – but don't worry, they don't bite the family!'

'Which family?' says Anna, unable to control herself. She looks away, in case he sees the tears forming. 'Men are so complicated, so duplicitous.'

'Now, now, Anna,' says Pierre, all pompous. 'Tut, tut, tut. You know men don't just go out and do this by themselves. There are often reasons. I had good reasons, or so I thought at the time. But women must collude with them. There are mistresses galore. You must know that – or perhaps you're not old enough yet.' Anna scowls at him. She feels like she has taken a punch to her stomach.

'Marceline knew what she was doing when she became my mistress long ago; your mother knew what she was doing when she became cold and rejected me. I have suffered greatly myself

– I was denied my children for years. You cannot think that I cut you off. No, I tried. I tried. Yet I am also to blame, but I am not the only one. No, it takes a woman, in fact two women – the woman who welcomes, and woman who rejects – as well as a man to break up a marriage.'

Anna feels sickened and guilty. 'I know all that. It's not exactly rocket science.' She hates the idea of her own life in any way being a reflection of her father's.

Pierre leans over the gears and pats her knee chummily. 'You do speak wonderful French, you know. Hardly any Manchester accent. As your papa, I am very proud.'

Anna cannot be with this foul, fat man for another second, and she certainly never wants to meet his killer Alsatians, his creepy family, or see his new patio. And he's probably a member of the National Front too, like Madame Canovas. She suddenly glimpses the town square and the station down a side street.

'Pierre? I know you'll understand.' Anna gulps. She's a little frightened of him. 'This has been a big day for me, very emotional. In fact, I'm quite upset.' There, she thinks, that's not a lie. 'But I don't feel, this time, that I can face coming home with you tonight and meeting my half-brother and sister. It will just be too much. Perhaps another time. I hope Marceline hasn't gone to too much trouble with dinner . . .'

'But Anna, surely . . .' He looks puzzled, perhaps shocked.

'Would you mind awfully if I just got out here, near the station?' The car is stuck in the rush-hour traffic and she opens the door. 'Thank you so much. It was . . . fascinating. I'll call you soon. Goodbye.'

There isn't a train until half past eight, so Anna collapses at a table in the fluorescent-lit station café. Her hands are shaking so much that she spills half her tea over her dress. How could it have been worse? How can they possibly share the same DNA, whole chains of it, binding them? Her temples are pounding, and the light hurts her eyes. She covers them with her hands and weeps into a pile of thin paper napkins. The waiter sees the wet clump of tissue, and kindly brings her some more.

'Are you all right? Can we help?' he says.

'No, I'm fine. I just made a mistake, that's all.' He brings her another cup of lukewarm Lipton tea on the house.

But it's not just a mistake, it's more damaging than that. Anna has lost all hope. She can no longer fall back on the perfect fantasy father when everything goes wrong in her life. Only now does she realise how much this absurd hope sustained her from childhood into adulthood, even when she never acted upon it. She should have left Pierre Ayer as fiction. Now that he's fact, the bottom has fallen out of her world.

On the train, she falls into an exhausted, delirious sleep, and awakes grubby, lipstick- and tear-stained, as they draw into Gare St Lazare at eleven o'clock. Anna takes a taxi to her lonely single room, and stands with her key poised at the street door, under the shadow of Nôtre Dame. It's now raining – plump, hot drops that mix unnoticed with her tears. At that moment, it is absolutely clear to Anna that this is not the life she wants. She has Olivier, and why should she throw away that chance of happiness, however shortlived or risky it may be? She calls him. It's just before midnight. He picks up on the first ring. He's awake, writing. 'I love you,' she says. 'It's that simple.'

'Oh good. I thought you might call,' answers Olivier. 'Was he unspeakable, then? Yes? I'm so sorry.'

Anna takes a deep breath and subdues her tears.

'Can I . . . can we?'

'Marvellous. That's settled, then,' says Olivier, with satisfaction. 'I will pick you up outside your room in ten minutes. I have a very fine bottle of Puligny Montrachet chilling, and some peeled quails eggs which are delicious simply dipped in a little rock salt.'

19

Olivier Malin

About nine months later, Olivier is sitting at his dining-room table reading the latest *Harry Potter* in French to Sabine, her friend Anouk, and Carmen the Brazilian concierge, who has come up to listen to today's chapter. The children are rapt, and making their way through a packet of mini lemon tarts. Everyone is very content, including Olivier. He likes living in the moment, being with his child and her friends. It helps him deal with the fact that his career is not progressing as well as it might, and he has more time on his hands. Indeed, he has been available every day recently for the popular four o'clock children's reading, ever since his book on the netocracy flopped and his author tour was cancelled, amid allegations of plagiarism. He suspects that Florence Vallon, that flighty little publicity girl from his publishers, took revenge on him by tipping off the press about his sources, from which he'd taken a few general themes.

Plagiarism and pies – those are the subjects that vex him in the small hours of the morning. Only the week before, a so-called 'satirist' – perhaps the very same one who has been pursuing his co-philosopher, Bernard-Henri Lévy – hit Olivier with a custard pie as he left the television studios with Bourdon after *Les Intellos*. Worse still, the satirist was accompanied by a photographer. Anna saw the photo of Olivier's dripping, shocked face and the headline in *Paris Match* and laughed, he felt, a mite cruelly. She said the verb *entarter* – to throw a pie at someone – had no direct translation in English, but that it was a *very* good word. Olivier shakes his head, puts the humiliation out of his mind, and concentrates on the *Potter*.

He leaves his small audience on tenterhooks for the next instalment. He pays the delightful Carmen to take a pile of his white shirts to iron – but the thing he misses most about his demotion downstairs is the loss of Luiza's housekeeping skills and delicious cooking. Anna would happily live on prosciutto alone – cooking is not an area of any expertise of hers – so he has become rather reliant on the hideously expensive *traiteur* in the street with its ready-stuffed scallops, onion tartlets and *pommes dauphinoise*. With some regret, he kisses Sabine and sends her upstairs with Anouk to Madison's apartment to be fed by Luiza. Through the open window upstairs, Olivier's finely tuned nostrils detect something delicious roasting, flavoured with a touch of garlic and marjoram.

What Anna refers to as the 'upstairs-downstairs' arrangement is working quite well now. Olivier is, he feels, a better and more loving father, now that his official hours are allotted. Sabine has emerged astonishingly in his mind not as a child, but as a person – and quite a complicated person at that. But there was a terrible time of darkness and turmoil earlier in the year. Sabine threw constant tantrums, and Anna became her emotional punchbag, since the child simplistically – and understandably – saw Anna as the catalyst for all that had gone wrong. Olivier felt like he was carrying a heavy backpack filled with remorse everywhere with him. And somehow, every time he was in the park with Sabine, she'd manage to fall off her bike, or cut her knee – almost intentional carelessness which perhaps expressed other hurts. Madison would look at them both witheringly when her daughter arrived back bandaged again. But now, at last, there is a vague sense of normality permeating the Rue du Bac – apart from the satirist with the custard pies who occasionally waits outside until the police move him on.

Olivier settles down to enjoy the rest of the quiet afternoon in his study. He likes to work when there is no one in the apartment, nothing to disturb the rhythms of his mind. His study is comfortingly familiar; the steel bookshelves and table have come from upstairs – indeed they fitted exactly, because his new study is directly below his old one. Sometimes, his head gummed up with theory, he opens his door and thinks he is upstairs, and is completely disorientated when he realises half the apartment is missing, and what is now there is filled with junk. Madison, in sudden minimalist, decluttering mode, has divested herself of tons of gilded mirrors, antique velvet chairs and *toile de jouy* curtains, and it is all coagulating downstairs with Olivier and Anna, who have neither the money nor the inclination to get rid of it.

Still, that's about to change, for Olivier has now decided to produce a major book, *The Philosophy of Love*, which will cite experts including Kierkegaard, Sartre, de Beauvoir, Heidegger, Nietzsche – and Malin, of course. Using passages from philosophy, literature, and life, Olivier will discuss the relation between love and desire, the place of love in self-realisation, the status of the Other in the relationship of love, and the typology of love as sensual or aesthetic (eros), and as friendship (philia). It is sure to be an enormous bestseller. A photograph of Olivier himself will grace the front cover.

He is very much relishing creating this book. He feels his own wide experience, as a man and as a lover, makes his analysis all the more accurate. Indeed, just a few more sensual experiences would make his philosophy portfolio complete. But as soon as he drops away deep into his writing, Anna bursts through the door, sits on his desk swinging her undeniably lovely legs, and quite derails his train of thought. Olivier cannot understand why all the women he has ever lived with are so bent on interruption. Do they lack concentration so much in their own scatty lives that they cannot understand its importance?

Anna is chewing gum, so her voice sounds odd. 'I'm going up to Montmartre tonight because Djamel's opening a new club up there. It'll be brilliant.' She snaps the gum. 'Do you want to come?'

Olivier puts his head resignedly in his hands and enunciates very slowly. 'I told you last month, and then I told you again last week, that it's the première of that reissued Bertolucci film tonight, and I'm giving an introductory speech.'

'Oh, yeah, I forgot that. I must start keeping a diary. But it's really important for Djamel that I'm there, and I think *Libé* will be covering it. I've styled the walls and cushions in a way which is sort of retro and Moroccan at once, all reds and oranges and bright blues . . .'

Olivier is irritated: 'We discussed this première ages ago. You are so adolescent. You have no sense of obligation, of what matters.'

'Well I do, actually. I have obligations to my friends, and you to yours,' says Anna, busily colouring in a huge flesh-revealing rip in her tight black trousers with Olivier's best Montblanc pen. 'But I am sorry I forgot.' She gives up on the trousers, takes them off, and tosses them in the wastebasket. 'I give up. That is too vast a hole to camouflage. We need to go shopping, you know.'

Olivier remains glumly silent.

'I'm starving,' she says, and heads off into the kitchen. He follows her. 'Stuffy old pedant,' says Anna lovingly, sitting on the kitchen countertop in her T-shirt and pants, licking yoghurt from a spoon. She has made, Olivier feels, some curious changes to the kitchen since they moved in. The walls are raspberry, the units shiny black, and on the far wall she has hung the huge painting of St Sebastian, discarded by Madison in her 'minimal-isation' upstairs. Today, Anna has made further improvements by draping the gilded frame with red, yellow and green light-up peppers on a plastic vine. The pained St Sebastian has witnessed a lot, and this evening is no exception. Anna hops off the counter, turns down the main light, and switches on the luminous peppers. 'I got them in Tati. It just works somehow. It brings it all together, doesn't it?'

'Christ,' says Olivier. It's like living in a circus. He shakes his head, mock-serious. 'You were just born with weird taste, weren't you? The aesthetic gene never quite fully developed.'

Anna looks hurt. Her skin has strange jewelled patches from the pepper lights. 'Your ideas are just old fashioned. You may not have noticed, but my business is aesthetics, and very successful it is too. My stall now does better than anything in the Porte de Vanves, and people are asking me to open a vintage shop, you know.'

'And you were in *Marie Claire*, I know, I know. Why does the apartment look like a municipal dump, then? Why is there a broken 1950s fridge filled with hats in my hallway? Why can't I move for your paraphernalia?' Olivier pretends to tear out his hair.

'I thought you wouldn't notice. I though you only cared for the life of the mind – and possibly the stomach,' says Anna, laughing and looking down at the waist of his trousers, which has become surprisingly tight these past months, thanks to the *traiteur*, or the true onset of middle age.

'Forget it,' says Olivier, feeling poked in his almost imperceptible paunch. He strides towards the door. He feels there is an embarrassing lack of dignity and respect here, and he can't quite take it. She's twenty-four, for God's sake.

'Olivier? Wait. Hey, I'm sorry.' She puts her arms round his neck and buries herself in his shirt. He sinks his face into her hair, which is freshly washed and smells of – he sighs at the inevitability – yes, it smells of bubblegum shampoo. And then there is the equally inevitable business of the T-shirt without the bra, so he can just see her nipples, and the pants which are really very small indeed. He luxuriates in Anna, he sucks in her life, her youth, her smoothness, and touches her skin which blooms and curves under his fingers. He kisses her deeply and lifts her up on to the table, conveniently behind. She's small and light; a sort of human soufflé. She's delicious beyond explanation, ephemeral. And she makes him feel truly alive. He cups her bottom in his hands; he puts his tongue between her legs. St Sebastian suffers all the more, in silence. Olivier makes love to Anna on the kitchen table.

After her bath, which Olivier estimates takes around two hours, Anna heads off to Montmartre in a most peculiar midriff-revealing top made of silk scarves, which she has sewn herself. Olivier puts on his dinner suit and bow tie, and gets back to work for half an hour before he has to leave for the première.

But his doorbell – also labelled Malin – keeps ringing with deliveries for Madison's first salon evening upstairs. Olivier's been invited, without Anna, but he doesn't think he will bother to go. He's impressed that she's able to carry off a salon at this time, however. Madison is busy at stressful theatre rehearsals for Beckett's *Happy Days*, but Olivier knows that like a well-oiled machine she will come home just in time to change, do Sabine's homework, and organise Luiza, the waiters and the canapés. He misses living with a grown-up sometimes.

Olivier walks down to the cinema on Boulevard St Germain for the première. He always enjoys being out in the warm spring in his evening clothes. He tosses his jacket over his shoulder and strangers nod admiringly at Paris's best-dressed philosopher. At the cinema, Olivier delivers a pithy and incisive analysis of the Bertolucci, taking into account its post-modern references, and leaves while the film is being shown. (He can't face sitting though it again – it's so pretentious and boring.) Outside the cinema, he pauses to breathe the warm night air. There's a soft splat, which throws him off balance, and his face and hair are soaked with wet, eggy foam. The cameras flash. It's another victory for the satirist and his custard pie, only this time – much to the delight of the assembled media outside the première – Olivier gives chase, swearing. From behind he's just a black suit running, with yellow, slimy, clownish hair. The *entartiste* jumps into his car, and is gone. Olivier dips his head in a nearby fountain until it is clean – Paris is very convenient for fountains at these tricky moments – and then marches angrily home. He calls Anna to share his indignation, but her mobile is turned off. God knows what interesting cocktail of drugs she's now consuming. He worries about her. Sometimes he feels as if he's her father.

Olivier gets in the bath, and relaxes. He can hear faraway music, glasses clinking and the roar of the chattering classes vibrating through the floor above. Up there, are his friends, people who appreciate him, proper intellectuals, not media whores. Besides, he could do with a drink. He dresses and goes upstairs. Luiza, back in her uniform again, greets him and takes him into a different world. Olivier's been used to handing Sabine over in the hall, and he hasn't been inside the salon for months. There's a wall missing, for a start, and everything is white, unless it's grey. The windows are uncurtained, flung open to the night, the floors are polished and bare, and the room is packed with bodies. There's a very odd sculpture, or perhaps it's an installation, at the end of the room, which looks like a garden shed frozen in time as it is blown apart. There are forks, spades, half-used bags of fertiliser and plastic buckets suspended by wires in the air, along with splinters of wood. On a plinth beside him is a wax sculpture of a human-thing which borders, he feels, on either the clever or the obscene.

No wonder she needed to knock through the two rooms, Oliver thinks, and hammers down a champagne cocktail, immediately taking another in his hand. He is much greeted as he walks through the crowd; a slim Bourdon, Rimbaud – all his old friends are there, and some new ones. Of course he cannot participate in much of the latest gossip, because it's about him and Madison. There is nothing Parisian high society does better than adapting to the ups and downs of relationships, always remaining sunnily polite to the participants. Often a woman will fall drastically from sight after separation or divorce, but not if she continues to fascinate on the stage or screen – or if she writes a revealing memoir and dresses well.

Behind him, Olivier overhears a much-Martinied Renée advising a girlfriend: 'Of course Olivier is not with anyone who's significant, socially or intellectually, so it won't last. Well, she's an amusing little thing, we even had her to dinner the other day, but . . .' Here Renée shrugs. 'You know how it is with him.' For a moment Olivier considers shoving Renée's Fendi baguette bag right down her throat, but his interest is drawn instead to an excitable crowd forming next door, in what was the dining room, but is now another vast white anodyne space with three murdered mannequins installed by Henri Mince at the fireplace, beyond the crowd. Perhaps there's some grand politician in there, thinks Olivier. He's already quite surprised by the famous faces that have turned up tonight, and some new ones he doesn't recognise; people of Anna's age, with ridiculous hair. There are also, he reckons, twenty young architects, who can be identified by their unwillingness to wear anything other than black. A tiny man in a yarmulke is having a huge argument about atomic particles with a woman padded in burgundy velvet like a sofa. Olivier makes his way through the commotion, and realises the centre of it all is a group of acolytes surrounding Madison. Well, it's her party, reasons Olivier, but he still feels that *he* should be the host, the star of the show.

Reneé sidles up to Olivier and asks if he has heard that Madison is being awarded a medal by the Elysée for her contribution to the arts. 'It's the greatest honour a Frenchwoman can receive – especially when she's not French,' says Renée. 'Well, in fact, the greatest honour is having a Hermès handbag named after you, but she'll probably have to wait a few years for that.'

Olivier feels a lurch of jealousy, slips away from Renée, and waves to Madison across the heads. She gives him a dazzling, public smile. Without any vanity he knows that she had noticed him the second he entered the room, in the way of spouses, or exes, who have a special radar for each other's presence. He hasn't seen Madison dressed up like this for a few months, and she's rounded out and glowing with summer-holiday health, her hair in a chignon, wearing a silk café-au-lait dress. The acolytes who have been to the exclusive previews of *Happy Days*, before it opens next week, are using phrases like *tour de force*, which are somehow very irritating to Olivier.

He goes up and kisses Madison on both cheeks, which feels strangely formal after their years of intimacy. But he finds himself taking both her hands, and congratulating her on the reviews, the medal. And he realises that he means it. Olivier is proud of Madison and what she has become once again through the amazing force of her own will. Does he mind not being part of her grandeur? A little. Does he still love her? Yes, but not in that way. From the warmth of his smile, he realises something: that Madison is happy, and has moved on. He feels forgiven, and the last shreds of guilt he harbours fall away.

But he is merely a guest. She moves on and he rides this disconcerting moment with another champagne cocktail. Then outside the bathroom, he meets Horatio Hervey with his dog Dorothy in her new Gucci collar. Horatio offers Olivier a line of cocaine, and that helps, too. Better. He's feeling better. The old Olivier is back. His eyes are flashing, and he's talking, talking to a crowd which has formed around him too, about the philosophy of love. It's a subject everyone has opinions on – he knows that from the Café Philo, and he recycles some of his best one-liners.

The crowd loves a bit of Sartre still – he is in some ways to philosophy what The Beatles are to music, a reliable old favourite. Interestingly, over time Olivier has discovered that very few Parisians have read Sartre properly, beyond Baccalaureate level, although they all claim they have. 'Well, of course we all know that *Being and Nothingness* details strategies for responding to the unrealisable ideal of love, strategies modeled on Hegel's master-slave dialectic,' says Olivier, sucking down more champagne. Everyone nods, rapt, thinks Olivier, suddenly giggling, but not as rapt as they were when I was reading *Harry Potter*. He sobers up and clears his throat. 'For Sartre – and you wouldn't expect this from a study of his own life – love emerges as an unrealisable ideal, doomed to failure. Masochism and sadism are the two basic responses to the failure of love.'

Now there's this pillar of a woman staring at him from the corner, listening, with a half-ironic grin. It's very disconcerting. Olivier continues his disquisition, while noting that she's wearing a black silk forties' suit, with an exceptionally tight waist and skirt. He finishes his mini lecture – even when quite drunk he never loses his grip on theory. Reality is, however, trickier. Unsteadily, he follows the magnetic lines leading to the tall woman. He introduces himself.

'Ute Mann,' she replies, all formal. She's *jolie-laide*, with a large nose, and a lean body like a greyhound. Under the suit jacket she is wearing nothing but a sculpted pink and black satin *Agent Provocateur* bra, but Olivier has to pay attention instead to the fact she describes herself as an 'unfashionably Freudian' psychotherapist. She's originally from Berlin – Olivier is already humming '*Mein Lieber Herr*' from *Cabaret* in his head – and has some thrillingly Germanic theories.

Olivier is both slightly scared and fascinated. He keeps talking: 'But frankly, for Sartre, masochism – whether real or imagined – fails because in the end death is the only answer, and sadism fails because there is always the possibility of rebellion.'

'But it's not that simple, is it?' says Ute, strictly. Olivier wants more. She continues in an attractive, throaty voice: 'I believe there is no female eroticism without a touch of masochism or sadism, but they can be easily interchangeable for most people. We identify consciously or unconsciously with both roles.' She looks at him knowingly. Olivier immediately feels a desperate need to put theory into practice.

'Do you mean that we are flexible, we can love like this without throwing our liberty into question?' asks Olivier, while thinking desperately, WWSD, what would Sartre do? Sartre would take the existential route, no doubt, and not let this potentially fascinating experience escape him.

'I must go,' sighs Olivier theatrically. 'It's past midnight.' He hands her his phone. 'Ute?' He smiles at her for a minute, until his meaning is deliciously clear. 'Would you mind just putting your number in there for me – I have come without pen and paper, but at some point, I would very much like to meet for a drink, to discuss the issue of the polarities of masculinity and femininity with you.'

His spine tingles and he suddenly knows he is being watched. Across the room, Madison shakes her head imperceptibly, rolls her eyes, blows him an ironic kiss, and is swallowed once again by her entourage.

20

Madison Malin

A satisfyingly thick, creamy envelope arrives addressed in copperplate. Inside is an invitation to the British Embassy Garden Party, known to be an outrageously grand event. The engraved card is for Madame Madison Malin, with no mention of Monsieur, but then he has rather fallen by the celebrity wayside while Madison has become an international sensation in the Beckett play. Madison props the invitation up on the white mantelpiece with all the others. It's that she-shall-go-to-the-ball moment.

There has been a pleasing outbreak of articles about Madison in serious papers like *Le Monde*, with sophisticated black and white photos. Everyone likes a narrative, and the one of Texan starlet becoming serious Parisian star is appealing to many nations, particularly the French, who like a public defection to their culture. *Oh Les Beaux Jours* is to become *Happy Days* for a short summer run to London, where Madison will play the part in English; she is, of course, '*L'Entente Cordiale* made flesh', according to the critics. In interviews, Madison is treated like a grande dame and says things like: 'Beckett said he dreamed in English, but he wrote in French, and I feel a curious rightness about the part, for I mostly think in English, and act in French. He wrote *Godot* and *Happy Days* in French first, and then translated them. So I hear the rhythm and the nuance of both languages in my head.' And it's true: she does, and she is happy.

She sees reflections in her own life, because *Happy Days* is about the power of denial – 'it's about a woman trapped in a mound of sand who is perfectly content, for God's sake,' says Madison to *Le Monde*. 'Winnie finds life a paradise, outwardly. By the end of the play she appears equally optimistic and satisfied, even though she is now buried up to her neck – and still in purgatory. It's the itchiest and most uncomfortable part I've ever played.' But the bit Madison likes best is when the character takes stock of the situation, that no news is good news. 'No better, no worse, no change.' She feels every night that when she squeezes out of Winnie's claustrophobic, fake sand mound and stands up as Madison for the applause, she has shaken off the same unchanging burden in her own life: 'To have been always what I am – and so changed from what I was,' as Winnie says.

Not that Madison's changed life is entirely without burdens or doubts, but mostly she can live with them. She was thrown disturbingly off-balance last week though, when she and Sabine were swimming in the wonderfully tiled Piscine Pontoise along Boulevard St Germain. The weekly swim began as normal. The pool is wonderfully old fashioned, and Madison was amused to see that a group of serious young priests had arrived from the nearby seminary. They slipped off their long black cassocks in the little blue-doored changing rooms round the walls, and emerged, their beautiful, untouchable bodies in exceptionally tight Speedos.

Madison was just thinking how very delightful it might be to sleep with a man again as they reached the deep end. But Sabine was so proud of her efforts at completing a length of crawl that she confessed she had a 'deep-end' secret to whisper to her mother.

Madison has been floating dreamily on her back, watching the sunlight flicker over the arched ceiling, expecting the usual tales of sleepovers, or secret dens. But Sabine said: 'Do you want to know something really, really secret? Like super secret? I don't think anyone can hear us here. I'm going to have a baby brother or sister to play with! I've always wanted a sister.'

Madison held on to the side of the pool, and drowned silently inside with a strange feeling of loss.

'How do you know? Who told . . .'

'Well, Anna kept going to throw up in the toilet, and one day I went in to bring her a glass of water because she was crying, and her face had gone a weird greeny yellow colour, and I was so worried that she would go away to hospital. So I told Luiza that Anna was sick, and I got very upset, but Luiza said not to worry because there was nothing wrong with her except that she is going to have a baby! But it's a big secret right now, until you can see the baby sticking out in her tummy. So shh,' said Sabine putting her finger to her mouth. 'Don't tell anyone.'

'I won't. That's wonderful, if it happens,' said Madison on autopilot. 'Now let's have a race to the other end.'

But later that day, as she was walking alone in the humid early evening to the theatre, Madison felt deadened, empty, truly cast off. Somehow there had been a conspiracy among mothers with adorable small babies in slings and prams to clog up her side of St Germain, all reminders that she would not have another chance. It was one thing watching Olivier move in with someone else, or even flirt with ridiculous Germans at her party, but having another baby seemed grossly unfair, a bigger betrayal – if it was true. She and Olivier had never tried for a second child. Somehow there had never been quite the moment or the inclination – both of them far too busy, far too unhappy. Now, though . . . but Madison stopped herself, shrugged, and shook her head to dispel its contents. There were people staring at her, half a dozen autograph hunters outside the stage door, so she concentrated instead on signing and smiling. By the time she had finished on stage, to another standing ovation, the empty feeling had been replaced by one of being deeply wanted and appreciated; she took the bouquets and flourished in the human contact that she had never experienced making films.

The next Sunday, Madison goes straight from her matinée performance to the British Embassy party, pausing only to replace her stage make-up and slip on what anyone would acknowledge is a perfect, white linen Costume Nationale suit. Her fear of arriving at such intimidating events alone, with 'Divorced' tattooed across her forehead, has begun to dissipate – once again she flows beautifully out of her car, into the inevitable wall of snapping photographers, and through the huge gates where the crowd, instead of parting before her, fawns around her. The embassy's butler is on special alert, and escorts her through the high-ceilinged, gilded salons, out into the gardens. She finds it curious, this attention, the way that fame breeds more fame, but she's not complaining. For once she feels she has earned this: it's been a long haul from Austin, Texas.

Madison has never been in the ambassador's residence before, a grand *hôtel particulier* off the Rue Faubourg St Honoré. Everyone who is anyone is there: government ministers, television anchors, famous explorers, members of the *Académie Française*, fashion designers, and, of course, actresses. There is, ridiculously, a military band in red-striped trousers and gold epaulettes, tootling up and down the lawn near the residence. Further away, there is quiet under the sun-dappled chestnut trees by the Henry Moore sculpture at the end of the garden.

You wouldn't know you were in Paris, it's so green, she thinks, and this is confirmed by the sound of tennis balls plocking on the grass court next door and a disembodied gentleman's voice saying 'Oh, bad luck!'

Perhaps it is because she is a tall blonde in white, she acts like a beacon. Madison is soon surrounded by acolytes. She's a little bored until she meets the French finance minister, who has three children, including a daughter the same age as Sabine, but never gets to see her children, except on weekends.

'Basically, my children have been raised by wolves – or ever-changing au pairs – for the two years I've been in this job,' says the exquisitely turned-out finance minister, getting them both another Bellini. 'With my teenagers, I talk most by text message, a language which I barely speak.' She sighs, mock serious. 'I have a budget deficit, a national bank strike next week, and my daughter has to make a model of the solar system this weekend, so you can imagine where my priorities lie,' she continues.

'The solar system?'

The finance minister nods resignedly. They walk off together under the chestnut trees, away from the crowds and the band. Madison suddenly tells this woman she hardly knows about Sabine running away, how it set in train a chain of events that altered everything, how she suddenly saw her life clearly. 'It was the worst, and in an awful way, the best thing that ever happened to us.'

A footman interrupts their intimacy with more cocktails on a silver tray, and the finance minister is usurped by the military attaché, a red-faced man with yellow stripes down his dress trousers and enough braiding and tassels for a roomful of curtains. He harrumphs excitedly around Madison. He's very pompous. He wants to reminisce about the many Shakespeare plays he has seen, not forgetting the ones he has performed in at Eton. While Madison is wondering whether he always got the part of second soldier, she is rescued by James Henderson, the British Ambassador, a man with surprisingly long sideburns, fashionable black-rimmed glasses, and a summer suit from Paul Smith, she guesses.

She met him a few weeks before, when they sat together at a grand banquet in the Elysée Palace, and he was wickedly and hilariously indiscreet. She felt as if she had known him for ages. At one point she asked: 'You were saying, Ambassador?' and he said 'James', and Madison felt he ought to add 'Bond' in that fantastic English accent, and she gave an almost undetectable snort of laughter. Yet Madison noted with interest, that Our Man In Paris was in his forties, young for such a prestigious post, divorced with two children in boarding school, and in dire need of the right sort of woman. Indeed, the Ambassador is the constant butt of comments of the sort that begin: 'It is a truth universally acknowledged that an ambassador in possession of a large embassy . . .' Madison considers James carefully. He seems very eccentric for someone with such a serious job. He's talking to her about Brownian movement at parties.

'I'm sorry?' she says, puzzled.

'You know, Brownian movement, the ceaseless random movement of small particles. Guests do that at social functions – believe me, I've suffered thousands – and then suddenly someone significant comes in, and the guests all point in the same direction, like tiny iron filings attracted by a magnet. Now, when you came into the garden, you had that effect on the crowd.'

'Oh dear,' says Madison, embarrassed. 'Could we not talk about that?'

'Well, you are not the sort of person who goes unnoticed, are you? And that is rather a splendidly cut white suit.'

James grins. Madison suspects he might be flirting with her in his English way, and feels it is better if she asks the questions. She discovers that his previous posts included Ulan Bator, where he owned a diplomatic motorbike with a Union Jack flag on the front instead of a car, and Kabul 'which had the worst politics and the best parties if you could get four armed guards to take you there'. He tells her the British acquired the embassy next door to the Ambassador's residence in Paris after the war by trading a set of old American movies for it, films being in short supply then, while empty buildings were plentiful.

'Is that true?'

'Well, perhaps some money changed hands too.' He shrugs. 'Sorry. I'm just in the habit of telling all these stories, all these anecdotes. I'm a trained diplomat, you see.'

'But you're not actually in your anecdotage yet, are you?' teases Madison. 'In fact, you're really too young to be in this job.'

They're laughing together now, focussed only on each other, much to the irritation of various diplomatic wives wearing too much perfume who keep sailing up and trying to interrupt them. Eventually James says: 'It's decidedly hot out here. I've been meeting and greeting people for two hours now, and I've got muscle fatigue from this rictus smile that I last maintained all day on my wedding day and that did not augur well . . . Anyway, shall I take you for a tour of the residence inside, Madison? It used to belong to Pauline Borghese, Napoleon's sister. She had absolutely no taste. Vulgar beyond belief.'

Madison is ushered by this man with manners from another century into Pauline's salon on the ground floor. They are alone, but for an occasional epauletted footman passing by. 'The British bought it from the Bonapartes in 1814. We've still got their clocks and chandeliers.' Madison is delighted, still appreciating gilding and grandeur, so long as it is not in her own home.

'That's her there,' says the Ambassador, touching Madison's arm to turn her around, and pointing to a portrait of a woman in Empire-line white. 'Of course, Pauline was said to be rather bulkier than that, but the painter was very kind indeed. And she had this specially made.'

He stands in front of a full-length mirror, its gold frame dotted with bees. 'Napoleon was very fond of bees,' says the ambassador as he hitches up his very British trousers to reveal ridiculous red-and-green-striped socks. 'See? It makes you look slimmer, your legs longer. But you don't need that,' he says, beaming. Madison looks at the marginally thinner version of herself in the mirror, and sees someone from the past who no longer matters to her. She likes this new body she inhabits.

Madison's phone rings. 'Oh, excuse me, I'm sorry. I should have turned it off,' she says, but the Ambassador shows no signs of going away to rejoin his guests. In fact, he stays right beside her, listening, in an undiplomatic manner.

'Hello?' she says. 'Hello?' But there's no one there, just the background of cars, a door slamming, and then Olivier's voice in the sudden quiet. Yes, she's still top of the automatic dial list on his mobile phone, although not in his life. The man needs technical help. And he's still doing business at the Hôtel Select. 'Versailles, please,' he says, 'and perhaps a bottle of red later, Madame?'

Madison switches off her phone and drops it in her little bag, the way one might handle a wet and very smelly fish. She knows there's someone new again, and she could not care less. She knows at that moment that her decision to leave Olivier was the best one she ever made. And she understands that this does not bode at all well for Anna or her baby. She actually feels sorry for her. Then Madison notices the Ambassador watching the shadows of changing emotions cross her face. He has an uneasy frown on his face.

'Is everything all right?' he asks.

'*Plus ça change*,' says Madison, and the Ambassador looks more worried. 'Oh it's nothing. Not my problem any more,' she says, laughing and shaking her head. The Englishman is puzzled, but he is looking expectantly at her, politely waiting. 'My ex-husband and his endlessly complicated affairs,' adds Madison. 'He's ridiculous.'

The Ambassador is incredibly cheerful at this news. He looks at her quizzically, but he's now in pursuit. He's got the scent and will not be deflected. 'Um, perhaps you would like to see the Duff Cooper library upstairs. I use it as my study, alone, at nights.' James affects a mournful look, but Madison is well-aware that he must socialise all the time in his job.

'I would love to see where you spend your lonely nights,' she says, giving him a knowing smile.

James leads her up the marble stairs, under the chandeliers, past the raised eyebrow of the butler, into the library and shuts the door. The room is quite dark and intimate, lit by the two green-shaded brass reading lamps over his enormous desk. There are gilded columns holding up the bookshelves, where volumes shine in rows of soft-coloured leather binding. He pulls out all the first editions of Beckett from the *Éditions de Minuit* and hands them to her. He has long, thin fingers.

'I saw you last month on stage. I went after we met at the Elysée, because I couldn't in my most outrageous dreams imagine you playing a dowdy old woman. But you were extraordinary, wonderful in that part.'

'Thank you.'

'And then I went back again, last week.'

'Isn't that overdoing it? Weren't you bored?'

'No. By that time, I was obsessed.'

Madison blushes and feels the blood rushing to her head.

There is silence. She slides down into a green leather armchair and surveys the strange Englishman, and takes some pleasure in slowly crossing her legs. He sits down opposite her, serious, smiling. Madison has not found anyone so attractive for a long, long time. She hardly recognises the feelings any more. Indeed, it is only now that she has come to terms with herself that she feels she can even look at anyone else. She stares at James, and she likes what she sees – apart from the sideburns, which need not be permanent, she reassures herself.

There is a knock outside. The butler comes in, taking in everything with his darting eyes, but betraying nothing in his face. 'Some of the guests are leaving, Sir. You may want to be on hand.'

'Thank you. I'll be down in just a tick,' says the Ambassador unhappily, and the butler shuts the door.

'James? I must head home,' says Madison, picking up her bag. The Ambassador offers her his hand as she rises on to her heels from the deep armchair. Madison can't decide whether he's old fashioned, or just fast-moving. But then he pulls her towards him, and kisses her, very gently, almost questioningly, on the lips.

Madison feels the last tiny shards of ice melting inside her. The answer to his question is a passionate one. But there's another bossy knock outside.

'Shall we go?' James asks Madison, and takes her arm as they go down the marble stairs together. Madison has a strange out-of-body experience, as though she's done this before, or will do it again in the future, but perhaps she's just read about it. 'I'm having a Nancy Mitford moment, but I can't remember why.'

'It's in *Don't Tell Alfred*. The former British ambassadress grandly descends the stairs in a white satin dress, shakes everyone royally by the hand, and then leaves the embassy for ever.' He pauses on the bottom step. 'You do this very well. I hope you're not acting. I hope you won't leave for ever.'

'No, I'm not acting. I'm perfectly sincere,' says Madison. She is even beginning to consider sideburns rather handsome. She feels elated, blissful, rescued.

The butler hovers in his black suit, messenger of doom. 'Better get on with it, then,' says the Ambassador, straightening his shoulders. 'Have to work that crowd. Once more into the breach.'

Madison nods, and holds out her hand to say goodbye. James kisses her with absolute formality on both cheeks, and then fails to let go of her fingers. He quickly brings them to his lips and kisses them too. The butler clears his throat and checks swiftly round to make sure the hall is empty.

'Madison? May I call you? Will you come here again soon?' asks James.

Madison smiles. 'Why not?'